REQUIEM FOR A HOLY ISLAND

I0692773

A Novel

ZECHARIA PLAVIN

REQUIEM FOR A HOLY ISLAND

A Novel

ZECHARIA PLAVIN

 SAMUEL WACHTMAN'S SONS    DEKEL PUBLISHING HOUSE

REQUIEM FOR A HOLY ISLAND

Zecharia Plavin
Copyright © 2015

Dekel Publishing House
www.dekelpublishing.com
North American rights by
Samuel Wachtman's Sons, Inc.
ISBN 978-1-888820-91-1

All rights reserved. No portion of this book, except for brief review, may be reproduced, stored in a retrieval system, or transmitted in any form or by any means – electronic, mechanical, photocopying, recording, or otherwise – without written permission of the publisher. For information regarding international rights please contact Dekel Publishing House, Israel; for North American rights please contact Samuel Wachtman's Sons, Inc., U.S.A.

Editor:	Hugo N. Gerstl
Language editing:	Kathleen Roman

Cover image:
A Beach In Hong Kong Island Photo © Creekmyst, Dreamstime.com

Cover design and typesetting by

For information contact:

Dekel Publishing House
P.O. Box 45094
Tel Aviv 6145002, Israel
Tel: +972 3506-3235
Fax: +972 3506-7332
Email: info@dekelpublishing.com

Samuel Wachtman's Sons, Inc.
2460 Garden Road, Suite C
Monterey, CA 93940, U.S.A.
Tel: 831 649-0669
Fax: 831 649-8007
Email: samuelwachtman@gmail.com

Dedicated to Marcey Gayer

TABLE OF CONTENTS

PREFACE

Between 2001 and 2010 I worked closely with Shlomo (Solomon) Jekabpils. We became dear friends, even calling each other "relatives" due to our common Baltic origin—I was born in Vilnius in Lithuania, while he was born somewhat earlier in Daugavpils, in southeast Latvia. Shlomo studied music in the United States where he started a career combining piano concertizing and musicological research. Due to the impact of the Israeli–Palestinian peace process that in 1999 seemed so promising, Shlomo—ever the idealist—moved to Israel. He became my colleague and subsequently represented Israel at numerous international academic forums, both lecturing and playing piano. However, the subsequent right-wing drift of Israeli politics resulted not only in him feeling exasperation, but deep-rooted anguish. In 2010, having been offered a senior position at a prestigious American university, he left Israel.

Early in 2008 Shlomo showed me a large number of documents salvaged from a remote island in the South China Sea. He asked me to help him understand the events referred to in this material. During the following two years we were in daily contact discussing the meaning of these documents. Both of us agreed that they deserved publication, but we differed on the form this publication should take. Finally two versions emerged: one, Shlomo's, was in the form of historical-anthropological research; the other, my own, was a novelistic presentation of the events referenced in the documents. However, I felt my task was to retain as much original material as possible, mainly just deleting repetitive details. Therefore the main body of my text preserves the diary-like nature of the documents as they appeared in the island archive.

Shlomo, after seeing my sketch in Hebrew, asked me to write in English so that this story could reach a wider audience including his dear parents, relatives, and friends scattered across English-speaking countries.

Shlomo himself published his own work in a series of articles in a professional anthropological journal. While the following is my work, the main narrator of the story is still Shlomo Jekabpils.

Zecharia Plavin

INTRODUCTION

The small archipelago known as the Paracel Islands seldom attracts the attention of westerners, especially since their interest in undeveloped, far-off places usually requires the presence of conflict or war. While there is indeed a simmering conflict in this region involving China, Vietnam, and partially the Philippines, the Paracels, which are sparsely populated and have no substantial riches, are barely noticed. In fact nobody in the West even paid attention to the fact that the northernmost island of the archipelago actually sank in 1995, resulting in practically all its inhabitants being drowned at sea.

I would never have known about the gruesome fate of this island and its people had I not attended an annual conference devoted to distant musical cultures that was held in 2003 in Southampton, England, where I was reacquainted with an old classmate of mine from Daugavpils, Ms. Nelly Zhdanovitch.

She was very upset. Instead of turning our reunion into a joyous celebration, she continually lamented the loss of the great love of her life, a man who miraculously managed to escape from

Pinto, the sunken island in the Paracel Islands. For some reason she believed that her beloved, Illirio Mariafels, was in Israel and implored me to find him. She cried so bitterly that I succumbed to her wishes and promised to do what I could upon my return home. Even after she had extracted from me the most solemn of promises, I was not eager to spend my time running across the whole country (however small Israel may be) searching for a man whom I did not know.

But on a visit to Paris the following spring I met the daughter of a deceased piano teacher who told me about her mother's extraordinary work on Pinto Island and about Illirio Mariafels, indeed a talented and heroic figure who constantly risked his life opposing the malefic rituals of his countrymen. This meeting forever changed my life.

* * *

In truth, I have always been in awe of heroic figures. I recalled this as I contemplated Nelly's plangent cries and my promise to her. And besides…there was another aspect. Reviewing the image of Nelly from our youth—near-sighted, unattractive, with thick, formless legs, dandruff accumulating upon her school apron, a continuously runny nose that she never bothered to clean, and the smell of yesterday's sweat permeating her presence—it was clear that she was not only ugly but disgusting. On top of all this, her sardonic, strangely haughty smile mocked our very contempt of her appearance.

But every now and then she turned herself into a ravishing beauty, and at these moments I, a lost, pubescent youth, found her irresistible. She tantalized me—for I could neither decipher the mechanism of her metamorphosis nor the reasons for it.

I could only observe it happening. Once, while reading a pocket score of Bartok's *Concerto for Orchestra* as she waited in the vestibule of the Philharmonia for her dowdy-looking coat, she transformed herself into a beauty right before my very eyes, standing tall above the crowd, poised and elegant, examining the phrases of the Hungarian master with the most rapt expression on her face. Even her third-rate glasses now appeared artistic and I—strangely enough—did not notice any dandruff on her shoulders at all.

My life, that of a music student, was one of intense longing. In addition, as a young Jewish Zionist I was waiting impatiently for my family to receive permission to immigrate to Israel, a document that took six full years to arrive. In the interim my parents lost their ardor for Israel and made plans to immigrate to America. Around 1969 Nelly's father, a high-ranking communist, got himself appointed manager of a top-secret military plant in his native city of Minsk and the family relocated to the Soviet Republic of Belarus, nearly two hundred kilometers away. Gradually I forgot Nelly, but not my dismay at being unable to understand her miraculous ability to self-transform.

Now in Southampton I saw the same bewildering phenomenon: an awkward, wrinkled, round-shouldered woman, wearing outdated clothing and glasses, all of a sudden become a seductive beauty when speaking of her beloved Illirio. In one mere second, she straightened up, her face smooth and radiant, providing an interesting counter motif to her bitter cries. Despite the tears that filled her eyes, she moved elegantly.

This time I fully understood that this transformation was caused neither by me nor my perception. I was electrified by her secret power. Ah, yes, there was another stimulus—she told me that Illirio was able to sing simultaneously in two voices. These chants produced, according to Nelly, a hair-raising, cosmic, supernatural effect. Although I could not quite bring myself to believe her story, I had heard about people from the Far East who could sing with two voices, and that had always piqued my curiosity. Anyway, she did succeed in planting within me an intellectual desire to find Illirio and later on this pursuit became my all-consuming passion.

But first things first—I need to relate the story of Pinto Island. I learned about its history in the course of my research in 2004–2005. Although the general history of the Paracel Islands is more or less known, at least to those with an interest in that particular Southeast Asian region, many details of the island have remained obscure to this very day. I will now fill in the gaps by presenting a schematic overview of Pinto Island and the Paracel Islands.

The first European to report sighting the Paracel Islands was Fernão Mendes Pinto, a Portuguese sailor and adventurer whose voyage crossed the region in 1537. The group's northernmost island was later named after him. Semi-circular in shape, it was the biggest island in the archipelago. While the island was almost flat, there was a prominent hill jutting above its southwestern edge. The island had fresh water springs with one located just at the foot of this hill. A thin strip of forest grew on the slightly elevated southeastern coast. Fernão Pinto did not see any people on the island at all nor any sign of animal life.

However, since around 1620 several hundred people of distinct Euro-Chinese extraction who called themselves Calvo-Pintoists steadily inhabited the island. Their language was a blend of Portuguese and Chinese and their written script employed the Latin alphabet. In the twentieth century the population of the island peaked at eighty thousand or more.

According to the national narrative, Calvo-Pintoists are descendants of the Calvo family whose progenitor, Vasco Calvo, a Portuguese sailor, was captured by the Chinese and forced to marry a Chinese woman. Members of the Calvo family suffered great humiliation in China because of their mixed ancestry. The third generation, having managed to escape to the island directly south of the southern shore of China, developed their own tightly knit community there. Their stringent code of ethics required that each youth of fourteen swear vengeance upon the Chinese for the humiliation incurred by the community's ancestors and to free the South China island of Hainan for future generations of Calvo-Pintoists. Regarding the latter, there were two schools of thought—one held that every adult had to fulfill the sacred national duty of combating the Chinese on Hainan Island, while the other preached a more gradual liberation of Hainan Island in the unforeseeable future. In spite of this difference, both factions concurred that the hill on the southwestern edge of Pinto Island had to be raised high enough for the islanders to observe Hainan Island from afar. This in fact was an impossibility given the resources that they had, for Hainan Island was 180 kilometers from Pinto. Nevertheless, each generation needed to contribute to the elevation of the hill by bringing more earth from other parts of the island to the hill's summit.

There was, however, another sacred duty—before entering into family life, boys had to perform two secret voyages to Hainan Island, which took a week to complete, in order to bring sand from there to solidify the growing hill. The Chinese frequently discovered these intruders and killed them on the spot, so Pinto Island youth grew up with the memory of a constantly expanding list of martyrs who had sacrificed themselves for the future glory of the nation.

There was a strict work discipline on the island with people toiling long hours diving for pearls and building seaworthy boats. The economy of the island was built on exchanging pearls for food and clothing with the commercial vessels that passed by Pinto Island. Later on an attempt was made to cultivate a greater variety of plants, and cows were brought over for milk production.

The great feature of the islanders was their glorious ventriloquist chant. The boys sailing in the raids to Hainan Island were obliged to sing these chants to express their hope for the glorious liberation of their future Hainan home.

In 1837 a group of five hundred islanders was sent to the United States in order to support Pinto from afar. "The 500" were supplied with sacred writings and were solemnly sworn not only to glorify Pinto Island for the rest of their lives, but also to indoctrinate their American offspring in filial devotion to the motherland.

"The 500" settled in the southern fields near Des Moines. They called their American settlement Pintoville. Painfully realizing that their traditional means of economic support—diving for pearls to be sold to passing ships in return for manufactured goods—was an impossibility, the community split into two groups. One integrated into American society, while the other devoted its energy to the cultivation of their ancient customs. Although these preservationists routinely cursed the integrationists for failing to abide by the Law of the Founding Fathers, they didn't object to living off their financial support. Yet in order for the preservationists to technically excommunicate the despised integrationists, they needed the sanction of the motherland, which never arrived (since the integrationists were the ones who sent money and equipment back to the island). Soon there was no intermarriage between the descendants of these two groups.

The Des Moines authorities quickly discovered the feuding community living in their outer suburbs and built a wall in Pintoville to divide them. However, both groups proceeded to destroy the wall, thereby intensifying the feud and stimulating violence among the rival factions.

Meanwhile, no European or Asian power bothered to establish control over Pinto Island. But in the early 1930s the French arrived with the purpose of establishing a meteorological station. Up to that time, the economy of Pinto Island had been based on simple barter that included the exchange of favors and assistance in construction of the small family dwellings that were uniformly made of clay with wooden roofs. The governing body consisted of four Sages or Teachers who issued moral commands that were to be executed without question. Their edicts were enforced by devoted youth who scrupulously obeyed the Sages and in return received public honor.

Their basic unit of economic value was the bucket of sand. Every family was obliged to supply one thousand buckets of sand annually for the elevation of the Hill. There were about two hundred iron buckets on the island that had been supplied by the integrationists in Des Moines way back in 1868. The buckets arrived on the island by special warship sent by President Andrew Johnson. (Consequently, Johnson's name was revered on Pinto Island and many local children were named after him.) Almost all of the buckets were the property of the Sages, although the most distinguished families, some fifteen or twenty people, obtained private possession of a bucket through special dispensation from the Sages.

The Sages sat in council and ruled by issuing commands that were required to be unanimously agreed upon. This governing schema created an atmosphere of unity among the islanders, despite the heavy loss of life incurred from the raids upon Hainan.

However, the island faced another severe challenge. Raging though seemingly random epidemics devastated the population. The Sages could not devise a plan to overcome the high mortality rate. As the island had no general health protection system and popular shamans operated as the only medical practitioners, the Sages taught that only the liberation of Hainan would bring relief from the island's suffering.

The arrival of the French in the early 1930s produced a miracle. After twenty-five Frenchmen and ten Vietnamese arrived, they started building fortified, heat-protected, waterproof three-story brick houses. They installed an electricity grid for nighttime illumination for the area surrounding their station. They also established two technological schools for youth as well as a scholarship fund designated to provide university education for gifted students. In the course of just a few short months, the small meteorological station had become a medical and technical relief center, instituting work projects for the improvement of life on the island like the construction of small hospitals and workshops and quality housing for the benefit of the islanders. Consequently, in 1938 nobody died from the epidemic nor from the monsoons that always flooded the shore and washed away flimsy housing. Moreover, any family who did lose its cottage was provided with a new apartment in one of the three-story waterproof brick structures built in the western part of the island.

In 1938, a narrow runway was constructed on the southern corner of the island, enabling small mail planes from Saigon to land. In November 1938, the famous author Antoine de Saint-Exupéry flew to the Island and remained there for two days as a guest of the Meteorological Station. Observing how shabbily the islanders were dressed, he recommended on his way back to Saigon that the French authorities send hundreds of thousands of shirts and trousers to the island population. The American integrationist diaspora willingly consented to finance the expense and soon the Islanders sported elegant white shirts and red trousers sewn by diligent Vietnamese.

The French, intrigued by the islanders' ventriloquist chant, quickly learned that the secret art of this type of singing was strongly protected by the Sages. In March 1939, a delegation of anthropologists outfitted with recording equipment arrived to study this wondrous chant and to capture its sound. Much later—by a different chain of events—they established a music school on the island where European music was taught to local children. They even brought two pianos. Local kids joyfully started learning the piano and also learned to play two-piano duets and four-hand duets on a single piano.

Even before the establishment of the music school, the Sages became upset with the foreign atmosphere permeating the island and started issuing public decrees urging people to remain faithful to the teachings of the Founding Fathers and to stay away from the French. But by 1939 many islanders had not only learned French, but the technological skills taught in the schools as well. While still revering the Sages, these adherents disobeyed their commands in practice.

With the start of World War II in September 1939, only one Frenchman remained on the island. The Sages started to recoup their power. They commanded the people to throw all their white shirts and red trousers into the sea and to participate more energetically both in building the Hill and in the raids upon the Hainan shore. They ordered that the bulldozer left behind by the French be used to dig the earth on the plateau and under the northern shore cliffs so that elevation of the Hill could be accomplished at a quicker pace. They also ordered that the people build more boats for the raids on Hainan.

At that point it became abundantly clear that the majority of the Islanders did not want to participate in these activities, but neither did they wish to be in active opposition to their brethren remaining faithful to the Sages' teachings. For some unfathomable reason, the island, never attacked by the Japanese, was left to its own devices throughout the war. The only problem was that the cessation of western commercial shipping in the South China Sea shut down the exchange of pearls for milk, gasoline, and even towels and underwear. The islanders had to rely on their own means of food production—which consisted mainly of catching turtles and fish.

But in 1945 with the end of the war the French returned, renewing their energetic building campaign. Once again the island flourished. More solid three-story buildings were built for the locals and the airplane runway was modernized. Good radio communication with Saigon was established. The Sages observed all this with silent rage, inflaming their supporters against the lapsed brethren siding with the foreigners. Still, for as long as the French remained on the island, relative calm between the two factions prevailed.

In 1955, following their defeat at Dien Bien Phu a year earlier, the French left the island and handed administrative control to the Vietnamese. But the Vietnamese were not eager to implement their rule. The island remained independent, though without any international recognition or the infrastructure of a state. Once again the Sages regained the upper hand and the quality of life on Pinto Island deteriorated with epidemics striking repeatedly and taking many lives.

* * *

Among the islanders who had managed to acquire a European education during the French presence was Constantius Tegularius (1922–1995), who had studied medicine in Saigon. Although he returned to the island just months before the French departed, he left to study educational systems at the Sorbonne for several more years.

In the late fifties at the request of the Sages, Tegularius returned home and was given unofficial authority to organize the development of the economy, the medical system, and schools. However, the Sages severely undermined his efforts by advancing their own project of building the Hill and raiding Hainan.

Knowing of the covert though wide-spread disregard for the Sages, Tegularius proposed a system of elections and the formal organization of a state. These proposals came at a time when he and a group of young doctors—his students and other associates—had succeeded in rescuing the island from the usual epidemics. After protracted negotiation and boycotts by the Sages, elections were finally held in 1978. Tegularius won overwhelmingly. Nevertheless, the Teachers proclaimed that his rule was still subject to their approval.

After four years in office Tegularius proposed new elections, aiming thereby to solidify the legitimacy of his authority's by backing it up by the demonstrated will of the people. The Sages saw this as a ruse to diminish their power and started a fierce campaign against the newly instituted political system in general and Tegularius in particular. Their instigations quickly deteriorated into civil war between the two camps, in the course of which much of the island was destroyed.

All this transpired as the American transport ship *President Harding* cruised the area as part of its routine security patrol, hence monitoring at close range the tragic course of events– the heavy rains, the consequent disintegration of the Hill, and seawater filling the huge craters created by ground implosions following the too-intense ritual digging. Fighting among the islanders went on until the very end of 1995, when the island totally collapsed and sank into the sea. Only one man—Illirio Mariafels, the gifted protégé of Constantius Tegularius (who was killed in the struggle)—escaped the island just moments before the ocean waters obliterated it by swimming southeast toward the *President Harding*.

PART ONE:

HOW IT ALL BEGAN

In June 2003 in my dual role as pianist and lecturer, I took part in the annual conference on distant musical cultures held in Southampton, England. I presented a paper on the music of Malta and Cyprus, performing works by Charles Camilleri and Christodoulos Georgiades. In reading over the conference notes, I discovered that not only was Nelly Zhdanovich coming, but she was also to be a keynote speaker at the gala inauguration of the colloquy. I was scheduled to follow with a performance at the end of that day.

Since the late nineties I had been vaguely aware of Nelly's successful rise to prominence following the critical acclaim that her articles on two-part chanting in the Far East had received. She was the first to write about two-part singing by one person. She soon became known for her brilliance and started receiving prizes awarded by various musicological societies. By the mid-nineties she had already attained full professorship at a midwestern American university. The short bio accompanying her publications stated that in 1989, under the auspices of a State Department program for aspiring Soviet doctorial students, she traveled to America. This was just before the collapse of the Soviet Union. Uncertain about her career prospects amidst the chaos that then engulfed vast portions of post-Soviet territory, especially her native city of Minsk, she opted to remain in America.

As I needed to prepare myself for the evening's recital, I could not stay for Nelly's keynote speech, although we had met beforehand at the registration coffee hour where we exchanged polite kisses. I noticed she looked tired, irritable, and strangely unkempt. It felt like once again she was proudly displaying her superiority with that sprinkle of dandruff on the shoulders of her dress. The lenses of her spectacles were so openly dirty I couldn't figure out how she managed to see anything. I was, however, relieved not to detect any odor emanating from her body.

Putting her right hand on my shoulder, she greeted me, "So you sit in Israel teaching little Zionist Chopins and Rachmaninoffs?"

"Yes", I said, and from that moment I tried to escape.

Suddenly she grew taller (and I was frightened), proclaiming out of the blue, "How I envy you!"I refused to react. Still grasping my shoulder and lowering herself to her regular height, she whispered, "You gifted little fool. Nothing's changed, right? The fool remains; there is only the question of the gift." She had already glided away.

Upon finishing my pre-recital warm-up, I overheard conversations in the foyer that at the opening session Nelly had created a scandal. I was too preoccupied with my own thoughts to react, but from what I overheard, I understood that she had resigned either from the Ethnomusicological Society that she belonged to or from some other prestigious organization. I could not care less. Forty minutes later, already familiar with the local Bechstein, I performed *Visions of Valetta,* the *Noospheres* by the outstanding Maltese composer Charles Camilleri, and *Six Concert Pieces* by the eminent Cypriot Christodoulos Georgiades.

The next day I did not come to the morning session, not because I was resting after the labors of a taxing recital; but because I was deeply offended by the faint applause I had received at my concert the previous night. In my judgment I played well, but all I got was a few hesitant claps lasting no more than twenty seconds. After the performance, having changed my stage tuxedo for a pair of ordinary jeans and a gray t-shirt, I mingled unrecognized in the white wine drinking crowd, peripherally intercepting crass remarks such as: "Well, what do you expect, this is not Chopin. People come to a concert to enjoy music, and that does not mean Camilleri," "This was a failure—we should have invited an international star, whatever the cost, to perform Chopin for us,"and "It's one thing to attend a conference discussing music from geographic regions far from the heart of Europe, quite another to have to listen to the stuff. One cannot be asked to do that!"

Throughout the next morning I paced the shoreline of Mayflower Park in silent fury. I could not bring myself to reason—I wanted to run from the conference straight away, even before reading my own paper that was scheduled for the afternoon session on the following day. It was already apparent that nobody was interested in my ideas; they showed that quite clearly during the concert. While walking, I engaged my colleagues in an imaginary Hunnenschlacht (Battle of Huns) wherein I beat them into oblivion. But this sense of false exultation betrayed the fact that

I was experiencing terrible self-defeat. I felt as though I were a miserable loser.

Just when the word "loser" occupied my heart, I spotted an elderly woman in a long, shapeless coat that trailed on the ground behind her—it was at least 27°C (80.6°F) and gloriously sunny—also promenading with lowered head. Suddenly I noticed the ridiculous old-fashioned glasses and started looking for an escape. Yes, it was Nelly, and yes, it was too late.

She approached me, again putting her right hand on my shoulder. "You played gorgeously," she said. "A wonderful recital, such music, such a wonderful performance…."

"Thank you," I said. "I am sorry for not being at your speech yesterday."

"You didn't miss much," she said. "I did not read anything."

"Then what did you do?" I asked.

"I resigned from all my honorary positions in the ethnomusicological establishment, asserting that all my research over the past six years—of which everyone in the music world was in such awe—was based on a great misunderstanding," she avowed. "It was all a terrible mistake," she mused, smiling strangely.

"Do you now know what that mistake was?" I asked, affecting nonchalance.

"No!" she said tremblingly, and suddenly started to grow alarmingly while at the same time looking more and more ravishing. It was unbearable. In front of me stood a tall, weeping woman of irresistible beauty. (Damn her! She made me love her again! Damned, cursed witch! Oh my god….) Patting me again on the shoulder, she said, "You will not understand much, but you have to help me." Then she smiled her sad smile, yet one of captivating beauty. Damn her. I could not withstand it. "You have to help me" she repeated.

"How?" I asked.

"You have to find my beloved Illirio Mariafels," she said.

"I do not know any Mariafels," I said.

"Go and find him. Find him for me," she commanded.

"How can I find a person whom I do not know—and where?" I was completely losing all self-respect. I did not even tell her that she had no right to make such requests of me.

"He's probably in Israel," she said. "He likes children," she continued. "His right arm is amputated at the elbow. He is tall...."

She started crying in earnest. I tried to comfort her. Damn her! As she placed her beautiful head on my shoulder, I breathed in the scent of exquisite perfume. "Oh, Nelly...."

"He is more than two meters tall with a head of thick, light brown hair. He has penetrating blue eyes that gaze toward the horizon...and a face, a face never to be forgotten," she continued, weeping. "And, he sings...."

"So?" I asked.

"He sings in two voices." Suddenly she collapsed into her usual stature and said, "Come this evening to my hotel, I will tell you more about Illirio."

She dragged herself away and I remained in Southampton.

* * *

Sitting in an armchair in the hotel foyer, attractively outfitted in a dazzlingly white track suit—damn her, she looked irresistible. She did not stand to greet me, so I cannot say whether she was tall now or just her usual stature, though I presumed she was tall. Waiting there without a book, newspaper, journal, or music score in her hands, she was simply beautiful.

"I am here", I said. "Please tell me your story."

"You sweet boy." Then, looking not at me but toward the side windows of the hall, she sighed and said melodramatically, "Yesterday I died. I no longer exist."

"So who is sitting in front of me?" I queried.

"A woman worthy of her beloved Illirio," she said.

"So you weren't worthy of him before," I intimated.

"Quite correct. I was a disgusting, stupid egomaniac." My effort to hide a smile was perhaps not all that successful. "Blow me off as much as you wish," she countered, "but you will help me find him, right?"

As much as I tried to evade making a straight answer, it was clear I would. She saw it. Damned witch.

* * *

This is her story.

I found him on Anticosti Island, a large, sparsely populated island in the gulf of the Saint Lawrence River. It was 1997.

At that time I had just received an associate professorship in anthropology at the University of Nebraska and was eager to

further my field research on singing customs of Native Americans. I was sure that their souls contained some rare wisdom that absolutely had to be brought to western light. I realized that the best chance of finding Native Americans still practicing their ancient customs most authentically would be to go to some secluded community, uncontaminated by mainstream culture. So in early June 1997 I sailed to Anticosti Island together with my two graduate student assistants.

I saw him just a couple of hours after we checked in at our hotel. My assistants remained at the hotel to rest while I walked along the shore alone. He was surrounded by a group of children on the edge of a pier that extended far out to sea. I did not overhear how he communicated with the children, but I immediately saw that they loved him. How attentively they smiled at him, sometimes waving their hands, as if imitating the wind itself!

He was far taller than average for a Native American, taller than tall. I think he was at least two meters tall. Or even taller. His right forearm was amputated and he did not hide the stump.

Ignoring all the well-honed guidelines of anthropological research, I went straight up to him and joined the group of children. As I got closer, I overheard a song, maybe a children's chorus, but with unusually low voices. I presumed this to be the low register of these strangely blond Native American children. When I came closer I saw that the children were not singing at all—their mouths were firmly closed. The tall man did not open his mouth either.

I was intrigued. Now I saw that I had erred—the children were of distinctly European ancestry. The tall man was the only non-westerner; perhaps he was of mixed origin. Eager to talk to him, I asked if I might join the group.

I was welcomed by two virile, highly mellifluous voices speaking French.

"Do you understand French?" Nelly asked me abruptly.

"No, not at all," I said in a mumble intended to convey discontent at the unwanted investigation of my personal abilities.

"Well, *I* do. But I could not understand where those two men who addressed me with such welcoming harmony were. The children smiled, and I heard them laughing softly. Yet no child had opened his or her mouth.

"Please do not be afraid, *madame*," two tender bass voices said with utmost concern.

But I *was* afraid—deeply afraid I was losing my mind. When the tall man with blue diamond-shaped eyes looked at me, I felt as though I were melting away. At that moment I felt myself to be an utter failure as a professor of cultural studies. For from my vantage point in the academic realm, these local people definitely seemed to be of inferior intellect, yet in a matter of moments this bizarre man had succeeded in disarming my mind completely; distinctly hearing two bass voices, I saw only one man. What was this surreal phenomenon I was encountering? Confused, shattered, unable to function, I turned into a pathetically scared girl. Apologizing for my aberrant behavior, I went straight back to the hotel on the mainland.

Later on, when speaking with my assistants, I told them that I had spotted an interesting case, a man surrounded by children who were singing with him in an unusual way, but I did not reveal the helplessness I had experienced. Their curiosity piqued, they insisted on accompanying me there the next day.

Together the three of us promenaded along the seashore trying to spot the tall man and children. Nobody was on the pier. After several days of stalking we still did not see anybody on the pier, so I returned to our original plan of interviewing city authorities about the Native American ancestry of local inhabitants. From these conversations, I understood that my ethnomusicological mission there was a failure, for Native Americans returned to the island only for a month-long hunt in October. They built a temporary camp in the forest on the island and then left. I was told to come back then if I wanted to interview anyone.

I also learned that only white people lived permanently on the island. So I released my two assistants and remained there alone. A week later, I visited the local St. Joseph's primary school (the only school in that vicinity) in an attempt to meet the principal and get his assistance in finding the tall man with the amputated left arm.

However, before entering the school I found *him* carrying a child who appeared to be sick into the main building. Noticing me, he nodded slightly and for some reason I started crying. I did not leave this time, and after a couple of minutes he reappeared to inquire in his harmonious French:

"Are you looking for me?"

"I…perhaps, yes," I said.

"Do you have some special matter to discuss with me?"

"M-maybe…."

"How can I help you?"

"C-could you answer several questions?"

"Yes, please, go ahead."

"Are you of European ancestry?"

"No, not really," he answered forthrightly, paying no attention to the intrusiveness of my question.

"Then what is your country of birth?"

"I am not exactly sure where I was born, but my homeland was Pinto Island in the South China Sea."

I pursued, "Why do you say your homeland 'was'?"

"Because this island does not exist anymore."

"Oh my god, what happened?" I was unable to control the expression of shock that crossed my face.

"It sank."

"What?"

"Yes. It disappeared into the sea."

"Were there any casualties?"

"Yes, practically the entire population perished."

I felt he was about to tell me some dreadful story that was clearly none of my business. My aim, after all, was to learn what he did with the children on Anticosti Island, and what those fabulous choruses that I had heard on the pier were. Perhaps it was some tradition that I should record.

"Would you please tell me about the children and the songs you sing?"

He looked at me with a sad glance and said, "Yes, what would you like to know?"

I asked him to sing for me.

He said he knew very few Canadian songs and only a handful of popular American songs. I asked him to sing his native songs. He sang me one. I was not impressed. I shivered, unable to hide my disappointment, claiming that it was getting cold.

He inquired politely, "Should we go inside?"

I nodded and quickly walked ahead of him toward the entrance. Suddenly the voices of two men asked me from behind, "Are you disappointed by what you have heard, *madame*?"

I looked back nervously, but only saw this one man with the strange, sad eyes.

"Who asked me that last question?" I said, frightened.

Looking down at me, he said, "I did, *madame*," again in two voices.

"How do you do that?" I asked like an amazed child.

"By combining ventriloquism with upper-chest breathing, while at the same time differentiating between cheek and tongue articulation," he explained in his usual one-tone voice.

"Can you sing in two voices too?" I asked, still dumbfounded.

"Yes," he answered.

"Are those songs originally from your homeland?"

"Well...."

"Sing me your songs," I begged impatiently.

So we agreed to meet the next afternoon on the pier where I hoped my quest for something groundbreaking would be realized. I was happy, perhaps for the first time in my life. What a fool I was."

"Did you ask him his name?" I questioned Nelly.

"Not then," she answered, visibly shrinking in size. "Come tomorrow, sweet boy," she said, now ugly.

"Yes, I will come after presenting my paper at the conference," I said.

"I will come to listen," she chimed in.

"You said you were dead, so remain that way," I reminded her in a slightly menacing tone; I did not want any outrageous behavior on her part to ruin my show.

"You are right," she demurred. "I will not come."

* * *

The composer Christodoulos Georgiades came from London expressly for my lecture, which was dedicated to his music. He played two of his short compositions—children's pieces—on the upright piano in the lecture hall, drawing wonderful applause. His performance unexpectedly turned my lecture into a tour de force. He was good indeed—both as a composer and a pianist. His playing was a combination of glitter and tenderness.

During the break people surrounded Georgiades to query him at length about his oeuvre. Standing nearby, I saw how happy this made Christi. I was glad for him too. As he was promising to send some scores to a number of well-wishers, I quietly left the room to go to the hotel to meet Nelly.

This time she was sitting royally in the armchair in the foyer, again beautiful in an eye-catching red track suit.

"How was your lecture?" she inquired.

I proudly reported, "It went surprisingly well. Georgiades came and played two pieces to illustrate my arguments and he was a huge success."

"Good for him," she rejoined. "And you left the admiring crowd just for me?"

"Do not interpret that as a complement," I rebuked. "Let's just get on with the story."

She smiled sadly. It was evident from her expression that my concerns with success were painfully alien to her.

"Please remember, I do not exist anymore…"

"Yes, and my task seems to be to return you to life," I responded to her sadness with sardonic bitterness.

"You sweet boy…"

"Go ahead; do not waste your inspiration!"

"So I met him on the pier and asked him to sing one or two of his island songs, turning on the tape recorder hidden in my pocket. While he sang, I ostensibly sketched some of his musical phrases on scoring paper. He was pleasantly surprised. I asked him about the meaning of the songs.

"He told me that these songs where about devotion to the Teachers and about a faraway land longing to be liberated. That evening he sang thirteen one-voiced songs: seven about the Teachers, three devoted to the faraway land, and the rest about a hill that was a gift from god to the people.

"Still I was impatient to hear his two-part singing, but as it was getting cold I decided to return to the hotel. The next day was to be my last full day on Anticosti. We agreed to meet that evening on the wharf, or in case of rain at the hotel."

"Did you learn his name at that stage?" I asked.

"No," Nelly answered peremptorily, disregarding the interruption. "He came to the pier and I asked him to sing the two-voiced songs and he complied by singing two wonderful songs. I asked him about his tradition of two-voiced singing. He answered vaguely, saying that there was no such tradition. I pressed him to sing some more two-part songs, which he did. He said they were songs of love for a woman, songs of love for children, and songs of love for the people.

"My acumen as an ethnomusicologist told me that the focus on love in this two-voiced tradition was what gave the songs their compelling power. When we came to my hotel later that night, he said that he was very grateful that at long last his songs had attracted the serious attention that they deserved. I smiled. He looked at once almost vulnerable and yet so virile.

"'I will help you,' I blurted out. 'I will help you build your life into a towering success!' His diamond-shaped eyes filled with tears. (I interpreted his emotion at that moment as simple, overweening ambition. Oh, how wrong I was.) I was getting ready to leave, my mind already focused on transcribing his songs and writing a paper on them. I remembered that the rules of contemporary research require that all recorded material be verified by the informant, so I asked him, 'Do you read music?'

"'Yes!' He answered readily.

"'I mean western music.'

"'Yes, I understood you,' he said in affirmation of his original statement.

"'Then I will send you my scores for authorization,' I said. 'What is your mailing address?'

"'St. Joseph's School, Port Menier.' He wrote down the exact address and that was when I learned that his name was Illirio Mariafels.

"On my long way back to Lincoln, Nebraska, I realized that I would have to return for another visit. I arranged for a leave of absence for the following August, but did not wish to inform Illirio in advance, wanting to surprise him and see his excitement. On the train it occurred to me that I might miss him, but no, there he was on the pier with the children, singing as usual. That was Fate's gift to me.

"As we walked along the shore of the mainland that evening, I asked him to sing his love songs, and he sang about a woman named Nissa. This time relying solely on my pocket tape recorder, I did not sketch out the music.

"As we walked around the village, he told me about some hero father figure who had died in order to save his life just before the island sank. I asked if he had some songs devoted to the heroes of the island, but instead he sang more one-voiced songs about the Teachers.

"He showed the utmost respect in his unique, tender way for my demands.

"I already knew what I had to do next—present this phenomenal man on stage at ethnomusicological conferences. Maybe I could even arrange a recording session with my commentary as liner notes. He was indeed my greatest treasure. I found a way to cling to his stump of a hand, and he loved that very much."

"Did you sleep with him at that stage?" I asked insidiously.

"You sweet boy, you ask such adult questions," Nelly's smile also contained a slight grimace.

"So?" I did not retreat under her withering sarcasm.

"I did not sleep with him on Anticosti. But he was already mine at heart."

"When did you first take him to the conferences?"

"In July 1998. But first I brought him to Nebraska, to our anthropology department. I asked him to sing for my colleagues and his voice produced such wild excitement. He wished to be presented to the faculty of the School of International Relations and Social Sciences, but nobody there was ready to listen to him. So he remained mine. I took him to my house. He was god's gift in my bed."

Nelly became silent, observing her feet while smiling to herself. I respectfully remained silent in honor of her moment of erotic reminiscence.

"He stayed with me until the semester resumed in Port Menier and I had him back in Nebraska for Christmas break. Appalled that he had no official papers, I procured him temporary residence documents, both for Canada and the United States. In February 1999 the article I published in the Ethnomusicological Review on two-voiced chanting on Pinto Island caused an uproar; nobody could believe that such chanting was possible. In July 1999 I took him to the annual ethnomusicological conference in Buffalo, New York, where I presented him on stage. People went wild.

"That fall I not only got my full professorship, but the gold medal from the Ethnomusicological Society, as well as many discretionary grants. At the US State Department I was presented with a medal of honor for being one of the five best researchers naturalized in America by none other than Secretary Madeleine Albright. At the reception she ironically commented that my family name, Zhdanov, was identical to that of the repressive Commissar of Culture in the Soviet Union. She got it wrong though—my family name is Zhdanovich.

"Then Illirio sang. In deciding to sing only his one-voiced ventriloquist songs in order not to produce too great a shock for Secretary Albright and her guests, he had hoped to create an atmosphere of compassionate interest in himself and his past that would lead to a short private audience with the secretary herself. He so eagerly wanted to discuss the plight of his sunken motherland and its lost culture. But Secretary Albright left immediately after the reception. He was still all mine!

"In December 1999 we went to Des Moines together to meet the American Pintoist community. He asked me to wait for him in the hotel. He returned three days later, his body covered with blood-soaked rags. One stab wound was most cruelly inflicted upon his stump. I never saw such a disconsolate expression as the one on his face! I got him to a hospital and I sat at his bedside for a whole week.

"I dared not ask him what had happened. He only said that he had sung his two-voiced songs and would not divulge anything further. I did not press him—after all, he remained mine. Returning to Lincoln, I wrote the St. Joseph's School for permission for him to recuperate at my residence, an obvious necessity that was duly granted.

"In February 2000 he returned to Anticosti and in April of that year I presented him at another conference in Tallahassee, Florida, where I received the annual Alan Merriam Prize. After he had sung his songs, he was surrounded by people who came to touch him or to be photographed with him. They asked his exact height, what kind of food he ate, and how many times a day. Some people wanted to see his stump, believing it to be some kind of machine that facilitated two-voiced singing. I stood nearby, smiling.

"He quickly learned to speak fluent English and he tried to tell the story of his sunken motherland. The people who were so enthusiastic about touching his body were remarkably indifferent to his history. Back at the hotel I saw how angry he was. He accused me of presenting him to callous academics who could only see him as some subhuman curiosity.

"I tried explaining that this was not callousness, but rather the scientific detachment of the intellectual community. He could not accept this. I cajoled that he needed to patiently go through the circuit of various academic conferences until his unique talent was acknowledged, just as polymaths and extraordinarily flexible acrobats had done. He did not say anything more.

"We went to sleep together, and at three o'clock in the morning when I woke up to go to the bathroom, I noticed that he was not in bed. He had left without saying goodbye, without even writing a letter. I was furious—after all, wasn't I the one who had helped him achieve the prominence that he now enjoyed? It was only through my dedication that doors were opening for him... he owed me!

"I lost him.

"In 2001 I visited the Pintoist communities in the Des Moines suburbs, incognito...."

Interrupting her story at this critical juncture, Nelly implored, "My sweet boy, please come tomorrow."

"But my bus leaves for London tomorrow at noon," I said.

"So come with your suitcases packed for an early breakfast; I will call you a taxi."

"Thanks, but I can call a taxi without your help," I said, not hiding my irritation at being drawn into all of this.

"Will you come, dear?" she asked with unforgivable radiance.

"Yes."

* * *

For our last meeting in Southampton, I arrived early the next morning. Nelly was not waiting for me in the foyer. I sat down in her armchair, hating myself for getting involved in her ridiculous story as though I did not have anything else to do in my life. As I waited, I observed several serious-looking senior citizens at a nearby table examining a map of Southampton. Suddenly two ladies looked at me with a frightened glance and then whispered loudly, "There's that pianist who played that awful contemporary music instead of Chopin." The ladies evidently felt that I was some kind of audio monster ready to kill them with repellent dissonances. Feeling trapped by their abhorrence for the modern classical repertoire, I grabbed for the nearest newspaper lying on a nearby table and feigned interest.

Finally Nelly, leaning awkwardly on the handrail, appeared on the stairs. She was wearing a wrinkled dressing gown, half-buttoned and revealing her repugnant breasts. From behind her unclean spectacles she smiled at me and invited me to her room "for a salad." I felt sick but followed her meekly, if only to avoid the senior citizen rumor mill in the lobby.

Seated at her small hotel table, I consumed a salad.

"You said you visited the Pintoist community in Des Moines," I said to recall the point at which she had dramatically dropped the story at our last meeting.

"Yes. I went there after going to Anticosti and realizing that Illirio was no longer there. I thought I might be able to understand something about him by visiting his countrymen in America."

"What did you see there?" I asked.

"Well, it's weird. It has two very distinct neighborhoods that are divided by an empty field. In the middle of that field there is a dense grove containing an eerie cemetery. The cemetery is surrounded by a shabbily constructed fence with two gates. One gate opens to the northeast, leading to a modern neighborhood, while the other opens to the southwest onto a filthy quarter of primitive one-story clay dwellings.

"A funeral was taking place on the southwest side as I passed by and I saw a dead body fastened to a stick lowered into a pit, but instead of throwing earth onto the grave, people poured buckets of water into the grave. Then they sang two songs. I am sure they sang it in a ventriloquist manner; they did not open their mouths."

"Did they sing the two-voiced songs?" I asked.

"No, I clearly remember it being a plain, simple chant."

"What did you do next?" I asked, hanging on to her every word.

"First I went into the dirty neighborhood. I did not see many people on the street, but the same plain chant emanated from every corner. The sloppily written street signs were in Latin letters. The language spoken by the few passersby that I did encounter was an unintelligible interpellation of shrieking, which may have been Chinese pitch accents and Portuguese. Soon I reached a public park in the center of the village. I encountered a strange yet grandiose scene: in the middle of the park was a tall, apparently man-made hill, with some grass growing on its sandy slopes. Many young children were busily uprooting the grass and throwing it down the slopes, while others dug huge ditches around the hill and lifted the sand to the summit in aluminum buckets. Some old men stood around directing the activity by giving orders to the children in song. It was a truly amazing scene and seemed to contain sacred significance. I left, not wishing to be intrusive.

"Crossing the deserted field, I then visited the modern neighborhood. I felt creepy crossing the field, as though I were treading on somebody's holy altar and that many pairs of unfriendly eyes were watching me from afar.

"The modern neighborhood consisted of three tall apartment buildings and several streets of cottages. There were several multi-story commercial buildings and two glittering pavilions, one for trade and the other for recreation. All contained clear inscriptions in Portuguese. I noticed many large billboards advertising commercial companies that could facilitate trade with China.

"I looked for the local authorities in the modern neighborhood. I was led by two boys who only spoke Portuguese to a one-roomed building where a young woman sat at the only desk in the room. I asked her about the neighborhood and she gave me a brochure written in Portuguese about the Pintoist settlement of Des Moines.

"When I inquired about recent street fights in the neighborhood, she answered that this was a frequent occurrence only in the southwest, not in the northeast. When I asked for information about the local council of the southwest, I was informed that there wasn't one; only the Teachers governed there and they would not speak to a stranger like me.

"I asked her if she was familiar with the tradition of two-voiced chanting. The young woman suddenly turned pale and asked me to leave immediately. 'For your own good, lady, never come back here and never ask about the two-voiced chanting!' I became really frightened and left.

"Upon examining the brochure I had been given, I learned about the Pintoist diaspora from the assimilationist viewpoint. The brochure spoke about the community's founding in 1837 and the subsequent split into two camps called "the Faithful" and "the Efficient." The text presented the existence of the two camps in a celebratory manner, describing them as a unique form of pluralism that the entire world should emulate. This pluralism was lauded as rich in genius, supported by a common love for the motherland. I learned that the central avenue of the northeastern enclave was named after President Andrew Johnson, 'one of only two streets in the United States carrying this eminent name.' I read nothing about two-voiced chanting."

"So maybe this chant was not part of the tradition on the Island?" I suggested.

"You may be right!" mused Nelly.

Suddenly she started growing taller and turning herself into a beautiful woman (damned witch).

"I think," she started sobbing, "I messed up not only the science, but my whole life!"

"What do you mean?" I asked, consoling her with as tender a caress as I could manage and then immediately changing my mind.

"I think Illirio carries a huge message in his special chant. And this message is not for me with my egoism and ambition to investigate; I should simply love him, and try to help him…I think I should devote my life to him…. Do you hear me, my sweet Solomon?" (This was the first time she had uttered my name over the course of our marathon conversations.)

"So you want me to find him for you and save your life."

"Yes! Don't you see? I am nobody now, and I will not return to my career. I will work at a grimy, foul-smelling gas station pumping gas until you find him for me!"

"How on earth do you know that he is in Israel?" I exclaimed, dumbfounded by the huge responsibility she had just placed on my shoulders.

From the pocket of her dirty dressing gown she removed a newspaper clipping. It was from a communal Jewish weekly in Los Angeles and contained an announcement for a visit by a Zionist activist from Kibbutz Bror Hayil who was coming to solicit financial contributions from the kibbutz's American benefactors. The announcement extolled the achievements of the kibbutz, mentioning in an off-the-cuff way two-voiced chanting.

I became furious. "And on the basis of this measly announcement you're sending me to find him?" I shouted imperiously.

"Look carefully at what is written," she said, calming me down.

I read the text under her pointing finger: "The unique two-voiced chanting developed by a visiting expert in the field especially for our Kibbutz Bror Hayil children."

"OK, give me your e-mail address," I conceded. "And let's be clear: I am not promising anything."

"My life is in your hands, sweet boy," she said from the summit of her beauty, and kissed me almost on the lips. Damned witch. The fragrance of her body was divine. Grabbing my suitcase, I immediately left the hotel.

I returned home.

On the flight back to Tel Aviv I was full of disquiet, ruminating over the terrible headlines in the newspapers from back home—a Palestinian suicide bombing and massive Israeli retribution. On both sides lay scores of bodies of dead children, elderly people on buses, and frightened families seeking protection in musty underground shelters. It was as though a feast of hopelessness had taken over the land, strangling everybody's soul in an ugly *danse macabre*, killing both the pure and the wicked, the innocent and the manipulative, the ambitious and the humble, the industrious and the lazy, the diligent and the adventurous, the sick and the healthy, the old and the young, the boy and the girl, the aunt and the uncle—all of us.

Although I felt my country should be more restrained in its spilling of Palestinian blood, I knew that this point of view was regarded with contempt in the corridors of power in Israel. Looking out the window and seeing the yellow lights of Tel Aviv on the eastern horizon, I wearily shook my head.

After thinking about it, I realized that if this man Illirio had indeed come to Israel (but why on earth should he??), then Kibbutz Bror Hayil would be the logical place for him to be. Most of the members of the kibbutz were Portuguese-speaking new immigrants from Brazil. The Portuguese language would be their common bond with Illirio.

Upon my return to Israel, my work required my full attention. So for the first few weeks I could not start chasing after Nelly's lost love. Coincidentally, while walking down Ben Yehuda Street in Tel Aviv I met Yuval Kariv, my Hebrew teacher from back in 2000, whom I recalled was a member of Kibbutz Bror Hayil. I asked him about a tall, middle-aged man with an amputated left arm who sang ventriloquist-type songs. He said he knew nothing about a man like that—he had left the kibbutz years ago—but promised to make inquiries.

I did not expect to hear from him. However, three days later Yuval called with news that a tall, one-armed man had indeed spent several months on the kibbutz some two or three years ago and then disappeared. He was much loved by the teenagers on the kibbutz and even helped the kibbutz psychologist calm down the little children during rocket attacks from Gaza. The psychologist, a woman in her early thirties, had since accompanied her boyfriend to the United States so it would be impossible to interview her, but some teenagers still remembered the man. Yuval had managed to get me some of their names.

So I came to that green, peaceful village situated on the fringe of the Negev Desert in January 2004, not really focused on Nelly's pleadings. I was in the middle of preparing for a recital in Paris that was arranged for me by a dear friend, Professor Mieczysław Narutowicz. I was also to give a series of master classes at the Institut des hautes études musicales de Paris (IHEMdP), the famous venue for aspiring young musicians. This time I did have to play Chopin (and also Schumann and Liszt). I traveled to Bror Hayil mainly as a respite from my intense practicing.

At the entrance to the kibbutz I found some boys playing soccer.

Soccer field at the entrance of Kibbutz Bror Hayil

To my utter amazement, they shouted to each other using a ventriloquist-type chant, even employing this technique when laughing. I told them that I was a friend of Yuval Kariv (only one boy remembered him) and that I had come to inquire about a certain character named Illirio, a tall, one-armed man who spoke ventriloquist Portuguese.

They immediately jumped upon me and started touching me affectionately. It was clear that they definitely loved this man and were eager for any news about him.

They told me that "Uncle Il" as they called him (*Dod Il* in Hebrew) was indeed there, and when he sat with them in the underground shelters, the children did not panic. It was there during the long hours in the shelters that he taught them this funny method of *pitum* ("ventriloquism" in Hebrew) singing. All of them knew some Portuguese, so they could communicate easily. He in turn quickly picked up Hebrew, pronouncing each word with such tender care. They told me that it seemed as if Hebrew sang in his mouth.

I asked them how he first appeared on the kibbutz. One of the boys told me that Uncle Il came by foot, while another one was sure that he swam all the way to Israel's shore.

"Where did he sleep?" I inquired. They showed me his deserted shack. I did not find anything interesting there. For some reason I had been hoping to discover a navigation chart showing the route from Anticosti Island to Ashkelon…well, I was dead wrong.

"So what happened?" I asked.

"One day he just left," the boys said directly.

"Didn't he say something before leaving?" I asked.

"No. Not to us," said the boys.

"Did Uncle Il have some friends here?" I asked.

"Yes, beside Margalit, the psychologist who left for America, there was Yekhezkiel."

"Who is Yekhezkiel?" I asked.

"Our old Yekhezkiel Rejinaldo is vice-chairman of the Kibbutz Council."

"Can I meet him?"

Two boys ran to his living quarters. I waited around listlessly for about an hour until they returned. They said that Yekhezkiel was attending a conference in Haifa. They did not have his telephone number, so I gave them mine and departed, not intending to come back. I was too busy with Chopin's *Sonata Opus 58* and with

Liszt (my Schumann was relatively easy), and in addition to that, I was overloaded with teaching. I had already done for Nelly whatever I could. I would write her a long, apologetic e-mail and she could now ask somebody else to find her boy toy in some other corner of the planet.

Three days later Mr. Rejinaldo called me. He was surprised that somebody who was not from the secret service was interested in Illirio Mariafels, whom he also considered to be an extraordinary man.

"Did he leave the kibbutz?" I asked.

"Yes," the vice-chairman replied. "And I am sure he left Israel too," he said, coughing with embarrassment.

"I think he left by sea. I mean, he literally swam to Cyprus… with his amputated arm. Once I saw him teaching our children to swim in our pool. I have never seen such might and such mastery. It was really superhuman." He paused.

"Well, let us not discuss things we are not sure about," I suggested. "Why did he leave the kibbutz?"

"It was the day after some heavy shelling in our area. Nobody was hurt, but the children were terribly frightened by the shriek of the homemade rockets landing in the nearby fields. Illirio sat with the children in the shelter and sang them wonderful songs, and the children responded to him, calmed down, and started playing. The next day the army retaliated brutally and *Maariv*, the afternoon daily, published photos of a Palestinian family that had perished in the attack.

"*Maariv* did not print photos of the dead bodies, but through their press connections in Gaza, they acquired and published pictures of the people who had been killed when they were still alive and in their prime. Illirio saw one particular picture of a beautifully smiling, vibrant young woman. He cut it out and put it in his pocket. By the way, he would not take any money from us for his services—all we could give him was a pair of discarded trousers with huge pockets. The very next day he came to me with that picture in hand and asked what I thought about the situation. I said we had no choice—solemnly intoning the Hebrew idiom *eyn brera,* which we say when we admit to perpetrating something awful that we wish did not have to happen.

"He said that my words killed all hope. I said that as an old-timer, I emphatically disagreed with our government's policy toward the Palestinians and had attended many, many protest demonstrations over the years. Yet self-defense is a natural human right, no? Showing me the blurred picture of the beautiful, smiling Palestinian woman, he said she looked like his beloved Nissa, the mother of his child. 'They are both dead now. And now this woman is dead too, together with her child....'

"He left my room and a moment later, on that a clear, silent evening, I heard a wonderful male chorus singing an unknown hymn. I was overcome with emotion. I was sure he had turned up the volume of his Walkman. Yet when I went out to see him off, I did not see the headphones of any Walkman on him. I hugged this tall, tender-hearted man and sighed, asking, 'What now?'

"'I cannot bear seeing how people kill hope,' he said. 'I will leave because I cannot be of any more help here,' he said, his voice full of remorse.

"'But on the contrary, you have been so helpful to our children,' I beseeched. I was really sad that such a great man wanted to leave us.

"'I could be of help when I had hope,' he said sadly. 'Wish me strength; I am going to swim a long distance,' he said. I gave him some meat from the kibbutz's communal kitchen and a few bottles of water. He rolled them into a tight package and attached it to his mighty waist. I hugged him again. He left without even a night's rest, walking straight to the Ashkelon shore."

I asked Yekhezkiel about the approximate date of these events. He said, "Early summer of 2001." I thanked him and wished him well. "If you find him, please call me," Yekhezkiel implored and hung up.

Several days later, as I was resting from the difficult scherzo in the Chopin sonata, I looked through the online archives on *Maariv*'s website and came across the blurred photos of the family killed by our shelling of Gaza. I downloaded the picture of the woman who, according to Yekhezkiel Rejinaldo, strongly resembled the great love of Illirio's life. Printing out a hard copy, I kept the picture in my drawer.

Photo from Maariv

While all this didn't have much to do with **Nelly**, it certainly shed some light on a vital part of Illirio's life.

Anyway, I sent Nelly a short message instead of the long, apologetic one that I had intended to write. I told her that while Illirio had indeed been in Israel, he vanished in June 2001. She thanked me profusely. I was free.

* * *

May 2004
Paris

I came to Paris in the middle of a beautiful spring–a dangerous experience for someone like me who is so easily overwhelmed by the city's seductive charms. The magnificent Parisian architecture with its large pastel-colored buildings, mansard roofs, and wrought-iron balconies casting dreamy shadows on the narrow cobblestone streets always arouses my acute urban sensibilities with an innuendo of a passionate *baiser* around every corner. Now transfixed by the perfume of the blossoming chestnut trees in the Jardin des Tuileries, all the sentimentality of Sinatra's "April in Paris" came to life.

Not being a globe-trotting star under perennial escort of a manager to steer me away from the temptations of the passing scene, I knew that I had to rely upon my own willpower to resist the allure of the Parisian streets so as to maintain the mental concentration required for practice before this concert. I locked myself inside the practice studios attentively polishing Chopin's descending double-noted fourths and lightning-fast multi-octave arpeggios. I did not allow myself even one promenade in the Jardin des Tuileries, instead stopping outside for only twenty minutes–no more!–to partake of the quintessential Parisian scene.

My program, coordinated to my host's wishes for "popular high-romantic repertoire only" started with Chopin's *Piano Sonata*, Opus 58—a defiant display of national glory protesting the dismemberment of Chopin's Poland by the adjacent Prussian, Austrian, and Russian empires. This defiance is obvious right at the start of the first movement, when after the dramatic descent of the B-minor arpeggio impetuous, energetic chords ascend to a high F-sharp. Chopin prescribes that this first movement be played *maestoso*. Everything in this magnificent composition— the lilting melody of the second subject in the first movement, the sparkling scherzo (reflecting the glitter of young Polish cadets dreaming of insurrection?), and even the somber largo with its extremely slow, march-like melody reflects Chopin's nationalist mood. And then the absolutely phenomenal finale—a fury of super-virtuosic heroism, again under the wing of a soaring melody...I always bear in mind that the world leaders assembled at Versailles for the Peace Conference following World War I wholeheartedly supporting President Woodrow Wilson's call for Poland's restoration, and that many of them came to Versailles after hearing the great Polish pianist (and later statesman) Paderewski perform Chopin in concert and absorbed his artistically conveyed political message to resurrect Chopin's *Patrie*.

Next on the program was Schumann's *Three Romances*, Opus 28. If Chopin's music is a depiction of national heroism, then Schumann's music is life as seen and felt from inside the human soul, the "life-pulse itself." In the first romance, I wished to recreate the atmosphere of noble Count Egmont's evening ride to meet his beloved Klärchen. The melody here evokes a proclamation of fate filled with a shadowy rumble—the rapid triplets dramatically representing not merely a lone riding knight, but also his emotional state of anticipation. In the second romance I wanted to convey a woman's love and tenderness by playing the extremely wide-ranging accompaniment in a soft, hovering manner. Yet both the accompaniment and the middle-register melody (which is decisively not written in the more standard feminine soprano register) indicate that this is not the love of a light-hearted, immature girl, but rather that of a great warrior-ally, a "Marianne." The third romance I played as a celebration of youthful spirit. The staccato chords, with one hand playfully imitating the other, that punctuate the composition show Schumann's ever-present fascination with youth.

I concluded the recital with the piano version of Liszt's *Orpheus* and his *Bénédiction de Dieu dans la solitude* after Lamartine. Liszt is a master of cosmic space whose musical tempests descend from awesome Alpine summits to reveal the presence of god in the human soul. As such, Liszt's music is frequently charged with epistemological motifs—like the bliss of the Elysian Fields that is found at the outset of the tone-poem, or the tender, persuasive chant full of humane values that Orpheus himself intones before the representatives of ancient barbarism.

From there I went into Lamartine's dialogue with god—an elevated contemplation of man's ability to overcome doubt and experience unification with the divine presence. Placing the melody in the low register to replicate the human voice, Liszt pairs it with a celestial double-noted accompaniment in a higher register—a very difficult challenge for a pianist! The stunning part—the merging of the noble low melody and the serene accompaniment in a swirling emotional vortex that then fades out into the silence of the infinite—always perturbs my own doubt-ridden soul and in my performance the intention was to transmit the transcendental humanization of the divine—god abiding in the human heart.

The audience at my recital at the Salle Camille Saint-Saëns was collegial, a group of eminent professors and students from the Institut des hautes études musicales (IHEMdP). Although the recital did not merit a review in the press, I did overhear some musicians critiquing my "virile, perhaps too virile Chopin" and my "clear, unsentimental Schumann." I was most interested in feedback about my Liszt, but I received none. Later upon quizzing my host, Professor Mieczysław Narutowicz, he fumblingly said, "Oh, my colleagues found it interesting!" Well, I got what I deserved....

Actually, I am quite familiar with this "no reaction" on the part of so-called musical confreres who rarely volunteer a helpful critique unless it is directed toward a member of their own circle. Musicians, it seems, are reflexively attuned to protecting their statuses against all outsiders. Usually there is no criticism of a visiting performer, especially if his performance is at least partially adequate and the performer is appearing at the behest of a superior colleague. On the other hand, senior musicians do readily express opinions on the performance of younger music students, especially in competitions or examination sessions; but these judgments usually focus on formal aspects of performance only—smoothness, fidelity to the score, finger articulation, cleanness of pedal application, adherence to the currently accepted stylistic canon defining a composer's music. The spiritual aspect of the performance is not only not discussed, it is not even acknowledged! In rare cases of rapture, jury members exclaim, "That was fantastic." When asked about the components of this "fantastic," they usually get irate and show open contempt for analyzing their feelings.

Yes, there was some presumption in my attempt to present my own musical perceptions to colleagues in this glittering center of culture from my non-star position—I would even call myself a fool trying by the force of my naïve vigor to break down the wall of their socially conditioned dissociation. Yet there were at least twenty piano students in the audience, and I felt that no wall existed between them and me. This was my space to live. In contrast to the estrangement evinced by my colleagues, I was treated with warm regard by these students; I heard many cordial words from them, and later, during the open classes, I felt an even greater warmth. It was a nice feeling.

For the next two days I listened to twelve students from IHEMdP exposing their own interpretations of Bach, Beethoven, Liszt, Scriabin, Schumann, Ravel, and Stravinsky. One student from Taiwan played the beautiful *Nocturne in E major* by the American composer Norman Dello Joio in the most exquisite manner; in his hands the melody, accompanied by a soft, persistent syncopation, had a tender, almost juicy sound.

The penultimate day of my visit to Paris was the strangest of all: Professor Narutowicz asked me to accompany him to a festive reception given by the directorate of IHEMdP. It was to be a tribute to the late Adélaïde Fourangier de Vermandois (known simply as Mme Fourangier), professor emeritus of piano at the school and France's eminent cultural envoy to faraway countries.

On our way to the reception Narutowicz told me a bit more about Mme Fourangier. She was born in 1924 and studied piano with the legendary, though controversial, Alfred Cortot, traveling to Switzerland where he made his home after World War II to do so. She was active in the early fifties throughout France, Switzerland, and Belgium as a recitalist, playing many solos with orchestras, especially the Karl Maria von Weber and Johann Nepomuk Hummel piano concertos. She was one of the very few concert pianists of that epoch who performed those lesser known compositions. She was in fact famous for her performance of Weber's well-known *Konzertstuck in F minor*. Quite early in life she married a scion of the French aristocracy, de Vermandois, gave birth, and then withdrew from the public eye. Rumor has it that she left both her husband and her baby daughter and went to live with a gifted emigré from the Far East, and then later left France. She reappeared in 1985, a quarter of a century later, and worked for eight more years as a senior professor at IHEMdP. Her last two years in Paris were especially successful; she attracted many students from China, Japan, and Korea, and helped them perfect their piano technique in a most spectacular manner. Professor Narutowicz suggested that Mme Fourangier had an uncanny way of penetrating the psycho-physical nature of her Far Eastern students and this is what produced their extraordinary progress. Professor Fourangier died in 1994. This gathering was to be a homage on what would have been her eightieth birthday.

When we arrived at IHEMdP, many of the school staff had already gathered in the beautiful reception hall. A large painting of Mme Fourangier in her later years was placed upon a high easel. I photographed this painting.

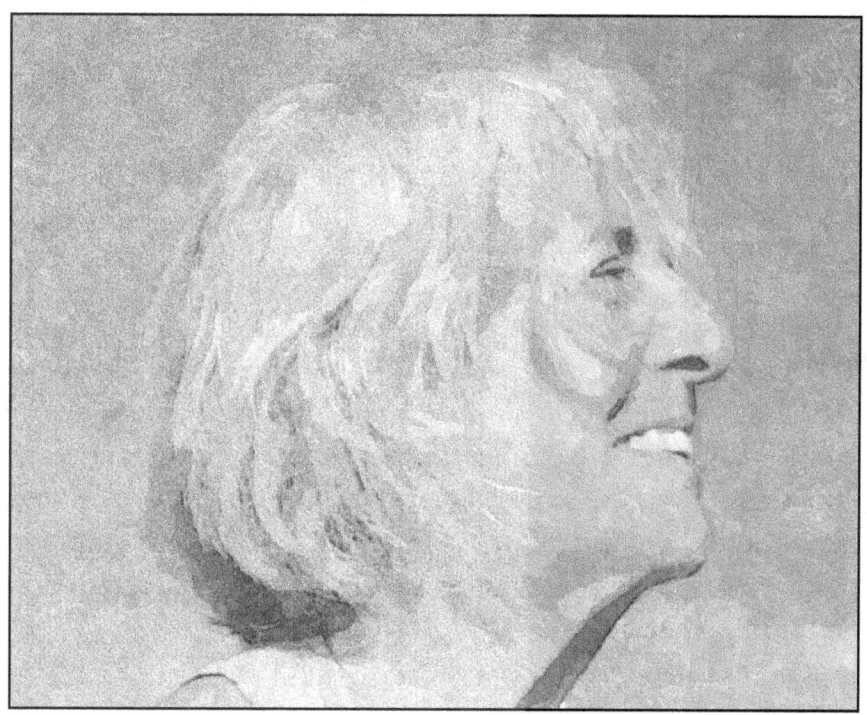

Mme Fourangier, painted by Gérard-Bénédict Murville

The director made a short speech honoring their eminent colleague, lauding her as France's cultural envoy to distant countries, and then people resumed their socializing. Having no knowledge of French, I found myself standing alone. I noticed one sad, exquisitely dressed woman in her late fifties sitting by herself in a chair near the window. She viewed the gathering from a distance with a polite smile. Professor Narutowicz noticed my glance and quickly led me over to that lonely woman.

"Permit me to introduce you both," he said smilingly. "Fleurette de Vermandois, daughter of the late Mme Fourangier; Dr.

Solomon Jekabpils, my dear colleague from…." My dear Mieczysław always seemed to hesitate when having to say where I am from.

"From Israel," I offered. Mlle de Vermandois smiled weakly and asked me several polite questions in English regarding my visit to Paris.

Inquiring whether she herself was a pianist, I found out that her interest was a charity for promising interior designers of apartment space. In pursuing a line of questioning about her mother and her humanitarian representation of France in faraway countries, I found out from Mlle de Vermandois that her mother was actually permanently stationed in only one place, an obscure island named Pinto that, according to rumor, had sunk sometime around the year 1995, about ten years after her mother had returned to Paris.

I was stunned. "Your mother worked on Pinto Island?" I exclaimed in surprise. My excitement was so palpable that it attracted the attention of other colleagues in the room.

"Yes, are you familiar with her work?" queried Mlle de Vermandois politely.

"No, not at all," I replied, trying to calm myself. "But I wish I could know more…did you live with her on the island?" I asked.

"I was never there," she replied. "My mother left me and my father when I was just three years old and went to live with another man. My position this afternoon is quite formal; I represent my mother as her legal heir. I do not frequently visit this institute."

"Did you meet your mother in Paris during her later years here?" I asked.

"Even after her return to Paris we met only occasionally. We became closer just before her death, when I cared for her during her illnesses. She had a son with that other man, and she took him to the island when she went there. On her deathbed, I heard her say, 'Illirio, my poor child.' I think that this must have been his name."

I could not believe my ears. "You know, by remarkable coincidence I recently ran into an old acquaintance who once met a man named Illirio in Canada…according to this acquaintance, Illirio does exist and he told her that he came from Pinto Island…." Mlle de Vermandois did not express one iota of surprise in response to this information.

"Wouldn't you like to know more about a possible half brother?" I asked with incredulity.

"Not really," she sighed. "But my mother did leave a large trunk containing many documents and artifacts that she brought back from Pinto Island. If you wish to examine it, you are most welcome."

"I would certainly love to, mademoiselle," I said with gratitude. Mlle de Vermandois graciously invited me to her Paris apartment the following afternoon.

When I arrived, Mlle de Vermandois opened the heavy wooden trunk for me and then left, saying that she had an errand to run that would keep her for at least three hours. I was alone with the trunk and its buried memories.

I slowly started searching through the contents—bundles of letters tied with ribbons, many with stamps from Saigon; curled, yellowing photographs of a smiling, middle-aged man in a white jacket smoking a cigar; melodies written in a child's hand, the margins decorated with childish illustrations. There were also clippings from French newspapers about French pilots flying to the Far East, and documents about a music school on Pinto Island. There were also several notebooks containing notes in Mme Fourangier's hand, apparently her sporadic diaries.

Seeing this, I was overcome by emotion. It was as if Nelly, that bewitching hag, had entrapped me from all sides. Not only was I now intrigued by all this Pinto Island material, I was caught up in deciphering it and finding Illirio for myself.

One photo of the man in the white jacket contained an inscription: Costas (Constantius) Tegularius, Acting Prime Minister of Pinto Island, 1978. Another later photo showed this same man embracing a tall, youngish man with diamond-shaped eyes. The inscription under the photo read, "To our angel."

There were several more photos, one of a severely wounded man whose entire torso was covered in blood and with a bloody mess where his left hand should have been.

This photo made me sick, but still I couldn't stop examining the contents of the trunk. Then Mlle de Vermandois returned and offered me tea. "I see the contents of this trunk excite you greatly," she commented in her dry manner.

"Yes!" I replied, not even trying to conceal my emotion. She approached me, tenderly touching my arm.

"Please call me Fleurette," she said. "May I suggest that you come to Paris so that you can study whatever is inside without hurry, say, for a week's time. You can stay here in my apartment, if you like. I will come to Paris to fetch you. I myself live in a château in the north. If you can make the time, I will invite you there as well."

"Thank you, Mlle…"

"Fleurette," she smiled with light sadness. "When would you like to come?"

"My dear Fleurette, I am happy to accept your kind invitation and stay here at your apartment for a week's time," I replied.

"You are most welcome, Solomon," she said. We parted.

Two months later I returned to Paris. I opened the trunk and was immediately immersed in the lives of two extraordinary men—Constantius Tegularius and Illirio Mariafels. I followed the heartbreaking story of Illirio's family, all of whom perished on the island, and I followed the strange, seemingly detached life of Mme Fourangier, who, with all her reserve, had nevertheless chosen to preserve the memory of the sunken island and its wretched inhabitants. I arranged the documents in more or less chronological order, photocopied them, brought them to Israel, and then translated them into English. Having omitted some less relevant pieces of information, I turned the main material into a readable sequence—in order to be able to better see the sad but heroic story in full human detail. I prepared a copy of this document and sent it to Fleurette. She was very deeply moved and suggested that I publish it to honor the lives of her mother and father. She asked me for the sake of her own privacy to change her parents' family names. This was the least I could do for her and readily complied. The best I could hope for at that stage was to send the relevant parts of this material to a journal of anthropological studies with the hope that they would publish it, thereby commemorating the culture and the recent history of the little-known Pinto Islanders who had perished in a self-inflicted calamity.

PART TWO:

FROM THE TRUNK

OF MME FOURANGIER

February 9, 1942
À ma fille
Adélaïde Fourangier
9 Rue Montignac, Vichy, Auvernes, France

Ma fille!

I am so proud of you!

You have at last reached the proper place from which to continue to progress toward a successful career as a concert pianist! Maître Cortot has accepted you as his student! I am sure your life in Vichy will be productive, especially now as he serves our glorious Chef d'État M. Petain as cultural supervisor! I am sure you will be protected and your path to glory will be assured!

I never had any doubt that you would be a great musician one day, and I am sure Maître Cortot will help you to achieve world fame! It is all in your hands now, my dear! Listen to every word the Maître speaks! Your success will bear the name of Fourangier across many continents, as befits the valor of your heroic father who died in battle for France just a year and half ago. All our neighbors including your proud teacher M. Antoine are enthralled by your success. My dear Adèle, if you could only see it! Next week I will send you parcels with cans of the best pork rillettes from our dear village. Please follow the mail notifications attentively. I will also send you a good new *chandail*—I knitted it for you myself!

Ta mere,

Mathilde Fourangier
7 Rue Les Batisses
Arronnes
Allier, Auvergne, France

The place where Mathilde Fourangier lived
with her late husband and their daughter Adélaïde

October 11, 1944
À ma fille
Adélaïde Fourangier
9 Rue Montignac, Vichy, Auvernes, France

Ma fille!

I am trembling with worry. I do not know what to wish for. Our motherland falls to pieces in front of our eyes, and new forces come to rule us. I am appalled that your great maître was arrested by the new rulers of France. How gloriously he served our motherland, just like our hero, Marshall Petain! Who are they, those new rulers? Godless chevaliers of fortune, stomping over our sacred homeland, prostituting themselves both to those money-obsessed Americans and our eternal enemies, those awful Brits. Listen, my dear daughter—run away to Paris and try to study in some privileged school under the patronage of these new rulers. People in our village say that they will rule France for a long time to come so there is no point in opposing them. Try, my dear, to listen to what the influential people in Paris say, especially where your future is concerned. Please write to me, my dear daughter, as soon as you can. How dearly I wish to receive your next letter from Paris!

Ta mère,

Mathilde Fourangier
7 Rue Les Batisses
Arronnes
Allier, Auvergne, France

March 12, 1945
À ma fille
Adélaïde Fourangier
30 Rue Cave, Paris, Île-de-France, France

Ma fille!

I am proud to inform you that your father, Jean-Pascal Fourangier, has been honored by the new government of France for his heroism in combat during the Battle of Abbeville. I received the Croix de guerre, 1939–1945, on his behalf. De Gaulle himself signed the congratulatory letter. What luck that your father served under this noble general's direct command!

I was informed that I will receive a small pension in honor of his memory. I hope this will allow me to stop knitting those tiresome *chandails* for the local market. Now, my dear Adèle, you can stroll the streets of Paris with your head held high—your father is a French hero!

Try to avoid mentioning M. C. and try to enroll in a good music school under solid governmental patronage.

Please write to me soon, my dear Adèle. How do you feel in your new Paris apartment?

Ta mère,

Mathilde Fourangier
7 Rue Les Batisses
Arronnes
Allier, Auvergne, France

May 14, 1945
À ma fille
Adélaïde Fourangier
30 Rue Cave, Paris, Île-de-France, France

Ma fille!

For some reason I have just received a letter from someone named M. Ilbert Dufour, the manager of academic studies at the Institut des hautes études musicales de Paris. Perhaps you gave them this address as your permanent residence. I think you should change that to your Parisian address—after all, the important people in France all live in Paris.

Anyway, I congratulate you—you have been accepted into the institute with a status of advanced student. It sounds very promising.

M. Dufour informs you that you have been assigned to the tutelage of Professor Sophie Halevi-Rabinowitz. According to M. Dufour, Professor Rabinowitz will return at the end of June from Switzerland where she lived in exile during the war, and he asks you to contact him then in order to receive her current address in Paris. Please do what M. Dufour says, my Adèle! I and all the villagers here are proud of you, our little Parisienne!

Ta mère,

Mathilde Fourangier
7 Rue Les Batisses
Arronnes
Allier, Auvergne, France

April 10, 1946
À ma fille
Adélaïde Fourangier
30 Rue Cave, Paris, Île-de-France, France

Are you mad, my daughter??

To use the spring vacation for a visit to that ostracized personality, M. Cortot? Do you think this can be kept a secret? I am sure there are plenty of people who will inform our present authorities that a girl from the most prestigious music school in Paris has gone to study under his guidance! What a disgrace! Do you want to destroy your path to glory, my dear? Think of me, Adèle, think of how much your heroic father and your humble mother sacrificed for you. How can you jeopardize all this? Promise me you will never visit this dreadful person again, and please write an explanatory letter to M. Dufour that your visit to Switzerland was not to study under M. Cortot, but only to pay him a courtesy call, as was his due. Nothing more! Promise me! Do not bring shame upon your mother!

Ta mère,

Mathilde Fourangier
7 Rue Les Batisses
Arronnes
Allier, Auvergne, France

April 22, 1946
À ma fille
Adélaïde Fourangier
30 Rue Cave, Paris, Île-de-France, France

What? You say you will visit Cortot again?

Why?

What's so bad about your current teacher, that Jewess, Rabinowitz? I am sure she teaches you in accord with M. Dufour's and the Parisian school's demands. Beware, my daughter—do not allow your career to slip away. Your aging mother cannot assist you to start all over again. Yes, you can always return to Arronnes, to your room at our house, and you will certainly get work—knitting *chandails*. But beware, my daughter, of how the villagers will mock you. And you will compel your poor mother to flee in shame.

Please open your eyes, Adèle, and change your ways immediately!

Ta mère,

Mathilde Fourangier
7 Rue Les Batisses
Arronnes
Allier, Auvergne, France

May 2, 1946
À ma fille
Adélaïde Fourangier
30 Rue Cave, Paris, Île-de-France, France

Adèle,

Your reply does not convince me at all. You say there is a big difference between the musical approach of M. Cortot and that of your current teacher, that Jewish lady. You even say that because her schooling is Hungarian, it is "heavy." So what? If M. Dufour's institute employs her, then her musical ways must be correct. You say she is of alien culture and does not reach the summits of Cortot's inspiration. Well, my daughter, didn't we learn after de Gaulle's return that there should be no alienation of the Jews? How can you expose yourself as a faithful student of a despised Vichy official? Do not bring trouble upon your dull head, Adèle. I think the time has come for me to prepare your room for your return and to prepare myself for the ignominy.

Do not be a fool and attribute too much importance to M. Dufour's remark that Cortot was and still is a great pianist. If Cortot were so great, Dufour would have him teach at your institute. Go back to your Jewess, Adèle, and never visit Cortot again!

Ta mère,

Mathilde Fourangier
7 Rue Les Batisses
Arronnes
Allier, Auvergne, France

September 8, 1946
Adélaïde Fourangier
30 Rue Cave, Paris, Île-de-France, France

Dear Mlle Fourangier,

I am seriously concerned with your visits to M. Cortot and with your summer studies under his guidance while remaining enrolled as a senior student at our institute. In visiting M. Cortot you violate two unbreakable axioms of our institution—you openly challenge the authority of Sophie Halevi-Rabinowitz, your professor at IHEMdP, and you openly compromise your own French citizenship by studying under a man whose collaboration with the Nazi regime has disgraced France.

Your behavior would normally require institutional sanctions. We at the school have assessed your pianistic achievements very highly and have thus included you in the select group of candidates for our highest diploma—the certificate of a concert pianist.

Your recent behavior has severely jeopardized your status. Besides, the Beethoven interpretations you presented the day before yesterday at our first after-summer concert show that you are deeply under the influence of M. Cortot; any further use of his performing idiosyncrasies in the concert milieu under the auspices of IHEMdP, or worse, on our behalf at other concert venues, will cause us all to think about your future at IHEMdP.

Music is a very transparent art—every incautious artistic decision causes fractures in an artist's reputation. IHEMdP must keep its reputation impeccable, especially in these times of national revival, when we as a famous French music academy aspire to a leading role in our culture, and when France herself struggles to resume her place of honor among nations.

Please consider your steps, Mlle Fourangier. For the present we shall not take any measures against you. But this is your last warning.

We at the institute will do our best to assist you in furthering your career in any direction that your talent may seem to indicate, but only if you comply with our wishes and completely change your behavior.

Honorablement,

I.D.

[*Ilbert Dufour* inscribed in pencil in Fourangier's hand—S.J.]

September 12, 1946
Mlle Adélaïde Fourangier
30 Rue Cave, Paris, Île-de-France, France

Dear Mlle Fourangier,

Please forgive me for this unexpected letter. My name is Jules de Vermandois. M. Ilbert Dufour invited me to your concert on September 6 at the Saint-Saëns hall at IHEMdP.

I loved your performance. I think you will be one of the most outstanding pianists of the next generation in France. I also liked the refreshing ideas that you brought to your performance, under the obvious influence of Alfred Cortot, the great Swiss French pianist.

M. Dufour told me of his discontent concerning your study under Cortot. I think I have some ideas that might help to mellow his dissatisfaction while allowing you to fruitfully build a future career with the aid of institutional support from IHEMdP.

I would be only too grateful if you would agree to listen to my ideas in this regard.

If that should be the case, please leave your reply at the office of M. Dufour in a sealed envelope addressed to me. I shall then gladly come to meet you at whatever time and place you suggest.

Sincèrement,

Jules de Vermandois
September 22, 1946
Mlle Adélaïde Fourangier
30 Rue Cave, Paris, Île-de-France, France

Dear Adélaïde,

With great expeditiousness I send you a summary of the ideas we discussed the day before yesterday at the Café de la Paix.

The core concept is the suggestion that a large part of your future repertoire consist of works from lesser known composers of the nineteenth and early twentieth centuries. Among the large quantity of their brilliant though not very substantial works, one still can find gems carrying ideas of nobility and lyricism, heroic bravura, and virtuosic glitter. Though sometimes lacking depth, music lovers of the present day would love to hear this forgotten music that nevertheless contains so much brilliance.

By specializing in this repertoire you could experiment freely, employing the considerable artistry you have gained from your study under Cortot without antagonizing the conservative musical establishment (Ilbert Dufour fully agrees with me on this point). You could delve into compositions of people like Ignatz Moscheles, Étienne Nicolas Méhul, and Johann Nepomuk Hummel with all your abundant ferocity. You can even go back in time and play works by the gorgeously expressive Carlos Seixas, a Portuguese composer of the eighteenth century. A pivotal composer linking those lesser-knowns to the greater, more famous ones, Karl Maria von Weber, is also well known in circles of the music-loving cognoscenti. His *Konzertstück in F minor for Piano and Orchestra*, Opus 79, recently played both by Lily Kraus and Claudio Arrau, has been very successful. Of course, you do not need to abandon Debussy and Beethoven, whom you perform so well, but do not make them the apex of your concert program.

This will allow you to appear as a musical explorer, a "time traveler of the musical soundscape," and thereby attract positive attention among influential music critics.

I was so happy to meet you, dear Adélaïde.

Allow me to invite you to my family château in northwest France. Please leave your answer at M. Dufour's office.

In case you kindly agree to visit, I shall personally come to take you there by family car.

Sincèrement,

Jules Vermandois

September 30, 1946
Mlle Adélaïde Fourangier
30 Rue Cave, Paris, Île-de-France, France

Dear Adélaïde,

You know, the last fifteen minutes in the car, already on the streets of Paris, when you started talking to me, it was as if the sun rose a second time, illuminating the evening hours.

I fully understand your ten hours of silence during our day together at my family home in Saulchery. I presume you were overwhelmed by the large dimensions of the château; perhaps I should have prepared you in advance for its scale. But I was too afraid that the moment I started to discuss my residence you would ask me to turn back...having witnessed your confusion upon entering my ten-year-old Hispano-Suiza car.

Thank you for playing the whole day on my late mother's Pleyel grand piano—and especially for filling this old, joyless house with your beautiful trills from Debussy's *L'isle joyeuse*. Somehow the brilliance of those trills brought the old walls to life again.

Our house manager, M. Gerardo Aguilar, would like me to convey how enchanted he was by your playing; I must join him in these sentiments. So in fact you did speak to us—though in the language of music—and made us so very grateful to you.

And then, in the evening hours in Paris, still in my old K6 car, you asked me to tell you who I am. I did not expect to earn this attention from you, my dear. I am grateful for that.

Here is my story—short and simple. I hope it does not disappoint.

I am 38 years old. Unfortunately and embarrassingly, I am rich, and—what is even more damning—I am a descendent of a medieval aristocratic family.

My full name (not intended to be funny) is Jules-Honoré Philibert de Vermandois. Our family house is called Château Abelard de Vermandois; its foundations were laid in the early fifteenth century.

Both my parents died together in February 1945 as they were supervising the cultivation of our winter wheat when the fields came under surprise aerial attack by the Americans. There was no possible escape. My mother and father died instantly.

I am their only son and heir. I studied agriculture in the well-known École supérieur d'agriculture international in Angers. I love agriculture and devote much of my attention to our private farms. Our produce is well known in France, Belgium, Switzerland, and on the Jersey-Guernsey Islands of La Manche.

Since 1928 I have had a pilot's license. In the war I volunteered for the air force, but in the confusion of May and June nobody would even talk to me, although I brought my own private plane to the mobilization station. With much embarrassment I was asked to remove my old-fashioned contraption from the field, its appearance causing nervous derision among the officers. My name never appeared on any military draft list (perhaps because of my "too high" status).

After the capitulation (I cannot accept the official term "armistice"), I served as a messenger linking Resistance groups in the northwest to the Free French command in England. To my great surprise, I was able to fly very low in complete darkness over the water, escaping the notice of the enemy. I attribute this to the special qualities of my old plane—its small engine hardly produces any sound. Besides, due to my many years of private flying before the war, I was intimately familiar with the topography of every *lieu* on the both coastlines of La Manche.

I am single—too timid, I am afraid, to reach out to find a true partner in these progressive times. I have almost gotten used to the idea of remaining single for the rest of my life. Perhaps by way of compensation, I have developed a deep love for music. At times it even succeeds in soothing my aching soul.

I support many charitable projects, and donate generously to IHEMdP. Ilbert Dufour (who became my friend during the Resistance) keeps me closely informed of the institute's activities. M. Dufour studied music and philosophy prior to the war; he was wounded in battle and cannot play anymore. I am glad that IHEMdP finds in him an able academic administrator.

I think I have presented myself in all possible fullness, dear Adélaïde. I hope to receive a word from you. You can leave a message at Ilbert Dufour's office or write to me directly at Saulchery. You know the address.

Chaleureusement,

Jules Vermandois

December 2, 1946
À ma fille
Adélaïde Fourangier
30 Rue Cave, Paris, Île-de-France, France

Ma fille!

I am so proud of you! You, daughter of the Arronnes villagers Jean-Pascal and Mathilde Fourangier, are being courted by none other than Sire de Vermandois himself! You know, since receiving your letter and informing our neighbors of the great news, people have started to treat me as though I were royalty! Not only am I now the widow of a national hero of France, I am the mother of the future Mme de Vermandois!

I am so glad he is already arranging concerts for you—and not only in France, but in Belgium too!

You say that you do not like him—his nose tilts unnaturally to the left, the elongated shape of his exquisitely polished fingernails repels you, that you do not like how he touches you.

Well, you will get used to his fingernails, his nose, and his damned touching too, *ma fille*! You will bow at his feet and do whatever he wishes—until the wedding, that is. And then you will command him. You will bear his family name with pride, and give birth to his sons, one after another, and you will squeeze out of him every possible gram of an international performing career by playing all those musical pieces he tells you to play!

Do not make me mad. Adèle, do not reject his wooing.

Ta mère,

Mathilde Fourangier
7 Rue Les Batisses
Arronnes
Allier, Auvergne, France

P.S. If you do reject him—god forbid—then do not show your face here again, Adèle. You will not have your mother to support you. Swear to me that you will not reject him!

November 29, 1947
Adélaïde Fourangier
30 Rue Cave, Paris, Île-de-France, France

My dear Adèle, my darling,

I think I have wonderful news for you—you will be invited to play recitals in Saigon in the coming spring. My dear, you will fly all over the globe!

Yours,

Jules

May 14, 1948
Mme Adélaïde Fourangier de Vermandois
Hôtel Saigon Palace
Rue Catinat 1, Saigon

Chère Mme de Vermandois,

Permit me to express my boundless gratitude for the piano recital you gave at the Opera Hall of Saigon yesterday. Your excellent performance revealed an entirely new world to me. While I always visit the Opera Hall whenever there are performances of European orchestral music, I do not regularly attend solo recitals. Yet yours shook my soul to the very core, bringing insight that I never could have imagined. I will never forget your glittering performance of *L'isle joyeuse* by Claude Achille Debussy with its fast, high trills and low, rumbling passages that so perfectly reflect the backstory that, according to the program notes, was inspired by a painting by the Rococo artist Watteau— the departure of a group of grandees to Cythera, the island abode of the goddess of love. The Debussy trills that pretend to be an expression of great joy deeply penetrated my heart. As an islander myself, I can poignantly identify with people who dream of such a lovely island. Under your fingertips, the evanescent glitter and joy that they anticipate on the island of love astounded me to the bottom of my heart.

Also your sumptuous performance of Hummel and Weber left me in equal awe; now at least I am aware of the loftiness and the discipline that infuses European culture. I did not know it is such a rich blend of gallantry and elegance.

From now on, I eagerly await your next performances in this region or, with god's help, wherever else around the globe that you may perform.

With utmost cordiality,

Constantius Tegularius
Second-year medical student at the École de médecine et de pharmacie de Hanoi, Section de Saigon
28 Rue Testard, Saigon
Residence: Teachers' Orphanage
House no. 10 in front of the French meteorological station
Pinto Island of the Paracel Islands

June 1, 1948
Mme Adélaïde Fourangier de Vermandois
Hôtel Saigon Palace
Rue Catinat 1, Saigon

Chère Mme de Vermandois,

Accept please my limitless gratitude for your second piano recital at the Opera Hall of Saigon. This time you captivated my heart by playing Weber's beautiful *Invitation to the Dance* and the many wonderful pieces by Moscheles that produced an atmosphere of capriciousness, as though we were all nonchalantly jumping. Your music became almost visual, projecting an image of human figures staring and gesticulated humorously at the audience.

I am the happiest man in the world because your music resonates within my heart. I must say that I was enchanted also by your presence as well; it radiates so much elegance and culture…the vision of your playing accompanies me now wherever I go….

With utmost cordiality,

Constantius Tegularius

October 15, 1948
Adélaïde Fourangier
Rue de Longchamp, 92200 Neuilly-sur-Seine
Paris

Chère Adélaïde,

This is a message for your eyes only. I hope you will consider it carefully as it is intended to promote your success as a pianist.

As one of your former instructors at the eminent Institut des hautes études musicales and the professor who for three years taught you piano literature and music history and who is now deputy director of the IHEMdP responsible for the public status of the institute's reputation, I must say that I was startled to detect so many blurred notes in the Beethoven sonatas that you performed two days ago at your Salle Gaveau recital. It seems to me that you are still too greatly influenced by Alfred Cortot, who should by no means be your sole source of inspiration. You should be aware that blurring passages in Beethoven seriously undermines the prestige of our school, from which you received a final diploma only months ago. After discussing your recital with M. Le President de l'Institut, we both came to the conclusion that you should not be allowed to perform works in the classical repertoire on the premier stages of France or elsewhere. If you decide to concentrate on a more peripheral repertoire, we will support your career in the future, if you should wish it.

I hope you will accept this advice in the solicitous manner in which it has been written.

Faithfully yours,

I.D.
Directeur adjoint, IHEMdP

February 28, 1949
Mme Adélaïde Fourangier de Vermandois
Hôtel Saigon Palace
Rue Catinat 1, Saigon

Chère Mme de Vermandois,

What a joy to listen to your wonderful playing again. Your performance of the Seixas sonatas was so moving, it was as though I were in the presence of a merciful queen who knows how to embrace her subjects with love and respect. I also admired your Baldassare Galuppi. I was overjoyed to learn that this Haydn contemporary was, like me, born on a small island, but managed to overcome his insularity by composing so much enjoyable music for listeners throughout Europe and around the globe.

I especially loved your performance of Hummel's polonaises— they are so full of elegance and humor. You have no idea how much my world is now in constant need of your wonderful sounds and your charm....

With great affection,

Constantius Tegularius
Third-year medical student at the École de médecine et de pharmacie de Hanoi, Section de Saigon
28 Rue Testard, Saigon
Residence: Teachers' Orphanage
House no. 10 in front of the French meteorological station
Pinto Island of the Paracel Islands

October 7, 1950
Mme Adélaïde Fourangier de Vermandois
Hôtel Saigon Palace
Rue Catinat 1, Saigon

Ma chère madame,

I have no words with which to thank you for your kind invitation to attend your public master class at Gia Dinh Arts College. I will definitely be there to absorb all of your inspiring words and every matchless example that you provide to local Vietnamese students. Oh, what I wouldn't give to be able to play the piano myself, just so that I might be taught by you....

Au revoir!

Constantius Tegularius

October 14, 1950
Mme Adélaïde Fourangier de Vermandois
Rue de Longchamp, 92200 Neuilly-sur-Seine
Paris, France

Ma chère Adèle,

I shall cherish our meeting for the rest of my life.

While the obvious concern for your students was truly regal (perhaps you should guide all the queens of the earth!) and while I observed closely your secrets of elegant, clean playing, I shall now cherish the tender feeling of your angelic hand leaning on my arm. From now on the river flowing through Saigon at Le Myre de Villiers embankment will be for me the most shining river in the world, as it has reflected your beautiful flowing hair and the unfathomable gaze of your soulful eyes.

Thank you for being open with me and telling me your life story so far—an amazing story of artistic growth in France's darkest times. I am also grateful to you for telling me about your prominent husband and about your little baby daughter Fleurette. (She should now be fourteen months old, I believe? I think that with time, little Fleurette will cry less and will allow you to practice more.)

I loved the little verse by Cesare Bocella from which you quoted—
"*Angiolin dal biondo crin*"—when you told me about your crying daughter; I went to the Saigon University library and found this little poem in its entirety. Permit me to finish this letter with its final words:

Angel fair with golden hair,

Lovely image of a flow'r.

Should my name e'er meet thine ear,

Sweetly lisp it to thy mother,

That her heart may hold it dear.

(I took the translation by Charles Fonteyn Manney.)

Be well, dear Adèle, and I hope to see you and listen to your playing again.

Your most grateful admirer,

Costas

March 5, 1953
Diary of Adélaïde Fourangier, first entry

I apologize for writing. I think keeping a diary is a sure sign of misery and defeat, for only defeated people keep diaries. But here I am—part of this repellent social club of the miserable.

I have to sort things out. It appears that my husband Jules has turned his back on me, siding with those "august" professors at IHEMdP, my so-called "alma mater." He accepts their opinion that I am an unworthy pianist. I suppose that was his view even while courting me during my final year at IHEMdP, otherwise why would he have insisted upon having a baby immediately? Fleurette, our child, looks upon me with merciless reproach: "Mother, you are unworthy!" Who told you that, little fool? Your loving father, that effete aristocrat who has absolutely no character flaws?? Awful…the whole world seems to be closing in on me.

Yes! I will play Moscheles and all those second-raters—until my time comes. After all, Cortot did NOT think I was worthless, that ridiculous-looking S.O.B., and he knows his art. I remember how his eyes glittered when I played Chopin for him in Lausanne—both of us knew that I was good! Well, he did inspire me…maybe him alone. True, I may still have to mature…but Jules certainly does not help in that regard. In fact, he abandons me, taking Fleurette with him!

Fleurette, April 1953

March 11, 1953
Diary of Adélaïde Fourangier, second entry

Why am I doing this? Why should I keep on wasting time with this inane scribbling?

Of course, I am ashamed of doing it. Instead of practicing and basking in the glory that I would have received after a concert I spend time with a pen, putting words on paper that will never become a public success—neither as a novel nor a dull autobiography. Only a pitiful soliloquy for no one's eyes but my own.

I readily admit that in keeping a diary I surrender to weakness, because it is so evident that writing a diary is an act of self-indulgence.

There is only one reason by which I can justify this activity: I need to clear my mind, and I have no one in the world to talk to. No one understands me at all. So now I have you, dear diary.

Before this I was actually always so proud of not needing anyone to talk to. I had no need to even *think* about my life—I was always so sure that I was on the right path. Nobody need break into my solitude with frivolous discussions "about life." I always felt that any outside interference in my affairs would only cause trouble.

But here I stand, with full awareness that although I always did the right thing, I now find myself in an intolerable situation where my career seems to be ending even before it properly got started.

Strangely, I do not feel any horror at this anymore, though my career was always my only dream.

But now I have to figure out what's going to happen to me. I have to bring my whole life before my eyes right now, in order to have the proper perspective on the future. OK, let's start.

I never had any attachment to my parents. I always knew my father was a weak drunkard whom my mother used to beat with her bare hands on Tuesdays and Thursdays and with a broom on Sundays after mass. It's good the poor man somehow found his way to de Gaulle's fighting unit so that he could die under "honorable circumstances."

True, my mother is a vain idiot, especially with her bouts of hysteria. What good luck that I do not live with her now.

So how *did* I live with them?

Very simple: since I was six years old, I played the piano in the vestry of our abbé. His assistant, M. Antoine (to this day I do not know his family name), taught me how to press the keys and how to read music. Later, when the local church acquired a new piano, they brought the old one to our home for me to practice on.

Then in 1933 I won the regional prize as the best young pianist in the southern villages of France and played several concerts in nearby cities.

My mother stopped hitting me.

Our abbé used his connections within the church hierarchy and arranged for me to play for Alfred Cortot, the greatest French pianist of all times. M. Antoine took me by train to Paris and brought me to Cortot's spacious apartment. Cortot frightened me—he looked like an emaciated country idiot, thin, ugly-faced, with a strange feminine haircut and bulging eyes. He also constantly smoked cigarettes that smelled awful.

First he and M. Antoine drank tea and then he asked me to play. I played two Czerny studies and two easy polonaises by Chopin for him. I also played the *Second Sonatina* by Schumann (from Opus 118); I noticed with a sideways glance Cortot's smile as he listened to this piece.

After I finished my performance, Cortot did not say anything to me, but leaned toward M. Antoine and whispered something to him, indicating several places in the scores of the pieces that I had just played. M. Antoine blushed and lowered his eyes. He did not raise his eyes until the end of our visit some half an hour later.

Then Cortot sat down at the second piano and showed me where I had misread the scores. All of a sudden he started playing a piano piece I had never heard (Later M. Antoine told me it was Chopin's famous *barcarolle*); he played this piece to the end. I sat nearby, trying not to lose my attention. I do not remember how Cortot played this piece then.

After finishing the *barcarolle,* Cortot looked at me (sitting very calm and polite), lit another cigarette, and played one of the polonaises I had just played for him.

This time I felt an acute shock in my stomach; the piece with which I was so familiar now sparkled with every possible light, bewitching me on every turn of melody and harmony. Cortot obviously saw my reaction.

"Did you like it?" he asked.

"Yes," I answered.

He looked at me with his ugly eyes and then smiled toward M. Antoine. "She is too young for poetry," he said softly. Then he asked where exactly my native village was, and then thumbed through an old notebook, its yellow, disintegrating pages nearly falling on the floor.

"Bring her to Mme Stefania Dylewska, she is the best teacher in southern France," he said to M. Antoine. He wrote a short recommendation to be forwarded to Mme Dylewska, and gave it to M. Antoine. Then we parted.

On the train ride home, M. Antoine trembled the entire time; I did not feel it appropriate to ask him why he trembled so much. But at the end of the journey he whispered, almost crying, "I do not deserve to be your teacher anymore; I misread the scores, and didn't notice your mistakes. I am not a good enough professional for you!"

Several weeks later he brought me to Mme Stefania Dylewska, a Polish émigré who taught piano in Toulouse, and whose studio was incorporated into the local secondary school.

So from the age of ten on, during the school year I lived in the dormitory of that school in Toulouse and only returned home for summer vacation. Cortot's letter produced wonders. I was placed in a private room with my own piano and a separate maid to take care of my needs.

I did not make any friends among my classmates. Anyhow, during my last years at school I hardly attended class, as I was only required to appear at mathematics class and Latin class twice a week. I could practice freely and solve harmony exercises, which the maid passed to me at the beginning of each week. (I gave her the solved exercises on Friday and she brought back the teacher's written remarks after handing me the new exercises. Usually I did well.)

I did not go to the cinema like the other students; I did not befriend the other girls or date boys—I disdained all that. All these things where for me a waste of time (I still think it is a waste of time to go to the cinema, or sip wine in a bar with a boyfriend). I used to overhear senior schoolmates making love— not in the dorm, of course, but in the village barns outside town when our school had its weekend excursions to experience the return of spring and to sing choruses *en plêne aire*.

The norm was that from among some twenty senior students, ten would remain for the choral exercises and the others would disappear for half a day, with no apparent alarm on the part of our teachers. They did not go far away, those bastards; they jumped into the first available moldering haystack in a local barn, and immediately started moaning. All those moans caused me painful, almost paralyzing disgust. I used to run away from those places as if pursued by a rabid dogs.

I hated sex and human intimacy too. I think I may have imbibed these feelings from early childhood, when hearing my sometimes half-naked mother attack my father with ugly cries in the kitchen as well as in their bed located behind a thin wall.

I felt huge relief when I started playing piano in the back offices of our church. Both M. Antoine and the abbé had inculcated in me the sense that I was special, free of human filth, pure, filled with the sounds of god's divine music.

When I would meet my schoolmates, or anyone else who happened to be around, I always had to overcome an inner shiver in order to communicate with them. Some invisible barrier always separated us. I always felt that behind any smile in my direction lurked a rude yell, an urge to overpower me and impose themselves upon me (just like my mother used to do with my poor father when she would try to seduce him in the kitchen by wrapping her legs around his waist).

I always looked aside when I felt someone's glance was too focused on me. I never could bear people touching me, even in the most formal manner. I always felt that every friendly touch contained a wish to overpower me, to throw me into a haystack and start moaning wildly in lusty, animal enjoyment.

And now if I allow Jules to touch me and enter me—I feel as though some horrible filth emanating from inside his body is penetrating me and invading my soul so that I am soiled and it is visible even from the outside.

Perhaps the only person who did not cause me to shiver when communicating with him, and feeling the modest contact of his hand on my elbow, was that young man from that god-forsaken Far Eastern island, Costas Tegularius. Strangely, I never felt threatened by him...perhaps because he is a trained physician, and they closely practice the art of touching people with respect.

Whenever I felt tired after hours of practicing, I used to lie down on my sofa and look at travel journals, dreaming about visiting faraway places, and playing my virtuoso repertoire to the grateful applause of a crowd.

Under Stefania's guidance, I won two prizes (in 1937 and in 1938)—both times second prize in the regional Southern France Youth Piano Competitions. Both times the first prize went to one Samuel Gustl, the son of a Jewish grocer from Toulouse.

This Samuel Gustl played with iron fingers and assured virtuosity—he played Liszt's studies and also Beethoven's sonatas. His energetic *Appasionata* was a huge success in every competition he entered, winning six competitions in just three years; whereas I took part in only two competitions because Mme Stefania said "it is not appropriate for a 'young lady' to expose herself in competitions too frequently."

For me Samuel Gustl's way of playing was exemplary; I knew that by playing in this manner—strong fingers, loud chords, clear sound, and energetic rhythm—I would achieve success and my future would be assured.

What did I aim for?

I never wanted to be rich, nor to be in contact with famous people, no.

I was not interested in fashionable clothing and jewelry, nor in choice cuisine.

Then what?

I think I just wanted to be free, that is, to move about freely and enjoy the servitude of others. Yes, I wished to be free and to be served. This is all I ever wanted. To come to some good hotel in Switzerland and to be asked what my wishes were and to answer, "an espresso, please, and then a photo camera to capture the beautiful mountain landscapes." And not to have to wait for a week for the photos to be developed, but to have them returned to me framed, or in albums within a matter of days.

Yes, I would like to travel—by sea or by air, and see people celebrating my successful performances.

Mme Stefania knew perfectly well what I wished for, and she led me exactly in this direction, straight to my target.

But then she left for America, even before the war started, and I had no teacher then.

I do not know what happened to Samuel Gustl during the war. I vaguely remember that he once said his father could not obtain an American entry visa.

Well, that's not my problem anyway.

I graduated in 1942, without taking piano lessons from anybody there; occasionally I played for M. Antoine and he constantly wept that he was not a proper teacher for me. He also bewailed the "too-sharp" playing style that I had acquired during my years with Stefania.

Then he arranged for me to study under Cortot in Vichy in private. It is not easy studying under a genius, especially when your own musical experience is as narrow as mine was at that time.

At first Cortot attempted to discuss the instructions that composers had inscribed at the beginning of their scores. I readily followed his lead, but he was not satisfied with my understanding of his intentions. So he himself started playing those pieces that I was studying under him. In doing so, he totally enchanted me. I have never heard—nor seen—such beautiful playing. Cortot used to send his hands to the keyboard with some inexplicable upswing, and then tenderly land his fingers, each one of them separately—after an additional small upswing—onto the keys. His sound was (and still is!) *unbearably* beautiful. And his music moved like some miraculous stream—glittering with infinite richness of color, and at the same time songlike. It was never whimsical, but it always somehow bypassed the strict formalities of musical rhythm.

At first I was devastated by the abyss between his mastery and my own poor abilities. I frequently sat frozen and was unable even to look at him when he suggested different musical solutions. But Cortot insisted that I employ only those means of playing that I felt comfortable with as an artist. This helped me a lot.

I understood that I would not be able to master his method of sound production, and he too was relieved when I returned to my energetic "Stefania-like" playing. No, he did not like this method of sound production, but he saw that I was no longer suffering in an attempt to imitate him. Now he showed me how to organize the musical stream, and I did it, comprehending music as a flow of soft rhythmical beats, always able to connect them to a melody that I could sing with my voice. I learned his ways of allowing Beethoven to stream forth, striving forward in a purposeful—always purposeful—manner; always arriving at the accent that was the central point of the musical idea.

In 1943 he taught me Chopin and Schumann—and I learned to give breath to their phrases. At that point Cortot started to lose patience with me: "Would you change your manner of piano touch, please?" he used to ask me curtly over and over.

I felt it was beyond my ability to explore this domain of his mastery.

Once I told him that Stefania's star student Samuel Gustl used to win competitions with a much uglier sound than I had when I studied under her. Cortot looked at me with a long silence, and finally said, "Yes, you should always do only what you fully believe in."

He kept teaching me until the early summer of 1944. Then he invited me to a last session and told me that if my wish was to become a true artist, I should always be myself, believe in my inner voice, and never submit to someone else's tastes. He gave me a cup of a good local wine, kissed my hand, and asked me to contact him "after the war."

I did.

Now what?

I entered IHEMdP with the aim of joining the circuit of concert pianists. The time vas very convenient—France lay in ruins, public morale was in confusion, and the new pro-left government was eager to sponsor the arts.

My assigned teacher Mme Halevi-Rabinowitz treated me with utmost respect and tenderness. She always agreed with my solutions, especially when I told her that I had received them from Cortot. However, she asked me to reorganize my sound production, suggesting the ridiculous high-wrist positions that were so popular in inter-war Hungary (she studied in Budapest in the early twenties). I refused to follow her; I could not imagine how I could succeed at this. I returned to my "Stefania" technique and even won a small competition by playing this way. Of course this silenced Mme Rabinowitz.

It all felt right now—I could play with strong, energetic fingers and was able to combine this with Cortot's musical phrasing. I felt I was on a true path. Then this rich man Jules appeared with his crony Ilbert Dufour, and both started driving me mad.

I knew I was trapped.

The problem was, of course, that I was also trapped within my body and by my sense of privacy. I had no other choice than to surrender to Jules and to become his plaything in return for my chance of advancing to a prominent pianistic position in the future. My refusal to marry him would cost me not only a diploma at IHEMdP, but would also result in a curse on me in France—nobody would support me after my ties with Cortot. Even escaping to the United States would not help, because first and foremost I would be known as the protégé of a Nazi collaborator.

So I had no choice other than to sell my body.

I was, of course, still a virgin then.

Jules did not become intimate with me before our wedding in the office of the Aisne magistrate in July 1948. My mother came for the fifteen-minute marriage ceremony and then left in a hurry. She feared that I would do something horrible at the ceremony (or later) and didn't want to witness it.

Next, I had to endure the "intimacy inauguration," letting a hardly familiar man of middle age lie on me, causing pain between my legs as he penetrated a cavity within me that until then I was not even fully aware of, and to smell his body, a mixture of fine perfume and the day's sweat...of course I trembled. I could not look him in the eye. With horror I imagined that he could notice my pubic hair. I did not wish to see him at all. The whole procedure took some twenty minutes, and throughout the ordeal I felt that I was taking an excrement bath. This is how it began, and it never changed. In between I gave birth to a nice girl, who, unfortunately, I could not bring myself to love. Poor girl. She is not to blame—but I can hardly smile at her. Yes, I know, I am a bad mother. But I should not have been her mother at all.

I hope one day I will find an escape from this trap. What is clear now, my dear Adèle, you made a Faustian bargain—you lost both your body and your career. And your dignity too.

Well, this is how things stand for now. So what is your next step, practical Adèle?

Well, first—I promise—no more long entries. I will never have the patience to read them myself, even for the sake of analyzing my own situation.

Second—I have to practice. I still have much piano work to do.

October 25, 1953
Diary of Adélaïde Fourangier, third entry

Today I received confirmation that I can give a recital at Salle Gaveau, in May of next year. I will show them I am worthy! I will play Debussy against the wishes of all, including those of "my dear" Jules, and they can shoot me afterward! There will definitely be at least one reviewer in Salle Gaveau who will like my approach, or at least define it as "authentic." Why, in our epoch everything has to be "authentic"; very well, I will supply authenticity in abundance.

And then if someone dares reproach me for deviating from the acceptable norms, I will show them this "authenticity" review. I <u>will</u> be respected—yes! [Emphasis in the original—S.J.]

December 23, 1953
Diary of Adélaïde Fourangier, fourth entry

Just received notice that my concert at Gaveau scheduled for the coming spring has been postponed until next season. Those devious hyenas, they lurk everywhere and plot against me. Jules will have to fix a new date. I will make him do it. How he will enjoy forcing me down the throat of his dear buddy from the glorious Resistance.

Meanwhile I will get through this somehow with my eyes closed, dreaming of that man from the far end of the globe…

December 5, 1954
Diary of Adélaïde Fourangier, fifth entry

Well, I feel fully prepared for my Gaveau recital. I know precisely what I am going to do—perform Debussy with a Beethovenesque interpretation, using phrasing that nobody has ever applied to Debussy. This interpretation is Cortot's personal gift to me. At least this is how I perceive it. The concert-going public will be amazed! And besides, I am playing three sonatas from Op. 2 by Etienne Mehul—no one would dare criticize my playing the music of our national hero from the days of the French Revolution! After all, so many people in the provincial towns of France and Belgium have applauded me over the last three months...thank god I could travel there alone and forget Jules's angry remarks and Fleurette's incessant crying. Jules should not be so proud of himself for arranging these concerts for me— after all, I have earned them by my professionalism too.

Wednesday, December 15, 1954
Revue de rencontres musicales à Paris

Yesterday's recital by Mme Adélaïde Fourangier de Vermandois at Salle Gaveau left, to tell the truth, a strange impression. Although the official heroes of this piano evening were Debussy and Mehul, two quintessential Frenchmen, patriots and inventors, the real, albeit formally unseen, hero was the strange caricature of Beethoven having been presented here as a barking street vender in the spirit of Pierre De Geyter, the author of the communist *L'Internationale.* Mme Fourangier started with *Ce qu'a vu le vent d'ouest* by Debussy, presenting it at a tempo twice as fast as usual, compounding it with steely phrasing and obviously intentional blurred passages as though it were a late Beethoven composition. What a bizarre spectacle! All the other Debussy pieces sounded so resolute and heavy to the point of conveying their opposite meaning. It was as though Fourangier de Vermandois were mocking the aesthetic values so dear to us, ripping our modern master from his French roots.

Likewise, Mehul's "sports-like" sonatas were treated as though the pianist wanted us to witness another bombardment of Paris. Let us not forget that Paris was too precious to us to allow it to be bombed again in the recent war. Hadn't we experienced these horrors enough during the Great War? Our art must be shielded from such gross misconceptions as those presented at Salle Gaveau yesterday. V.B.

[*Vincent Bénichou* inscribed in pencil in Fourangier's hand—S.J.]

December 16, 1954
Mme Adélaïde Fourangier de Vermandois
Rue de Longchamp, 92200 Neuilly-sur-Seine
Paris, France

Ma chère Adèle,

I hope you'll allow me to address you by the diminutive of your beautiful first name that has now become the beloved prayer that I repeat each night before closing my eyes.

I was at Salle Gaveau the day before yesterday, sitting at the edge of my seat as I hearkened to your phenomenal musicality—huge, blistering joy burst from your fingertips. I inhaled your Debussy almost physically, your energetic Mehul pieces pointing out to me with scorching clarity what my life's task must be—to help my people modernize and breathe in freedom. Hopefully this will cure their mental illnesses and turn them into a productive nation whose labors will be recognized throughout the world. Your playing, like a spectacular aurora lighting up the skies, showed me my life's direction...I hope that one day you may see the people of my little island.

I was appalled to read the harsh review your concert received in the *Revue de rencontres musicales à Paris*. The music critic was so nasty that I thought he must have been suborned to write in this repellent way. I want to assure you that my ears and my heart are full of your music, just as my eyes and soul are full of your beauty.

I am now in Paris studying education at the Sorbonne. I was lucky to get a scholarship through the former French high commissioner to Indochina, M. Léon Pignon, a very goodhearted man whose acquaintance I had the good fortune to make while studying medicine in Saigon.

I send you tender gratitude for your music, my dear Adèle.

Wishing to see you and hear you perform more and more, with all my heart.

Costas
Maison de l'Indochine
57 B, Boulevard Jourdan
75014 Paris

December 18, 1954
Adélaïde Fourangier
Rue de Longchamp, 92200 Neuilly-sur-Seine
Paris, France

Chère Adélaïde,

I think we have reached the point where a deep reappraisal of your situation is in order.

In my capacity as deputy director of IHEMdP, I cannot conceal the inability of our institute to support you in your piano career anymore. The devastating review of December 15 in the *Revue de rencontres musicales* leaves no doubt that you must disappear from the Parisian concert stage for a long time.

I am the last person to advise you how to implement this idea. However, if one day in the future you evince the maturity to perform the standard repertoire in a more acceptable manner, it would be better for you to introduce yourself anew, with no trace of your present reputation.

Please keep me informed of your future steps.

Sincerely,

I.D.
Directeur adjoint, IHEMdP

December 23, 1954
[hand-delivered letter—S.J.]

Adèle,

You must by now be asking yourself about the whereabouts of Fleurette and of myself. Well, at the time of your touring in Périgueux, Villeneuve-sur-Lot, and Bergerac, we left Paris. I felt I had to withdraw to our family castle so that I might consider our life together in a more careful vein.

To tell the truth, I am tired of your unmitigated anger toward me, especially since I do not understand the motivation behind it. Surely you must be aware that I do everything possible to support your career, allowing you to concertize throughout France, Belgium, and Switzerland according to your wishes. My readiness to heed to the warnings of Professor Ilbert D., the deputy director of your eminent music school, is dictated solely out of care for you.

I do not accept your anger toward me when I tried to raise my suggestions concerning your interpretations of Debussy and Beethoven and your accusations that I side with M. Ilbert D.

as if in so doing I betray you. I think in his criticism of your ways Ilbert has a point, and he truly wants to help you. You, on the other hand, immaturely reject his position without trying to analyze it. I feel I have not the fortitude to absorb your mercurial fits of temper.

Moreover, I cannot accept your indifference to our dear Fleurette. I am sure you are on the wrong road, Adèle, and I feel that neither our little Fleurette nor I can make you change. I am tired, Adèle. I want my life back, without the interminable pain and frustration I constantly feel in my heart. And I see the great pain I cause you, dear Adèle.

When I first saw you on the concert stage of the IHEMdP and when I met you later at the Café de la Paix, I thought I could serve you as a devoted knight would serve his beloved lady. I thought I could bring all the advantages of my position with all its connections to help you to develop what you most deserve—the career of a concert pianist. I thought I could perhaps contribute some of the wisdom acquired during my long years of loneliness toward shaping your future. Perhaps I could not free myself of inborn paternalism, a sin inherited together with family riches. I thought I could convince you of better ways to pursue your goals, presumptuously believing that I saw the situation more clearly than you did. Perhaps I failed to understand that your gifts are part of your character and I should not interfere in your decisions, and—moreover—I shouldn't meddle in your professional life. Perhaps I was too vain to grasp that I should not meddle in your life….

My dear, please forgive me for such an emotional outpouring.

Because we both adore you, Fleurette and I will happily welcome you whenever you wish to visit us. Yet, unfortunately, it is most evident that we do not make you happy. Therefore I have decided that we each have to give the other space to lead our own lives.

Jules
Saulchery (Aisne)

October 6, 1955
Diary of Adélaïde Fourangier, sixth entry

Maison de l'Indochine

I was not aware how sweet the life of a professionally invisible person could be, especially for a woman. I move through the streets of Paris and absolutely no one recognizes me, walking in or out of the Maison de l'Indochine, nobody greets me with a "hello."

Yes, I am living with Costas, that romantic. I think he is the only person in Paris who respects me as a professional musician. And I do not even need to practice for that. I have already done all the practice necessary. Now I can relax. He is so fond of my hair—I preen in front of the mirror for hours while he studies at Rue des Saints-Pères. As far as I understand it, he is quite successful, and I hope eventually he will get some position here in Paris. Then we could marry, maybe. Maybe not. Who knows. His doctoral dissertation is already finished—he works fast and efficiently. He is very gifted. With his Vietnamese medical training, he is able to support us here as a junior therapeutist at one of the state hospitals in the southeastern quartier of Paris… suppose we do not remain in Paris, then what? Maybe we could go to Guadeloupe or Martinique? Surely they need doctors and pedagogues there, and maybe musicians as well.

Only one thing irritates me—his stories of his native island, a shitty crackpot land. Yet he is so homesick… what a bastard he will be if he goes back there!

March 8, 1956
Diary of Adélaïde Fourangier, seventh entry

Maison de l'Indochine

Shit, I think I am pregnant. I am not sure though. Anyway, I do not mind. I will visit a gynecologist soon.

April 8, 1956
Diary of Adélaïde Fourangier, eighth entry

Maison de l'Indochine

Yes, I am definitely pregnant. I will tell him soon. Meanwhile, the presentation of his doctoral thesis is set for next week. Half of the pedagogical society of Paris is planning to be present for the open discussion of his ideas. I will be there too, just to watch. I think he will be very successful.

Letter on a double page
[received April 15 in the early morning hours, signed for by Fourangier—S.J.]

March 5, 1956
To Etienne Duvernoix, *pilote de Aigle Azure*
From Jean-Luc Lefebvre, *ancien Meteo France*
L'île Pinto, Paracel

My dear Duvernoix,

Please forward this letter to our dear friend Costas T.; his address should be:

Monsieur Constantius Tegularius
«Maison de l'Indochine»
Address: 57 B Boulevard Jourdan
75014 Paris

My dear boy,

Etienne tells me you are already greatly successful in Paris. At this stage you are already highly qualified in three vocations—electrician (I remember sending you to Lycée Chasseloup-Laubat in Saigon to pursue study during the day there while apprenticing in the French army's electricians' workshops in the late afternoon...), respected doctor, and now philosopher-pedagogue.

My boy, your native island is in trouble—huge waves of epidemics kill droves of your compatriots. I have never seen all four ruling Sages in such a rage. The last epidemic broke out half a year ago, after the eldest Sage commanded that the islanders pour sewage into the only remaining fresh-water well, proclaiming that human contents are sacred both from without as well as from within. As a result, the island has attracted overseas flies that have attacked everybody and poisoned hundreds. Sage no. 2 and Sage no. 4 have expressed venerable opinions that only fervent prayer to the ancestors can stop these flies; Sage no. 3 says that our youth should be sent to the Chinese island of Hainan in ever-greater numbers so that the sacred ground that they bring can be used to alleviate the suffering here. Meanwhile the Chinese shoot the boys en masse. It is a slaughter. The boys' glorious ventriloquist chanting does not help, only a quarter of the boys sent out return from the journey, and most of those are wounded. Many others subsequently die of fly bites.

In your absence, my boy, some parents have evinced growing concern for the future, particularly for the future of the children. They speak of you with great hope. They visited the eldest Sage and told him they want you to come back. They say that the eldest Sage nodded in consent. They have asked me to convey to you the following urgent message: hurry up, my boy—the island is in great need of you.

As you may know, the French are leaving Indochina. I alone am remaining on the island out of love for you and some of the other kids that I've met here. Etienne, the pilot,—you remember him—will fly to the island for the last time on April 19, so please be on board his Dakota and come back here.

You are the island's only hope now, my boy.

Yours with love,

Jean-Luc

P.S. I am remaining on the island with all my up-to-date equipment and my CG Pettersson boat. (Do you remember your first journey on this wonderful boat to begin your studies in Saigon?) But how can I sail the seas alone now?? And where to??

April 16, 1956
Diary of Adélaïde Fourangier, ninth entry

Maison de l'Indochine

Damn it. He left right from the Département des sciences de l'éducation immediately after his damned doctoral dissertation was accepted. That pilot Etienne took him right from Rue de Saints-Pères. What a fool I am! I could not even tell him that I am carrying his child, that bastard. Well, he will never know that he is a father. Let him go; I am so tired of all these men. Can I go back to Neuilly-sur-Seine? I am not sure…it seems that I am following in the footsteps of Madame Bovary. How I hate them all. Gone are Cortot, Mehul, Beethoven, and Debussy, and those ridiculous champions of vanity like Moscheles, Kalkbrenner, and Hummel. I do not practice any more. What a mess. But I will give birth to this little bastard.

I think the father of this fetus is the first human being to give me warmth, tenderness, and—well—love! True, when he first approached me in Saigon I did not feel anything special. But this was the first time in my life that I did not feel my usual revulsion.

Yet to my surprise, here in Paris I started to wish to be touched by him—to feel his tenderness firsthand. I first felt the pleasantness of his body when he bowed to the ground to pick up the pocket score of Hummel's third piano concerto that had dropped out of my hands. Inadvertently his shoulder touched my leg. At that time the tenderness running up my body provoked in me a strong compulsion to embrace him.

Well….

I think C. and I made love well, so I will always feel that I have something real in my life, and maybe, maybe it will all work out. I cannot even return to my poor old mother—she does not know anything. She still believes I am with Jules…. I will wait here until I am asked to leave this apartment. After all, C. has paid the rent until September. So maybe I can remain here until then.

December 3, 1956
Diary of Adélaïde Fourangier, tenth entry
Hôtel Château d'Esclimont

ILLIRIO BORN IN THE EARLY HOURS OF THURSDAY,
NOVEMBER 15, 1956!

Well, I can live here for a while, because the owner of this château
is a friend of Jules who accepts me now as his own friend even
though he knows that I am not living with Jules anymore. Thank
god Jules does not know that I gave birth to a bastard (he goes
about our separation as though it were he who is offended). He
would immediately divorce me and then undermine my career
forever.

Now what will I do with this baby? The female hotel staff help
me. They assure everyone that I found him "somewhere in the
street." Perhaps I should give the baby over to some reliable
orphanage...but somehow I just can't, I don't know why. What
family name should I give the child that authorities would believe?
I need to think things out. Meanwhile he sleeps so innocently,
sweet little bastard. His diamond-shaped eyes are exactly like
his father's. I will have no difficulty saying that I found him on
the street...I'll say there was a torn note pinned to his chest,
with what must be his name written on it...I'll have to invent
an exotic, memorable name for him. What in the world am I
doing? I should be playing the piano instead of being involved
in this mess.

January 30, 1957
Diary of Adélaïde Fourangier, eleventh entry
Hôtel Château d'Esclimont

I found a good name for the boy—outlandish, but still "normal"
enough: Illirio Mariafels. The first name is a cognate for Illyrius,

who was the son of the fierce Cyclops Polyphemus (that's his father from a godforsaken island somewhere in the vast nowhere) and the beautiful nymph Galatea animated by Venus (that's me). And his second name, Mariafels, is a monastery where, according to the dictums of my old mother, I should now be living.

February 28, 1957
Diary of Adélaïde Fourangier, twelfth entry
Hôtel Château d'Esclimont

Everything's fine, Illirio is now in the good care of the sisters at the Maison Sainte-Thérèse. It is just near my former house in Neuilly. I gave them Illirio as an *enfant trouvé*, and at the same time signed an application to adopt him. Very smart, Adèle! They gave me the right to visit him whenever I want—that is, until his true mother is found…very well. This boy will never be a tool of someone else's will to overpower or subjugate me as Jules was always trying to do. I will love him and he will return my love.

I can now resume my career. I have to rise again, to pursue my dream to be prominent and forever free.

March 6, 1957
Mme Adélaïde Fourangier
c/o *M. le Directeur*
Maison de l'Indochine
57 B, Boulevard Jourdan
75014 Paris

[*received on May 14, 1957,* inscribed in pencil in Fourangier's hand—S.J.]

My love,

Every moment that I think of you, I inhale the memories of your wondrous beauty, your shining eyes, and your divine body. Your gaze follows me wherever I go and whatever I do, and it gives me the power to overcome hell.

I was so happy the day that I received my diploma from the Sorbonne and you were present in the hall to witness it. I wanted to be able to kiss you fully on the lips before Etienne Duvernoix took me away on his Dakota.

My silence is not of my making, my beloved. Our island is cut off from the external world. Our insignificant Pinto people—and the truly noble Frenchman Jean-Luc, who has decided to devote himself to us—are now just a small suffering bubble in the middle of a large ocean.

If this letter reaches you, it will be thanks to Jean-Luc's heroism, for he is taking it now to Saigon by boat—alone!—to find Etienne, or another of his pilot friends who can pass it on to you, my dear. You see, he is risking his life for my love of you, your beauty, your eyes.

How are you, my dear?

I am working feverishly day and night, trying to cure my people, both in body and in spirit and—as god is my witness—I am succeeding. And that instills hope in me. My hope is that I may see you at last, here on our small piece of land.

Our spiritual leaders—the old Teachers—have agreed to give me the authority to organize the islanders against the fly-borne epidemic. At my insistence they have agreed to fill up our current wells and to dig several new ones, and, most importantly, not to pollute them with our excrement.

With a silent nod they gave me temporary permission to do this. The flies immediately disappeared. I also am given authority to open European-style academies to give our youth training in mathematics and astronomy. I argued with them that these disciplines like our glorious ventriloquist chant are nothing more than the inner voices of our Teachers. I won a nod of approval from the two old Teachers, no 2 and no. 4, and a no-rejection or a non-nod from Teachers no. 1 and no. 3. (no. 3 is very much devoted to no. 1).

My love, if you come one day, you will see an island that is a shining garden filled with joyous, healthy, friendly, and satisfied people. They will be leading fulfilling lives—according to the American psychologist Abraham Maslow's principles—and one day the world will recognize our abilities too. One day, my love, we will establish a music school here and you will teach your beloved Debussy, Beethoven, and Moscheles. We will teach our youth to write down their wondrous chants and these too we will bring to France and the entire world.

I am not alone in working here day and night, my love; the parents of the children whom I have cured help out with utmost devotion, especially those parents who studied with me in Saigon at our beloved Lycée Chasseloup-Laubat and at the Université de Saigon. We have started building better housing too, and our dear Jean-Luc supervises the work with patience and good will.

The only big problem remaining here is our Hill. Some parents have asked me to go to the Sages and ask them directly to abandon the idea of erecting it. That, of course, is impossible. In order to stop this work one needs to obtain not only simple nodding on the part of the Sages, but a unanimous proclamation in writing. For the present all we can hope for is unofficial consent for the project's delay. I think I may have told you, my love, that erecting a Hill to enable us to view the shores of the Chinese island of

Hainan is our national project. To do so we have to bring much more earth than we have on our small island. So we send our best youth by boat to bring earth from China while we dig our own soil here. I am afraid that in the process we endanger our island by opening it up to flooding. Besides, the soil on the Hill does not harden sufficiently, so in case of flooding one cannot even expect to be saved by climbing up to its summit. At the moment though, the erection of the Hill is now almost completely frozen—the Sages know well that as long as I run the island I will not agree to any work on the Hill. They grudgingly accept this, because they know that I alone have the knowledge of how to drive out the flies.

I look forward to a bright future and many parents support me. I only hope one day—one gorgeous day—a boat will bring the most beautiful lady in the world here (or will she arrive in the plane of our dear friend Etienne?). Then our island will blossom, with you having your adoring Costas at your feet, loving you with all possible tenderness.

Costas

March 8, 1957
Adélaïde Fourangier
Rue de Longchamp, 92200 Neuilly-sur-Seine
Paris

Ma chère collègue,

Your letter arrived at a very auspicious moment; how providential that it was so attuned to my own thoughts as to how I might contribute my own musical training to the cultural wellbeing of society—especially the wellbeing of my Armenian compatriots living in France and throughout Europe. I think your proposition to join forces in a series of recitals of piano duets would find support among the members of the Union générale arménienne de bienfaisance, which is very active here in Lyon. (Coincidentally, I have been provided with a two-piano studio under its auspices.) I think we can prepare excellent musical programs suitable for a variety of tastes and interests from compositions spanning various epochs. I think for a successful tour we should right from the beginning include works by Armenian composers: Khachaturian, Harutiunyan, Babajanyan, and arrangements of Soghomon Komitas. Thank god my country is rich in wonderful works for two pianos! I know the Armenian expat community would line up for these performances with utmost eagerness.

I await your early visit to Lyon to start working.

Cordialement,

Sirouné Avakian
c/o Centre Culturel UGAB
Adresse: 12 Rue Emile Zola
69000 Lyon

July 31, 1957
Adélaïde Fourangier
Rue de Longchamp, 92200 Neuilly-sur-Seine
Paris

Chère madame,

Your request to adopt Illirio Mariafels, a male foundling of foreign race, born around December 1956, has been proceeding in due course. You are requested to submit your husband's signature in order to complete the official adoption procedure.

Sincerely yours,

Benoît Bettencourt
Chef de services
Maison Sainte-Thérèse Orphelins Appretis d'Auteuil
40 Rue La Fontaine
75016 Paris

October 6, 1957
Adélaïde Fourangier
Rue de Longchamp, 92200 Neuilly-sur-Seine
Paris, France

Dear Adèle,

Thank you for your letter.

Well, I will never cease to marvel at the sudden turns in your life. Now this new baby…I must admit, my dear, you stun me. What caused you to take such a phenomenal step? May I hope that this heralds a general turn in your feelings or in your world outlook?

Upon your request, I have signed the forms required of "us" to adopt that foundling boy of yours. I hope one day to see the baby at Saulchery. I hope your love for this charming young soul will bring you back to Fleurette, and perhaps will allow you to see your own life in fresh perspective.

I hope you know what you are doing. Because of the deep love I still feel toward you, I cannot refuse your request, but even knowing you as I feel I do I cannot at all understand your motive. After all, you claim you have your career; your recent successful concert series with Mlle Avakian under the auspices of the Armenian diaspora organization in France is an excellent development. Why do you need an adopted baby of unclear origin when you have a very fine child of your own whom you rarely see? I hope there is no hidden reason—an idea that I drive away with all possible vehemence. Anyway, I have mailed the signed documents to M. Bettencourt at the Maison Sainte-Thérèse.

Be well.

Jules

P.S. Fleurette is growing and developing very well. She dances Spanish sarabands under the devoted guidance of our dear Gerardo Aguilar, the house manager. Monsieur Aguilar is still as fond of you as he always was from your first "silent" visit to our house back in 1946.

November 6, 1958
Adélaïde Fourangier
Rue de Longchamp, 92200 Neuilly-sur-Seine
Paris, France

Adèle, *ma chère amie,*

I could, of course, tell you this at our next rehearsal; however, I would like to put some of my feelings down on paper in such a way as to commemorate them. I would like to thank you with utmost affection for our collaboration during this most productive year. Thanks to our joint talents, we have been able to successfully promote Khachaturian, Harutyunian, and Komitas, not only among my Armenian brethren in the western diaspora, but also among professionals and cultured people throughout Europe. Our most recent concert in Neuchatel a week ago at the hall of the Lyceum Club International will remain in my heart for a very long time. Our performance of the *Harutyunian-Babajanian Armenian Fantasy* and the *Poulenc Sonata* for two pianos have been wonderfully received. True artistic achievements! I think with further discussion and additional work we will soon be able to bring Beethoven and *Lindaraja* by Debussy to that same high level.

I remain in utmost admiration most cordially yours,

Sirouné
Lyon

November 8, 1958
Diary of Adélaïde Fourangier, thirteenth entry

What exaggerated self-esteem this woman Sirouné possesses. She evidently thinks that her understanding of Beethoven and Debussy is better than my own…. Is this just her personality or does she feel that her understanding of the music is deeper because it is her own personal cultural heritage??

February 23, 1959
RADIOGRAMME Pinto-Meteo-Saigon-Paris
À Madame Adélaïde Fourangier, Asie du Sud-Est
c/o *M. le Directeur*
Maison de l'Indochine
57 B, Boulevard Jourdan
75014 Paris

My love, I hope to be in Paris by the end of May. No day passes without my dreaming of you. No epidemics any more. Much hope all around. Etienne will write to you soon. Costas.

April 20, 1959
Mme Adélaïde Fourangier de Vermandois
Rue de Longchamp, 92200 Neuilly-sur-Seine
Paris, France
[hand-delivered letter—S.J.]

Madame,

I visited your residence in your absence, having been received by Mlle Marie, your au pair, and observed your charming little son happily playing with her.

I am writing you at the request of my young friend Costas Tegularius, your devoted champion. He intends to visit Paris in the near future and he has asked me to report upon the situation on Pinto Island to you from a French point of view.

First of all, regarding myself: I am a native of Cherbourg, born in 1921. After serving as a pilot in the Free French squadron affiliated with the British, I joined the Aigle Azure company at its inception in 1946. I now undertake occasional round-trip flights from Saigon to Paris. I met Jean-Luc Lefebvre, the meteorologist, at the end of 1945 in Saigon. The eminent gouverneur-général of French Indochina, M. Pierre Pasquier, had personally sent him to Pinto Island in the early thirties to establish a meteorological service there. One rainy day in December 1945, Jean-Luc told me about where he happened to be stationed and about the mixed Portuguese Chinese population of the Island—most of whom, having unique diamond-shaped eyes, belong to a distinctive human group.

The islanders live a very secluded life maintaining their own peculiar religion, a combination of Confucian veneration of elder Sages and their own self-centered perception of themselves as a people of exceptional wisdom, the level of which they consider to be far above the wisdom of other peoples on the planet. Being on the island for so long, Lefebvre has developed a strong emotional attachment to the local people. I think you could readily say that he has distinct fatherly feelings toward the gifted young orphan Constantius Tegularius. Jean-Luc has devoted all his resources to helping Tegularius develop his outstandingly selfless personality. This fatherly devotion brought Jean-Luc to construct a narrow runway on the stones of the island's eastern shore (with his bare hands!) rightly figuring that in so doing his beloved boy could travel to Saigon by plane, eliminating the sea voyage that is so perilous even in his extraordinary Pettersson boat.

I supply you with all these details with only one purpose in mind—to convey Jean-Luc's generosity toward his foster child. Constantius Tegularius, a child of simple parents who died as a result of one of the island's frequent epidemics, is a man of extraordinary compassion and ability. He loves you with all his heart.

He dreams of bringing you to the island to inspire the locals with your playing, just as you inspired him during his medical studies in Saigon. He feels that perhaps you could open the hearts of the Teachers (this is the term the islanders use for their eminent Sages) and free them of their dangerous, wrongheaded beliefs. At least your playing—and possibly your teaching (he told me about the wonderful master classes you taught in Saigon nine years ago)—could bolster the self-confidence of parents who dream of a better future for their children and for the island.

Tegularius follows in the footsteps of Jean-Luc; he has already built a house for you with his bare hands, with the hope of turning it into a music school complete with two concert pianos and practice rooms for other musical instruments.

As you may know, these islanders have an extraordinary tradition of religious ventriloquist chanting. Jean-Luc thinks such a tradition could attract the attention of musical researchers from France and possibly you could facilitate their coming…but these are still dreams, premature of course.

The main thing is that due to his superhuman effort, Tegularius has eliminated the periodic epidemics that have plagued the island, installing a modern sanitation system with the help of some of the Saigon-educated parents. The Sages have tacitly agreed to let Tegularius organize civic life on the island and to establish some schools featuring western-based curricula.

Some Pinto expatriates from the United States (as far as I know, there is a veteran community of Pinto expatriates in Iowa) started sending some equipment to their motherland, and Jean-Luc brings it in from Saigon (on his Pettersson boat!). I sometimes assist him by bringing in the heavy equipment in my Douglas DC-3. Several months ago, I transported hospital equipment and even printing machinery—the islanders will now have their own press, and probably a newspaper! Jean-Luc, though in his sixties, is himself still very strong and he brought new radio equipment to the island in order to reestablish radio contact with Saigon. In theory, you can now receive short messages in Paris from Tegularius right from the island. You will be able to answer them via telegram to Jean-Luc Lefebvre, c/o Aigle Azure—Indochine, 65 Rue Le Loi, Saigon. Our people will immediately transmit them to Pinto Island.

In other words—and these are the words Tegularius asked me to say to you only if I felt that I could say them honestly—the island is becoming ready for you.

At this point, I will finish my report to you, my dear *madame.* I hope I have conveyed to you the spirit of life on the island. I also hope I was able to tell you something about who Constantius Tegularius is—the most heroic person I have ever met, and someone who loves you with all his heart.

If you want to, you can always learn about my whereabouts at the main office of Aigle Azure on 70 Avenue des Champs-Élysées, Paris.

Chaleureusement,

Etienne Duvernoix
Pilote

April 22, 1959
Adélaïde Fourangier
Rue de Longchamp, 92200 Neuilly-sur-Seine
Paris, France

Adèle, *ma chère amie,*

I write to you upon the arrival of the news that Salle Gaveau has agreed to give me a recital in early spring 1960!

The Union générale arménienne de bienfaisance has asked me to agree to their efforts to organize additional recitals for me featuring Armenian, French, and American programs before and after the planned Gaveau date. I have asked them to refrain from any further action until I contact you and get your response. The union gave me ten days to figure out the situation. Let us discuss this at our next rehearsal here in Lyon.

Tendrement,

Sirouné

April 23 1959
Diary of Adélaïde Fourangier, fourteenth entry

Damn that Sirouné—after all I've done for her!!

If Costas invites me to his damned island I will go with him and I will even take Illirio there. After all, Illirio is *his* child (although I would not be such a fool as to admit it to him and allow another man to rule me through our offspring).

April 22, 1959
Adélaïde Fourangier
Rue de Longchamp, 92200 Neuilly-sur-Seine
Paris, France

Ma chère Adélaïde,

Thank you so much for writing to me and for fondly remembering our musical meetings in Lausanne after the war.

I am so sorry to hear about all the impediments you have encountered along your career in France. As you doubtlessly know, I am in no position to help you at present; my activities in the service of the Vichy government during the last war and my concerts in Germany still render me persona non grata in France, although I have lately been allowed to perform there and to give open classes there. And besides, I am old.... I remember very well our discussions at the piano—of Beethoven's "flux"— and I recall how you blurred passages in order to achieve this "flux." Yet in piano works by Moscheles, you managed to achieve this flux without blurring any passages. Magnificent!

I think you should try piano pedagogy, my dear, just as I have done. I think your pragmatic approach will assist you in achieving great success in this field.

Be well!

Bien affectueusement à vous en hâte,

Alfred Cortot
5 Avenue de Jaman
1005 Lausanne
Suisse

May 18, 1959
Adélaïde Fourangier
Rue de Longchamp
92200 Neuilly-sur-Seine
Paris, France

My love, I cannot think rationally, not even for a moment. Your eyes, your glance, so direct and so shining; your beauty—follow me with every step I take.

I am writing these words in the truck that is bringing me to our friend Etienne Duvernoix's plane. I shall ask him to pass this little letter to you. I hope—I am sure—Etienne will take you and Illirio to our beautiful island on one of his next flights.

Illirio…you did not tell me you had adopted a boy…thank you for sending me the photo of him! He is so extraordinarily beautiful, with his ever-questioning eyes! If I hadn't known that he is your adopted son, I would have thought that he is a child of our island (our child??)—the shape of his eyes reminds me so much of the eyes of the little children on the island. Yes, I will accept him as my own boy, believe me, my love. And I am sure my dear old Jean-Luc Lefebvre will love him as his grandchild. And he will love you too, my beautiful angel!

The truck is now approaching the plane—I must finish this letter. Etienne is flying now to France to bring several huge boxes of vaccine, medicine, and surgical equipment to us here. We will cleanse our island of any malady or dangerous microbe in advance of your coming, my love. I am eagerly waiting for you two! If not on this flight, then on Etienne's next one!

Costas
Sent from Aigle Azure
70 Avenue des Champs-Élysées, Paris

May 31, 1959
Adélaïde Fourangier
Rue de Longchamp, 92200 Neuilly-sur-Seine
Paris, France

Adèle,

Thank you so much for informing me about your plans. Needless to say your letter caused me great anxiety.

You ask me for two favors that are on the surface contradictory: first, to divorce you while retaining my guardianship of our beloved Fleurette, and second, to assist you in getting a long-term international assignment on behalf of IHEMdP.

Well, my dear, the divorce procedure is the easier request of the two. I suggest you come to Saulchery as soon as possible. I will prepare all the formalities in advance. Be assured, my dear—I will behave well, I will never say an angry word about you. This poor knight of the sorrowful countenance will always bear in his heart those couple of years he could assist his queen and lady. We shall be fine, Fleurette and me, dear Adèle....

We can sign all the necessary documents in the presence of a lawyer representing the local government of the department of Aisne. You will be able to play with Fleurette, if you wish. Please inform me when you wish to come.

I shall write immediately to Ilbert D. I hope he will be as cooperative as he has been in the past—after all, we have always supported him and his school and will continue doing so in the future.

Yours,

Jules
Saulchery (Aisne)

July 10, 1959
Adélaïde Fourangier
Rue de Longchamp, 92200 Neuilly-sur-Seine
Paris, France

Adèle,

I am glad we are through with that unpleasant divorce procedure. This means that I will not be required to finance your life anymore. This will be so in accordance with your own wishes. I also appreciate your willingness to sign the documents assigning me sole custody of our beloved Fleurette.

I am also sorry that little Fleurette did not recognize you and did not wish to play with you. However, I find that it would really be better for Fleurette not to grow up in a loveless relationship with her mother. It seems to me now that it would really be better for the two of you to live far apart from each other.

Yesterday I received a letter from Ilbert D. He accepted my request to provide you with long-term assignment in the Indochina islands as an envoy of IHEMdP. I think his text has independent merit, so I attach it to my letter.

Be well, Adèle. I wish you a long and productive life. I hope that one day you will return to Paris with a new reputation and that you will be warmly received.

Jules
Saulchery (Aisne)

July 6, 1959
Jules-Honoré Philibert de Vermandois
Château Abelard de Vermandois
Saulchery (Aisne)

Mon cher ami,

I have received your very interesting proposal to send dear Adélaïde to Indochina's offshore islands for a prolonged assignment as a piano *pédagogue* representing IHEMdP. I am glad to inform you that your proposition has met with great favor here. Dear Adélaïde will be advised to establish a ten-year preparatory school for local youth and to inform us of its progress on a yearly basis. We shall pay her a monthly salary in internationally converted francs equal to that of our senior preparatory school teachers. We shall arrange transfer of payment through a Saigon bank.

If the process goes smoothly, in three years' time starting in 1963 we shall send one of our supervisors to her school to assess its professionalism. In all probability we shall send M. Lothair Döpps, our brilliant alumnus.

I would like to assure you, dear friend, that M. Döpps, a young, talented Alsatian, has proved his outstanding abilities as a specialist in piano pedagogy since his last year of study at our institute and thereafter. We have already sent him to oversee foreign music schools and he has delivered the most astonishing results. We gather that his visits so energize the local piano teachers and make them and their pupils work so much harder, so that they do indeed maintain our high IHEMdP standards.

But first Adélaïde has to establish herself in her new place. In order to assist her in her voyage, we shall pay for one-time air transport of her belongings, including her two pianos, to the designated *lieu*. The only reliable organization known to us that brings both cargo and people to Indochina from Paris is the Aigle Azure company. We shall contact them and organize the whole transaction. Dear Adélaïde should then contact them in three days' time in order to implement the arrangements.

Please send my best wishes to dear Adélaïde; I will be most interested in reading the incoming mail from her in this important placement.

Yours,

Ilbert D.
IHEMdP

July 26, 1959
Diary of Adélaïde Fourangier, fifteenth entry

Here I sit in this empty house. The ancient chairs of the Vermandois dynasty that I tricked myself into being part of and an old French country dining table and the modern kitchen will remain here, in Jules's (formerly "our") Paris residence. Well, to tell the truth, everything remains here—Persian carpets, books, heavy wooden shelves produced by medieval masters of carpentry. And the glorious dinnerware…. Only my two Pleyels with their piano stools, my scores of Beethoven with notes in Maître's hand, and the works of my dear Moscheles will go with me into—into oblivion.

But the house was never my house even if I used to live here. And now it will empty *of me*. In these last hours that I am here

I am like a ghost moving around in it. The day after tomorrow even the ghost will vanish...the sound of little Illirio's babble in the room overlooking the garden will disappear. We will be gone as if we had never lived in France, as if...as if I had never performed at Salle Gaveau...as if I had never concertized in France's beautiful small cities and in Belgium's ancient towns. Yes, my so-called "benefactors" and "friends" have all exed me out of existence.

Yes, it is good that Fleurette will not know her mother—because how would she feel if she knew that her mother was unwanted in her own country... a ghastly shame...I leave this place without tears, without sadness. I am as cold as ice, because there is nobody here to whom I could show any affection. Indeed, could I ever be warm without my Pleyels, without the admiration of my audiences—masses of them? No, nobody can accuse me of coldness—the accusers should themselves be accused.

I shall take this little bastard Illirio with me to his naïvely passionate if provincial father—if he embraces the child with affection, maybe I will tell him after all that Illirio is indeed his child. And if he is not welcoming toward the child?

I hope somebody will be warm to him there. After all, aren't we going to *his* historic homeland? Enough!

Enough of this spineless emotionalism...I should start thinking about piano teaching. I hope they speak French there....

August 20, 1959
Diary of Adélaïde Fourangier, sixteenth entry

On board the Pettersson boat with M. Jean-Luc Lefebvre

I have asked Etienne Duvernoix, the airplane pilot, to allow me a couple of days in Saigon to rest—the flight was too tiring for me. He took the pianos and the boy to the island right away and arranged for Jean-Luc to take me by boat. Etienne is a good man; I feel Illirio is safe in his hands.

What a nice boat this Pettersson is…heavy wooden block construction, everything polished, two big rooms for passengers, enough room for a big refrigerator, a spacious, clean toilet, big portholes in the cabins, and a nice tobacco smell. The sea is calm, only the powerful sound of the engine fills the air. We are heading northeast.

* * *

Jean-Luc shut off the engine. He says he must catch some fish for the islanders whom he says are badly administered. He claims that without the selfless concern of several key individuals— including "heroic Costas," as Jean-Luc calls him—the islanders would easily die of hunger. There are no big animals on the island, only reptiles that with proper preparation are somehow edible. Jean-Luc has cast his net and is now leisurely smoking his pipe. He's a taciturn man in his early sixties…I wonder if I will live to his age?

* * *

The sky is covered with gray clouds; it's drizzling, which brings me blissful tranquility. Yes, I am exiled, expelled not just from Paris, but from the civilized world. In my homeland, my name is a sign of disgrace. I am an outcast. Why? Because some powerful people did not like my performance of Beethoven?? Should someone be exiled for this…? But actually I prefer being exiled to being Jules's caring wife, that stupid aristocrat from the north, and a good mother to that perpetually crying Fleurette.

Eh bien, Fleurette…alone now, without a mother…do I even know her? Do I remember how she laughs, or eats ice cream, or plays with her dolls? No, I do not remember a thing…I abandoned her because I needed the adulation of the public…and now here I sit in a wooden boat at the ends of the earth without any adulation and without a daughter. Who am I? Where am I? On my way to an obscure island whose inhabitants eat turtles!!

But I don't even cry—I feel nothing, nothing…maybe I would like to play a bit of Moscheles, but for whom?? Costas? He has no discernment as far as music goes. Well, maybe I am wrong. Actually I think I *am* wrong. But anyway, his only desire is to have me, playing the piano or otherwise. Well, at least he will not criticize me or exile me somewhere else (although where else could I be exiled? Tahiti? I am sure all positions there are already occupied).

* * *

Jean-Luc says Costas has prepared a two-room clay house for me and for my school. It even has electricity, which Jean-Luc produces on a dynamo generator that works off a small well on the rock. This is the same power source that serves his own meteorological station, which is nearby. He says the islanders are not aware of the existence of this source, only Costas and a few others know about it. He says electricity is very scarce on the island, but Costas has organized a public works project to produce electricity on a larger scale from coal from South Vietnam, supplied in exchange for pearls that the island boys are adept at collecting by hand.

Well, I better not listen to Jean-Luc any more before we get to the island or I will die before we even arrive.

* * *

I think I should write a letter to Fleurette so that she can read it when she grows up. But can I do it?

Jean-Luc is now pulling up a huge catch of fish and throwing it into the rear tank of the boat. Now he's starting up his engine and we power on with the entrapped fish desperately beating their tails. Awful. Tomorrow at dawn we will arrive on the island. So help me god.

PART THREE:

ON THE ISLAND

October 1, 1960

I have been here now for more than a month. What an unbelievably crazy world! From now on I will try to write at least once a month in order to summarize my experiences—who knows, maybe sometime in the future Fleurette and Illirio will read this account.

We approached the island early in the morning. The rising sun briefly came out from behind the clouds and brilliantly lit up the rocky coast. To the left, on the western corner of the island, I saw a tall, strangely shaped hill; to the east, there was a forest that disappeared into the rounded coast. Several dozen teenagers were standing on the cliffs that rose perhaps twenty meters above the shore, and they were waving pink handkerchiefs to greet our approaching boat. Behind them stood Costas with his hair flowing and his strong arms embracing the shoulders of a few of the youths.

Soon I heard the singing—a magnificent two-part chant. Never in my life had I heard such sound, a two-voiced chorus of the same melody repeated over and over just an octave apart—a rare phenomenon in folksinging. I immediately memorized the sonorous tune:

Two-part chant

The chant won me over immediately. Not only had I never felt this way before—as though my heart were leaping out of my body toward that tune, savoring its resonance, its purity, its embrace. It made me reconfigure in my mind how to play Beethoven, although this joy I postponed for a later date. So under the spell of this radiant music was I that only when we reached the shore did I discern that in this remarkable chorus the girls and boys were singing with their mouths closed.

"They greet you with their traditional ventriloquist chant," explained Jean-Luc, perceiving my amazement. Taking my suitcases, he led me to the door of my residence, a sorry two-room affair consisting of a small bedroom with a Vietnamese bathtub (made of special stone) and one portable lamp, and beyond the entrance corridor a larger room containing my two Pleyels. This was to be the "conservatory." There was a small annex behind the house that had a field toilet and a kitchen with a furnace, a small table, and three backless stools, the furniture all handmade by Jean-Luc. Well well…I will now have a perfect opportunity to understand the early post-Neanderthals.

The first few days were hectic. On the first day, we toured Jean-Luc's meteorological station that was contained in several small army-like barracks. It was outfitted with several high antennas, radio transmitters, and other equipment whose exact nature is still unknown to me. Beneath the barracks was Jean-Luc's house—a clay structure just like mine, only it had just one room that served as bedroom, kitchen, and guest room. The bathroom located behind the house had a modern shower and toilet that included sewage devices and water filters. I was relieved to see a washing machine.

The shelves in Jean-Luc's big room were overflowing with books in French and Portuguese. Near his bed stood a good, strong, portable lamp. I guessed he must have been an avid reader. What else can one do in such a godforsaken hole as this? I noticed that his library was very up to date, for the copyright on *Les sciences de l'homme et la phénoménologie* by Maurice Merleau-Ponty that was open on one of his shelves was 1958.

I innocently asked Jean-Luc whether he had ever heard of Alfred Cortot. Without a word, he opened a cabinet to reveal his modern phonograph and a shelf containing long-playing records. Most of them were French chansons by Edit Piaf, Alibert, Marie Dubas, Francis Lemarque, and Yves Montand. But there were also three classical music records—one of *La Marseillaise*, the Berlioz version, and another containing works by Chopin played by my teacher, Alfred Cortot. The third record—how else?—was Beethoven's *Ninth Symphony*, conducted by Toscanini (the well-known televised recording of 1948, with the NBC symphony orchestra, of course).

When I walked outside, I heard a soft gurgling sound and looked for its source. Both Jean-Luc and Costas smiled at my investigations.

"This is our secret well. It is a small source of pure water and independent energy," said Jean-Luc.

"In the future we will build desalination facilities across the entire island and you won't need this little trifle," exclaimed Costas, laughing loudly.

"Well, until that happy day, I will cling to this little well," said Jean-Luc with his characteristic sad smile.

"Are there other Frenchmen on the island?" I asked.

"No other Frenchmen live continuously on the island now," Jean-Luc answered, "but until 1955 sometimes French people from Saigon did arrive for a week at a time. We used to work together. Do not worry, I do not feel alone here," he smiled. "And—Costas…." Jean-Luc looked lovingly at Costas.

"Are you *that* close?" I asked.

Neither of them answered.

On the second day, even before I saw Illirio, Costas took me for a long walk along the island. We walked nearly fifteen kilometers— almost to the Sages' compound—and then returned along the opposite coast. I was completely exhausted and could not walk for two days. Can you imagine that there is neither car- nor horse-powered transportation? People either walk, or in urgent cases they are transported in wheelbarrows pulled by the youth.

Before starting out on our hike, Costas gave me a wonderful pair of Parisian sport shoes. "Look behind you!" he said, pointing to a tall, steeply sloping hill just beyond Jean-Luc's residence that was partially covered with grass. "This remarkable hill is handmade," he explained. "According to our island dream, we have to raise the height of this hill until we are able to see the coast of Hainan Island, which belongs to China.

"How far away is that?" I asked.

"Some two hundred kilometers to the northeast."

"How much taller does this hill have to be in order to fulfill the dream?" I asked offhandedly.

"Much, much taller than it is now," Costas said, smiling. "By my calculation, no less than another two kilometers in height."

"But the base of that hill does not seem wide enough to provide the foundation for such a tall structure," I noted. "Is it safe to build so high?"

"I have no idea, but in any case, I do not believe that the Hill will ever rise more than another few hundred meters. The whole idea is fundamentally absurd. Hopefully we will never complete the Hill because we do not have enough building material to do so."

"What is the aim of observing the Chinese territory?" I asked, my curiosity mounting.

"The idea is to watch the movements of their people."

"Whatever for?"

"To detect the proper moment for sending our forces over to occupy Hainan."

"Why would that be necessary?"

"Because our Sages maintain that Hainan belongs to us," answered Costas.

"The Sages insist that the islanders dig the soil along the northern coast and bring it here in buckets and wheelbarrows," said Jean-Luc.

"Well, I do not see how they can promote their grand aims to occupy Hainan by simply sending our people with their ridiculous buckets to put sand on the Hill," shrugged Costas.

* * *

In twenty minutes we reached the northern coastline. I noticed a little pier with several unusually large rowboats. Several people were occupied in burning and bending large timber planks for some more boats.

"Are those boats for fishing?" I asked.

"No, these are the boats our youth sail to Hainan to bring some of its soil back here," explained Costas.

"Is it safe to sail that far in rowboats?" I asked.

"No, it is practically impossible to survive such a trip. During the last ten years very few boats have returned intact."

I was shocked.

"Why are you so eager to have soil from Hainan?" I asked.

"It has symbolic meaning. In accordance with the teachings of our Sages, soil from Hainan, even in small quantities, has the power to fasten the local sand that is poured onto the Hill. In any case I do not think this madness will continue after the current generation of Sages."

"Are the Sages the actual leaders of the island?" I asked.

"Yes, but they do not interfere in its day-to-day life. They issue orders through their apprentices, and it is the apprentices who supervise the execution of their edicts. In cases of utmost necessity, these apprentices can be bribed," Costas smiled, although his voice was full of sad irony.

We walked along the edge of the sea. I took note of the little clay structures to our right. Many people moving quickly in all directions were carrying timber planks and pieces of metal or were pushing wheelbarrows containing construction material. The scene was abuzz with energy, accompanied by the people's ever-persistent humming.

Approaching one large clay house on the outskirts of the area, Costas, with a big smile on his face, invited me inside. It was his hospital! There were several beds in each room, and only few were unoccupied. A different room contained a laboratory. Although I am surely not able to assess its professional quality, I definitely saw much modern-looking equipment. Several people with serious expressions wearing white lab coats were looking into their microscopes, while others were constantly going into the adjacent room to check on the patients.

In another room that Costas very proudly showed me, newly arrived surgical equipment from Paris was being installed. All the personnel spoke perfect French, and I was glad to be able to exchange a few words with them. All of the staff had studied medicine in Saigon and were Costas's protégés. All those present—especially the patients— greeted Costas with the utmost reverence and cordiality and he returned their profuse greetings with his jaunty smile. Costas beamed as he walked me through the hospital. Then he invited me into a small cabin, announcing, "This is my place!"

I saw a sparsely furnished room with a single bed, a stool, a small table, many books, journals, a small radio transmitter, a phonograph with my recordings of Moscheles and Mehul made in the early fifties, and a minuscule kitchen. Both the hospital and Costas's cabin had electricity.

"We also have a nearby well, so we have good drinking water, and we are able to generate electricity day and night. It is enough for now." As it was around half-past twelve, Costas suggested that we have lunch at the hospital. He immediately took to opening several boxes of canned food and soon we had a good beef soup with preserved vegetables. I drank the local water. It was my first time and I found it incredibly refreshing!

Costas smiled. "Be grateful we did not dine outside."

"Why?" I asked.

"Because then you would have been served turtles and seaweed, or perhaps roasted mice made with turtle oil."

"Stop tormenting me," I said.

"And the water would have been brought to you from one of our 'official' wells polluted with feces, which would have presented a great challenge to your health."

"Enough!" I said in disbelief.

After a short rest we continued our journey. Around half-past two we approached a larger area containing even smaller houses. Here not only was the humming stronger, but the air was full of the stench of roasted turtles and mice. Unbearable! Here the island widened considerably and the sandy area on the northern coast rose gently southward in an elongated ridge covered by forest.

A very large basin opened before us; inside it crowds of naked people were running around with iron buckets and wheelbarrows. Several extremely dirty, naked people pushed their carts very near to us. To my horror, I noticed that their bodies, especially their bellies, were covered with insects. The sight was unbelievable!

"What are these people doing?" I asked, unable to restrain my trembling.

"They are excavating sand for the Hill," explained Costas. "Look at them—don't you see the procession of wheelbarrows going in the direction of the Hill?"

"Why are they so dirty?"

"According to the teachings of our Sages, everything on our island is not only clean, but sacred. So there is no need to wash oneself," explained Costas. He added remorsefully, "This aspect of the holy teaching has caused many epidemics on the island."

"Are your Sages mad?" I asked, my incredulity rising.

"Well, yes," sighed Costas, "but it is only through such madness that the cohesiveness of our people is maintained, especially since we have no contact with the outside world." Costas sighed again. "You know, we do have an ever-growing community of parents who calmly and quietly push the Sages' teachings aside and slowly begin to modernize our island. They claim 'the future is in our hands.'"

"And you are a part of this community of progressive parents?" I asked.

"Yes," sighed Costas, "you see, I operate in direct contact with the Sages, trying to arrange not only the modernization of the island, but also the reform of their teachings. For example, your arrival here on our island had to have their unanimous approval."

"And exactly how do I fit into their teachings?"

"I led them to believe that you, a consummate western musician, will study our ventriloquist chant and spread word of its divine nature throughout the world...and you will keep the little kids busy so that their elder brothers and sisters can study at the Sages' compound."

"What do the elder brothers and sisters study?" I asked innocently.

"Why, they study the Sages' teachings, isn't that self-evident?" laughed Costas with a tone of mockery in his voice.

"For how many hours?" I asked.

"From dawn until sunset," answered Costas. "And then they eat roasted turtles."

"You said 'elder brothers and sisters'; where are their parents?" I queried, totally baffled by the story I was hearing.

"Most of these children are orphans. Their parents died in the frequent epidemics that plague our island. The children live in orphanages." Costas sighed deeply. "I was one of them myself."

"Where did you place little Illirio?" I asked, the horror of the situation suddenly dawning on me. "In one of those orphanages??"

"Yes, but, my love, please do not worry. This particular orphanage is clean, it is run by progressive parents. Didn't you see how clean the hospital is?"

"I don't care. I want Illirio back at our place tomorrow morning!" I said in a tone that brooked no argument.

Costas smiled. "It will be arranged; but do not worry, the place where he is now is run by caring professionals. He won't be alone and this way he will be able to learn our local Portuguese dialect!"

"And what will happen when he grows up? Will he be sent to the Sages to study their naked teachings in the dirt??" I trembled with fury.

"No, my dear, in that distant future, the current system will be far behind us," Costas said reassuringly with his habitual smile.

"Anyway, bring Illirio to me tomorrow morning!" I said, continuing in my imperious tone.

"It will be done!" he said definitively. "Come, let's cross to the southern coast. We won't be able to see the Sages' compound today."

We turned right and passed through a densely populated area. The ubiquitous humming was now deafening, but I noticed that the hummers never opened their mouths. I mused on how unusual this sound production was.

We passed a large two-story house. A tremendous noise emanated from inside. From time to time adults (dressed, thank god) ran out with large packets of leaflets. Others, empty-handed, ran back into the house and soon reappeared with new packets.

"This is our local newspaper," explained Costas, "the one printed under the auspices of the Sages."

"Who brought the printing equipment and the paper?" I asked, unable to contain my surprise. "Your friend Jean-Luc?"

"Oh, this does get complicated," smiled Costas. "These materials as well as modern goods and clothing are supplied by the expat Pintoist community in Des Moines. They're delivered by speed boat from the Philippines."

"Des Moines? In America?"

"Yes, my dear," said Costas. "But please do not underestimate our progressive parents. We have our own leaflets too, and we distribute them much more diligently than this 'official' newspaper."

"Are you also helped by the expatriates in Des Moines?" I asked, hardly restraining my sarcasm.

"No, my dear, our faithful Jean-Luc supplies us with paper and printing materials from Saigon. And he brings us some clothing, as well."

"Who pays for all this?" I asked.

Costas did not answer directly, but instead said, "You will soon see."

Then we entered a forest that was several kilometers wide. How wonderful it was to breathe in the fresh forest air! The only disheartening thing was the complete lack of birdsong. I had to make do with the buzz and whirr of insects instead—a new, sparse forest music to which I tried to acclimate as quickly as possible.

After hiking for an hour and a half, we reached the island's stony southern coast. The approach to the water was difficult.

This part of the island was completely empty, no clay houses, no humming, no stench of roasted mice and turtles. Only the soft lapping of the waves. Suddenly we overheard the animated chatter of young adults. Boys were jumping into the water and disappearing for long stretches of time.

"Who are they?" I asked Costas.

"These are our pearl divers," explained Costas.

"Are they also fulfilling the Sages' orders?" I asked.

"No, this is a voluntary activity," said Costas.

"How come?" I asked with feigned perplexity.

"Well, about two hundred years ago, the Sages came to understand that it would be best to overlook this activity," answered Costas, scanning the horizon.

"Why?"

"Do you see that small dot in the distance?" asked Costas.

"Yes…."

"It is one of the American cruisers on patrol."

"So?"

"Our boys collect pearls, swim to the cruisers to sell the pearls, and then they return with dollars."

"And you give these dollars to Jean-Luc who buys goods in Saigon for your progressive parents."

"You are so right, my dear, but most of the dollars the youth keep for themselves in order to buy medicine and canned goods for their parents, as well as to pay for their studies in Saigon," he added, now very serious.

Costas noticed how tired I was. He asked one of the young men to bring a wheelbarrow. In a moment he ensconced me in it and pushed me all by himself back to my new residence in Jean-Luc's compound. When we arrived it was already dark. Costas left me to dine with Jean-Luc, promising to bring Illirio the next day. In parting, he suggested that we not hurry to pay the required official visit to the Sages. Jean-Luc was of the same opinion. Costas managed to postpone the visit by a whole month.

I was so tired that after an hour I retired to my quarters to luxuriate in my new Vietnamese bathtub and then fall asleep into my new bed for a long, calm night.

The next morning I busied myself exploring my small kitchen. Unexpectedly, I heard the sound of small children's voices coming from the piano room. I discerned the motif of the chant with which I was greeted upon my arrival being awkwardly played on my two Pleyels. I entered the piano room.

Two pairs of eyes gazed at me. Two tots of about the same age, almost twins, stood in front of me, holding hands and examining me intensely. The girl had brown hair and slightly diamond-shaped turquoise eyes, just like Illirio's. Illirio smiled and said to the girl, "Adèle, my mother!" He remained motionless, waiting for the girl to react.

"Nissa!" said the girl finally, pointing to herself and bursting into peals of laughter. Then both kids jumped on me, hugging my knees.

"Ask Nissa if she is hungry." I instructed Illirio.

"Nissa is always hungry," answered Illirio, laughing.

"Then let's go to kitchen and eat something."

"We eat roasted mice!" said Illirio.

"Let's eat something more appealing now, perhaps some fruit, maybe dry bread," I suggested. Illirio told Nissa something in Portuguese.

"Yes, fruit!" laughed Nissa, still holding me by my gown.

For the first time in my life I acted just like a good mother, quickly opening the boxes of foodstuffs that Jean-Luc had left for me and trying my best to set out an improvised yet "princely" breakfast.

The kids jumped on the meal, demolishing it in just two minutes. I kept preparing more food, and they kept on eating. Not until the third round was their hunger sated.

I was beginning to wash the dishes when Nissa approached me (holding Illirio by the hand) and said something that I did not understand. Then she sang that familiar chant, already able to do so without opening he mouth. Illirio said:, "Mother, teach us to play this tune!"

"Both of you?" I asked.

"Both of us," said Illirio.

"Both of us," Nissa repeated laughingly in French.

I finished washing the dishes and we all went back to the piano room. Instead of placing the kids on the piano stools in an orderly way, I myself sat down on the chair and put both children on my knees. I started to play the melody of the chant. Both of them laughed while looking attentively at my hands. Then I started singing this melody. Nissa immediately put her little hand to my face, covering my mouth. Now I was the one who laughed. Illirio told her that his mother didn't know how to sing from her belly. Nissa immediately started showing me how she contracted her belly muscles. It was so funny being taught by a four-year-old that I burst into prolonged laughter. After playing the melody several times, I showed them with great exaggeration how I put my fingers on the keyboard. Both kids laughed and easily reproduced the melody. I showed them how to play it in octave unison. They copied me with great joy. I got up to bring over some simple scores that I had brought with me from Paris. Glancing over the pages, I overheard the kids—now seated very low at the piano on the chair I had vacated—transposing their chant by a whole tone, and then trying to pick it out a fifth higher. I was amazed at how they instinctively knew how to do this. I left the pedagogical material aside and returned to the piano. I placed them both back on my knees and played a five-tone scale, encompassing an interval of a fifth. They laughed and played this scale and other similar short scales all by themselves. I didn't interfere by showing them the correct hand positions.

Then Illirio started singing (with an open mouth) "Frère Jacques."

"What's that?" asked Nissa when he got to "*Din, dan, don. Din, dan, don.*"

Illirio said in Portuguese, "Mother's song."

I started playing it, and the kids picked out the tune, one an octave higher than me and the other an octave lower. It was a delicious feast that I did not want to interrupt. We kept playing for two hours, and then we went to the toilet and returned to the kitchen for another meal. While the kids napped on my bed, I practiced Gabriel Fauré. His melodic turns and spicy harmonies brought the gazes of Nissa and Illirio standing hand in hand to mind. Music suddenly acquired a new, almost cosmic meaning. I never experienced such inspiration before. I even cried.

Later in the evening Costas came by to take the kids back to the orphanage. I said assertively that the kids should stay here with me. Costas immersed himself in thinking. The kids started getting nervous. Finally Nissa said, "Let's go!" I understood that I would not have the kids that night or even the next day.

Costas said, "We didn't give much thought to the manner in which you would work here. We were just so thrilled that you were coming." He lowered his eyes. "The orphans are well cared for by the educated parents," added Costas. "They are kept clean, taught to read Portuguese, and even a little arithmetic."

"They are hungry," I said adamantly.

"But we cannot just take them out of the orphanage and disregard all the other kids," said Costas.

"So how many children do you have in that orphanage?" I asked.

"About seventy," he replied.

"Let me propose that I see all seventy kids to check their musical abilities. I will teach the more gifted kids piano, and we will have choral practice for the others. We will sing French songs open-mouthed. All the kids will visit me twice a week and have their main meal here too. Can't we have meals for them here on my behalf?" I asked.

"Well, I hope Jean-Luc will help us with that, but we must think not only about this particular orphanage, but about the entire child population of the island," said Costas.

"My dear Costas," I retorted, quickly losing my temper, "with all due respect, I will not be able to teach all the children on the island!"

"Then what do you propose?" asked Costas.

"I suppose we could start with this particular orphanage, and in the coming years expand the musical education further, perhaps by bringing in more teachers."

"A good idea," said Costas. "This is just what I will say to the Sages."

Together with Jean-Luc we outlined a work plan for the coming months. Now Jean-Luc had to sail to Saigon to bring cargo of canned food for my "school." To the extent that I understood anything about what went on around there, it was not a moneyed economy. Jean-Luc left the next day and returned six days later. Meanwhile I had Illirio and Nissa with me at my home three more times. Together we learned "Ah! Mon beau château!" (both kids were absolutely happy to play and sing the "*tire-lire-lo*" verse with their mouths open), "*Comptine des bisous pour Maman,*" and "*J'ai vu le loup, le renard, le lièvre.*" Nissa had of course never heard of a *loup*, a *renard*, or a *lièvre* (a wolf, a fox, and a hare), and Illirio tried his very best to explain what these creatures were to her. How we laughed and laughed. The kids advanced in their piano technique very quickly and I even started to say a few short sentences in Portuguese.

* * *

November 9, 1960
Clipping from a local newsletter
As Notícias de elevada (*The Elevated News*)
Comunicado do Gabinete dos Sábios (Communiqué from the
Office of the Sages)

All four Sages received Senhora Boulger for three short separate
meetings.

Sages no. 2 and no. 4 spoke to Sra. Boulger together for twenty
minutes. Sage no. 3 spoke to Sra. Boulger alone for ten minutes.
Sage no. 1 spoke to Sra. Boulger alone for five minutes.

Sra. Boulger was brought to our elevated island to spread the
word of our talents throughout the world via her powerful
network in France. France is a country northeast of Portugal, the
motherland of our beloved forefather Fernão Pinto. Sra. Boulger
was brought to our dear island by Constantius Tegularius, who
acts to purify our people from weakness and helps them to get
inner strength after drinking the sacred water from our bathing
wells.

Sages no. 2 and no. 4 informed Sra. Boulger how best to reveal
the talents of our youth.

Sage no. 3 informed our guest of our customs and the mode of
behavior expected of her while on our island.

Sage no. 1 spoke with Sra. Boulger on philosophical themes.

Sra. Boulger is expected to remain on our beloved island for
many years. She will reside at the end of the island, near our
guest, the technician Jean-Luc Lefebvre, who is our semi-faithful
resident.

On behalf of all Sages, the secretaries accompanied Sra. Boulger
to drink our water. On their return, the secretaries reported
that Sra. Boulger took a large, festive gulp from Well no. 2. The

secretaries awarded Sra. Boulger with a bucket of sand as her contribution toward the building of our extraordinary Hill.

In the evening Sra. Boulger returned to her residence at the end of the island.

November 9, 1960
Clipping from another local newsletter
Posto dos Nossos Pais (*Our Parents' Post*)

Our Sages received the eminent guest of the island, a professional musician and teacher, Sra. Boulger. In France she is known as Sra. Fourangier; in spite of that, our Sages have decided to call her Sra. Boulger.

Sra. Boulger brought two large instruments to our island that produce music that is popular on the other side of the globe and inspires many people there. Some children have already started learning under Sra. Boulger's guidance. In due course many more children will start studying with Sra. Boulger.

Our great friend Jean-Luc Lefebvre will provide the necessary equipment for these new studies.

Sra. Boulger says that the course of study for our youth may take ten years. After completing such a course of study, our most gifted students should be able to play the highly inspiring music of humanity's greatest composers. Some might wish to continue their studies overseas.

November 15, 1960
Diary entry by Adélaïde Fourangier
A visit to the Sages

This island is far worse than even I could have imagined. At least this is my impression from visiting the Sages—two old, almost completely blind maniacs with long, scruffy, repulsively loose beards. Apparently their grip on the islanders' hearts is overwhelming. Costas tells me that all four idiots keep this poor island in danger of constant epidemics and prevent the islanders from developing themselves.

On the morning of our visit, Costas came early and brought a tube of antibiotic ointment with him. "Before getting dressed, cover your body with this ointment," he commanded. I obeyed. Then he gave me a thin condom and asked me to put it on my mouth and inhale. This was strange beyond all belief.

"Why am I doing this?" I asked.

"The Sages will probably ask you to drink our polluted water, so you can just pretend to do so, using this little trick: after gulping the water from the well, just take the little sac out of your mouth and wait until you can discretely throw it away." If I hadn't realized it before, it was now clear to me that we were in the domain of maniacs. Finally, Costas asked me to dress all in white; I did so without even asking him what the purpose of this masquerade was. He brought a wheelbarrow. We both sat down on its little bench and two strong young men conveyed us to the Sages' compound. They ran quickly like the horses in the American pony express. At every kilometer the runners were replaced by another pair of young men. In two hours we reached the fence surrounding the compound.

November 9, 1960, late evening
[letter written in Tegularius's hand—S.J.]

My dear Adèle,

Please keep this letter for future reference—I try hereby not only to capture the spirit of our visit to the Sages, but also to infer what is expected from us in our public behavior on this island in the years to come. As long as the Sages, with the help of their numerous secretaries, dominate the public sphere of this island by imposing their vision upon us, we have to respect their wishes—at least in public—for our own safety.

I will now give you the chronological account of our meetings with the Sages.

The first Sage to receive us was Sage no. 4. The official local newsletter writes that both Sages no. 2 and no. 4 received us; this is wrong, as you well remember. Sage no. 2 is ill, but in order to maintain tranquility on the island the Sages conceal this information from the islanders. As you may well remember, both Sages no. 4 and no. 3 spoke only with me in local Portuguese in your presence; Sage no. 1, however, did not come to meet us at all.

Sage no. 4 made several queries about you: Do you copulate? What is the nature of the instruments you brought from the other side of the world? What is your attitude to the teachings of Sages?

On your behalf, I replied that you are a single, childless woman, a virgin by evidence of all those who know you in Paris. I told Sage no. 4 that the instruments that you brought to the island are called pianofortes; they are very popular on the other side of the globe, especially among powerful people. I added that our brethren in Des Moines like pianofortes too. I said that these instruments enable people to make music without singing. This will magnify our wonderful local musical traditions and inspire our students to perform heroic deeds. I told him that you have heard much about our island and the insightful teachings of our Sages, and that this knowledge made you eager to come to work with us here.

Sage no. 4 told me the following: "I shall agree to her"—yours, dear Adèle—"presence on the island under several conditions. First, this woman will keep to her domain and not travel to other quarters of the island; she will not copulate with anyone; secretaries will be sent to the vicinity of her house to observe her celibacy. If anyone notices that the woman is copulating, secretaries will come to her house and start to copulate with her in order to produce children. Second, this woman"—they mistakenly call you "Boulger," my dear; it is wrong, but I cannot change that now—"will study the oral teachings of our Sages, and teach our islanders to manipulate the pianoforte according to our musical traditions. In the event that she deviates from this line, our secretaries will come and burn her pianofortes."

The meeting with Sage no. 3 began with the same questions regarding your sexual activity.

I explained to Sage no. 3 that this matter was already discussed in detail with Sage no. 4, and being a virgin, you have agreed to live in strict accordance to his instructions. Sage no. 3 demanded proof of your virginity. I told him that if your privacy were to be violated, France would send soldiers to occupy the island, demolish our Hill, and harm the Sages.

Sage no. 3 asked by what other means could I prove your virginity. I suggested applying to the French medical bureau; I added that such an appeal might result in prolonged litigation and that virginity confirmation might arrive only after ten years, not to mention that such a request would present our island in a most unfavorable light in Paris. Sage no. 3 agreed to adopt Sage no. 4's practical formula: to send secretaries to your vicinity in order to observe your way of life.

On behalf of Sage no. 1, Sage no. 3 asked how you would promote the good name of our island in Paris and around the world. I told him that you have been sent to our island with the blessing of one of the world's greatest music schools that happens to be located in Paris. I also informed him that once every three years a special envoy from Paris is supposed to visit our island in order to listen to our talented students. I expressed my sincere conviction that some of the children would certainly excel and the envoy would then write superlative reports to his superiors and this would promote the reputation of our island. Maybe even one or two youngsters might eventually travel to Paris to further their studies, and this would also spread the word about us in that region. I expressed my abiding belief in your wonderful talent and the power of music to uplift the soul.

Sage no. 3 consented to all that I had said. He reminded me to help protect your celibacy and demanded that you publicly drink from Well no. 2 (the less polluted of the two). He also ordered that upon your drinking, his secretaries would bestow upon you a bucket of sand so that you could prove your loyalty to our ideals by contributing this bucket of sand to the elevation of the Hill.

Sage no. 3 also proclaimed me to be your protector on the island. I should add that all four Sages have made me "Chief Operator" of the island—a curious but efficient appointment. In this capacity I can act to modernize the island, and I have some administrative power as well. I hope to make you feel good here, my dear, for many years to come.

November 15, 1960
Diary entry by Adélaïde Fourangier, continued

The last pair of boys stopped the wheelbarrow at a distance of a kilometer from an elevated ridge of dry sand. Costas told me that this was not really sand, but dry seabird feces called "guano" that provides good building material for the island's structures. To our right scattered on the field in no apparent order were many open gray tents. The girls and boys who were seated on wooden benches inside the tents held black slates and chalk, and they were writing down their teachers' words. The teachers, mostly men, although there were some women, all wore gray sweat suits. The oldest adolescents received their lessons from completely naked men who had clouds of flies buzzing around their bodies. Nobody seemed perturbed by this.

To the left, hundreds of women in gray sweat suits grilled turtles over open charcoal pits. A nauseating aroma hung in the air. Costas gave me a thin piece of cheesecloth to cover my nose and head as we entered the open guano gate. It turned out that we were still not at the Sages' compound, but only in precursory territory. Here in many small clay structures similar to my garden residence sat naked secretaries, covered with feces and flies, performing their paperwork in an exaggeratedly fastidious manner. The air was full of the sound of their ventriloquist humming combined with the buzz of the flies. In the distance alongside the guano fence, I noticed dark stains on the ground that attracted especially wildly buzzing flies.

"These are our former drinking wells, now full of feces and without much water left in them; they are the symbols of laborious homage to our glorious Sages' teachings," explained Costas, his irony tinged with disgust.

We then approached a high fence made of modern metal latticework; we entered a small gate and found ourselves surrounded by people in clean white sweat suits with ridiculous figures of naked men covered with flies printed on the front of the sweatshirts. These people were running from one small metal barrack to another, storing manufactured goods that they hurriedly carried in wheelbarrows.

After a fifteen-minute walk, we noticed an elegant two-story wooden country house with a large glass-enclosed veranda surrounded by a well-groomed lawn. I noticed that to the left of the house was the harbor where a large boat named *Pintoville* was docked; the white-costumed men hastily unloaded goods from the boat. I also noticed that behind the house stood two more elegant houses; one of them, situated close to the seashore, had a tall antenna protruding from its wooden roof.

We entered the enclosed veranda and waited for over half an hour before an old man in a shining white, silky gown appeared before us. It was clear that his eyesight was weak. He sat down on a big chair behind a large table and looked far above us. Then he started talking to Costas in the local Portuguese dialect. His voice, soft but powerful, was at times angry. I remained silent throughout the entire interview. I can't imagine that the old man actually saw me. Two secretaries dressed in white with images of filthy, naked male bodies on their chests came in and wrote down the Sage's words. They did not record Costas's words. Then the old man left the verand——slowly. We waited for another half an hour until another completely blind old man was assisted to the veranda. He uttered several words and was taken away.

We left the compound, accompanied by several white-clothed secretaries and three or four naked secretaries who had flies buzzing around their smelly bodies. We walked for about an hour until we reached the wells. When we arrived, Costas instructed me to double the fold in the cheesecloth that covered my head in order to make it less transparent. Then he whispered to me to put the condom in my mouth, making sure to cover my teeth. As we approached a large pool of obviously unclean water, the secretaries started singing their ventriloquist chant. I bowed and "gulped" some of the sacred water. The secretaries exploded in rapture and immediately ran away. I quickly spat out the condom and removed the cheesecloth. The last remaining secretary gave me a bucket of sand and then he ran away too.

"This is the sand that you are required to put on the top of our Hill, thereby contributing to our national effort," explained Costas. I was getting more and more perturbed by the inanity of it all. Why had Costas brought me to an island run by insane fanatics who were enthusiastically killing their people with their sacred customs? Just to amuse himself or because he was lonely for Paris and civilization? At this point, however, my position was very weak: I had no other place on the globe to live. My current misery did nevertheless provide me with some income, however invisible, coming from Paris and landing somewhere in Saigon. My suffering on this crazy, moneyless island would one day make me—in case I did survive here—a rich woman...I must somehow learn to control my anger!

Saturday, December 17, 1960
Diary entry by Adélaïde Fourangier

While I have been on this island for only twelve weeks, every day I experience an intense feeling of liberation. Although confined to a small quadrant of this backward and filthy little place, my deliverance from the scrutiny of my august French compatriots who always judged and belittled me is such a relief that no matter what this stupid island holds in store for me, I will always revel in this marvelously redemptive feeling.

Yesterday about seventy children, some of the parents, and workers from one of the orphanages came to my home for their first-ever piano recital. It was supposed to be a low-key examination to find out which children were the most suitable for piano instruction. As my house was much too small to accommodate all the curious parents and children, I opened the windows and asked the parents to put some benches in the yard so everyone could hear. I played two pieces by Ignatz Moscheles: the melodious Piano Study, Op. 70 in A-flat major, and Fantasia in E-flat, Op. 13.

Ten days ago, when I started preparing for this performance, I thought of also playing *Moonlight Sonata*, especially since the beautiful, tender middle movement displays all the color of the instrument that I would have wanted this audience of neophytes to hear. But the thought of investing so much effort into polishing Beethoven's delicate phrasing only to have it go unappreciated by these novices was too much to bear. So I went with Moscheles whom I have performed so often that I could do it in my sleep.

There were at least twenty children who must have liked the music because not only did they listen wide-eyed—as though hearing an exciting tale—they even accompanied my playing with their ventriloquist manner of singing. But before I had finished playing the first piece, most of the other children ran away and a short distance from the benches began throwing mud at one another. So it was patently obvious which children I should start teaching.

But afterward the parents of ten of the children who ran around throwing mud approached me in great distress and asked me to teach their kids too. So fervently did they implore, insisting that under my tutelage their children's lack of interest would turn into consummate virtuosity, that I relented. I clearly felt, though they did not explain it directly, that they were less interested in the musical accomplishments of their children than in the possibility of sending them far away from this godforsaken place. I could not refuse their plea, and besides, at this stage I thought I was too much of a newcomer on the island to antagonize anyone, so I arranged short lessons on Friday afternoons for these ten children as well.

To sum up, my weekdays—at least for the time being—will look like this: Every day except Friday I will give four or five forty-minute individual piano lessons with a twenty-minute break between lessons. On Tuesdays and Thursdays I will also teach these students pitch-training and sight-reading vocal music, what we professionals call solfège. I have divided the piano students into two groups, and each will receive one forty-minute lesson in solfège a week. On Wednesday evenings there will be a chorus rehearsal. On Fridays I will spend my time with the students whose parents approached me to insist on their lessons. I have grouped them into three classes of four, four and two, and I will give each group a half-hour lesson—that's about all they can manage before they start jumping up and wanting to go outside.

The pedagogy will not be easy—each child receives only one lesson a week, and this is his or her only opportunity to touch the piano. Yes, it is preposterous; I only can hope that in the future these primitive conditions will improve.

The good thing about this schedule is that it enables me to use the morning hours when my mind is freshest for my own practice. I think I have found a way to improve my technique by using some of the methods that Cortot tried to teach me (and failed!). Perhaps now when no one austerely oversees my work as he did I can advance at my own pace and achieve the results that he expected of me.

Friday, December 23, 1960
Diary entry by Adélaïde Fourangier

Five days ago, on a Monday afternoon, I gave my first lessons. As agreed, local parents and some people from the orphanage brought children ages five to fourteen for individual lessons. Over the course of the week I saw twenty students. And now I just completed my first day with the children whose parents begged me to take them in spite of their visible lack of enthusiasm. I invented a new technique—we sang together, then clapped to the beat and imagined that we were throwing mud at each other. At most they evinced only feeble interest at the start of the lesson, and their attention soon flagged. Should I exclude them from my school as I originally planned? They definitely do not belong here. But…I do not dare break their parents' hearts. I shall have to rethink how to motivate them.

Anyway, not knowing any Portuguese with which to communicate with any of my pupils, I was at a loss until little Nissa and Illirio spontaneously began translating the words of their "*Mama Musique.*" These two stay with me all day long, so naturally they absorb the instruction much more quickly than the others. During the intermissions between lessons, the two of them eagerly scamper onto the piano stools and pick out island chants that they know by heart. What a delight to observe them!

On Wednesday (the day before yesterday) our music school attracted some unwanted guests—naked secretaries smeared in excrement. There were at least fifteen horrible men outside the house gesticulating in an impudent, swaggering manner, and shouting something in vulgar-sounding voices. Although I immediately slammed the windows shut, the repulsive smell of their bodies still managed to penetrate the room. How amazed I was to see how calmly the children reacted to the secretaries' presence. I, on the other hand, quite visibly panicked. When I couldn't bear it anymore, I went outside to try to convey to the secretaries through hand gestures that they had to leave. Upon seeing my ridiculous charades, the naked secretaries burst into raucous laughter and approached the closed windows in bold mockery, leaving feces-covered handprints all over them. Feeling threatened, I sent all the young students away. Nissa and Illirio ran away with them. Our first children's chorus rehearsal ended fifteen minutes after it started.

Was I being overdramatic? Of course I couldn't help but see how my hysterics frightened the children—some of the younger ones wept when I stormed out of the house to confront the secretaries (who still remained nearby, leaning against my dreadfully dirty windows). I remained inside alone and trembling as though imprisoned. Then miraculously becoming detached from the scene, I began witnessing my own panic. I know this feeling well; it has helped me many times in the past. I was then able to notice, for example, that the naked men did not attempt to break into the house or attack me, which they easily could have done. No, they remained outside, close to the windows where I could see them, ugly laughing men.

Perhaps some of the children told their parents what a maniac I had been and they notified Costas, for about an hour later he and five of his associates showed up.

I saw how Costas softly addressed the secretaries. Afterward most of them withdrew, but a few others remained and they continued imprinting my windows with even greater fervor. Costas pushed one of them away. In a moment a huge fight erupted. The naked men who had initially left returned with clubs and started beating him and his people. Though tall and seemingly able, the secretaries' movements were sluggish. After about ten minutes Costas and his men succeeded in driving my attackers away. Costas, his shoulder wounded, was now bleeding heavily. His associates bandaged him as I began cleaning the windows, opening them to eliminate the stench. Right away Costas called out to me, ordering me to close all the windows. Everyone but me knew that the feces attracted poisonous flies and the very first thing to do was to protect the house with disinfectant spray. Costas asked someone to bring some from the hospital. Luckily, it rained just an hour later so the air smelled clean and fresh once again. I asked Costas to remain in my house. He agreed. With such a wound he could not move around very much anyway.

Sunday, January 1, 1961
Diary entry by Adélaïde Fourangier

Though still in pain, Costas is recuperating. He remained at my house for two days to rest, lying quietly on an inflatable mattress that his associates had brought from the hospital. He was so silent that I was sure he was sleeping under his thick hospital blanket. His associates had placed the mattress in the narrow corridor between the two rooms of the house. There were no lights there, not even space for a chair. As there was no way I could even sit next to him, I remained in my bedroom, gazing into the darkness where he rested until well after midnight when I too succumbed to sleep.

At dawn I heard the sound of water streaming from the bathroom. I went to check and saw Costas standing naked under the shower without his bandage. His wound was huge and still bleeding. He cleansed it, at times applying ointment on the inside surface of the wound, his face contorted in pain. When he noticed me, he stretched out his left hand and gently pulled my sleepy body toward him under the warm stream of water. Having no desire to resist, I allowed him to remove my already wet night robe. In our embrace, his blood covered my shoulder. I could then feel his terrible pain. As I caressed the skin around the wound he received while defending me, he covered my body with kisses as tender and as mighty as a knight's.

For a long time we held each other in complete silence. Then we made love on my wet robe on the floor; he was powerful, soft, and loving. I felt how much we wanted each other and now we were joined in blood (so to speak). We stood up and washed ourselves under the shower. Costas then pushed me brusquely out of the bathroom (which, after our tender moment, startled me). All this transpired without a word, without even a whisper.

In the morning his associates brought him a fresh bandage and dressed his wound. Although all of us were fussing around Costas (and he was still completely silent), I somehow felt that I had proprietary rights.

Only after breakfast did Costas start to speak. Strangely, his voice was deeper and more tranquil than usual, while to my amazement, my own voice had become lower too—a clean, low mezzo-soprano without any huskiness. As we spoke, I heard how the resonances of our voices intertwined and knew, completely knew, that now we were truly a couple. (It felt so different from our time in Paris when I used to make love so mechanically. I certainly did not feel united with him through our voices as I do now. Perhaps this is my own personal way of validating our love.) Then Costas interrupted my heavenly musings by reminding me that under the bargain he had struck with the Sages, our intimacy was life-threatening—in fact, his role was to ensure that I lived in complete celibacy.

I told him that I hadn't forgotten that exhaustive letter that he had written me after our meeting with those old crackpots.

"How will we manage?" I asked.

He caressed my hand softly and smiled. "At dawn, my love, when our guardians sleep their sacred slumbers and commune with our exalted Sages in their dreams."

"All of them?" I asked.

"Yes, all of them, just at dawn," he smiled, adding, "but the only place we can be together is in this narrow corridor between your two rooms. Not only is the sight of our lovemaking dangerous, but the aroma remaining in the air also attracts unwanted attention. I noticed your hurt expression when I pushed you out of the bathroom at dawn. I had to do it because if we had remained together, our bodies would have emitted a sweat permeated with the fragrance of love. The secretaries would undoubtedly have discerned that pungent scent, and it would have been the end of us."

"Enough," I said.

During the day, some associates from the hospital and some professionals from the parents' quarters came to consult with Costas. However, around six o'clock in the evening he sat down at the outdoor kitchen table and helped me prepare an evening meal, doing so with only his left hand. Although I saw how acute his pain still was, he uttered nary a word of complaint. All this time we discerned several naked secretaries lurking a small distance from the house and casting piercing glances at us. Costas remained quiet.

In the evening he took the kitchen broom, wrapped it in a towel, and placed it under the blanked of my narrow virgin's bed. Then he led me into the corridor where his mattress was and we both lay down like teenagers. At last he said in a soft voice, "My love, tonight let's just talk, and then we will fall asleep in each other's arms."

"We can only talk because if we make love, either the secretaries or the flies will detect the scent," I said with deep, analytical understanding.

"Yes, my love," he murmured.

"So what will you tell me tonight in order not to attract the flies, *mon prince charmant?*" I asked.

"First, I will tell you something about the flies," he said.

"Should I prepare a fresh towel for vomiting?" I asked.

"I will be brief," he said. "We have two sorts of flies—the smaller ones that feed on human excrement are like all the other flies of the world, a constant annoyance that propagates infection. And then there is the much bigger type of fly that carries poison in its thorax. This poison attacks the human respiratory system and can kill people in the course of several hours."

"What might be the cuisine of these much bigger flies," I asked, "if not human excrement?"

"Surprisingly, they are relatively indifferent to typical human excrement," Costas explained, "but they are acutely attracted to the fluids of human ecstasy that remain in human feces after defecation. The big flies go absolutely mad when they find such 'especially enriched' feces in drinking water. After feeding on it, they start to murderously attack people in the vicinity."

Costas's words caused me horrible nausea that took several minutes of silence to overcome. Costas understood and remained silent too.

"What sort of ecstasy are you talking about?" I asked, already exhausted by the topic.

"Mainly two—religious and erotic."

I took the towel and pressed it to my mouth.

"Wait, there's still another point here too—the secretaries' behavior," said Costas.

"Oh, really?"

"I think you should know this, my love…"

"Oh yes, I can already guess—the secretaries have the same acuity as the big flies, they feel the ecstasy in human excrement…"

"That too," answered Costas. I was surprised that he took my sarcasm for perceptiveness. "But—"

"But what?" I had lost my last ounce of patience and was becoming snappish.

"Perhaps you have asked yourself whether we should expect some punishment from the authorities for beating their holy men and driving them away."

"No, I did not have enough composure to think about that, I was just so glad that you came in time to rescue me. But as I was alone without anyone for god knows how long, I did ask myself why on the earth would they come here in the first place and smear my windows with their feces?"

Costas nodded. "OK, here is the explanation, as briefly as possible," he said. "At the end of sixteenth century…"

"Ah, you mean *that* brief of an explanation?" I teased.

"It really will be brief."

"Go ahead."

"There were only around one hundred people in the second generation of islanders. People were frequently hungry. The general mood was one of embitterment, with many wishing to leave the island and ask the Chinese to let them back into Hainan. Fighting over food with heavy injuries and deaths occurred daily. There were four very strong men on the island who used to separate the brawlers. They were also able to withstand the collective anger of the embittered populace. When they grew older, they proclaimed all inhabitants of Pinto Island to be holy brothers whose eternal aim was to return to Hainan when an increase in their numbers would allow a successful fight against the Chinese. They of course could not specify what that number might be, but until that time all islanders were to purify themselves by pursuing a life of brotherhood, with no islander hitting a fellow inhabitant, thereby preserving the idea of sacred unity. They imposed collective ventriloquist singing (known in certain remote regions of China, especially in the northwest, and transmitted by scholars to the progenitor of the Pinto Islanders, Vasco Calvo), which produces such an ecstatic mood that the urge to strike one's fellow inhabitants just disappears.

"The Founding Fathers"—this is what Costas called the first four Sages—"proclaimed that there would be no police or indeed no court on the island that would in any way mitigate the effect of this ecstasy. They wanted the aura of holy brotherhood to reign supreme over all. They also discovered that the scent of human excrement carries a stimulant that triggers interpersonal harmony. So they initiated and enforced the dreadful body and spirit rituals that you will observe soon.

"Then they required that thirty men from among their most ecstatic supporters devote themselves entirely to the study of their teachings and act as the islanders' spiritual guardians. In order to inspire full confidence in the hearts of all the other islanders, the first Sages insisted that their new disciples—the secretaries—walk around completely naked, serving all others by personal example."

"Why is this damned nakedness so important?" I asked.

"In order to show that they have nothing to hide, that even their bodily urges are harmoniously united with their relations to others."

"Ah yes, and by covering their bodies with feces they show even more harmony."

"Yes, my love."

"Oh, and this is what has created the atmosphere of spiritual unity here?" I was already having difficulty imagining the dimensions of all this.

"Yes," Costas went on, staring into the distance, "and then the first Sages introduced universal education for all children, decreeing their own elevated teachings to be the sole curriculum.

"After the first Sage died, they invented a method for promoting another man into their ranks, creating two additional classes of secretaries, the gray-suited ones and the white-suited ones. The men in white are the more senior and a new sage is selected from among their ranks. But since the naked secretaries are upheld as living examples of the highest decency, they alone are encouraged to walk around the island displaying their own unity of body and soul in order to inspire others with the profound wisdom of the Sages."

By this point I was dumbstruck.

"How can there be any nobility in these naked idiots?" I rasped in the nightly whisper that we were forced to use. "They wander around producing ugly sounds, carrying huge clubs with which to beat people, and they stink. When they themselves are beaten nobody, not even those who believe in their inherent nobility, bothers to come to their rescue. What kind of depraved idiocy is this?"

"So you're looking for the existential logic of our existence here?" asked Costas in an amused voice.

"Nothing amusing here," I said, "and stop patronizing me, I'm warning you!"

Costas accepted the rebuke.

"Well, as the Founding Fathers grew older and their physical force diminished, and in spite of their noble teachings of brotherhood and the eschewal of violence, they equipped themselves with huge bludgeons just to make sure that order was maintained. The older and weaker they became, the less they could intimidate the other islanders. So they gave clubs to the naked secretaries and watched to see what would happen. The naked secretaries started attacking anyone who seemed to be afraid of them—maintaining that only sinners needed to be afraid. In this way the secretaries maintained that they were still acting in complete accord with the ideology of the Founding Fathers. To their way of thinking, the beatings reinforced the lofty spiritual order that could never be contaminated.

"But then one of the Founding Fathers became so physically frail that when a few secretaries came to this elder's abode with some now-forgotten request that was refused, the infuriated petitioners hit him with their clubs, and the elder died of his wounds. So the new council of Sages revised its security policy: the naked secretaries were required to subsist on a nutritionally deficient diet of grilled turtles, which caused them to be sluggish; the gray-suited secretaries received axes (acquired from passing ships), while the white-suited secretaries got huge swords. At the beginning of the eighteenth century, the Sages themselves already had in their possession pistols and rifles acquired from sea pirates cruising in the vicinity. So 'divine equilibrium' was achieved with the white-suited secretaries fearing the Sages, the gray-suited secretaries fearing the white-suited ones and their swords, the naked secretaries fearing the gray-suited secretaries and their axes, while the general population was cowed into accepting the teachings of the Founding Fathers by the naked secretaries' clubs. In case the Sages grew too old and frail and were incapable of handling their rifles, they were protected by personally devoted white-suited secretaries who were armed with guns. Both the gray- and the white-suited secretaries were obliged to keep strict personal hygiene and never indulged in the feces rituals. Their health and well-being (needless to say, the Sages lived in meticulously clean residences) served as a sign of the rectitude of the general order on the island."

"Why does nobody come to protect the naked secretaries when they are beaten?" I asked.

"In the Sages' view, if the naked secretaries are attacked, it is a sign of insufficient zealotry on their part," explained Costas. "Technically speaking, the general population, if properly organized, could overpower the naked secretaries, but most islanders fear staining their consciences by thinking badly of them. In the people's humble state of mind, the secretaries cannot detect any of the fear that provokes their violence. So the existing madness replicates itself in an endless loop.

"This 'divine equilibrium' is the core achievement of our Founding Fathers. It is accepted as the best possible social arrangement in the world—in fact, it is revered as being prophetically inspired. The island faith presumes that in some future millennium, the divine teaching of our Founding Fathers will be accepted by all mankind."

It took me quite a while to recover from the disgust and incredulity generated by Costas's short tale, but when I did, I confronted him savagely. "Why did you bring me to this island? We cannot live together, we endanger Illirio, and there is a constant threat of death. Why?"

"You are right, my love," said Costas, guiltily lowering his head. "I should not have done it. I felt—"

"You are simply an egoist, a bestial egotist." I now felt so deceived that I wanted to pound on his chest, but he was too close for me to deliver a strong blow.

"When I heard you playing in Saigon, I experienced such elevation of soul—so much more genuine than that produced by our Sages' teachings—that I thought your enchanted music could free us from this damned ecstasy of righteousness."

"What? My playing the piano did that?" I asked with even greater incredulity.

"Yes, just as I experienced liberation and release from this ecstasy through your music, I thought it might happen for the others as well, and then if you taught our kids—"

"You really think my playing has that much power?" I asked.

"Oh yes, my love, undoubtedly," he assured me while bestowing soft kisses on my hands and fingertips. And yes, I returned his kiss.

* * *

Yesterday both Costas and Jean-Luc came over to celebrate the New Year with me. Costas is still visibly in pain, but he is already able to work with both of his hands. Since the beginning of last week three of his associates patrol my house during the children's music lessons. These men do indeed bring huge clubs. They beat every secretary who comes within fifty meters of the school.

Monday, January 2, 1961
Diary entry by Adélaïde Fourangier

I think I should mention here that we have arranged a set of signals so we can notify each other of our predawn assignations. Costas comes over at least twice a week to consult with Jean-Luc; he indicates his presence by switching on the light in Jean-Luc's back porch, which I of course can see from my bedroom window. If I don't wish to see him (when would that be?) I switch my lights off, otherwise they remain on. We are now Hero and Leander of Greek mythology, though I hope without the tragic consequences. I am offended by the whole situation, feeling more like Costas's call girl than his wife, but I hope he will find a way to "normalize" our married life in spite of the insidious bargain he struck with the Sages. I surely don't want to harp on this theme in the future. Meanwhile, I hope it will not affect the tenderness of our present relations.

Friday, January 20, 1961
Diary entry by Adélaïde Fourangier

For the first two weeks of January, our routine has been as follows: approximately half an hour after the first sounds of the piano issue forth from my house (I do not yet practice in the mornings), the naked secretaries appear, usually at least ten of them, laughing horribly and moving toward my classroom windows. Costas's people accost them about fifty meters from my house and beat them with huge clubs. The secretaries try to fend them off with their own clubs, but their fighting methods are too awkward. The wounded secretaries fall down, bellowing wildly, shattering any serenity that might have prevailed in our learning environment.

Although I could not see the beatings (they all occurred behind a row of bushes), I heard them and know that children should not be exposed to these dreadful outcries. I told Costas that I would stop teaching if my work had to be accompanied by these bloodcurdling sounds. He accepted my ultimatum and told the people on patrol to disarm the secretaries with pepper spray, though he grimly remarked that that was much more dangerous to both the secretaries and to us than the beatings. For a while this allowed me to carry on with the lessons without outside interruption. But the secretaries soon became increasingly attracted to the chemicals in the spray and now dozens of them, ugly, naked, and dirty, gather in the bushes near my house every afternoon. With horror I noticed the huge flies buzzing around them. So now I was forced to choose between beatings and a widespread plague. Instead I insisted that Costas remove the secretaries from the entire area surrounding my house. Smiling sadly, he agreed to it. Since the day before yesterday the naked secretaries have been beaten at a distance of two hundred meters from my house. We no longer hear their cries, so now it's all perfectly "OK."

I fully realize now that the secretaries are not people with whom it is possible to have a reasonable conversation. Suddenly I felt sorry for them. When I saw Costas next, I told him how I'd had an attack of conscience over the beatings those naked maniacs were receiving because of me. So Costas sat me down for another talk to supplement my knowledge of the order on the island.

"These several thousand secretaries, repugnant in your eyes, are our national DNA, the carriers of our wisdom, our spirit, our character," he intoned with an inflection of awe in his voice. "They have no need to listen to any of the ordinary people around them. That is not part of their raison d'être."

"So they listen to no one?" I asked in bafflement.

"Only to their superiors in the Secretarial Order," he answered.

"What do these naked ones do," I asked, "when they're not persecuting me—masturbate day and night?"

"No, most of the time they sit at their little tables on the eastern side of the island copying the Sages' writings and learning them by heart. Then they pass the copies to the secretaries dressed in gray who collate and revise them and return the revised documents to the naked ones for further memorization. Those who chant these writings the best teach the youngsters, thereby transferring our sacred knowledge and spirit from generation to generation," said Costas.

"You can't be serious," I said. "These smelly men smeared in feces are your teachers?"

"As I told you, these are the commandments of our Sages whose dictum is the indivisible unity of soul and body, both from within and without. To renounce these teachings would be tantamount to killing our spirit."

"And who needs this spirit?" I asked. I paused to grimace and then added, "Or this 'divine equilibrium'?"

"We do, because this has become the essence of our existence," he said assertively. "The naked secretaries come to your house to put their feces on your windows with the simple aim of counterbalancing your spiritual energy, your foreignness. Equilibrium must be maintained!"

"I absolutely refuse to take you seriously." I almost laughed in his face.

"You may consider my words to be sarcastically bitter," sighed Costas.

"So you say," I mocked, "but you can't deceive me. I feel you from the inside. I can differentiate between the bitterness and the filial devotion in your voice." My own voice was now acrid. "You deceive only yourself. In your heart you are as devoted a son of these shit-covered Sages as everyone else, differences in ideology notwithstanding!"

"As a scientist I know that adherence to our tradition brings with it a high price—mass death, and now with ever-growing frequency. The most numerous victims of the fly-borne epidemics are the naked secretaries themselves, so the general population reveres them as martyrs."

Challenging him directly, I asked, "So what do *you* propose as a solution to this quagmire?"

"In liberating our people from mass death through the institution of western hygiene, we also liberate ourselves from deadly traditions," Costas averred.

"Just who are the 'we' you're talking about?" I queried.

"Well, there are many people here besides me who realize the absurdity of our traditions," he said.

"How many?" I persisted.

"I am sure it's a majority by now."

"Do people openly repudiate the Sages?" I continued my interrogation.

"No, that would be way too disrespectful, but many people simply disregard the ideas the secretaries chant and just concentrate on their own work, whatever that might be—fishing, catching turtles, building, childcare. Those who have studied in Saigon continue to study mathematics, physics, and radio engineering using the texts they brought back with them."

I felt exhausted. I clearly remember that I sighed deeply (and Costas sighed too—though perhaps for different reasons).

"How come the secretaries don't attack me inside my house?" I asked. "After all I *am* afraid of them!"

"Because your body and personal abode are protected by the spirit of our Sages, my dear virgin," said Costas. "Please remember our meeting with them!"

That's how this man finally defeated me.

April 15, 1961
Comunicado do Gabinete dos Sábios

We hereby remind everyone that in the spirit of our Founding Fathers, celebration of the commandment to fulfill the supreme duty of uniting body and soul will commence in two weeks.

Everyone is required to bring their holy excrement to our public wells and to defecate there with joy while performing the sacred chant. All other sources of drinking water must be consecrated in the same way. The sacredness of our island totally depends upon this duty.

April 21, 1961
Posto dos Nossos Pais

Our honorable Sages call on us to fulfill the traditional consecration of body and soul. We ask that everyone observe these rites with utmost caution, since this duty usually causes extreme hazard. We therefore urge that anyone interested in implementing the Sages' appeal do so in a symbolic way ONLY. The long-standing recommendation of the Parents Movement is to send just two or three representatives to the wells and to request that they simply bow over them—nothing more.

April 23, 1961
Cassettes recorded by Jean-Luc Lefevbre

Great apprehension prevails among the parents. Every rational person knows that mass adherence to those mad Sages' orders will produce a new wave of death. The horrible taste of this devil's lottery—who will die? and, most cruelly, whose children will perish?—is on everyone's mind. For two days now there have been deliberations in the council of the Parents Movement (those who studied in Saigon and some of their friends) on the appropriate course of action to take. Emotion boiling at white-hot heat often overcomes rationality.

Four mothers decided to demonstrate at the gate of the Sages' compound. Yesterday they held a vigil, silently and respectfully holding placards that stated, "Beloved Sages! Please postpone these rites!" An hour went by before they were attacked by naked secretaries and bludgeoned to death. Their bodies were left to rot in an open pit near the guano fence. As a result, today's debate continued even more vociferously. A group of parents confronted Tegularius with the death of the women, contending that he knowingly sent them to certain death, whereas compliance with the Sages' orders might not have caused their deaths. The debates deteriorated into the usual hysterics and acrimony. Three people fainted. One died on the spot from a heart attack.

May 1, 1961
Cassettes recorded by Jean-Luc Lefevbre

As could be expected, the mass defecation rituals at the wells was followed by an onslaught of poisonous flies. The epidemic started straight away. Luckily for us, the monsoon rains chased away the flies. This time there were only eighty-four dead from among the island population.

May 2, 1961
Comunicado do Gabinete dos Sábios

We greet the people after the satisfactory completion of the rites of the Festival of Unity of Body and Spirit. While some sinners have died, there were many fewer deaths than in previous years—a clear sign that our island is now purer than in the past. From the spirit of our Founding Fathers we have a clear sign that we now gloriously tread the path of righteousness—the path of our venerated Sages.

May 9, 1961
Posto dos Nossos Pais

Thankfully our purification rites are over. But we need to ask ourselves whether, with eighty-four dead, this ritual with all its elevated piety is the proper form that adherence to our sacred island tradition should take. Among the dead were several friends from among the technical workers, thirteen children who did not even enter the well area, and many honorable secretaries. We soberly propose that in the future, CELEBRATE OUR RITES IN A SYMBOLIC MANNER ONLY.

Tuesday, June 20, 1961
Diary entry by Adélaïde Fourangier

Today we completed the first year of study at our school. Good pedagogic practice tells me that I should prepare a progress report to guide our future work. So here it is.

All of the students (thirty, to be exact) have just performed an end-of-year concert in the presence of Jean-Luc, Costas, and some parents from among his associates, though most of the children participated in the concert only as choral singers (under my own rather clumsy baton).

Trying hard not to be a bragging mother, I must nevertheless admit that both Nissa and Illirio possess outstanding musical talent, rare even in terms of European culture. During the concert Nissa proudly performed Beethoven's *Sonatina in G major* and Illirio played Kuhlau's *Variations in G major*, Op. 42, and Schumann's *Song of the Reapers.* Very good playing by both of them. Five other children also showed good achievement; they played shorter pieces by Georg Philipp Telemann and Johann Sebastian Bach.

While the majority of students have difficulty concentrating and do not evince much patience for western music, they do nevertheless sing pleasingly in the ventriloquist manner of their native culture. I write down the melodies of the chants and then we execute them on the piano. Using this methodology, I may be able to open them up gradually to western music. Gathering them in groups, I let them perform their favorite songs on two pianos with four hands, myself conducting. Sometimes Nissa conducts and that is indeed a moving scene to watch.

I've also learned how to tune the pianos. Who would ever believe that I could do it!

Tuesday, July 18, 1961
Cassettes recorded by Jean-Luc Lefevbre

Since little Illirio's appearance on the island, something in my heart has changed. I have lost all repose; every day I worry about his and Nissa's future. Formerly I just enjoyed looking at the children here openheartedly, taking a distant view of the bizarre local customs and the mad devotion to the Sages. While I've always loved Costas as if he were my own son, I never felt the palpable worry about him that I now feel for Illirio and Nissa. How blissfully they walk around the compound holding hands together. What will be their fate on this island of too many early deaths?

Thank god I was wise enough to help arrange semi-secret lessons of mathematics, physics, navigation, and electrical engineering for those who want to learn these subjects and better themselves; there are about 350 people on the island who have already pursued a higher education in Saigon. At least 120 others are currently studying there now. I remember talking with the islanders even before the Second World War, seeking out those willing to build a better future for themselves. My French colleagues who were then stationed here on the island by my side used to make fun of me, calling me the Colonial Preacher and deriding me as one who despises native culture.

To them I was a zealot eager to impose my truth upon hapless natives. Our disputes frequently ended in acrimony, as I was then really offended by their accusations of imperial arrogance on my part regarding my caring attitude toward the locals. I think my protective feeling toward these innocents is what has caused me to remain on the island....

I remember one episode back in early 1934 (Costas was a young boy then). After visiting the well area during the excrement festivities, I helped one woman who was injured in the stampede to walk to her cabin. She leaned heavily on my arm and wept. Actually, she cried so hard that she almost choked. She told me that all of us would die before the night was over because of the onslaught of the big flies. I told her that according to our meteorological forecast there should be heavy rain in about two hours and that would disperse the flies. She looked at me in disbelief. As she could not walk rapidly, we approached her cabin right before the downpour. The rain was indeed so heavy that no flies remained in the air. We had been saved (at least those far enough from the wells were, because later some flies returned to the wells). As we entered her cabin, the woman looked at me in awe. Collapsing onto her bed, she glanced at me like a drowning passenger from a ferry boat who had been tossed a lifesaver— her belief in the sublime authority of the Sages still remained intact. Feliciana, as she was called, later died of her injury—no one could help her, though I begged my French colleagues to send her to Saigon to get medical treatment. They adamantly refused to interfere in local matters and prohibited me from doing so either. Poor Feliciana! She had one devoted young son, Constantius. He was already living in the orphanage, since the secretaries had proclaimed Feliciana to be insufficiently faithful and took him from her. After her death I took the boy to our station. Nobody dared take him from us.

On her deathbed, Feliciana called over some of her friends and we started discussing the situation on the island. Since then I have had a wide circle of friends among the natives here, and felt then as I do now that following my heart does not lead me in wrong direction.

After Feliciana's death, I quietly started organizing local youth who wanted to obtain a western education by transporting them to Saigon on my boat. It didn't bother me that the Vichy government was occupying Vietnam at the time. I only cared for the well-being of the people and the possibility of their creating a better life for themselves. Since 1947 I have fostered a network of evening classes where parents gather their children and their friends from among certain reliable orphanages for small-group instruction in European technology. I am proud of establishing this network (may the Sages drown me in their feces!). The secretaries were and still are clueless of its existence, certain that the studious children whom they see pouring over their books are studying the revered Sages' teachings, since every time they approach these evening gatherings the children start humming. Many children, though not all, really like this surreptitious education. Some have even learned decent French since the textbooks all come from Saigon.

Maybe these kids will one day liberate the people from their tragic devotion to the Sages. Who knows? And while this is my general worry, somehow my anxiety about Nissa and Illirio is different, almost as if I had a personal connection to them, as if they were Costas's kids...my own grandchildren.

Friday, July 21, 1961
Cassettes recorded by Jean-Luc Lefevbre

I do not like wandering around the island anymore. Until 1955, when there were more Frenchmen here, I felt totally comfortable doing it. Although I now know many residents and even some of the secretaries and the women who grill turtles, I still prefer to stay in my own locale. I can no longer quietly observe how these people harm themselves. Sometimes I walk to the Hill from whose height I can look over at the marina and see the teenagers busily constructing the boats that will take them on their ill-fated voyages to Hainan. The idea of "freeing" Chinese territory because many generations ago a few of their Founding Fathers allegedly lived there is suicidal in every sense. How can these primitives even imagine overcoming the several million inhabitants of Hainan, not to mention the support that Hainan would receive from the billion mainland Chinese? Obviously this is only a ritualistic game, but for years now, out of the six boats carrying about forty boys, only one boat returns with some eight survivors. True, all of those who participate in the mission are deemed heroes and great honor is bestowed on the survivors, not to mention the communal elevation as the solemn chanting of the names of the dead youths begins. While it may be impossible to dissuade adolescents from dreaming of heroism and adventure, where is the supposed wisdom of the Sages? What can be their motives for sacrificing these young boys' lives? I already shudder to think that when Illirio comes of age, he will want to sail to Hainan and be designated a hero. *Ô mon dieu.*

Sunday, August 20, 1961
Diary entry by Adélaïde Fourangier

Illirio and Nissa visited me today. Illirio enthuses about the heroic sailings of the older teenage boys. He makes it sound like a holy mission, a children's Crusade. I was amazed to hear the precision and clarity with which he talks about the ancient homeland and the collection of holy soil for the Hill. He's just a boy, not even five years old!

Saturday, September 23, 1961
Diary entry by Adélaïde Fourangier

Jean-Luc and Costas came to dinner at my house. Jean-Luc brought canned vegetables, juices, and some fish from his recent catch, which I grilled on my outdoor woodburning stove. Jean-Luc told us about the exciting developments throughout the world that he monitors on his shortwave radio—both the Soviets and the Americans have succeeded in sending people into outer space and bringing them back to Earth alive. Illirio's enthusiasm for the journey to Hainan still reverberating in my mind, I suggested that this sense of human indomitability and the refusal to accept "realistic limits" is precisely what impels Pinto Island youth to undertake the heroic sacrifice of sailing to the motherland. Costas lowered his gaze as I talked, while Jean-Luc's entire face assumed an expression of pain. "These are terrible actions," he said, and immediately explained: "This is a ghastly way to get rid of dozens of the strongest and most devoted youth. I am sure the Sages encourage this craze out of fear of an insurrection that these young men might initiate once they become fully aware of the Sages' autocratic rule. I have not one iota of doubt about it," Jean-Luc insisted with conviction.

"You are wrong, Papa, and you know that," said Costas tenderly.

Jean-Luc did not answer, but only shook his head sadly. I did not know what to think and so asked Costas for his opinion. Opening his palms, he began with his usual sigh.

"This is but another dreadful custom of our island. I hope it will be eradicated by the time Illirio comes of age so that he will not feel obligated to go there."

"Have you been there yourself?" I asked.

"Yes, twice," said Costas, and I noticed the slight wrinkle of pride that suddenly appeared on his lips. I have to admit that I was also caught up in his exultation. Most likely Jean-Luc noticed this too, because his eyes filled with exasperation and sadness. Perhaps the severity in his gaze helped me to regain my senses.

A few moments later, I asked Costas, "How come you didn't tell me anything about the dangers these teenagers face in sailing to Hainan? You see Illirio and Nissa frequently—they would listen to you. Why don't you inform them of the ridiculous stupidity of their Hainan dreams?"

"I cannot treat them as exceptions and expose them to the wrath of all their peers, not to mention that of the secretaries," answered Costas in a sad voice.

Now I felt anger rising in my heart. I knew we were fated to have a tough talk about this sometime in the future and already anticipated the acrimonious fallout. I promised myself that I would not allow Costas to evade the moral duty of putting an end to this madness. Our festive dinner party ended in gloom.

Tuesday, November 21, 1961
Diary entry by Adélaïde Fourangier

We have started a new school year. I now have thirty-five pupils, fifteen of whom I teach in three groups of five combining singing with piano instruction. The rest get individual keyboard lessons.

I have noticed an amazing thing: Illirio tries to sing in two voice registers simultaneously—the lower voice is produced by using the local ventriloquist technique, and onto this he superimposes sounds produced in the throat and cheeks. Using French folk tunes that I taught him in the lower register, he transfers the local chanting into a higher pitch. Amazing! And this from a boy of only five!

February 8, 1962
Diary entry by Adélaïde Fourangier

Illirio and Nissa amaze me; they copy the music for my older students and study it as they copy. I see how Nissa and Illirio sit at the piano and teach each other their independently acquired secrets.

February 20, 1962
Diary entry by Adélaïde Fourangier

Illirio composed a counterpoint melody to a French song. He wrote out the polyphony and now tries to perform it using his double-voiced technique. In those short intervals when he actually succeeds, the effect is one of cosmic grandiosity, and that in spite of his soft child's voice.

Tuesday, February 21, 1962
RADIOGRAMME
À Madame Adélaïde Fourangier, Asie du Sud-Est

The eminent pedagogue Dr. Lothair Döpps will visit your school to evaluate the progress of your students on June 25–28, 1962. Please arrange for his accommodation and prepare your students.

Ilbert D., *Directeur adjoint,* IHEMdP

Sunday, February 24, 1962
Diary entry by Adélaïde Fourangier

I informed Costas about the approaching visit of M. Döpps. Costas said that in the interest of preserving the music school he must take Döpps to the Sages' compound for an official visit.

Friday, May 25, 1962
Diary entry by Adélaïde Fourangier

I will have only my most advanced pupils play for Döpps. The main repertoire items will be Johann Sebastian Bach's preludes and Haydn's minuets. Illirio and Nissa will play Beethoven and Mozart. I have only a few pieces of early twentieth-century children's music, so only one child will play Bartok's *Slovakian Boys' Dance*.

The less advanced kids will do the four-handed accompaniment for our chorus. The culminating event will be Illirio's original two-voiced singing. We will naturally have a recital of ventriloquist chanting performed by the older children's chorus. I think it will be a good presentation.

Saturday, June 30, 1962
Comunicado do Gabinete dos Sábios

Our Sages received Senhor Loreno Dos, who came to visit our island to get an impression of our music school and its gifted pupils. Upon returning to his homeland, he will spread the fame of our island and its elevated ways. Senhor Dos expressed his deep gratitude to our great Sages for receiving him.

Friday, July 6, 1962
Posto dos Nossos Pais

Our island was recently visited by Professeur Lothair Döpps of France (whose name was interpreted by our Sages as Loreno Dos). Professeur Döpps is a specialist in music pedagogy and came to listen to the pupils of our beloved music teacher, Adélaïde Fourangier (whose name is interpreted by our Sages as Senhora Boulger). M. Döpps listened to our music pupils for three days and made notes that, as he explained, will later be transcribed into a formal report for his colleagues. It is no doubt an important professional advance for our music school.

Wednesday, July 25, 1962
Cassettes recorded by Jean-Luc Lefevbre

As a Frenchman, I was happily predisposed to meet the distinguished music professor from Paris. After all, Paris is Paris, a world-class city. And I was so sure he would have fresh news of the end of the war in Algiers! How eager I was to hear all the details. But I was deeply disappointed. M. Döpps was disinclined to discuss anything with me, a "retired meteorologist." Etienne Duvernoix, who brought Döpps, told me that he is Alsatian. Etienne never stays on the island for more than several hours since the naked secretaries always attempt to smear his plane, both the interior as well as the exterior, with feces. Their pranks tend to damage the landing gear as well. As usual, Etienne wished to depart immediately and then return a few days later to take Döpps back to Saigon. However, the eminent pedagogue insisted that the plane remain on the island for as long as he himself remained here. So Costas sent cordons of parents to protect the plane, and used the entire stock of currently available narcotizing spray to neutralize the attacking secretaries.

M. Döpps brought a modern TV with him and gifted it to the islanders. Etienne and I immediately erected a special antenna on the northern slopes of the Hill and succeeded in receiving broadcasts from Hainan, though the quality of the video was extremely poor. Anyway, immediately after Döpps's departure, the secretaries destroyed our antenna.

M. Döpps insisted on having meals with Etienne and myself (but without Adélaïde). The house, especially erected for his visit, had a toilet, electricity, and fresh drinking water.

I am not sure that he formed a positive impression of our music school. At dinner, he repeatedly interrupted the meal to scribble some comment or other in his notebook, as though he had just recalled an incident that had to be included in his report while at the same time apologizing for the impoliteness. He excused this rude behavior by saying that he puts professional duty above all else. He said frowningly that his notebook contained many observations regarding the problems of our children's music school and it was his duty to record them all. I was happy to see him leave and only regretted not being able to enjoy a few more good hours with my old *copain* Etienne.

Thursday, August 2, 1962
Diary entry by Adélaïde Fourangier

I am deeply concerned about Döpps's visit here. Only now, a whole month after his departure, can I resume my journal writing—this is how long it has taken for me to regain my composure.

Döpps, in fact, did not say much; he mainly sat with an extremely dour expression on his face, frequently tapping on the table he asked me to set in front of him as he listened to the children.

Sometimes he leaned in my direction and asked questions such as, "Is this the only choice of repertoire that you could select for this child?"

"Is this the way you prefer them to play scales?"

"Why do you continue teaching them when they do not have an instrument at home on which to practice?"

Formally speaking, he did not display any enmity to me. However, something in his bearing radiated total contempt— not only toward me but toward the students. Before the first pupil, an eight-year-old boy, started playing, he greeted him in an overly mellifluous manner, and then immediately said that he did not have time to listen to all three of the short pieces that the child had prepared. I translated his message for the boy as he sat down at the piano. At the beginning of the second piece, Döpps said, "Enough!" The child did not hear and kept on playing. Döpps hit the table with his right hand. The startled child stopped playing, burst into tears, and ran out of the room. Döpps sat motionless for a minute, and then turned to me. "What are you waiting for? Send in the next student!"

So I called the next student, another boy, age nine.

He started his first piece, Jean Baptiste Lully's *Gigue in E minor*, a difficult piece for a child. Döpps interrupted the child seven bars before the end of the composition and asked him to leave the room. Then he sat silently for another minute.

"Should I call the next student?" I asked, at a loss.

He tapped the table with his pencil, lowering his head in deep reflection.

"No, bring in the previous student," he said peremptorily.

When the first child appeared, the tears on his cheeks now supplemented with mud, Döpps, with his super-mellifluous greeting, repeated all of his previous speech. But now he reprimanded the boy for not respecting his superiors by appearing with mud on his face. These last words were uttered in an openly intimidating manner. This time, however, the child did not lose his composure and played his first piece (Haydn's *Minuet in C major*) and then started to play his second. Döpps interrupted him again at exactly the same spot and looked worriedly at his watch. Then he sighed self-importantly and said (again in his mellifluous voice), "Unfortunately, we do not have time to listen to your entire program. I am sure you understand our important professional responsibilities, don't you?"

The child left the room, not crying this time, but totally bewildered. So was I.

Döpps did not evince any interest in our choral productions and was oblivious to the originality of Illirio's double-voiced singing. His main interest, or, more accurately, his main focus of criticism, was the recital by the ten children who performed piano solos on the first day. His only relatively good word was reserved for Nissa's rendition of Mozart's country dances. "Reasonable playing," he commented.

I do not even wish to imagine what he will say in his report to Ilbert D.—it's just too depressing to think about. What can I expect? To be sent off to some even more remote place on the globe? Could there be such a place? Or will they decide to stop paying me a stipend? In that case I will return to France and resume concertizing with my beloved Moscheles and Hummel...I suppose Ilbert D. would much prefer that I stay here even at the expense of the monthly stipend that is accumulating compound interest in my savings account in Saigon.

I thanked Döpps for his attention, which he accepted in full seriousness. But I was partly serious too—after all, Döpps not only brought me spare strings and the spare piano parts that I needed, but also more music from Paris. And now, a month later, I can start to breathe again.

Tuesday, September 25, 1962
RADIOGRAMME
À Madame Adélaïde Fourangier, Asie du Sud-Est

The collegial council of IHEMdP has received a full report on the state of affairs in your music school that was prepared by Dr. L. Döpps. *M. le Directeur adjoint* was deeply saddened to hear of your pupils' low level of achievement. He intends to send Dr. Döpps to you again in two years' time (1964) to check on your students' progress.

Tuesday, September 25, 1962
Diary entry by Adélaïde Fourangier

Damn them. Damn them all, filthy Parisian bastards! To hell with them all!

Monday, August 5, 1963
Cassettes recorded by Jean-Luc Lefevbre

I have just returned from a trip to Saigon. I brought over twenty-four Pinto Island teenagers to study the rudiments of engineering at Lycée Chasseloup-Laubat. I feel that besides the canned goods that I bring back to the island, my transporting these youth to Vietnam on my beloved Pettersson is my main contribution to the future of Pinto Island. This way the kids can at least obtain the modern education that they could not otherwise receive on the island. On my way home I had two wonderful days of fishing.

Monday, September 30, 1963
Diary entry by Adélaïde Fourangier

Once again we start a new school year. By now, I speak the local Portuguese dialect rather well—an achievement in its own right. But actually, I wonder if my work here has any value? I mean, even if Döpps, his value system, and his judgment are all wrong—I still have to wrestle with the question of my teaching western music here. As the children are not at all familiar with European culture, the musical ideas expressed by the European masters will always be alien to them, even if some ten or twelve students intuitively appreciate European melodies. Should I enlarge the place local melodies have in my curriculum? And do they need me here for that? After all, they have their own educational system.

Anyway, my work is frequently interrupted both by alarms about spreading pandemics and by fights with those naked secretaries. I have no idea what the end of all this will be.

And Costas? He, like a saint, believes that the island is on the high road of progress. In my opinion, he is deluded, although admittedly he has organized a revolution in agriculture. At his urging many parents have started to cultivate little plots of land that produce vegetables, so now the local diet contains something other than grilled turtle and fish.

For me, the only bright spot is my work with the children. I feel they do grow richer and wiser, even if they are studying an alien culture. Still, I do my utmost to cultivate their local chanting too by transcribing it to the piano and playing it back to them.

Illirio himself now writes wonderful piano music that the children perform. Nissa does this as well, although she composes less than Illirio. She has a wonderfully boisterous manner of playing—a sheer delight to listen to. Nissa is a joyous girl, a rare quality on this island. She is gifted in many spheres—she is excellent in mathematics, she reads French, she runs and jumps as though powered by some turbo jet. Each time she somersaults into the air, I am breathless waiting to see whether she will land on her feet. It is no coincidence then that she plays music in such an energetic manner, and with such fine attention to detail. An amazing girl! I would be proud to bring her to play for my revered Alfred Cortot. (How is he? Is he still alive? If only I knew.)

I tremble at the thought that when Döpps comes again, he will once again invalidate everything I do.

Friday, October 18, 1963
Diary entry by Adélaïde Fourangier

Several days ago, while practicing in the early morning (naked secretaries beaten somewhere far away, so "no disturbances"), it finally occurred to me how I might produce a better sound. I feel I am on the right track, because today, having rearranged the acoustic balance between the two hands, giving more impulse to my left, I was able to give greater range to the sound dynamics not only while playing piano, but also with forté and fortissimo. Now I can better create the effect of space and this will surely bolster the artistic value of my Fauré.

Sunday, November 24, 1963
Diary entry by Adélaïde Fourangier

I was working on my arpeggios using the new technique I
developed when Jean-Luc came running in, breathless, to
tell me that the American president John Kennedy had been
assassinated. He says that all America is stunned. I do not
know anything about politics; what should I think, what about
his poor widow? Is she a mother? How old are her children?
Was President Kennedy a good husband? Did he make his wife
happy? Jean-Luc raced back to his wireless before I had a chance
to ask him. I will surely forget to ask about Mrs. Kennedy when
I see him again.

Saturday, November 30 1963
Diary entry by Adélaïde Fourangier

I think we have to acquire two upright pianos and bring them
here. After all, the children do have to practice during the
week—that damned Döpps was right. I am ready to buy these
pianos with my own money if the islanders do not have the
resources to acquire the instruments. I shall inform Costas of
the need to visit Saigon.

Friday, December 27, 1963
Cassettes recorded by Jean-Luc Lefevbre

Costas has succeeded in opening several small schools run
by Saigon-graduate parents to teach French, mathematics,
navigation, and radio technology. No visible protest from the
Sages so far.

These parents have also erected new two-story clay houses
that have clean running water. This independent fresh water

system took two years to construct, but out of fear of secretaries' wrath, the circuit of the water pipe only covers the small western part of the island, the same locale where the new high-quality housing is being constructed. Costas reached an agreement with the Sages under which all the sand excavated in the home construction would be turned over to the secretaries who now fill their buckets with it and bring it to the summit of the Hill.

The day after tomorrow Adèle and I will sail to Saigon to buy two pianos. Costas has already brought me two sachets of big pearls to pay for them.

Friday, January 10, 1964
Diary entry by Adélaïde Fourangier

On Wednesday Jean-Luc and I returned from Saigon with two old upright Gaveaus. Both are in good shape, and I am sure they will serve the children for years to come. Costas's people took the pianos to the backrooms of the hospital so the children will be able to practice in the afternoon hours, each a full hour twice a week under the supervision of the hospital personnel.

In Saigon I managed to visit the opera house. As I stood there leaning against its front wall, I remembered my days as a concert pianist. How long ago that was! Somehow I had the feeling that one day I would return to my former glory.... Never mind. The opera house is still beautiful, though I have no idea what the present activity occurring within its walls might be. I assume it's not music.

Monday, February 10, 1964
Diary entry by Adélaïde Fourangier

Illirio and Nissa play Schubert's impromptus wonderfully (no wonder—they practice daily in my house in the evening hours).

Upon hearing a Piaff recording at Jean-Luc's house, Illirio made his own two piano arrangement of *Non, je ne regrette rien*, which he plays with Nissa.

Illirio continually implores me to come with him to the marina to watch the ceremony of greeting the heroic teenagers who have just returned from Hainan. What should I do? I guess I must go with him. But, oh my lord, I tremble each time the thought of that damned marina enters my mind.

Friday, February 14, 1964
Diary entry by Adélaïde Fourangier

I went down to the marina and saw two boats approaching the coastline. Their arrival was accompanied by loud ventriloquist humming from at least a thousand girls and boys who had been released from school just for the occasion; they were accompanied by secretaries wearing gray, apparently their teachers. A crowd of naked secretaries had also gathered somewhat farther to the east, their feces-smeared bodies covered with medium-sized flies. The secretaries in gray, on the other hand, looked quite clean, and the numerous youngsters with them also appeared to be tidy and clean.

The first boat to touch land contained six or seven teenagers who were proudly waving their arms and holding little boxes in their raised hands. The youth aboard were chanting:

> The soil of Hainan,
> The soil for our Hill,
> For our Sages.

The other boat attached to theirs by a rope appeared to be empty. "We salvaged the bodies of ten of our heroic comrades;

the other thirty-five drowned at sea," chanted the arriving teenagers in unison. When no one descended from the second boat, I realized—much to my horror—that it was full of corpses.

I looked in Illirio's direction. He had brought a high stool with him in order to observe the proceedings from behind the crowd. Although he did not say anything, he was evidently ecstatic. This, more than anything else, terrifies me.

Friday, March 20, 1964
Comunicado do Gabinete dos Sábios

A week ago our festive semi-annual unity rites commenced. As a sign of transcendent benevolence, Sage no. 3 agreed to be brought to our sacred public wells in order to oversee the body-and-soul unification ceremony firsthand. The first part of the ceremony was performed by 365 heroic secretaries. The unification drinking rite continued until late afternoon. Masses of chanting islanders came to greet Sage no. 3 and asked him to convey their best wishes to Sages no. 4, no. 2, and no. 1. Our dear Sage no. 3 of course agreed to their humble request.

March 30, 1964
Diary entry by Adélaïde Fourangier

The eastern part of the island is under a terrible onslaught of poisonous flies. According to reports by parents, hundreds of people are dead. My music school is open only twice a week now, with very few children attending. I try to convince Illirio that playing the piano and composing is far more important to the development of his soul than preparing for a futile journey to Hainan. How utterly useless.

Yet both Illirio and Nissa love music and make wonderful progress. They practice Schubert's four-hand piano pieces together for hours, particularly now since the school is empty of pupils. Illirio has also composed several two-voiced chants with piano accompaniment; he both plays and sings with true mastery. He sounds like a one-man baroque orchestra. Amazing!

Friday, April 14, 1964
RADIOGRAMME
À Madame Adélaïde Fourangier, Asie du Sud-Est

Dr. Lothair Döpps, the eminent pedagogue, will visit your school to evaluate the progress of your students on June 22–25, 1964. Please prepare your students and arrange for Dr. Döpps's accommodation that at least meets the standard set by his previous visit.

Thursday, April 30, 1964
Diary entry by Adélaïde Fourangier

Yesterday Costas visited me after classes ended. It was his second visit today after our pre-dawn rendezvous. He feels how concerned I am about Döpps's forthcoming inquisition. No, my hands do not tremble. But he could sense that I was distracted and worried during that short hour before sunrise that should be ours alone.

So he arrived for "a working visit" during my last pupil's lesson while both Illirio and Nissa were still here. We started talking in their presence. It was a difficult, rambling conversation.

"This time, if Döpps finds fault with my work, the institute will certainly fire me," I said dryly, "and in that case, my presence here on the island will become illegitimate. We will have to part, my dear prince."

"Why?" asked Costas in astonishment.

"Because your august Sages have accepted me here only insofar as I am the official representative of the damned IHEMdP," I answered curtly.

Costas lowered his head and asked in a soft voice, "Don't you see how valuable your work here is?"

"Valuable!" I flared up. "Haven't I lived on this island long enough to know what's valuable and what's not?" I paused, then continued in a more controlled tone. "Everything is valuable— or rather, tolerable—if your exalted Sages accept it, and their devoted, spineless disciples—like you, my dear—implement it."

Placing my right hand on his shoulder with feigned sympathy, I felt a slight tremor in his muscles. Had I gone too far? Years of suppressed anger had suddenly burst out of me. But I saw nevertheless that I really had hurt him.

"We cannot even live together like a normal couple," I continued more softly, "exchanging views at the breakfast table while eating slices of damned dry bread or local cucumbers, or even wash ourselves together in the bathroom. For years now our relations have been deprived of any normalcy."

"If you only knew how I dream of such a future," Costas said entreatingly.

"My dear, there will be no such future," I retorted without conceding an inch.

He sat with his head buried in his palms.

"You must accept that I will have to leave if Döpps delivers a report to Paris that disqualifies me."

Looking deeply and respectfully at me, it seemed that Costas finally realized that our future together was in the hands of a complete idiot. Wisely he did not to ask, "What will you do in Paris, perform Hummel and Kalkbrenner in front of admiring crowds? Or play concertos by Moscheles and Field with the Boston Philharmonic?" because if he had, that would have severely bruised our relationship. We both knew that if I returned to France at that moment, I would perhaps only be able to get a job as an accompanist for some amateur chorus in the villages of northern France where they still chant baroque hymns.

Costas was considerate. Rather than asking provocative questions, he only lifted his eyebrows as though searching for an idea. "Don't you have any thoughts as to how to proceed with Döpps?"

"No, do you?"

"I think you should become familiar with his approach to piano pedagogy," he proffered, "not to emulate it—no, no, by no means—I see how magnificent you are as a teacher—but in order to have a conversation with him on his own terms. What do you think?"

(Costas always ends his sentences with "my love," but for the sake of brevity I will omit them all here.)

"Just how should I familiarize myself with his teaching methods?" I probed.

"As we both know, he earned a doctorate in piano pedagogy during the time you were giving concerts with that Armenian pianist Sirouné Avakian, don't you remember?"

"Yes, of course I remember. How foolish I was to end my collaboration with her."

"Well, you came here instead," he reminded me coyly. "So our task should be to find some knowledge of what Döpps wrote in his dissertation; after all, he was promoted to be IHEMdP's international piano pedagogy supervisor on the strength of his research."

"I am not interested in reading his thoughts," I said in disgust. "That man with his outrageous behavior. His very presence revolts me."

"Maybe so, but at this stage we cannot ask for someone else to come in his stead; besides, we're not even sure that they have anyone else."

"So what you propose?" I asked.

"Let's send a telegram to IHEMdP asking that a copy of Döpps' dissertation be sent to the island."

"I object," I said emphatically. "To ask for such a thing right before his visit would be morally corrupt sycophancy."

"Would it be 'morally corrupt' to ask Döpps himself to bring a copy of his work?" asked Costas.

"The very thought of immersing myself in his writing makes me sick," I replied.

"All right then," said Costas, "let's ask that the abstract of his dissertation be sent by radiogramme, as a prelude to his forthcoming visit. Then you can decide later on what the next steps might be."

"If you wish to send them such a request, you are free to do so," I said with resignation.

"Shall I sign the request in your name?" asked Costas with a twinkle.

"OK, sign my name," I sighed. This man had won me over again. In spite of my harsh criticism, I do admire Costas's work and his ingenuity. I know I should give him as much moral support as I can. So no more talk about my leaving just yet. Victory in hand, Costas left my house and turned toward Jean-Luc's in order to send the telegram.

Thursday, May 7, 1964
RADIOGRAMME
À Madame Adélaïde Fourangier, Asie du Sud-Est

We passed your query on to Professor Döpps himself. His response was: sending his doctorate or a summary of it ahead of his professional visit to your school or bringing it in person would inevitably distort his objectivity in judging your school's achievement. He suggests sending you a summary of the dissertation by telegram two months after his upcoming visit to your school. He asks for your acceptance of the abovementioned proposition.

Saturday, May 9, 1964
Diary entry by Adélaïde Fourangier

I was right! Nevertheless, I went to Jean-Luc's house and asked him to send a confirmation of my wish to receive Döpps's summary toward the end of summer. Damn that summary.

Friday, July 10, 1964
Cassettes recorded by Jean-Luc Lefevbre

I just had a delicious lunch with Costas and Adèle. But instead of enjoying the tasty meal prepared with vegetables from our local fields—a joy to comprehend no less than to savor!—we devoted ourselves to a discussion of the abhorrent M. Döpps and his effect on our music school and on dear Adèle herself.

Adèle maintains that this man despises everything she does. She is afraid that his biased report will create a negative impression in Paris. She particularly worries about the fate of four or five pupils whom she would like to send to France for further professional study. She says that their future is totally dependent upon Döpps's good recommendation and that he completely ignores their achievements, not to mention the fact that he is absolutely indifferent toward Illirio's amazing double-voiced chanting, insisting that Adèle not bother him again with vocal performances. Costas is beginning to worry about Adèle's mental state.

Tuesday, September 22, 1964
RADIOGRAMME
À Madame Adélaïde Fourangier, Asie du Sud-Est

In light of the negative assessment of your work by Dr. Lothair Döpps, our institution is weighing suspension of your employment with us.

Ilbert D., *Directeur adjoint,* IHEMdP

Thursday, September 24, 1964
RADIOGRAMME
À Madame Adélaïde Fourangier, Asie du Sud-Est

As promised, receive herewith a copy of "General Principles of Good Adolescent Piano Instruction: A summary of the dissertation of Professor Lothair Döpps."

General overarching principle: Aesthetics of expression is a function of social status. The higher the social rank of the pianist, the freer the range of expressive tools—dynamics, tone color, and tempo—may be. Immoderately expressive performance by an adolescent is not only an act of immodesty, in most cases it is one of insincerity. Such playing shows disrespect toward adult professional supervisors. In light of the above, a child or an adolescent should play only within a moderate dynamic range, never surpassing the forté level, and never softening the performance below the level of simple piano (in order not to compel superiors to make special efforts to listen to them). There should be minimal rhythmic freedom; adolescents should not perform pieces with dramatic recitatives (for example, Beethoven's 17th Piano Sonata, Op. 31, No. 2, known as The Tempest). Although passages should be played with strong fingers, their force should be tempered and maximally equaled by the restraining force of the wrist muscles.

During a performance, children and adolescents should sit very still, with an upright back, never swaying or bending toward the keyboard.

As piano music education is aimed at cultivating a concert career only for the crème de la crème, the atmosphere of the studies should be highly competitive. All students should play the same pieces and their performances should be frequently judged by their superiors, who openly inform weaker students of their meager—or nonexistent—ability to reach the concert stage and public acclaim.

The secretariat of IHEMdP asks Madame Adélaïde Fourangier to confirm the transmission of this message as soon as possible.

Friday, September 25, 1964
Diary entry by Adélaïde Fourangier

Oh yes, I confirmed that I received their message. What a rotten salad! Are they sane at IHEMdP? Thank god I am no longer there! Yes, it's true that I felt this feeling of liberation from them right from the beginning of my life on this island. And now they hunt me down here! What an ugly comedy!

Wednesday, October 14 1964
Copy of **RADIOGRAMME**
À M. Léon Pignon, ancien haut commissaire,
Ministère des affaires étrangères, Paris

Sir,

I hope you remember me. I was one of your technical assistants in Vietnam while you served there in during 1947–1948. I used to repair your car and you liked to debate me on the subject of the welfare of Vietnamese people. At the time you expressed both benevolent attention toward my small native island, Pinto, which is a remote part of the Paracel Islands, as well as solicitous concern about the fate of its people. You may recall that you wished that one day I would lead the people of my island to a better, more enlightened future.

I am trying with all my heart to fulfill your wish. We have created a system of sustainable agriculture on the island and a medical system that includes a hospital with several good physicians, including surgeons and anesthesiologists, all alumni of the excellent Saigon Academic Medical School. We have also established an excellent music school under the supervision of the talented French pianist Adélaïde Fourangier, a former student of Alfred Cortot and an alumna of the Institut des hautes études musicales de Paris.

The institute supports our music school by paying a monthly stipend to Mme Fourangier and regularly sends its inspector, Dr.

Lothair Döpps, to assess our school's achievement. We residents of Pinto Island treasure the work of Mme Fourangier and would like to receive additional opinions on her contribution to our cultural life here. I fully understand that any effort on our part to ask for a change in policy at IHEMdP would be understood by the institute as unprofessional and undignified. We do, however, wish that someone in addition to the inspector could get a firsthand impression of our children's abilities. We think that if the present inspector, Dr. Döpps, could bring video equipment with him, that would enable presentation of authentic material for evaluation by a larger circle of music pedagogues that would be most beneficial.

I would be deeply obliged to you, sir, if you could help facilitate this.

Votre affectionné,

Constantius Tegularius

Sunday, December 6, 1964
Diary entry by Adélaïde Fourangier

I am so angry at myself for allowing Costas to send that bootlicking letter to the former governor of Vietnam. I do not believe in personal begging.

And I am right—almost two months have passed since the dispatch of his ridiculous letter (I am not even sure it ever reached Léon Pignon), and there's been no reaction from there at all. Next time Döpps comes, he will finish me, I'm sure. I have to rethink my future now.

Wednesday, March 3, 1965
RADIOGRAMME
À Madame Adélaïde Fourangier, Asie du Sud-Est

Our inspector, Dr. Lothair Döpps, will arrive for his next visit with a video camera. The expected date of his arrival is June 1966. Monthly payments to your account in Saigon will continue for the time being.

Ilbert D., *Directeur adjoint*, IHEMdP

Wednesday, January 19, 1966
RADIOGRAMME
À Madame Adélaïde Fourangier, Asie du Sud-Est

Due to his ill health, M. Ilbert Dufour has resigned. Our new vice director in charge of external communications is Dr. Marius Villeneuve. Dr. Lothair Döpps's visit to Pinto Island has been postponed until 1967. Your monthly payments will be continued.

Tuesday, August 9, 1966
RADIOGRAMME from Marius Villeneuve
À Madame Adélaïde Fourangier, Asie du Sud-Est

Professor Ilbert Dufour has passed away at age 78.

Tuesday, July 12, 1967
Diary entry by Adélaïde Fourangier

The third Döpps visit clearly bore a farcical nature. He came with two cameras and two tripods. He asked me to postpone student examinations for a day in order to place the tripods in their proper position; he requested two powerful spotlights to illuminate the piano room. We have no such equipment on the island and the only possible alternative was the special illumination in the surgical theater at Costas's hospital, which he emphatically refused to part with. Döpps in a fury demanded that we call IHEMdP to report the setback. Upon being told that we had no telephone communication with the outside world, he demanded that an urgent telegram be sent. When Jean-Luc patiently explained to him that it would take at least a week for the earliest possible reply, Döpps's imperious mood strangely changed. He started talking to me in the friendliest manner. But nevertheless, his usual fixation on detail continued; he asked that some children pose in front of the cameras and then return home. He incessantly moved the tripods and looked into the camera lenses, becoming very sweaty and tired. He worked until evening and then came to Jean-Luc's for dinner. He twice interrupted the meal to run back to check the positions of the tripods (each time Jean-Luc waited forty-five minutes for Döpps to return).

The next day he filmed my ten good students, incessantly changing the position of the cameras and asking the children to begin their pieces anew. In the evening he refused either to film or listen to our choruses or Illirio's two-voiced singing, claiming that he had no mandate to do so.

On his last day, he announced that there definitely were two advanced pupils in my school (neither Nissa nor Illirio, should I thank my lucky stars for that?), but as he was mandated to take three pupils to France, he said that the next time he visited he would arrange a competition for the third spot.

Tuesday, September 19, 1967
RADIOGRAMME from Marius Villeneuve
À Madame Adélaïde Fourangier, Asie du Sud-Est

Our three senior colleagues have reviewed the videos taken by
Dr. Döpps and their impression is that your level of teaching
and your pedagogical approach meet IHEMdP standards. Your
monthly payments will therefore be assured for the next two
years.

Friday, January 17, 1970
Diary entry by Adélaïde Fourangier

For a long time I have repressed my fears concerning Illirio's
fate, but now I can't help being terribly anxious. Illirio is going
to Hainan. He is not even fourteen, but he is tall and strong
and nobody believes that he is still thirteen. For the last two
weeks I have tried to persuade Nissa to discourage him from
participating in this preposterous adventure, but she adamantly
takes his side. But yesterday as she was caressing him, I overheard
her whisper, "You will return, right?" He emphatically told her
yes as if there could be no doubt. Oh, what horror!

Wednesday, January 21, 1970
Diary entry by Adélaïde Fourangier

I cannot sleep, I cannot eat, I cannot think, I cannot breathe
normally. I tremble all the time. I sit near the children at the
piano and do not say very much. In my distraction, I allow the
unmotivated students to sit and do nothing, while others just
look out the window. One girl brought a book to read (I noticed

it was in French, but I could care less). Please, god, have mercy upon my son—please do not let him die, I beg of you.

I have no fortitude....

Saturday, January 24, 1970
Diary entry by Adélaïde Fourangier

He is back, alive. Out of forty-one boys, only eleven returned. It is unbearable. When I first saw Illirio, I tried speaking to him, but his smile is now an artificially proud grimace. He refuses to talk, but I can see the dark horror in his eyes. I left the beach where the crowd was enthusiastically greeting the boats. I will attempt to sleep. What new nightmare will befall me?

Sunday, January 25, 1970
Diary entry by Adélaïde Fourangier

I had a strained talk with Costas. I told him these sailings are madness and that they must be stopped at any cost. He replied that the atmosphere on the island is so permeated with national heroic mythology that no one, least of all him, is capable of dissuading the youth from undertaking these dangerous trips. His only idea for a solution was to send an even greater number of teenagers to Saigon each year. However, as the war in Vietnam becomes more intense, all remaining French personnel, especially teachers, are leaving the country. So there is even less of an intermediate remedy for this madness.

I told him that someone should stop these teenagers the moment they leave the coast. He said, "You say 'someone,' but I am the only one here listening to you. Do you wish me to stop them?"

Not having a ready answer, I turned my back on him—angrily.

Tuesday, January 27, 1970
Diary entry by Adélaïde Fourangier

Yesterday after class Costas came to me again. Our previous talk had visibly moved him. He entered the piano room when the last student had left and immediately started with, "I fully agree with you that these sailings to Hainan should be stopped. But can they realistically be stopped now? Just imagine, if I come with some fifty of my associates from the hospital and from the orphanages, and perhaps from among our strong pearl catchers, and if we succeed in blocking the departure of forty-five strong youngsters—suppose we even prevent them for reaching the beach—what next? The next day they would surely come again, and so we would have to come again too. And then another day, and so on. Should we completely stop our work at the hospital, our teaching (where the slow process of enlightenment through education actually does take place), our electricity production, and water purification? Should we stop catching pearls and be unable to exchange them for medicine and vital goods?"

"So now you have only several dozen people to rely on?" I asked. "I thought you said that the majority of the population sympathizes with you."

Costas sighed in evident exasperation.

"It is more complicated, my love," he said. "I think that roughly half the population really wishes us to be a modern society, insofar as they understand modernity:—to keep life like in Saigon, they say. But they are terribly afraid. The emotional attachment to the Sages is still so strong that if they abandon their teachings altogether, they feel that Pinto will become culturally and morally bankrupt. They all know that the first

Sages saved the islanders from all-out, total war, and they are afraid that forsaking the Sages' teachings will result in such a loss of moral compass that civil war will once again break out."

"And you, Constantius Tegularius, you personally, what do you think?" I asked, enraged.

"I think—" Costas started to answer.

"Ah, you think," I interrupted. "You just manipulate me. You do not have a personal stake in the issue like I do. You are one with the spineless idiots who hide behind the supposed loss of your 'moral compass' so that you don't have to see the iniquity of the Sages for what it is: child sacrifice," I shouted at full volume.

"Believe me, I hate the current situation just as much as you do."

Suddenly I felt that I could force Costas to give up his ingrained devotion to the Sages.

"So? Are you ready to abandon your reverence for the Sages for our love?" I asked with all possible firmness.

"I just hope that soon we will have the opportunity to live normally," said Costas.

"Oh please, your words are so empty," I shouted, enraged. I can't remember a time when I was so livid.

"My love, you ask me both to live with you normally and to stop the trips to Hainan," began Costas. "These are two very different things. Living with you in the open under our present circumstances will bring certain death for us both, just as it did for the tragic lovers in Verdi's *Aida*. Don't laugh at me, this situation is very similar. The naked secretaries would drag us all over the whole island until we reach the Sages' compound and there they would beat us and throw us into a pit of fresh excrement. We would be smothered there. Perhaps sixty people at most would dare to defend us. And they would be killed immediately. In that case, our hospital would remain without personnel. People would once again start dying of curable diseases. So we would be foolish to do so.

"You may not believe me, but day and night I think about how we can save our youth from death on Hainan. But again—at this stage only a few parents of the departing youngsters would join me in physically blocking the trips. However, in the traditionalist camp, hundreds, perhaps thousands, of secretaries would beat these parents to death. Please remember that our side has no weapons. We cannot overpower all the secretaries with our little reserves of pepper spray."

"So it's hopeless," I said.

"No, not completely. During the epidemics many people panic and are ready to oppose the Sages."

"So your task is not to combat the epidemics, but to make sure that they occur so that they can be used to incite the weakminded?" I said in another angry outburst.

"My sacred task is to eliminate the epidemics; but sometimes they are so strong—especially when there is no rain—that we do not have the resources to do so. We have already been in such situations and I have come to understand that in such moments it is my duty to act not only as a doctor, but also as a public figure."

"So, answer my question. Do you respect the Sages?" I said pointedly.

"No, I think they are disgusting criminals," Costas replied without hesitation.

"How many people can say this as openly as you do?" I asked.

"Around two thousand at least."

"You just said that only sixty would accompany you to stop the youngsters sailing to Hainan. So where are those other two thousand?" I asked.

"There is still a difference between saying things—and at other times not saying them—and actually giving yourself over to physical combat and possible death," said Costas. "Sixty people are ready to fight and die, while the other two thousand are warm sympathizers."

"How many people do you need to overthrow the Sages?" I asked.

"A clear majority, around forty thousand," Costas answered.

"What is their attitude toward the Sages at present?" I asked.

"First, about a third of our population are diehard followers of the Sages, whatever the circumstances. Then there is the less devoted, silent majority who maintain that while the Sages are remnants of a glorious tradition that should be preserved, restrictions on their power that enable public hygiene and personal development definitely need to be instituted," Costas responded, happy that he could fend me off for a little while.

"So you are waiting for some catastrophe to prevail, in order to convince the fence-sitting majority to depose the Sages?" I asked.

"As a physician, I am obliged to prevent a catastrophe," answered Costas in total seriousness.

"I see," I said, "you're committed to combat the epidemics and in so doing sustain the Sages' power, but you know that your medical and organizational powers are frequently too meager to overcome them, so in those cases you have the duty to persuade your countrymen to end the current regime."

"Exactly," said Costas grimly.

"If you would not combat the epidemics so wholeheartedly, you would cause the majority to help you overthrow the Sages much sooner," I observed. "In the final reckoning, you would save more lives that way than by helping the Sages keep ruling."

Costas looked at me as though I were some demonically inspired Machiavelli. "Please do not play games with my conscience, my love," he said almost in a whisper.

I realized I was hurting him. But by now I had lived on the island for almost ten years and my responsibility toward the innocent children who came to study with me was no less than his to his Parents' Association. So I asked one last question, now in the same grim tone that characterized Costas's last words: "Do you see any positive future arising from all your efforts?"

This time I tried to caress his forearm. He stepped back, as though rejecting my attempt at reconciliation, and said, "I do not know. I know only that if I do not try, we will all die."

"Go and get some rest," I proffered. "I won't bother you more," I said.

He went back to his cubicle at the hospital, not stopping at Jean-Luc's.

Thursday, April 2, 1970
RADIOGRAMME from Marius Villeneuve
À Madame Adélaïde Fourangier, Asie du Sud-Est

Professor Döpps will arrive in early June 1970 in order to audition your students on June 6–7. Please prepare your pupils and arrange decent accommodations for Professor Döpps.

Sunday, July 5, 1970
Cassettes recorded by Jean-Luc Lefevbre

If I had never known France on my own and had only met this Döpps, I would have to conclude that France is a madhouse. On second thought, listening to the shortwave radio broadcasts, I often feel that France is indeed a madhouse—those attempts on de Gaulle's life, those absurd student demonstrations, and lately this odious "Markovic affair" involving the president's wife....

Anyhow, Döpps has organized a competition to choose the third child to be taken to France to further his or her studies. He announced that he himself would accompany the three kids to France on Etienne's plane immediately after his visit. Of course, the news created pandemonium on the island with all the parents of Adèle's pupils coming to the school with packed bags of children's clothing and pearls to prepare their offspring for immediate departure to the other side of the world.

Döpps auditioned twelve children and after reflecting for half an hour in solitude (pacing around the garden behind Adèle's house, one hand supporting his chin, the other held behind his back), he approached Adèle and whispered the name of the chosen student in her ear. She immediately invited the parents of that girl to her room and then asked all the other parents and children to disperse and to keep sending their children for music lessons.

But the parents did not disperse. All the parents were enraged, as all parents wanted to send their own child to France to safeguard him or her from the dangers of life here. Some parents approached Döpps with raised fists; a threat of violence hung in the air. Adèle shielded Döpps from the angry parents with her own body (Costas happened to be performing an urgent operation in the hospital at the time so he couldn't rush over as he always does).

Döpps—pale but calm—slowly moved toward the plane accompanied by the three young teenagers. He asked that the parents not accompany them to the runway. They acquiesced in piety. Absurd. The whole situation is absurd.

Monday, September 7, 1970
RADIOGRAMME from Marius Villeneuve
À Madame Adélaïde Fourangier, Asie du Sud-Est

After serious discussion, our collegial council recommended sending the two boys from your Pinto Island school to the Cambrai School of Music with full accommodation. After being tested, they will be enrolled in the local high school as well.

In view of the expanding war in South Vietnam, we strongly recommend that you transfer your bank assets from Saigon back to Paris.

P.S. Professor Döpps left the girl who was selected for the third spot to further her education at the National Music School of Saigon. As per Professor Döpps, she will study there until achieving the necessary competence required to be taken to France.

Sunday, September 27, 1970
Diary entry by Adélaïde Fourangier

The three of us—Costas, Jean-Luc, and I—have been in Saigon
for three days.

How the city has changed—American soldiers walk around
everywhere, the cafés are full of them! The faces of the locals
are sad and full of stress. At the same time, there is no evidence
of decay in the condition of the buildings in central Saigon.
Rue Catinat with its Hôtel Majestic and the Palace Hôtel (where
I used to stay in the late forties) looked even better than in my
time; Bach Dang Harbor, however, is very dirty, but then that
was also the case twenty-two years ago. We also got a glimpse of
the new US embassy, a gleaming white fortress situated behind
a high fence. Upon reaching the Opera House I was amazed to
see how neglected and decayed it was—a dingy shadow of its past
grandeur. Although it now serves as the parliament building, it
looks more like a large whorehouse in a shadowy suburb. How
it pained me! Can this building ever be an important venue for
concerts of classical music in the future?

I went about closing my local bank account in Saigon and
transferring my money back to Paris (the bank teller wept as
he carried out my request). I bought some music scores, books
for myself (Merleau-Ponty, Albert Camus, and *Mon mal vient de
plus loin*, the French translation of Flannery O'Connor's latest
collection of short stories, *Everything That Rises Must Converge*),
and some Stendhal and Hugo for Nissa and Illirio. Costas
exchanged pearls for several small radio receivers and other
radio equipment (in light of the deteriorating situation in
Vietnam, he is eager for every islander who wants to to be able
to listen to shortwave international radio programs). He also
bought some medicine and medical tools.

I found the girl that Döpps had left behind in Saigon sitting in the corner of the cafeteria in the National Music School. She was frightened and starving. She told me that she waits in the cafeteria until the other students finish their meals and then she surreptitiously collects the crumbs from the their plates hastily thrown into the garbage receptacles. I took her back to the island. On the way back, Jean-Luc stopped the boat and fished. We had a nice, relaxing two days on board.

Wednesday, November 25, 1970
Diary entry by Adélaïde Fourangier

Illirio and Nissa are now fourteen years old. Illirio is tall, strong, and still growing. Nissa is tall too, and she is developing into a beautiful woman. Both of them assist me in teaching the little kids. Both have a special proclivity for helping weaker pupils progress. Illirio is now working on Beethoven's Piano Sonatas, Op. 22 and Op. 31, No. 3, both difficult. He has developed a noble and virile playing style. Nissa plays extraordinarily well too; she is now working on several Liszt studies—the *Il Lamento* and the *La Leggierezza,* and Ravel's *Une barque sur l'océan.* They both should become concert pianists. Illirio has completely mastered the double-voiced singing technique that he created and now successfully teaches it to other children. He also composes a lot of choral music for us. He has learned to repair radio equipment from Jean-Luc, so one day he may build a system that will allow all of the islanders to communicate with the outside world.

Thursday, February 5, 1971
Comunicado do Gabinete dos Sábios

With deep grief we announce the passing of our beloved Sage no. 2. The entire world is shattered by this tragedy. After the solemn body consecration ceremony that will be performed in the Sages' compound, the entire populace of our sacred island is invited to express its grief with even greater zeal for the performance of our solemn unification rites. This time islanders will unite their bodies and souls not only with the spirit of our ancestors, but also with the sacred body of our beloved Sage no. 2. The rites will start the day after tomorrow at noon at our public wells and will continue until the elevation of a new Sage.

Friday, February 6, 1971
Posto dos Nossos Pais

With great sorrow we announce the passing of Sage no. 2. We advise our compatriots to take all precautionary measures during the funeral ceremonies to avoid mass infection, which may cause immeasurable suffering and death.

Saturday, February 27, 1971
Diary entry by Adélaïde Fourangier

Costas visited me yesterday at dawn and this is what he relayed about the funeral services for Sage no. 2. Masses of people began assembling at the wells at first light in anticipation of some breakthrough announcement, which finally happened around five o'clock in the afternoon. A huge procession of secretaries dressed in gray left the Sages' compound carrying a large palanquin inside of which was the throne where the new Sage no. 4 was seated (the former Sage no. 3 was promoted to the second position, while the former Sage no. 4 now became third). The air was full of drum-like humming. The palanquin was slowly brought to the Well no. 1 and raised far above it. As secretaries dressed in gray constructed a huge tripod with their bodies, a hole opened in the palanquin's underside and some feces gloriously fell into the center of the pool. A joyous chant arose from the crowd and 250 naked secretaries bowed around the walls of the wells and repeated the action of the new leader. As Sage no. 4 was returned to the Sages' compound, about half of the secretaries dressed in gray returned there with him while the others started pushing the crowd toward the well, forcing them to drink. Several parents from our movement tried to prevent this while others, dressed in protective overalls, jumped into the water dragging huge nets and attempted to collect the excrement. Most of them were killed by the secretaries' bludgeons. This scene continued for two full days with more and more death caused by people stampeding toward the wells.

The severe rain that started at the end of the ceremony drove away the flies that had already started to swarm. Medics from the parents' group buried the dead immediately so epidemics did not break out. In total, a hundred and twelve people died in the process of remediating the wells.

Sunday, March 28, 1971
Diary entry by Adélaïde Fourangier

Illirio is going to Hainan again—I am horrified. An icy chill envelopes me. I try speaking to him, but he always dismisses me with his detached glance. How formidable this look is. I cannot bear any of this.

Wednesday, April 7, 1971
Diary entry by Adélaïde Fourangier

Please, god, please. Please, *Deus, miserere filii.*

Friday, April 9, 1971
Diary entry by Adélaïde Fourangier

Illirio returned, thank god. I saw the boat approaching the coast with seven surviving teenagers—five uninjured, and the remaining two severely wounded. Four teenagers happily waved their arms; Illirio was bending over his wounded comrades. As I approached, he did not make eye contact with me. Nissa went and kissed him and he returned her caress. Then he helped carry the stretchers with the wounded boys. From there he went to the cemetery—by himself; both Nissa and I waited outside— to bury the bodies of his dead friends. When I approached him afterward, trying to give him a kiss, he said he had more work to do and asked me to leave.

Costas came by this evening and told me that in a few days he was going to visit the American warship that was cruising nearby. He said he had to get more medicine and the American ship was the most reliable supplier. He said he would explain it all to me later and left for the southeast coast. I am too tired now for a new wave of worry. My hands have just stopped shaking.

Thursday, April 29, 1971
Diary entry by Adélaïde Fourangier

Costas was here and told me about his visit to the American cruiser called the United States of America Military Transport Ship *President Harding* or as it is referred to here, the USAT *President Harding*. Costas says the ship patrols the waters east of Pinto Island, twenty-five kilometers from the coastline. Costas exchanged a large amount of pearls for several cases of medicine and equipment that were subsequently delivered by our fishermen who sailed out to the ship. (I am not sure, but as far as I understand it, Costas actually *swam* to that *Harding* ship with a bag full of pearls tied around his waist. And he then swam back all alone, telling his people afterward which goods to load onto their fishing boats.)

Sunday, March 12, 1972
Diary entry by Adélaïde Fourangier

Horrible. I thought that Illirio had already fulfilled his norm of madness by sailing to Hainan twice. That turns out to be false. He is going off to that damned place again. I think he is haunted by a death wish. Though I see him almost every afternoon at my school, I cannot utter a word to him. My whole body shakes and my mind is paralyzed. I saw Nissa secretly crying. This young man will kill us both.

Sunday, March 26, 1972
Diary entry by Adélaïde Fourangier

Illirio has returned. His facial expression transmits dark inner resolve. His comrades look upon him with hostility. It appears that he saved six youths against their own wish to die on Hainan's shores. The faces of these six express unbearable shame. All in all, eleven teenagers returned home with twenty-nine bodies of their dead comrades. Another nine drowned at sea.

Sunday, May 7, 1972
Cassettes recorded by Jean-Luc Lefevbre

After laboring in my radio studio, I sometimes walk around in the garden at Adèle's house. I like listening to her practicing Fauré, Moscheles, and Hummel. Occasionally she plays Beethoven and twice I overheard strains of Debussy and Ravel. For some reason she belittles her own true ability with Fauré; I myself am a great Fauré aficionado and I can truly say that she plays him magnificently. I want to ask her to play more of this great master's work. What a gift the art of piano music is….

Tuesday, May 9, 1972
Diary entry by Adélaïde Fourangier

I must regain my concert playing form. Such a long time has passed since I last performed that now I have difficulty keeping the minute details of scores in my head. I must somehow regain my old abilities. I have to retrain myself to bring my attention to flow along the musical score properly.

Monday, June 19, 1972
Diary entry by Adélaïde Fourangier

Again we had an excellent end-of-year concert, which was attended by Costas, Jean-Luc, some parents, all my students, and their friends. Having studied piano with me for nine years now, there are students who are capable of playing very advanced material. (Ah, Jean-Luc brought another Gaveau upright to the island. Now the hospital backrooms sound like a real music school, with cacophonous, intertwining melodies from the three simultaneously played pianos pouring out of its windows. The poor hospital workers…it must drive them crazy, but sometimes they might overhear a decent Chopin, and hopefully that could be uplifting.) My plan is to send some of the most advanced students to France, bypassing our dear Professeur Döpps, though the war in Vietnam casts a bleak shadow on their chances. But perhaps once peace arrives…. I am talking about

Nissa, Illirio, and three others. Though none of them dreams of going overseas—they see themselves as devoting their lives to the betterment of the people on the island here and now—what noble youth!

Anyway, at today's concert Nissa marvelously performed Chopin's *Third Ballade,* the brilliant Charles-Marie Widor's *Toccata,* and Beethoven's *Sonata* Op. 90 in E minor. Illirio, exhibiting his nearly symphonic sound played Beethoven's Op. 10, No. 3 in D major. Our younger students performed Haydn and Rameau, some of their own original compositions, as well as pieces composed by Illirio. Illirio now also has a four-kid chorus, each child singing in two voices. The effect is at once stunning and upliftingly friendly. Thank god no naked secretaries came by to interrupt us.

Saturday, July 22, 1972
Diary entry by Adélaïde Fourangier

I just tried out my solo program for Costas. I returned to some of my old pieces, adding Fauré's *Third Impromptu in A-flat major* and the short *Fifth Impromptu in F-sharp minor* (strangely named since the real tonality of F-sharp minor appears only in passing; the piece is actually atonal). I also played his darker *Ninth Barcarolle,* Op. 101. I made many mistakes and stumbled much more frequently than I would have wished. But at least my mind worked without stress, and that is important. Still I must improve. Costas is a good partner to grow with since he understands music (definitely much better than many of my august colleagues in France) and he understands me. During the performance some secretaries appeared behind my house. Costas went out to shoo them away. As four of them refused to move, Costas doused them with narcotic spray and then dragged their limp bodies two hundred meters from the house. When he came back, I resumed the concert, although it was a pyrrhic victory because Costas was so exhausted from his effort of removing the annoying secretaries that he really couldn't concentrate on my playing.

Tuesday, August 15, 1972
Cassettes recorded by Jean-Luc Lefevbre

I was once again walking around Adèle's house in the morning listening to her practice. I just now begin to realize how hard her work must be; I noticed she repeated one passage from Mozart's *Variations on a theme by Gluck* at least thirty times, mostly slowly, but sometimes quickly, each time delicately changing the colors and accents in the left hand, and then, probably after reaching a satisfying variant, she started adjusting the triplet passages in the right hand in order to achieve the interplay between the sparkling accents that she wanted. Although this passage takes no more than fifteen seconds to play. she deliberated over it for at least three-quarters of an hour. Each change was delicate, but noticeable (I can't imagine how tiring—both physically as well as emotionally—this prolonged process of polishing a work must be). Finally I gave up listening to her painstaking travail and walked toward the Hill. When I returned she had apparently just finished polishing this excerpt. I was tired, but all of a sudden I heard the same passage pouring out from her windows. But now it had acquired a supernatural effervescence. How noble her work is; every melodic turn, every eloquently performed passage casts a cleansing spell in the air, as if the life around us were being freed of its ugliness, its stupidity, its madness.

I used to feel sad for Adèle, isolated on this tiny island in the middle of nowhere, unable to travel or perform for people who could really appreciate her talent and repay her stunning performances with encouraging applause. She doesn't even have the stimulation of peers with whom to engage in musical conversations. How does she manage? Strangely, she never expresses any bitterness. Perhaps she finds refuge in Hummel and Moscheles whose music exudes solidity and balance. Perhaps her predilection for these composers is itself an indicator of her state of mind; I wouldn't know. But I do know that it is in Fauré that her true talent shines.

As someone who lives alone, I spend many hours reading and listening to the radio. Thank god my radio equipment is sophisticated enough to receive shortwave broadcasts of classical music from all over the world. In my childhood and youth in my native Bénouville, I used to sing in the local chorus and attended all church concerts. The great Charles-Marie Widor once gave a concert in our village, and I, just nine years old, was overwhelmed by the power of his music. Since then wherever I could I visited concert halls and churches with good organs. And, of course, I developed a great love for orchestral music. So I am actually quite familiar with both Hummel and Moscheles, though not specifically with the pieces that Adèle plays. Also I heard quite a lot of Hummel in France. His *Trumpet Concerto*, always a favorite of military bands, was a tour de force for virtuosi trying to demonstrate their superb technique in making the trumpet sound even more brazen than I am sure Hummel himself would have wished. The trumpet in this concerto, though in good taste, can be extraordinarily (almost *too* extraordinarily) proud. Maybe Hummel's classicism has some qualities that resonate with Adèle, once again I do not know. I will have to ask her. Anyway, when I hear her playing

Hummel, I hear audacious pride tempered by civility. And I like that very much—it is so gratifying, so uplifting….

I am less familiar with Moscheles—I recently heard an astonishing performance of his supposedly well-known *Third Piano Concerto* by the Philharmonia Hungarica under the baton of Othmar Maga with the distinguished Michael Ponti as soloist. I detect in Moscheles rare combinations of ebullience and mellifluous melancholy. I think these traits are intimately familiar to Adèle too—her own renditions of Moscheles sound so sincere and engaging.

But Fauré has the rare mark of a genius. I think his own particular romantic melancholy, peppered with spicy harmonies, radiates some kind of profound wisdom. It is as though he is standing apart from the world, yet exposing himself to its vicissitudes. Fauré was definitely a lyric. The tender music he wrote rarely rising above a simple forte, never reaches the level of a fortissimo. Yet the spiciness of his harmonies and his typically prolonged dissonant sonorities—though still within the dimensions of nineteenth-century culture—suggest a departure from the period's open emotionalism. In other words, in his music he created his own, better world, where cleverness, understanding, and tenderness blend as in an expansive twilight. This at least is how I perceive his wonderful *Ballade for Piano and Orchestra*. How I wish Adèle could return to Paris and play it there—it would be an uplifting experience for her and even more so for her audiences. Here, far from the cultural vortex of Europe, she has developed an unusual ability to create the effect of space in her playing, allowing the difference in sound volume and color between the high and the low chords to create a feeling of vast expanse. Whenever I express my admiration for her playing, she demurs, trying to brush off my praise.

Lying in bed the other day, I thought what meaning could Fauré's tenderness have in this war-torn conflict zone? With such colossal bloodshed is there any place for his gentle, caressing tones? On the other hand, Fauré himself fought in the Franco-Prussian War. He knew suffering. Yet he did not allow his music to bear the scars of acute pain and wild screams. On the contrary—he brings solace to those in pain.

Tuesday, August 29, 1972
Diary entry by Adélaïde Fourangier

Yesterday I played a full recital: Moscheles, *Piano Sonata in D Major*, Op. 22 in three movements; Hummel, *Piano Sonata No. 8 in A-Flat Major* in three movements; Mozart's *10 Variations on a theme* by Gluck in G Major, and three pieces by Fauré (the Third and Fifth Impromptus and the *Ninth Barcarolle*). It went reasonably well. My small audience was composed of Costas, Jean-Luc, Illirio, Nissa, and all my current and former students. After prolonged negotiations, the Sages sent six high-ranking secretaries dressed in white whose presence fortunately caused the smelly, naked ones to stay away.

Monday, September 11, 1972
Comunicado do Gabinete dos Sábios

On August 28, a rite of foreign sound took place at the school of music. It was held in presence of our honorable white-clothed secretaries who report that these foreign sounds do not in any way compel our people to deviate from obeisance to the elevated spirit of our Founding Fathers. In fact, this foreign rite should be understood as a mind drill that may actually assist in the study of the teachings of our noble Sages.

Wednesday, November 15, 1972
Diary entry by Adélaïde Fourangier

Recently I observed Nissa's choral conducting with our students. She is a born conductor. Our ebullient Nissa, with her super abundant energy, has taught herself to conduct the chorus with consummate restraint, though her movements are clear and expressive. She also conducts Illirio's compositions for two-voiced singing. She produces a phenomenally uplifting effect. Listening to her conduct, I feel that I am being transported to the heavens.

Nissa tells me Illirio started building a house for them both. She says it will have a bathroom, electricity, and filtered drinking water. Well, they are sixteen years old now, almost adults. May god bless them.

Thursday, April 26, 1973
RADIOGRAMME from Marius Villeneuve
À Madame Adélaïde Fourangier, Asie du Sud-Est

For security reasons Professor Lothair Döpps will no longer visit the island. Your stipend will continue.

Tuesday, October 16, 1973
Diary entry by Adélaïde Fourangier

Jean-Luc now frequently informs parent groups about the events in Vietnam. He says that a truce has just been reached that stipulates full withdrawal of all American forces. It is becoming clear that South Vietnam, until now open to communication with the outside world, will become a closed territorial jail just like all the other communist countries. Without the presence of the American army, the North Vietnamese communists will soon overrun the South Vietnamese regime and turn the whole area into a closed society.

Distress spreads among many local parents—they now have no place to send their children to escape the island. Yesterday I asked Costas what prevents the Vietnamese communists from occupying Pinto Island. Costas explained that the Vietnamese communists fear the Chinese communists. I then asked him why the Chinese do not occupy us.

"They are afraid of our epidemics," he said with his sad smile. "No foreign force can occupy us."

"Well, strategically that is a colossal achievement," I wisecracked.

In no mood for my sarcasm, Costas snarled, "Do not anger me, my love," and then marched away.

Thursday, November 1, 1973
Diary entry by Adélaïde Fourangier

Together with Jean-Luc and Costas, I visited Illirio and Nissa in their new home on the western edge of the forest. Illirio has built a comfortable two-room abode with a good bed, several lamps, a nice toilet, and a nicely polished stone bathtub. Though only seventeen, these two are starting a new family nest. Still, they look completely mature and wise, with Nissa's bubbling humor adding special charm. Jean-Luc brought a bottle of his cherished pinot noir, and we drank from plastic cups that Costas pilfered from the hospital reserves. We sang many melodies in four-part harmony, including one from Beethoven's *Consecration of the House Overture*. Costas made me dance—after all these years, I was completely out of shape. At first I blushed in embarrassment.

Aren't I a serious professional? But then the music, the wine, and Costas's ardor overcame me, and coming more and more under the enchanted spell of the party, I twirled around the room with abandon. Have I failed as a role model? Perhaps I should have set a better example for Nissa, especially since she—when overexcited—starts jumping around and throwing plates laden with food high into the air? Surely there is no place for that in Paris, where I hope that both she and Illirio will go to pursue their careers. Next time I must duly reprimand both her and Costas. We stayed for a couple of hours and then Costas escorted me home, although he first made his ridiculous detour to Jean-Luc's. When did he say things would change? Oh yes, soon, soon, my love.

Sunday, November 4, 1973
Cassettes recorded by Jean-Luc Lefevbre

I attended the housewarming party that Nissa and Illirio threw at their new home. What a cute couple they are! Illirio is over 6'8" and extremely strong. Nissa is very tall, too—she is surely well over 6', I am sure. They fill the space with a wondrously joyful presence—as if sparkling vivacity were built into them.

Costas and Adèle were already there when I arrived. All of us sat around their little table joking. When I came, Adèle stood up and in full seriousness started to bless the new couple. She then awkwardly interrupted herself to bring in a very large bowl of freshly prepared salad made with homegrown tomatoes. Then she wanted to resume her blessings. As a lapsed Catholic, I could understand her motivation, but Nissa could not stop laughing and jumped over to the kitchen stove where a huge omelet was cooking. In a moment she started cutting pieces from the omelet still in the pan, placing them on plates, and throwing them onto the small wooden table where we were seated. Three plates landed exactly in front of our place settings, with omelet pieces, slices of dry bread, and salad intact. One plate flew a little bit sideways; Illirio promptly caught it and threw it back to Nissa, who threw it back once again, this time so it landed right in front of Costas.

Costas exclaimed, "To eggs!"

And we all loudly shouted, "To eggs!"

Illirio then sang an operatic hymn (in full voice), "*Puteus nunquam scire ubi ova*" (we shall never know where the eggs are from). Nissa joined Illirio and then took over the main melody, Illirio supplemented it with his double-voiced wizardry, and Costas added his own "*O-kho-kho-kho-kho*" refrain at various places as the music permitted. Adèle and I sat spellbound and motionless. The frivolity didn't stop there, for Nissa then started to dance around us, quickly raising both Costas and Illirio to their feet. Costas took Adèle's hand and started waltzing her around the room. Adèle was visibly confused and this caused Nissa to laugh even harder. "Mama confused, Mama confused!" she half laughed, half sang.

Then Nissa and Illirio sang their amazing vocal arrangement of Strauss' (fils) beautiful *Heimaths-Kinder Valse*. Costas now whirled Adèle around the floor with even more fervor as he finally allowed himself to express his passion for her publicly and she, infected by his enthusiasm, openly gave herself to her *prince charmant* (this is how she calls him in the presence of others). While they danced, Illirio—singing—threw the nearly emptied plates to Nissa—who kept singing too—and she caught them expertly as she stood in the kitchen. Not a plate was broken, not a remaining crumb fell to the floor.

Then Costas threw Adèle into the air and gallantly caught her, and went on throwing her up to the ceiling. He always caught her with utmost tenderness. Witnessing the emergence of Costas's long-suppressed love, I, old man that I am, rhetorically asked, "Who are the newlyweds today?"

"Costas and Mama," laughed Nissa and jumped outside to turn several high somersaults. The evening ended with our singing the opening bars from Beethoven's *Consecration of the House Overture*. Then we left the young couple to themselves.

Monday, December 24 1973
Diary entry by Adélaïde Fourangier

Epochal news: Nissa is pregnant! I need to prepare myself for becoming a grandmother. It's about time. I myself am approaching my fiftieth birthday.

Nissa tells me that Illirio works all night on a secret project, frequently returning home only after dawn. Keeping silent about his absences, he refuses to tell her where he goes. She worries that he is planning another trip to Hainan, although he most emphatically denies it, stating that he has put all that madness behind him. So Nissa knows no more about what's really going on than I do. Costas says that he too knows nothing.

Saturday, March 2, 1974
Diary entry by Adélaïde Fourangier

Costas visited the *President Harding* again and returned with more medication and newspapers from around the world. All of them were dated and not worth reading, especially since

Jean-Luc supplies us with fresh news. However, among the old newspaper clippings was one that attracted my attention—I attach it herewith:

An article from May 1972
THE PINTOVILLE POST
(a newspaper published for residents of Pintoville, Des Moines)

Last March the traditional sports regatta took place in the northern waters off Pinto Island. The best and strongest of our youth, ages fourteen to nineteen, took part in the festive sail. The "Hainan Regatta," as it is reverently called by the islanders, is a wonderful way for our youth to develop navigation skills and endurance. Participation in the regatta is their greatest dream.

The sail includes landing on the shores of the island of Hainan, the historic homeland of our Founding Fathers. As is well known, the Chinese communists now rule this territory and use every pretext to incite conflict with the regatta's young sailors. Sometimes Chinese naval forces fire on our innocent teenagers who are only expressing their devotion to our glorious tradition, and this uncalled for aggression causes their untimely demise in Hainan coastal waters.

Our representatives in Des Moines and America at large seek to draw the attention of the US president to these belligerent acts, asserting that they must be stopped, if necessary, by American military force.

In spite of this unpleasantness, we look forward to more regatta sailings and one day we hope to enjoy their complete success.

[remark below written in pencil in Fourangier's hand—S.J.]
Costas says that the American Pintoists are informed of events

occurring here by the Sages firsthand. They have direct radio communication via the satellite dish installed at the Sages' compound.

Friday, April 5, 1974
Cassettes recorded by Jean-Luc Lefevbre

Illirio has built an underwater rope structure to hold back the boats sailing to Hainan. He asked me to verify the strength of the system. So last night I accompanied him down to the marina and sailed out on one of the boats. At a distance of two kilometers from the shore when my boat should have been ensnared by a rope that was hooked to its keel, it did not stop—instead, it dragged the long rope farther out to sea.

When I returned to the marina, I advised Illirio that his plan might work if he were to install columns of concrete and steel below the seabed of the cove. He said he would try, but couldn't manage to install more than four such columns before the next sailing. I told him to do at least that and that later he could install more. He asked me to help him get construction material from Saigon.

Yes, I told him I would assist him, with deep pain in my heart, although glad that he felt close enough to me to make me his confidant. I know that neither Adèle nor Costas have any idea of what he is doing. He swore me to secrecy.

But the more I think over Illirio's project, the more a dark horror rises in me. I hardly remember the last time I had cold hands, and now not only are they ice cold, they tremble. Considering Illirio's plan as just an audacious prank, I reasoned that the only ones who could possibly hurt him if the plan succeeded would be those half-retarded, naked secretaries who rarely gather in any one place in large numbers. True, they do gather en masse at the marina to greet the returning fools, but if Illirio's contraption were able to stop the kids from sailing out in the first place (at least four out of the planned six boats), then the whole event might indeed be revealed as a farce, and then in all probability there might not be a festive mass gathering for the return of the remaining two boats (if in fact they were to return at all).

However, when I realized that Illirio's daring project would undoubtedly be perceived as an insurrection, not tens but thousands of naked secretaries would be sent to beat him and he would in all certainty be killed...how could I live with the thought of Illirio dying as a young man? Better I die myself, and as soon as possible. What do I care?

But perhaps I should do something more practical than dying? The power in Illirio's urge to stop the suicidal sailings of our youngsters is obvious. Of course he must know that a single operation will not suffice. But sure that a failure of the voyage at its very onset would be understood as all failures are understood here—as a well-deserved failure, a penalty for the wrongness of the original intention—he thinks it will reverberate throughout the island. In his mind, as the island mentality is one of heightened emotionalism, the impact of the operation will be very strong.

But my knowledge of this island's distorted mentality gives me the foreboding that the Sages will overreact—since no one has ever dared to stop the sailings either by force or even by direct criticism.

Should I stop Illirio by all means? In doing so, I will surely kill his *élan vital*—and this is tantamount to killing his soul.

I have several possible courses of action—to break my promise to Illirio and tell Costas about his plans; to bring my Pettersson to the marina and extricate Illirio if necessary by ferrying him to burning Saigon (where he will either die under bombardment or at the hands of the communists); to deliver him to the *Harding* where he could request asylum, although in all probability he will just swim back to the island; or just to wait for the outcome of this plan, and if Illirio dies, I will kill myself too.

Yes, the last option is my only choice. I'm old and have lived long enough. I know how to die quickly and certainly. I have the means.

Wednesday, May 1, 1974
Cassettes recorded by Jean-Luc Lefevbre

This was my last trip to Saigon. I felt such terrible anxiety in the streets. The noise of the departing American helicopters was deafening. This time I saw only a few American soldiers in the near-empty cafés. I did not run into any of my long-time friends—everyone had already left. I procured as many bags of cement and construction aggregate that I could load onto my Pettersson. Illirio will be able to mix the two together to form concrete. I also added a number of steel rods, large pieces of rubber, and extremely long ropes. I left the city immediately. Fortunately, I wasn't bombed.

This time I did not stop to fish. I brought my Pettersson directly to the marina and left it there for Illirio to unload. He worked all night and then brought my boat back to its usual harbor by the Hill.

May 10, 1974
Diary entry by Adélaïde Fourangier

Illirio no longer comes to work at the music school; Nissa says that she also sees him only infrequently, and when he comes home at dawn, he is taciturn and tired.

In spite of her advanced pregnancy, Nissa now replaces Illirio at the school. She looks so tired and unhappy.

Tuesday, July 2, 1974
Diary entry by Adélaïde Fourangier

On June 24, Nissa gave birth to a son, a healthy three-and-a-half-kilo baby. They named him Alfredo-Vasco, his first name in memory of my revered Cortot, the second in honor of the nation's progenitor. They call him Alfi.

Yesterday we held a family reception for the baby at my house. Many naked secretaries came and clung to my windows, leaving marks of ugly, stinking excrement. Costas immediately reached for his spray, but I quickly stopped him, fearing for the safety of the baby. Nissa's pupils who came by to congratulate her miraculously saved the day; they began singing their two-voiced chant, and in a moment all the secretaries withdrew, smiling. They left affectionately touching one another's shoulders. Illirio was visibly stunned, though he did not utter a word.

The moment the secretaries left, Nissa and I cleaned the windows with the disinfectant that we always keep in the storage shed. We then returned to our table for two more happy hours of singing; how I wish Illirio would smile more—after all, he is the new father in the family.

Thursday, July 4 1974
Cassettes recorded by Jean-Luc Lefevbre

"Likki, don't do it."

"Why not, Grandpa?"

"Because it is stupid and hopeless, son."

"On the contrary, it would be even more stupid and more dishonorable not to do it, Grandpa."

"Ah, honor…. You are the father of a baby; aren't you old enough to know that games of honor only cause disaster? Think of your wife and your child. Do you wish Nissa to become a widow and Alfi to grow up without a father? You are exposing yourself to mortal danger!"

"What mortal danger?"

"Don't you understand?? If you succeed in this endeavor, the Sages will regard your act as one of insurrection against their teachings. They will send those stinking fools to kill you."

"I am ready to die, Grandpa. I have faced death before."

"Are you crazy??"

"We are all walking corpses here on this island, Grandpa."

"Then why have you been so careless as to allow Nissa to get pregnant??"

"Because if we act wisely, we do have a small chance to survive."

"I would call your prank an act of desperation, not one of wisdom, Likki."

"It's not a desperate prank; it is an attempt to expose the whole rite as an openly perceived farce."

"Ah, so now you are a theatrical *régisseur*, my son? I have dreamed of bringing Nissa, Alfi, and you to the Philippines from where you could continue on to the United States and develop good musical careers there. You surely must know that both you and Nissa possess great talent, Likki."

"The world does not lack great musicians, Grandpa. They will manage without us. Our people need us more here."

"So you have decided to turn Nissa into a widow?"

"Don't play with my feelings, Grandpa. I hope I will survive, and that we will all thrive here. But in order to do that, someone has to show that the will of the Sages is not the overpowering spirit here on the island. Let me tell you what happened on our last Hainan escapade."

"Go on."

"We landed in full daylight, and surprisingly attracted no one's attention, though the seashore was full of people. The Chinese soldiers patrolling the shore sat around nonchalantly playing cards and drinking tea. Their rifles were strewn in a pile, not in their immediate reach—they didn't seem to be disciplined soldiers. Our idiots decided to dig the soil just under the feet of these soldiers. After a few minutes of this the Chinese soldiers recognized who we were and kicked three of us in the bellies with their boots. The three teens started bleeding and attempted to crawl back to the boats. Seeing that, our uninjured men pushed them back to where the Chinese soldiers sat and used their hands as shovels to dig more soil to fill their boxes. The injured ones groaned in pain. Then the Chinese soldiers stood up and went for their rifles. They began shooting at the uninjured teens. Two were killed on the spot. I dragged several more to the boats. For this my crew considers me traitor, as though I were a Chinese collaborator. Grandpa, since my last trip to Hainan, I have been considered the enemy. My fate is sealed. This plan, Grandpa, is not foolish. If I wish to survive, if we wish to survive, we have to act now."

"I am with you, Likki."

"I love you, Grandpa."

WARS BEGIN, 1974–1978

Thursday, August 22, 1974
Comunicado do Gabinete dos Sábios

Our Sages call for renewed effort to erect our magnificent Hill and remind everyone that this sacred duty brings us closer to liberating the land of our Founding Fathers. Every islander who has reached the age of fourteen is required to bring three buckets of earth to the summit of the Hill. Since this duty has not been regularly performed for many years, everyone is now required to bring ten buckets of earth to the Hill's summit. Our glorious teenagers are reminded of their ultimate service to the nation by bringing soil from the land of Hainan to reinforce the Hill. This soil is the best and truest glue to make all the other soil brought to the summit of the Hill adhere together. Therefore the task of our brave teenagers is of paramount importance in keeping the spirit of our forefathers alive.

Thursday, August 29, 1974
Posto dos Nossos Pais

While the Sages have called upon us once again to renew the effort to build the Hill and to send our youth to the shores of

Hainan, our Founding Fathers' land, we in turn call upon all islanders to fulfil this call in a wise manner. We strongly suggest refraining from impulsive, unplanned digging, but rather to collect soil for the Hill at new housing construction sites where much ground has already been excavated. We also recommend extending the soil gathering campaign into a gradual, year-long process. As for the collection of "glue" for cementing the earth at the top of our ever-rising Hill, we recommend collecting sand from the bottom of the sea several kilometers to the north of our coast. We maintain that the cementing quality of this sand is much higher than that of the soil taken from the shores of Hainan. While we support the sailings of our heroic youth to the north, we suggest limiting the distance of the journey to twenty-five kilometers. At that point, diving competitions for bringing up the largest quantity of sand from the bottom of the sea could be held. These would not only keep our glorious tradition alive, but would also preserve the life of our youth.

Friday, September 6, 1974
Cassettes recorded by Jean-Luc Lefevbre

Yesterday morning at dawn I visited Illirio's secret underground pit. I must say I was impressed by its design; it contains five concrete columns with huge cable drums that are capable of winding thick ropes of extraordinary length. Through specially built apertures covered by waterproof rubber hosing, the ropes extend two thousand meters underwater and hook the bottom surface of the boats intended for departure. Illirio maintains that this time six boats will be departing for Hainan and his equipment is designed to stop only five. "I cannot allow more deaths," he rasped solemnly, "but I do not know how to prevent the last boat from sailing." His resolve left me speechless, but it also made me terribly afraid for him.

Tuesday, September 17, 1974
Cassettes recorded by Jean-Luc Lefevbre

I woke up to strange, loud shouting noises that I had never heard before coming from the area of the marina. I got dressed quickly and went to the shore to have a closer look and saw at least two hundred youngsters throwing themselves on the ground wildly tearing out their hair and pummeling the earth with their fists. I could not determine whether these shouts were expressions of wrath, laughter, shame, or maybe all three together. Soon some naked secretaries came by and started defecating all around. Were they blessing the situation? Looking toward the sea, I saw six motionless boats full of wildly gesticulating teenagers at a distance of about two kilometers. The commotion went on for a whole hour. Then two secretaries dressed in gray approached the shore and called for the teenagers in the boats to row back to the marina. I could not help smiling; Illirio's plan had succeeded admirably and no one had gotten hurt! I have just returned to my place to wait for the arrival of my fantastic grandchild.

Tuesday, September 17, 1974
Diary entry by Adélaïde Fourangier

It is late evening now, half past ten. Nissa and Alfi have just left. Nissa told me that Illirio left home the day before yesterday and has still not returned. Poor girl, she is trembling. No one has any idea of where he could be. I wonder if his nightly disappearances have anything to do with this? What is this young man thinking? He is the father of a family; can't he show any responsibility!?

Now I myself am starting to feel a freezing fear—what could have happened to my son??

Today was strange—it began with hundreds of youngsters running around the marina shouting wildly until about noon. Luckily by two o'clock, when I had to teach, it was already over. I wonder if this errant noise is somehow related to Illirio's disappearance. How? This young man is so unruly….

Wednesday, September 18, 1974
Diary entry by Adélaïde Fourangier

It is seven o'clock in the morning now; I have just returned from Nissa's house. How she trembles—Illirio has still not returned. She said that some boys from the orphanage told her that yesterday, when pounding the ground in frustration at the aborted sail to Hainan, one of them felt that he had struck not solid ground but a wooden board that had been covered with sand. That boy laughed off the incident, saying that the loud vibrations from the spot had attracted the attention of naked secretaries who enthusiastically covered the place with feces. Thinking that this had something to do with Illirio's disappearance, Nissa was now on her way to find that pile of shit, poor girl. I volunteered to remain with Alfi, but she asked me to return home, leaving Alfi with a hospital babysitter instead.

I slowly returned home feeling an icy frost rising in my body. Is my son, god forbid, dead? And has my daughter-in-law (or whatever the valid term for that relationship is on this shitty island) gone mad? At this early age?? She is not even twenty! And where is Costas, for heaven's sake? That dreamer is wandering around somewhere with his water desalination ideas, or cutting up someone's body instead of searching for his son. Oh my god, I am going crazy myself.

September 18, 1974
Cassettes recorded by Jean-Luc Lefevbre

Gasping for breath, Nissa came running into the meteorological station and told me that she had discovered Illirio's body. Based on the orphan boys' description of the locale, she had discovered the underground pit containing the rope drums where Illirio's unconscious body lay. His left forearm was cut off at the elbow and blood was dripping from it. Through intense force of will she had somehow dragged him out of there, but that was all she could manage. We ran back to the spot only to find a horrible sight—naked secretaries were dancing around Illirio's limp body. I was afraid he was dead. I looked at Nissa. Lifting his right wrist, she nodded to me that there still was a pulse. As we lifted Illirio, the secretaries started defecating on the tracks left by his body as Nissa dragged it over the sand. For the first time I was grateful for these idiots—they had covered the signs of Nissa's actions so that this place still remained unknown to the "authorities" (if that is a proper term for these madmen).

We immediately got a youth-drawn wheelbarrow cart to bring Illirio to the hospital. Nissa ran alongside the wheelbarrow youngsters while I followed behind at my slow pace. Some children present at the scene had run to alert Costas and Adèle. By the time I had gotten to the hospital, Costas was already there. A few moments later Adèle burst into the room. She fell on Illirio, taking his head to her lips. It was then that I saw the depth of her maternal love. She didn't care how mutilated he was, only that he should survive. Tegularius saw this too. Although he didn't say a word, he cried. Illirio had not lost all his blood because by some miracle he had knotted a tourniquet around what was left of his arm. Costas's operation cauterized the wound and tied off the major arteries and veins. Then he sewed up what remained of the severed arm. All of us, Adèle, Nissa, the baby, and I waited anxiously in the hospital.

Now I realized that Illirio's intractable decision to stop *all* the departing boats meant that he had decided to save the lives of the sailors on the sixth boat by turning his own body into a rope drum, leaning upon one of the concrete columns to gain leverage. Having fastened one end of the rope around his left arm, he probably didn't realize that the torque of the uncoiling line would shear off his forearm. Late in the afternoon, an exhausted Costas came out of the operating theater and mumbled, "He will probably live," adding, "Nissa saved his life." She immediately burst into tears and Adèle embraced her. Adèle took Alfi to the music school to enable Nissa to remain with Illirio.

Monday, October 14 1974
Comunicado do Gabinete dos Sábios

We recently witnessed an evil attempt to disrupt the glorious sailing of our heroic youth to the sacred shores of Hainan. The evil man behind this crime is none other than Illirio Mariafels. His satanic intelligence has brought the contempt of our Founding Fathers' spirit upon us. Illirio Mariafels should be dead, finding a well-deserved punishment meted out by the blows of our heroic secretaries. However, Sage no. 1—in his elevated wisdom—has granted clemency to Mariafels and will try to free his soul from the devil's grip. He will forever bear the stamp of disgrace—his stump will always inform all passersby of his arrogance, his breach of the Founding Fathers' spirit, and his presumptuousness in violating the will of the Sages. Everyone here is ordered to spite him, to never touch him or even speak to him. His wife will abandon him. He will not see his child. So he will live until the day—and our great Sage no. 1 says that this day is not very far away—when he shall crawl to the Sages' compound and beg to be accepted to the order of naked secretaries, asking only to be their feces bearer. Sage no. 1 is the wisest and most elevated son of our Founding Fathers; we bow to his decision.

Wednesday, October 23 1974
Diary entry by Adélaïde Fourangier

Illirio lives. My son is indeed an idealistic fool, much like his father. He will now bear the ugly mark of his senseless devotion to these stupid people until the end of his days. Now with a stump instead of an arm, any bright future he might have had as a pianist is over. Even if he could perform, there is no repertory for a solo right hand. Maybe now he will devote his one useful hand to caressing his wife and angelic baby and abandon this revolutionary stupidity of his.

Thursday, October 24 1974
Posto dos Nossos Pais

While we are all very glad that Illirio Mariafels's dramatic attempt to stop the teenagers who were supposed to sail to Hainan ended without fatalities, and while we commend the selfless motivation behind Illirio's act, we think that the sailing ritual should be changed gradually and not impetuously. A decision on this matter needs to be made by consensus rather than being resolved by one man, however virtuous, acting alone. We applaud the merciful ruling of Sage no. 1. We hope that as a result Illirio Mariafels, a young parent with a demonstrably strong conscience, will contribute much to the future well-being of our island.

Monday, October 28, 1974
Diary entry by Adélaïde Fourangier

Yesterday Costas brought me a page from the Sages' *Posto dos Nossos Pais* and showed me the appalling decree ostracizing Illirio. The man may have saved the lives of at least forty youngsters on their damned island—sacrificing his own arm and his career as a concert pianist in the process—and they deign to punish him. Perhaps I should be thankful that they spared his life, the life of my foolish son. Taking into consideration that Illirio is the chief coordinator of electrical works on the island, I wonder how they will be able to implement their decree. Nevertheless, I am frightened, seriously frightened. Costas says that the effect of the curse will evaporate in several months' time. I think he is wrong. He misunderstands both the Sages and his own people. As an outsider, I see how absolutely the "Founding Fathers' spirit" rules over them all. Oh, how I hate those Sages!

Tuesday, April 15, 1975
Cassettes recorded by Jean-Luc Lefevbre

After the ban the Sages imposed on Illirio last October, I thought his life on the island would in effect be over. I started thinking of how I might take him, Nissa, and Alfi out of here. Afraid for his life, not to mention Nissa's and Alfi's, my thoughts stumbled into the usual obstacles: Bangkok is too far for my Pettersson and for my own dwindling powers, likewise the Philippines. Vietnam is sealed. China and the adjacent Paracel Islands are certainly not even a possibility. The only viable option remains the American ship that endlessly cruises around, but I was sure that Illirio would only swim back to the island.

Rethinking the Philippines option, actually, it is not too far; the problem is that I am becoming too weak to sail there. However, if there were a real need I could, I hope, find the strength to make the trip, not to mention the problem of gasoline. I used to buy gas in Saigon, bringing extra drums of it for additional trips. That is how I amassed the reserves for my fishing trips. But now, cut off from my gasoline supply, my reserves are low. Yes, Costas could bring me a small quantity of gas from the *Harding*, but it would not allow me to make the five-hundred-nautical-mile journey to the port of Laoag in the Philippines and back. So actually it is gasoline that is the acute problem, not my health.

Incidentally I have noticed that from the time when Illirio first started going for his short walks outside the hospital, both children and parents smile at him and even shake his hand, as though grateful for his valorous action. I feel profound relief at the fact that the edicts of those mad Sages do not totally cow all the people here anymore. It seems that Illirio can live here even with their curse upon his head...I must thank Costas for that change in attitude—he has found his way into people's hearts and succeeds in dispersing their fears. I remember the time when whatever those madmen decreed was taken as ironclad law by these docile, unquestioning people.

So, all of us will remain here. For the time being, that is....

Friday, May 2, 1975
Diary entry by Adélaïde Fourangier

While recuperating, Illirio does multi-kilometer swimming exercises, employing his right hand and stump with special body development techniques designed by Costas. A week ago just by chance he came to the marina with his children's chorus as the boats bound for Hainan were about to set sail again. The children started singing Illirio's two-voiced chants and upon hearing the sound, all the teenage sailors stopped their preparations and became extremely friendly toward each other. Abandoning their boats, they all returned home to their orphanages.

Illirio works with the children's chorus twice a week. On the other days he builds shortwave radio receivers and distributes them to our parents so they can now listen to overseas news. As more awareness of the world outside Pinto develops, dialogue on a wider scope of ideas is more prevalent. There are animated disputes and political discussion groups have even been formed.

Sunday, October 19, 1975
Cassettes recorded by Jean-Luc Lefevbre

Illirio's two-voiced chant has turned out to be an amazing weapon against fanaticism. I cannot for the life of me understand how it works, but as a scientist I cannot deny my own observations of how, over the course of a few minutes, it dissolves antagonism. Yes, I did see it! The most amazing thing is that once they've experienced the noble impact of these chants, those who used to express outward signs of ill will never do so again. Maybe this chanting should be incorporated into the overall strategy of my dear Costas and his supporters.

As Adèle explained it to me, Illirio places French folksongs into the bass register and superimposes local chanting melodies onto the upper voice. She compares this to medieval European organum singing, although according to her it is produced by an entirely different bodily effort, whereas in the olden days in France people gathered in groups of three or more, and each sang his or her own melody, supported by his or her own diaphragm. Here, on the other hand, each singer uses both his or her stomach muscles and—separately—his or her cheek muscles. Amazing.

Though only a few of the secretaries have been exposed to the benevolent effects of this two-voiced singing, and only very few parents have listened to this music as well, the atmosphere on the island is now far more tranquil than at any other time that I can recall. People are generally friendlier and more children are willing to study the sciences in our parents' schools. French is now slowly being introduced as a foreign language. So far sailing to Hainan has been put off, and I have noticed that the frequency of the Sages' bulletins has also decreased. Above all, Costas looks happy.

Tuesday, December 9, 1975
Diary entry by Adélaïde Fourangier

I have never seen Costas in such high spirits. He is brimming with ideas for the island's betterment and there is no anxiety in his heart. For the first time we spent the whole night together. Nobody disturbed us.

Our little Alfi is already running around, uttering a few words in the local Portuguese dialect and in French. He has beautiful diamond-shaped, sky-blue eyes, just like his parents. Some of our older pupils watch over him in a nearby room while Nissa works with the chorus. Yet he always finds a way to burst into the room and sing as Nissa conducts. He lifts his hands when he sings, imitating his mom. What a child! His preference for low sounds is what amazes me most. It seems that he is already preparing himself for his father's two-voiced chants…. And his eyes are always so shiny and welcoming. How I just love to bask in his glance….

Monday, February 16, 1976
Diary entry by Adélaïde Fourangier

This morning I was awakened by a terrible humming in the area. At first light I saw naked secretaries running around wildly defecating everywhere. Many were handing out leaflets calling for people to fulfil the duty of unification of body and soul, which they claim has been willfully neglected as a result of deliberate instigation by unfaithful souls dwelling on the island.

Coming with his children's chorus to chant to the secretaries who were going berserk, Illirio started one of his most effective hymns—*Irmãos, nós sorriem um para o outro* (*Brothers, We Smile upon One Another*), but to no avail. All of them had placed cotton plugs in their ears. On the empty packages of earbuds scattered on the ground was the inscription "Iowa Cotton Wool." These bastards had made themselves deaf with American help. The stench outside is getting more and more unbearable by the minute. And unfortunately there is no sign of approaching rain.

February 20, 1976
Cassettes recorded by Jean-Luc Lefevbre

"What do you think of the situation, Koty?"

"It's so horrible, Papa. We cannot keep on pretending that our task is only to help people die without prolonged suffering. We do not have the right medicine to neutralize the flies' poison. We cannot drive this horrible plague from our island."

"But, Koty, I see how valiantly you attempt to prevent the fly onslaughts with your mass disinfection campaigns and the methods of house protection you have invented."

"All our efforts are futile, Papa. If we really want to succeed, we have to destroy the Sages' power, which means that we may risk war. Papa, you always know what is going on in my heart, so you know how much I hate war with all its senseless death."

"But people will die from the epidemics anyway, many of them."

"True, but now they will die because of my will. It is too unbearable, Papa."

"So do you have an alternative strategy?"

"No. Do you?"

"No, but I do know that you will need the Pettersson as your life-support vessel. But now we are cut off from gasoline supplies. And the Philippines, where we could acquire some, is both too far for frequent trips and beyond my dwindling powers to assure a safe voyage."

"Thank you for the advance warning. If we need your help to reach the Philippines, I will ask my people to assist you in navigating the boat. Maybe Zeferino, the young electrician, could be a good copilot. I will talk to him."

"Koty, the trip to the Philippines is a long one. It can take four days in one direction in normal weather conditions. Every productive roundtrip might take no less than ten days. In case of war, you will need a more reliable supply source for ammunition, food, medicine, and technical equipment, not to mention gasoline. You'll have to devise a better solution than sending the Pettersson on long, open sea voyages."

"Papa! You've just given me an idea. Perhaps we could travel to the Philippines once or twice in order to arrange imports that could then be brought here by their sailors. Even if they refuse to dock at our port because of our epidemics, we could rendezvous with them in open sea forty miles off our coast. We could then collect the goods in our little fishing boats. The Pettersson could sail out only to carry the larger pieces."

"Like what, Koty?"

"Like armored troop carriers, Papa."

"Don't make me laugh, Koty. You sound ridiculous. The Pettersson is way too small for taking on a single armored vehicle."

"Yes, but we can import them in parts and reassemble them here."

"In that case the Pettersson will certainly be able to bring over two armored vehicles. God bless you, Koty, with all your tricks. Though I hope I won't see the day when you employ armored vehicles on your island."

"I don't think we'll import armored troop carriers after all, Papa. But there is *some* military equipment that we will have to import, even though I am the first to decry it."

"May god help you, son. Trust your heart."

"I love you, Papa."

Sunday, February 29, 1976
Diary entry by Adélaïde Fourangier

An epidemic reigns supreme. The skies are literally blackened with millions of poisonous flies. People everywhere are getting bitten. They die out in the open. Costas and his associates run around the island in protective overalls spraying disinfectant and dragging the afflicted to nearby trees in the attempt to alleviate their suffocation. I see these suffering people through my window. Luckily, several months ago Costas and Illirio framed my windows with double glass and installed a special air filtration system. As long as I am at home, I am relatively safe. But I worry about our little Alfi. Infants are so vulnerable. Nissa and Alfi should remain here with me, but Nissa says she is needed at the hospital, and prefers to have Alfi nearby under the care of the hospital babysitters who she assures me are very competent. True, their house is near the hospital, but still, it is only partially protected by double windows and protective netting. My son, a principled democrat, cannot permit himself the hypocrisy of fully protecting his own house while his neighbors' homes are not as secure. So his own family has to wait until he finds the time to upgrade everyone's home (he only protected my house fully because it serves as a school). I doubt that Alfi is safe there, but what can I do? I can't take Alfi to my home by force. If I try, I will only cause Illirio pain. And besides, he is still nursing, so there is no food for him here anyway. So he stays where he is.

Friday, March 12, 1976
Diary entry by Adélaïde Fourangier

Since mid-February nobody has come to my school. Today I covered myself with double cheesecloth and went to visit Jean-Luc, but he was not home. As I was afraid to leave the area to look for him, I left him a note and returned home. Three hours ago he came over to my house and gave me the sad news that our sweet Alfi had died.

Yesterday Alfi was attacked by a swarm of flies that had somehow penetrated the protective cheesecloth that is always placed over his crib. Nissa was helping in the hospital and Alfi was being cared for by a hospital babysitter. The flies literally sealed the toddler's mouth and nose. He was immediately brought to the hospital where his mouth was cleansed of flies, but there is no effective medicine against their poison on the island. They tried treating him with an anti-infection aerosol, but that only caused constriction in his respiratory system. Alfi struggled for the entire night and shortly before dawn his little heart stopped beating. I saw his body wrapped in white linen lying alongside twenty-four other small, still corpses. Nissa was not there. She fainted and was receiving treatment in a room nearby. Illirio stood alongside the motionless body of his son, caressing him with his stump, his face pale and seemingly devoid of emotion. Later he approached me and embraced me with his right hand. We held each other in a silent hug, immediately after which he left.

Friday, April 16, 1976
Cassettes recorded by Jean-Luc Lefevbre

Four days ago Costas and I sailed to the USAT *President Harding* and obtained a small stock of antibiotics and other vital medicines that were donated to us as a gesture of goodwill. But we need so much more and it can only be obtained with the approval of the American government. This needs to be Costas's next urgent task.

I am afraid once again that I am the messenger of horrible news. Upon our return, we learned that just yesterday Nissa had died while burying dead secretaries on the eastern side of the island. She was attacked by flies and succumbed. We were told that driving her comrades away, she dug her own grave and fell into it. As part of their rituals, naked secretaries danced around her as she expired. Later her body was covered with earth. One of the eyewitnesses to the event, the pearl catcher Ferrao, quickly found Illirio and told him that there was a piece of paper in her hand. So Illirio dug open her grave and recovered the note. Ferrao told me that Illirio remained silent as he read Nissa's last words, his face a mask of stoicism. Ferrao has just left my home, after informing me of what had transpired.

Friday, April 16, 1976
Diary entry by Adélaïde Fourangier

In my former life—did I have such a life once?—it used to be Good Friday. Now according to this island's satanic calendar, it is the Feast of Death. Nissa is dead. Nissa, my beloved daughter, my dear, wonderful, brave, beautiful girl. Nissa.

Yesterday Costas came bearing this dreadful message. He sat down on my bed and cried like a small child. He brought me Nissa's little mirror with *Alfi* inscribed on its frame and an old British sports journal with a guide to somersaults that he himself had given her after visiting the *President Harding*. What should I do with the journal? Perform somersaults myself? Nissa—you shouldn't have died, my girl.

Saturday, April 17, 1976
Cassettes recorded by Jean-Luc Lefevbre

Yesterday evening I went to Adèle's house. She sat alone at her table, her diary open in front of her. She sat straight up with her hands on her knees as though meditating. Her pencil, still in her right hand, flickered in the moonlight. As I approached her I saw a steady flow of tears falling from her chin down her blouse to the pencil. I tried to touch her, but she remained still, almost as if she were lifeless. I called her name several times, but she did not answer. I went to the door and sat down myself. Suddenly I found myself crying too. My hands became wet from tears. Pulling myself together, I went into the bathroom to wash my face and when I came out, I met Costas at the door coming in. We hugged and then I left. Before closing the door, I saw Adèle putting her head in Costas's hands.

Sunday, May 30, 1976
Diary entry by Adélaïde Fourangier

It is dreadful. My school is closed, with the number of dead at over eleven thousand—many are children, especially babies.

My windows are now covered with blankets impregnated with antibiotic spray. I get my food directly from Jean-Luc's greenhouse in a tightly sealed case.

Of course nobody sails to Hainan now, though many people come with buckets to the Hill, as if doing penance. Many die either while climbing or descending the slopes. Costas's associates wear face masks and drag the bodies on wheelbarrows to a burial ground north of the marina. I can see the funerals from my highest window.

Thursday, July 1, 1976
Diary entry by Adélaïde Fourangier

Yesterday a council meeting was held in my piano room. There were eight of us—Costas, Jean-Luc, Illirio, Parent Eulálio (father), Parent Valeriano (father), Parent Leocádia (mother), Parent Leonor (mother)—all sitting along the walls of the room just like the children used to. A strange flashback for me.

I was asked to practice Debussy's *L'isle joyeuse* (how grotesque!) very loudly so the secretaries running around outside the school could not hear the parents' conversation. My guests still took precautions even though my house is now surrounded by a steel fence preventing the secretaries from approaching my windows.

To open the meeting, Costas said that as the direct result of the Sages' demented policies, the island had now reached a critically dangerous state. Eulálio said the Sages must die. Costas reiterated yet again that the aim of the meeting should be to find ways to protect islanders' lives, not instigate more death. Leocádia said the Sages' fanaticism prevented them from being concerned about the welfare of the islanders. Leonor asserted that any effort to fight the Sages would only bring more death, especially among the unprotected children. Valeriano said that the Sages had rifles in their compound. As a former assistant to a French weapon manufacturer in Saigon, he was familiar with the sound of automatic gunfire and unequivocally stated that he had heard those frightening sounds coming from behind the compound's guano fence. Leonor repeatedly warned everyone not to fall victim to the irresponsible adventurism of Costas Tegularius and his followers. Valeriano countered with the statement that they were already victims of Sage-inflicted death.

Illirio said that practically speaking, there were only two available paths of action: change the Sages' ideas or oppose them by force. Costas asserted that with regard to the second option, the military equipment in the parents' possession was inadequate for the task. Illirio asserted that he had trained nearly three hundred children in singing his double-voiced hymns and this could be used to overpower the secretaries. Costas replied that the secretaries had learned to plug their ears with cotton wool to prevent being influenced by the chanting. And besides, there would soon be a new call from the Sages to build the Hill and dig the soil on the island, endangering not only the new island housing, but also causing salt water to penetrate the island's aquifers.

Jean-Luc asked how many islanders could be counted on to support Costas. No one could give a clear answer. Jean-Luc then asked how many people were in the service of the Sages and how many of them died annually. Costas said that in his estimation, at least five hundred secretaries died of fly poisoning every year, but since at least eight hundred babies were brought to Sage orphanages during the course of a year, the secretary population remained stable. Jean-Luc then asked how many people lived on the island in general. There was no reliable answer, as no census had ever been taken. Costas proposed arranging a discreet census conducted by trusty pearl-catching youth who could circumspectly register every individual. The census could be completed within one month. All present agreed that it should be done.

Leonor, the pacifist, thanked everyone for not approving any decision that involved bloodshed. Valeriano suggested acquiring nonlethal weapons. Jean-Luc brought up the idea of Tasers, a recently invented device that delivered an immobilizing, nonlethal electric shock. Leocádia asked where these instruments could be obtained. Costas informed her that the only way to get them would be to travel to the Philippines and from there to import them directly from the United States, paying with dollars received in exchange for pearls. Jean-Luc stated that with the collapse of the South Vietnamese regime, the island's historic link to Saigon had been severed and that his pilot friend, Etienne Duvernoix, would not make deliveries. He further iterated that Tasers could not be obtained from the USAT *President Harding*. All of the parents at the meeting then looked to Jean-Luc, who promised to sail to the Philippines to get the Tasers. Illirio volunteered to join him. Costas said that Eulálio and Zeferino, the young electrician, would also sail with Jean-Luc.

Friday, July 2, 1976
Cassettes recorded by Jean-Luc Lefevbre

Well, *vers l'avant un vieux bonhomme*—forward march, old man. Having promised, I must attempt it. Thankfully Illirio will join us—so there will be four of us altogether, including Eulálio and that young chap Zeferino.

Sunday, September 19, 1976
Diary entry by Adélaïde Fourangier

The epidemic has petered out and calm has returned. My school has opened its doors again; twenty-one of my pupils were among the many thousands that died. All the surviving students and even some former students come now to play funerary music. We are thinking of preparing a memorial concert. Each surviving student took it upon himself or herself to play a piece of music to honor the memory of a specific pupil. We arranged a large board of grief on the left wall of my classroom where the names of the kids who passed away were inscribed and with some reminiscences about them made by their surviving friends.

Here is what Aloisio and Duarte (both eight years old) wrote about Demetrio, who was just eleven years old:

Demetrio was our great friend and leader. Once he led us to the top of the Hill at night. He had matches. He lit a bonfire and we all sat around it. Demetrio told us not to sleep. We did not sleep, only a little. When we woke there was no more fire. There was light in the sky. It was morning. We saw a plane—high in the sky. Demetrio said the plane came from China. It appeared every morning. We asked him to show us the plane again. He led us to the Hill three more times, but we did not see the plane. Demetrio said that clouds were covering the sky. We asked why. We were afraid. Did we do something wrong? Demetrio said the Sages send clouds to protect us from the plane. The plane has bad people in it. They should not see us. Demetrio was our great friend. He loved our music teacher Adèle very much. We love her too.

Here is what my pupil Candelária (thirteen years old) wrote about her friend Djanira (fourteen years old):

Djanira knew a wonderful place to sit and make up fantasies. This place is on the southern shore, where the forest almost touches the waterline. There are plenty of large stones crammed between the trees and the water. Our pearl catchers rest there before diving. Djanira always liked to look at Arnaldo, who is strong and friendly. Sometimes she stared at Balduino too and did not look at Arnaldo at all. She told me once that it was too dangerous to look only at one man, because death could take him and thereby break her heart. She told me that there is a persistent rumor on the island that death collects its preferences and places them deep inside the Hill, and that the Sages knew where the secret door leading to the Hill's inner chamber was and they had the key to lock and unlock that door. Therefore she was not very much afraid that the death would take Balduino. She was sure that the Sages would eventually let him out. But she was afraid that death would take Arnaldo. When I asked Djanira why she was so afraid for Arnaldo, since Arnaldo would also be able to escape from the Hill's inner chamber, Djanira had nothing to say, but she started to cry. I loved Djanira very much.

Here is a list of the children who died—I will add my own brief description of those who impressed me in some special way:

Agostinho—age six

Aliciana—age eleven

Belmiro—age fourteen

Britesia—age nine

Constancia "the little"—age seven

Constancia "the older"—age fourteen. She was one of three students from the secretaries' orphanage. She was always terribly dirty, with feces staining her clothes. We arranged for her to take a special shower before entering our classroom, and I personally gave her newly laundered clothes each week and sent her dirty clothes to the public laundry located near the runway. Although not talented, she practiced sincerely. She had learned the Mazurka from Tchaikovsky's *Album for the Young* (Op. 39) and used to play it incessantly—with sloppy rhythm, though—to the naked secretaries who were being treated at the hospital. They respected her very much.

Demetrio—age eleven, a boy with a sly smile. He was especially good at Bach's *Inventions*. The intricacy of the polyphony made him laugh. When he played Bach's music, I used to wonder why nobody else thought of it as music of joyful exploration. Why always morbidity? But I am no longer in a position to judge the world—I no longer know what is happening over there. Maybe they have already started playing an exuberant Bach....

Deolinda—age fifteen

Djanira—age fourteen, a lazy coquette

Eleuterio "the little"—age seven

Eleuterio "the sailor"—age sixteen, and a veteran of two voyages to Hainan. He was our young Louis Jourdan, handsome and brave with the persona of a movie star—a heartbreaker and champion of all champions in every field. Except music. He insisted on playing Chopin's demanding études and could never master them. He invented a "method" of blurring the left hand passages in Chopin's famous *Revolutionary* étude, which reminded me of the puerile "inventions" that I myself had once introduced into Beethoven's sonatas during my post-war career in France under the egoistic pretention that it was inspired by Cortot. No wonder they hated me there!

Fernanda—I loved her so very much, Fernanda. How intelligent and serious she was! She grasped tasks quickly and with assurance. What a wealth of imagination she had. Although not as flamboyant as Nissa used to be, she definitely boiled over with talent. She had already started to study Chopin's extraordinarily difficult *Allegro de Concert* (Op. 46). I heard her play three pages of it in full glory. She was seventeen, my great hope.

Fernão and Roldao—twin brothers, age eight

Ilda—she was just eight years old, a child from the eastern part of the island. She would come with nicely shaped little pieces of turtle meat wrapped in pages from the Sages' newsletter. She was always eager to share them with the other students. She wanted to remain for that purpose for many hours in my room. I was able to convince her to deposit her treasure in my container, and in the evening my most senior student would take it to the hospital for the nurses to dispose of. She lived with her mother and two other siblings (I never saw them). Her father was a naked secretary, proudly performing his defecation services across the island. Her mother used to send me a set of clean clothes for her, so that I could help her change in my bathroom, and send the used ones back, usually wrapped in the Sages' newspaper.

Laurinda—age thirteen

Olginha—age thirteen, the only girl with a well-groomed braid; the others didn't even seem to brush their hair. Poor Olghi was not even touched by the poisonous flies; she died in a stampede on her way to afternoon classes. People had noticed a large swarm of flies and started running away in a panic. She fell down and was trampled to death.

Olivinha—age thirteen, a nasty girl

Rufino—age sixteen, he was an orphan from the eastern side. He never knew his parents. Actually, he was Illirio's student, studying choral chanting and composition under him. He had promised his guardians, the naked secretaries, that he would learn how to write out the local chants so that he would be able to supply the Sages "with a professional analysis of the local music." Evidently the Sages were interested in sharing this knowledge with the outside world of lower creatures. I always felt it was a cover-up for Rufino's secret desire to escape the control of the Sages and become part of the Parents' Movement. Poor boy.

Sabion—age eight

Teodósio—age fifteen, he had a real talent for harmony. He used to invent gorgeous sequences of chords and always asked me to tell him about the instruments in the orchestra. He frequently visited Jean-Luc, who played his old records of classical music for him. Once deeply moved by a transmission of Schubert's *Rosamunde Overture* that he had heard on Jean-Luc's shortwave radio, he kept on imploring Jean-Luc to record it for him whenever it was transmitted again. Jean-Luc promised to do so and Teodósio waited for the recording with stoic patience. No, Jean-Luc did not record this piece, yet when he heard of Teodosio's death he said that he would tape the *Rosamunde* in Teodósio's memory. Teodósio, Teodósio....

Monday, November 1, 1976
Diary entry by Adélaïde Fourangier

Another meeting was held at my home with the same people attending.

Here is the census data that they asked me to write down.

Current population: Approximately 85,000 people (plus an unknown number in the Sages' compound)

8,000 secretaries (including teachers)—approximately 2,000 of them married

8,000 single women working in turtle-cooking kitchens and orphanages

2,000 male pearl catchers

23 female pearl catchers

1,500 male lumberjacks, mostly living with their spouses in little clay houses (although some live in common barracks)

1,500 fishermen, mostly married

2,000 builders of guano fences and barracks, mostly married

25,000–35,000 children in orphanages and 10,000 in parents' homes

2,000 parents who have obtained a Saigon education (and their spouses)

12,000 parents (male and female) working either on water installations, in schools, or in electricity production

7,000 old and lame people

A special discussion was devoted to estimating the number of people in the Sages' compound. No one on this side of the barrier has any direct knowledge of what happens in the compound area since it is heavily guarded and sealed from the general population. The Kremlin, as Jean-Luc calls it. Several facts, however, are known—there were no children in the compound, very few women, and hardly any turtle-grilling industry. Since the Sages import food directly from America (via the Philippines), it is impossible to estimate the population by the quantity of food passed to them from providers on the rest of the island. The only way to estimate the number of compound dwellers was to analyze their consumption of drinking water.

Since the compound has only two small wells, their main supply of water must be pumped in from the two wells in the central square of the island and presumably thoroughly cleaned by an elaborate device visible from the guano fence.

There was a huge uproar when Valeriano mentioned that the Sages probably never drank water mixed with human feces. Eulálio and Leocadia emphatically urged us to tell this story to all Pinto Islanders. Costas stopped them, proclaiming:, "My friends, nobody will believe that the installations inside the compound are in fact water filters, and that the Sages trespass the very laws they decree for us. We have only four water specialists who understand what they see there, and even theirs is only an indirect impression. These filters were built many years ago by visiting American expatriates and given to the Sages in firm belief that they were performing sacred labor.

"But what the hell are these Sages thinking *in principle* if they themselves are not keeping the damned Founding Fathers' spirit?" shouted a totally enraged Eulálio.

"In my view it is very simple," answered Costas. "The Sages are absolutely certain that drinking feces-polluted water is god's gift to Pinto Islanders. And in order to keep the Founding Fathers' spirit alive, they have to preside over the functioning of the island. So they must keep themselves healthy, sacrificing their own honor to serve us so that we can reap the benefits of god's gift. The Sages have captured our wretched population in an inescapable mental trap—drinking this feces-polluted water is considered a holy act and those who die of it are those whose minds are consumed by carnal sin."

After some speculation it was suggested that the Sages' compound contains around six thousand men. For the sake of strategic analysis, it was assumed that all of them were—or could be—armed with rifles.

With this factor in mind, Costas asserted that the data show that the parents' camp was still a minority and that fighting the Sages would end in catastrophe. However, were there to be another epidemic (and how could there not be with the defecation rituals still in force?) many lumberjacks and fishermen would desert the Sages' camp, and this would allow Costas to approach the Sages with a clear demand to stop these morbid consecration rites. And even if naked secretaries were to assault the people in Costas's camp, they could be disarmed without being killed by attacking from the rear with Tasers. Upon hearing these words, Leonor exclaimed, "Tegularius, you are our beloved leader, thank you for avoiding bloodshed!"

In addition, there was talk concerning nonlethal weaponry. Having traveled to the Philippines, Jean-Luc, Illirio, and Eulálio had brought back forty-six Tasers along with their recharging equipment (each Taser cost an amount equivalent to a week's haul by the island's most able pearl catchers). Costas asked Illirio and Eulálio to train strong parents in their use.

Jean-Luc voiced the opinion that forty-six Tasers would be inadequate to ward off a violent conflict. Illirio proposed tunneling into the Sages' compound in order to reconnoiter and discover the true amount of rifles that they had on hand. I shouted, "NO!!!" Costas blocked Illirio's suggestion, adding what everyone already knew, that the Sages were supplied with armaments purchased by the Pinto diaspora in America. Costas expressed hope that soon a representative from the island's progressive community could visit Pintoville and bring about a change in attitude regarding what is really going on here. Illirio was made to promise not to dig a tunnel on his own.

Overruling Leonor's exhortations, it was decided by a majority vote that some two hundred rifles with ammunition should be acquired as soon as possible. Eulálio resolutely exclaimed, "Finally we are on the right path!"

Costas sadly summed up that from now on, the island would face the possibility of fratricidal war, pronouncing the verdict, "My conscience tells me that we have no choice other than to defend ourselves. The Sages are no longer our brethren, but agents of evil."

As the meeting ended, the naked secretaries noticed the light in my piano studio and approached the fence; I played another Debussy piece—this time *La Cathédrale Engloutie,* although since the crazy secretaries wear ear plugs they obviously could not hear anything. Or maybe they do occasionally take out their ear plugs? Anyway, they quickly left the area. My guests left half an hour later.

Costas remained for the rest of the night. What a sad night it was.

"I fear I will become a killer," he moaned.

"Don't exaggerate," I responded.

"I will inevitably have to give orders to kill people, and I will become a monster, no longer worthy of you," he said, already with a robotic iciness in his voice. "I cannot even ask you to love me because I do not want you to love a killer."

"Why do you play at theatrics," I said, cutting into his lachrymose monologue. "You are saving your people."

"Saving them, well…" he chuckled morosely, "…look, ordinary people value inner peace more than they value their lives. They want some force that will lead them, shape their value system, organize their space and time. Certainty brings tranquility to their hearts. And being a doctor, I can say that tranquility is actually healthier than happiness, which is, at best, only a passing sentiment, and a very short one at that."

"Aha, Goethe, 'Faust,'" I commented jocularly. Sarcasm is sometimes my only recourse with Costas.

"Yes," he continued as if he hadn't heard me, "happiness is a very strong emotion, like a lightning bolt to the heart. In fact, it is so strong that when prolonged more than several minutes—maximum ten—it can be lethal. But rarely do people experience such elation. Maybe a first love, maybe the birth of a longed-for child, maybe a reunion with a dear friend, or a miraculous escape from a deadly trap. The worst case scenario is experiencing this when viewing a venerated leader. But afterward people calm down. Remember Beethoven's *Le Retour,* the third movement of his *Les Adieux* piano sonata...."

"Please go on, *mon prince,*" I said in quiet admiration.

"It captures in music the concept of human happiness, as inscribed in the sonata's full title: *Les Adieux—L'Absence—Le Retour.* The happiness that Beethoven conjures is almost unbearable, and at the end of this movement it becomes clear that life *must* return to its normal flow."

"So?" I asked.

"This normalcy, this continuation of a happy moment is more important to the human soul than are the wildest moments of happiness, for in this quieter mode a person functions at his or her best. Look, even comparing the blazes of inspiration to moments of happiness, even then one needs normalcy to digest and implement the ideas that appear during moments of inspiration. And let's not forget that most people do not even fulfill their own ideas, but rather other people's. And if they succeed at that—they are satisfied. If they die fulfilling their leader's wishes, they die happily, because they have devoted themselves to goals that they find both satisfying and assuring. People need this quietness, my love."

"And you think you will come and destroy it," I said.

"Yes, my love. And not only that—now I will begin to kill them too."

"Do you want me at your side?" I asked.

"Yes, my love."

"You have me."

"The question is, who is the *me* that you will have?" he said and sighed. And then he added, "I think you should return to France."

I pretended to attack his cheek with my fist as if to fight him and said, "Go drink some tea, and then take a cold shower. You smell like sweat." I pushed him to the kitchen and deliberately fell asleep before he came back. He left at quarter to six in the morning.

Monday, January 17, 1977
Comunicado do Gabinete dos Sábios

Our great Sages remind the islanders that due to disturbances on our sacred island, no work has been done in elevating the Hill. Our Founding Fathers' spirit cannot tolerate such unpardonable delinquency. Every islander older than fourteen years of age is hereby called upon to bring twenty buckets of earth to the summit. Everyone may dig in any open place, especially under our walking paths where the ground is more blessed.

Monday, January 24, 1977
Posto dos Nossos Pais

We call our brethren on the island to devote maximum energy to the restoration of their lives and health, taking note of the necessity to care for our children, heavily traumatized by the death that surrounds them. Therefore, we call upon our brethren to employ discretion with regard to the ecstatic calls emanating from behind the guano fence.

Wednesday, February 9, 1977
Cassettes recorded by Jean-Luc Lefevbre

My old friend Etienne Duvernoix flew over from Bangkok bringing with him two hundred automatic rifles, ammunition, and vital quantities of gasoline. Costas's people quickly unloaded the cargo so that its presence went unnoticed. I looked at Etienne and realized how old I myself must be. Etienne intends to sell his plane to a flight history museum; he has kept on flying only to supply such people as ourselves with vital goods or to occasionally keep in touch with those enclosed in their own cocoons. His hands have recently started to tremble. He joked that his old pal Jean-Luc made the wrong bet in life by remaining on an island populated by half-mad people instead of spending his old age as a military pensioner in a Parisian suburb near the Saint-Cyr academy where we both trained. "Well," I said, "in that case, I would hardly have been honored by your visits." Both of us laughed, but truth be told, I no longer know the difference between laughter and weeping. In old age I think they become the same.

Monday, March 28, 1977
Diary entry by Adélaïde Fourangier

The island is now the embodiment of Danté's *Inferno*, with naked secretaries dancing around their own excrement like wild apes. They have lost all resemblance to humans; they run around, buckets in hand, digging up the ground. Their heavy buckets clanging and bumping against each other disgorge the sand they hold in the course of the wild dancing. When they finally notice, the fly-covered secretaries jump around in ecstatic paroxysms of laughter. Their excavations along the coastline have created massive flooding, polluting the aquifer. Poisonous flies hover all around the island and only the strong rains protect us from the magnitude of death caused by the previous epidemic. Still, many die; most of them secretaries.

Leonor came to me with the news that a large demonstration of lumberjacks protesting the call for additional "compensatory" consecration rites took place at the entrance to the Sages' compound. According to Leonor, secretaries wearing gray shot at them from inside the compound and killed forty-nine lumberjacks. Leonor feels strongly that anti-Sage *agent provocateurs* called for this demonstration. She blames Costas and his activists for causing the deaths of innocent husbands. She implores me to convince Costas to stop the anti-Sage agitation. I promised her that I would have a talk with him about it.

Monday, April 11, 1977
Diary entry by Adélaïde Fourangier

Last night I had that unpleasant talk with Costas about Leonor, telling him that she had begged me to speak with him on her behalf. I asked if there was any truth to the claim that he agitates against the Sages. My very question angered him. He asserted that while he does not agitate against the Sages, everyone knows his opinion: the Sages' behavior is unpardonable. I interjected that this was enough to agitate the highly emotional, fearful islanders and make them demonstrate against the Sages. He countered by saying, "It is sad that the demonstrations are so feeble and that so few people take part in them."

I remonstrated that his answer was proof that he does in fact wish to inflame the already high passions on the island, insinuating, as Leonor did, that the naïve lumberjacks went to the guano fence inspired by his agitation and paid for it with their lives.

"That is insane!" shouted Costas. "They demonstrated peacefully against the Sages' murderous policies that have killed hundreds of their comrades in the forest. How is it that when maniacs shoot at them from behind a fence killing forty-nine, Leonor blames me for creating the mess?"

Feeling that I had fulfilled my promise to represent Leonor, I now realized that I needed to assuage Costas's own agitation. I took his hand in mine as gently as I could and was relieved to hear him sigh.

Continuing with more self-control, he asserted, "Leonor's views are quite popular, at least among a quarter of the island's population. Their position seriously undermines our efforts to pressure the Sages. While I do not wish to antagonize Leonor, I still believe that her naïve pacifism is a folly we cannot afford.

We are, after all, all islanders, and a better future should be our common goal." Then he left.

Thursday, June 9, 1977
Cassettes recorded by Jean-Luc Lefevbre

Illirio, Eulálio, Zeferino, and I have once again just returned from the Philippines and brought back fifty-eight more Tasers. We have also brought very long pipes that Illirio says we will need to defend our territory if armed secretaries attack us. It's undeniable—I am getting weaker; I'm having more and more trouble driving the boat. Etienne is right, I am an old man. Luckily, Illirio, Eulálio, and the young Zeferino are very strong and capable. They had to haul the cargo from the shore by themselves. I needed to rest on the boat. Illirio's presence is always beneficial—his perceptive overview of every situation and his knack of finding the right method for overcoming every difficulty are rare gifts. Blessed are those who are in his company.

Tuesday, August 30, 1977
Diary entry by Adélaïde Fourangier

The situation on the island will most certainly disrupt the start of the new school-year. How tired I am of teaching under these stressful conditions. Even though I personally am reasonably well protected, the problem is the children. They are so vulnerable, especially those in orphanages on the eastern side where their so-called "guardians" heartlessly neglect them.

Monday, September 5, 1977
RADIOGRAMME from Marius Villeneuve
À Madame Adélaïde Fourangier, Asie du Sud-Est

We request a report on your pedagogic achievements. We recommend that you hold a piano competition among boys and girls aged twelve and older to determine the most outstanding performance of Bach's *Preludes and Fugues.*

Wednesday, November 2, 1977
Cassettes recorded by Jean-Luc Lefevbre

I think that some kind of revolution is finally taking shape here. While the defecation feast goes on unabated, three weeks ago several dozen young men from among Costas's progressives came to the wells and pushed the defecating secretaries away. They were immediately beaten; two young men died on the spot. Other young men have obstructed the digging of soil in the forest that has caused young trees to fall. They too were beaten.

Leonor gathered her supporters in a mass protest against Costas, whom she accused of causing bloodshed and death. Naked secretaries, seeing the milling crowd, started hitting everyone with their sticks, killing twenty-six mothers. Leonor accused Costas of bearing ultimate responsibility for these killings. Costas's supporters who came forward to protect the women were bitten on their hands by the mothers who had received a direct order from Leonor to do so. Then Illirio with his children's chorus approached the altercation and they started chanting. The scene miraculously calmed down. The secretaries, who apparently were not wearing their ear plugs, started smiling in a friendly manner and withdrew to the guano fence surrounding the Sages' compound. Costas's people brought water hoses and washed down every dirty secretary they succeeded in catching. They actually thoroughly and painstakingly cleaned all those poor, feces-covered idiots.

After three days of quiet, the wild digging renewed. This time secretaries dressed in gray and armed with rifles accompanied the naked ones. Efforts by Costas's young men to stop the digging ended in their immediate death. Costas's forces started a military-scale operation, attacking the armed secretaries with Tasers and disarming 458 of them. Costas's soldiers pulled the cotton ear plugs from the secretaries' ears and brought them to the marina in the northwest where Illirio's pupils sang them two-voiced hymns. The captured secretaries dressed in gray immediately morphed into friendly creatures. This time, however, our people kept them there in the marina. The newly pacified secretaries displayed ravenous appetites for healthy food and began consuming huge quantities of vegetables. This in turn soon became a strategic problem, as the stock of fresh vegetables quickly dwindled. Costas's people were compelled to resort to serving them meals of grilled turtles, the diet that had created the secretaries' mad fervor in the first place.

Meanwhile, more and more squads of armed secretaries dressed in gray have been wandering around the island shooting down Costas's people. Dozens of young men have been killed. But then a large group of pearl catchers attacked the armed secretaries and overpowered them. Taking the initiative in combat and using the rifles that they had captured from the secretaries, the pearl catchers started killing more and more of them. Leonor's mothers intervened, once again biting our fighters' hands. Their effort to cling to the bodies of our fighters made them easy targets for the secretaries dressed in gray. Not wishing to harm any of the mothers, our fighters tried to push them away as gently as they could, but that only energized their adversaries. In the foolhardy process of imploring our youth to stop angering the Sages, forty-nine mothers died and their intervention not only caused the battle to continue much longer, but as a result seven pearl catchers were killed in enemy crossfire.

During the past ten days, our boys have captured at least seven hundred rifles with enough ammunition to last for several days of battles. I feel that the tide is slowly turning in our favor. At this moment it occurred to me that we had a very prosaic problem— not enough fish to feed our people. Amidst constant skirmishes Costas came in his blood-stained doctor's gown and asked me to sail out urgently to bring in some more fish, although he could not spare any assistants to help me with this task—every male was either shooting or bleeding. Costas himself gave orders from his hospital theater. My son has indeed turned into a warrior.

I went fishing for four days and when I returned I realized that Costas's people had freed a third of the island's territory from the secretaries' grasp. This area included the Hill and the marina. It turned out that 784 neutralized secretaries had been captured and forced to listen to the two-voiced chanting.

Thursday, December 22, 1977
Diary entry by Adélaïde Fourangier

Unusual calmness has descended on the island. For the first time since my arrival twenty-seven years ago, I was able to walk freely around the western part of the island. Not only that, I was warmly greeted by many people. I noticed a system of water pools being constructed to serve as a communal laundry. A large number of men and women were energetically washing children's clothes by hand and hanging the dazzlingly white laundry out to dry. All the children on the western side now wear clean clothes. I also saw that the island paths had been cleaned; there was no sign of any suspicious stuff lying on the ground. At long last Costas comes to me every night! He needs a long-deserved rest.

Thursday, December 30, 1977
Diary entry by Adélaïde Fourangier

Costas told me that twenty-nine fishermen with their families from the eastern part of the island came ashore with their catch and requested to be allowed to join our side. They were warmly welcomed.

Tuesday, January 31, 1978
Diary entry by Adélaïde Fourangier

The blessed tranquility continues. We reopened the music school; nineteen children of various ages have started coming to play piano again. Illirio teaches them his two-part chanting (he says with great musical sensitivity that this artistic solution happens to be the most effective strategy for disarming secretaries). Parents have started to build new clay houses with electricity, and fresh running water is now piped throughout this side of the island. Public toilets have been erected and are regularly sanitized. Finally everything is clean. Four parents who learned English in Saigon have started teaching the language in the schools.

Six days ago, another group of 129 fishermen with their families came to our shores and asked for asylum. They told the parents that secretaries on the eastern side of the island have been digging huge underground tunnels under western territory, preparing to carry the soil to the Hill under the protection of secretaries dressed in gray and armed with automatic rifles. Upon hearing this, Costas immediately ordered his people to construct new housing farther to the west and to move the people already living in endangered areas. The work started immediately.

Costas also gave orders to start intense combat training among our own people with the rifles that our side now possesses. Two days ago, 490 additional fishermen—again with their families—from the east came over to us, asking to join our side while at the same time providing more information on the war preparations taking place on the eastern side.

Leonor's camp is in a panic. She announced that she would lead a procession of mothers chanting hymns of repentance to the eastern side of the island. Beating themselves for their sins, the mothers would ask the Sages to accept their supplication as expiation for the sins of the western islanders. Costas convened a meeting at the now enlarged hospital and asked all representatives present for their opinions on Leonor's actions. Both Valeriano and Leocádia maintained that Leonor had no right to do this without the consent of the larger group. Eulálio held that Leonor's behavior and that of the mothers she led was so unpardonable that they should all be killed. Costas quickly countered that nobody on the island deserved to be killed, that a better life should be the destiny of every islander. But when hearing the hysterical groans of Leonor and her supporters, the opposition succumbed and agreed to permit her group to go to the Sages.

Thursday, February 9, 1978
Cassettes recorded by Jean-Luc Lefevbre

Leonor and fifty-eight other women participated in the women's campaign for clemency. Thirteen of them were killed by rifle fire just seven hundred meters inside eastern territory (the two territories are now divided by a newly erected guano fence). Most of the others were either wounded or were beaten to death by naked secretaries. Two wounded women crawled back to the western part of the island under cover of darkness and were brought to the hospital. Although they could not stop crying, they did not utter a word about what they had endured; their spirits were deeply confused and shattered. Luckily, their wounds were not fatal. Leonor herself died at the hands of the chastising secretaries and her pacifist mothers' movement died with her.

Friday, March 3, 1978
Cassettes recorded by Jean-Luc Lefevbre

At dawn on February 17, two thousand naked secretaries carrying buckets of soil crossed the new mid-island guano fence into the western section. They were accompanied by a thousand armed secretaries dressed in gray. After advancing three hundred meters into western territory, they encountered a double obstacle—two four-meter-high barriers of loosely woven rope (Illirio's invention!). As soon as they started climbing the rope barrier, western youth started pulling on the ropes, causing the secretaries to fall and the soil in their buckets to spill out.

The secretaries dressed in gray started shooting left and right but they too got stuck between the ropes. Thirty naked secretaries managed to avoid being caught in the rope barrier and they ran full speed with their buckets toward the Hill (without rifled protection). Some youth and fishermen assaulted them with Tasers and once they were immobilized, the youth pulled the cotton wool plugs out of secretaries' ears and started the double-voiced chanting. The naked secretaries calmed down and when they could move they ran back to the rope barrier with friendly smiles on their faces. Their brothers dressed in gray shot and killed them all. Then Costas ordered the secretaries dressed in gray to be shot, and they were all killed.

The following night Illirio and the young men mended the ropes and buried the dead secretaries. In addition, they dug a deep ditch alongside the rope barrier and covered it with a sand and tree branch camouflage. Illirio also persuaded Costas that a third line of defense behind the rope cordon needed to be built. His plan required that a large number of boats, all filled with combustible material capable of being ignited in a manner of seconds, be placed across the entire width of the island in order to deter a full-scale invasion.

It was Costas's job to persuade the fishermen to give up their boats for the defense of the freedom of the western part of the island. Gathering them on the northwestern coast, he solemnly promised the fishermen that their boats would be returned immediately upon the cessation of hostilities. Nobody believed him. Almost everyone considered it as a pretext to deprive them of their livelihood. As a result, 286 fishermen immediately sailed back to the eastern part of the island. However, 294 noble fishermen did hand over their boats to Costas's men. The remaining fishermen were asked to sail out for fish, bringing their vital catch to the runway area on the southwestern coast where the fish processing plants were located. In the end, 240 boats were carried onto land and filled with dry tree branches. This dry material would serve as tinder for the locally made alcohol that was placed in the narrow pipes purchased in the Philippines thanks to Illirio's foresight.

Many of Costas's young men lay in ambush waiting for the secretaries to attempt to breach the ropes again. However, at dawn two days later, all of them were shocked by a deafening roar never before heard on the island. Two armored troop carriers charged the rope line and easily broke through it. Both armed secretaries and naked secretaries with buckets full of soil followed. With mathematical precision, Costas's men ignited the alcohol in the pipes just seconds before the armored vehicles reached the line of boats. Both exploded upon contact with the wall of fire.

The naked secretaries who survived rushed to the Hill while the armed ones ran toward the houses of the western islanders, shooting indiscriminately. Costas ordered his men to fire on the attackers, but their resistance was strong. The battle raged until darkness when the western youth managed to drive the secretaries back to the guano fence that now divides the western and eastern parts of the island. The western side suffered fifty-nine casualties. Several hundred secretaries were killed. Costas's youth collected the rifles from the killed easterners, burying their bodies on the northern coast near the new guano fence. The naked secretaries returning from the Hill were captured. Upon hearing the two-voiced hymns, they asked to remain on the western side. They were placed in captivity in the marina area, but they were not treated as combatants. Upon examining the burnt-out frames of the armored vehicles, Costas's men found the following inscription inside: "To our beloved brethren in the homeland, from your proud expatriates in America." Currently all is quiet on the island.

Monday, March 6, 1978
RADIOGRAMME from Marius Villeneuve
À Madame Adélaïde Fourangier, Asie du Sud-Est

We have not received a report of your teaching accomplishments and look forward to receiving it soon. We also look forward to learning about the results of the piano competition to identify the best performer of Bach's *Preludes and Fugues*. We also recommend teaching your advanced students compositions by Jeanne Demessieux (1921–1968), especially her unpublished piano compositions that we now actively promote. We advise acquiring copies of these excellent pieces.

Friday, March 10, 1978
Diary entry by Adélaïde Fourangier

Jean-Luc is seriously ill. Tormented by high fever, constant shaking, and swollen joints, he can hardly move his arms and legs or even speak. Costas took him to the hospital and is treating him with antibiotics. Illirio brought some children over and they sang French folksongs for him—the old man was deeply moved. Now, lying in bed, unshaven, he does look old and frail. He says he is eighty. We never asked him when his birthday was. Now when I asked, he just smiled and answered that all his birthdays had passed and he was now living in open time. It was meant, I suppose, as a wise joke.

Friday, March 24, 1978
Diary entry by Adélaïde Fourangier

Jean-Luc is better now after his antibiotic treatment, but he still remains very weak. Costas sent two electricians—the experienced Goncalvo and the young and strong Zeferino—to Jean-Luc's meteorological station to assist him in operating the Pettersson and the radio receivers and to work the vegetable and fruit gardens.

Wednesday, April 12, 1978
Diary entry by Adélaïde Fourangier

Yesterday I was witness to an extraordinary event: the approach of a flotilla consisting of four fishing boats, two large, motorized lifeboats, and eight smaller boats. The last contained armed secretaries dressed in gray, their guns pointed directly at the beach. The fishing boats landed first and the unarmed fishermen submitted themselves to a search by our coastal patrol. They delivered the message that two Sages were aboard the lifeboats and they wished to meet with Costas.

When Costas arrived at the scene, he told the messengers that all the armed secretaries had to come ashore and be disarmed. They complied. Then Costas demanded that if the Sages wanted to discuss the fate of the island, they too had to step ashore. Immediately twelve secretaries in snow-white robes carried two palanquins from the lifeboats onto the shore. The blind Sages sitting motionlessly on their thrones were dressed in silken robes that were even more glaringly white. As Costas approached them, everyone else withdrew so that they could converse in private. After the discussions, the Sages were conveyed to their lifeboats; the secretaries who had been stripped of their arms joined them and the flotilla sailed away.

Toward evening on the same day, I assisted Jean-Luc in returning to the hospital. He was so frail that he could hardly move and his fever had returned. Youngsters placed him gingerly in a wheelbarrow and ran him to the hospital. Goncalvo and Zeferino now remain permanently at Jean-Luc's residence.

Thursday, April 13, 1978
Cassettes recorded by Jean-Luc Lefevbre

I am glad to still be able to record the summary of the meeting that took place late at night on April 12. I took the Dictaphone to the hospital and put in batteries to allow me to make several short recordings (although the best way to make such recordings is on equipment that runs on electric power, which I have at home). I was strong enough to be able to get up and join the participants. For my convenience it took place in the room next to the place where I am receiving medical treatment at the hospital.

Costas relayed the suggestion of Sage no. 1 (passed to him by Sages no. 2 and no. 4 with whom he recently met), which was to call elections so that his candidature for the position of "island holder" could be put to a public vote. In the event that Costas receives a majority of the vote, the Sages would appoint him to the position. In this capacity he could improve conditions on the island for everyone, but his power would be subject to the following limitations:

His directives must be approved by the Sages.

There must be two annual sailings to Hainan, three annual week-long festivals of digging and building the Hill, and four annual week-long festivals of putting human feces in drinking water ("consecration of drinking water").

Secretaries must have immunity from prosecution.

Education must remain solely in the hands of the secretaries.

Schools must only use the curriculum sanctioned by the Sages.

Armed secretaries must be allowed to protect the waters of the western wells.

Two-voiced singing must be forbidden.

The Sages demanded that a response be delivered within four days to the four deaf, naked secretaries whom they had left on the western side for that purpose.

The discussion went on for hours until finally at one o'clock in the morning when still nothing had been resolved, Costas urged his people to get some sleep. Discussions would resume in the evening. I think he did so in order to give me some rest....

Saturday, April 15, 1978
Cassettes recorded by Goncalvo

At the end of last night's meeting (held April 14, the second meeting in three days), Grandpa Jean-Luc once again fell ill with rheumatic fever. Our leader Costas Tegularius and our colleague Illirio Mariafels stayed with him in the hospital all night long. Zeferino and I intend to remain at the meteorological station to operate it together. Several hours before the discussion in the wider forum that was scheduled to take place that evening, Grandpa Jean-Luc, Costas Tegularius, and Illirio Mariafels had a lengthy private discussion regarding the Sages' proposal. I was called in to massage Jean-Luc's feet and to bring him tea as well as the André Petit cognac that he had stored in his cellar. Here is the account of the exchange that I recorded at Grandpa Jean-Luc's request. (Grandpa Jean-Luc has asked me to keep recording the history of the island on his Dictaphone. I am honored to do so.)

The Sages left behind four totally deaf (apparently their ear drums had been pierced), unarmed secretaries to wait for

Tegularius's written yes-or-no answer that was to be delivered by midday three days later. Grandpa Jean-Luc opined that the Sages were once again showing that they had no heart, but it was not his place to advice Tegularius and Mariafels. Tegularius said that the idea of being elected to the position of "island holder" based on popular majority should not be rejected out of hand. Mariafels said that in reality, this proposition was an act of demagogy (a word he had learned from his adopted mother Adèle), for in fact the Sages were exploiting western democratic processes in order to coopt Tegularius's popularity and make him their slave.

Agreeing, Tegularius said that nevertheless it was important to avoid all-out war because for more than half of the people on the island, the Sages were sacred symbols who epitomized the meaning of life. It was all that they knew. He thought that there was no way that he could supplant the people's mystical yearnings with his own broader, humanist outlook without first educating them and obtaining their acceptance. If the process of solidifying the island behind him by improving the quality of life on the island could be initiated by means of an election, what would be so wrong with that?

Grandpa Jean-Luc said in his sad voice that it was erroneous to believe that the Sages would allow his administration to be independent. Upon uttering these words, he closed his eyes and Tegularius and Mariafels assumed that he was thinking quietly. Mariafels said that in his view the Sages would attack the western part of the island regardless of any detente between the two sides and that they should use the time judiciously to prepare the defenses along the entire width of the separation line with their newly acquired rifles. In his view, the attack could start the moment the deadline passed.

While Tegularius agreed in principle that there would be an attack, he speculated that no pitched battle would occur immediately since the easterners, having suffered heavy loss of military equipment (not to mention loss of life), had to be resupplied. They needed the ammunition donated by our Des Moines brethren and that would take several weeks to arrive. Therefore, a powerful attack could not occur until then. The two men concurred that an immediate defense system across the entire width of the island should be organized. It was then that they realized that Jean-Luc had suffered a heart attack.

Sunday, April 16, 1978
Diary entry by Adélaïde Fourangier

Papa has had a heart attack. He gives me so much, this dear man. He understands music no less than Costas. And he loves us so much. What a true and noble man! With his quiet goodness he spreads care and humane love on this mad island. Just by his presence, his benevolence, his friendliness, his readiness to help, he has saved so many people. His fair-mindedness dissolves hatred, this saintly man. What will become of us without him? Please live, dear Papa.

Monday, April 17, 1978
Cassettes recorded by Goncalvo

The final discussions in the wider council included Tegularius, Mariafels, Eulálio, Leocádia, and Valeriano, all of whom had voting power, and several parents were present, as were nonvoting debaters. The majority tended to favor giving the Sages a negative answer, since they felt strong enough to repel any military onslaught coming from the east. Mariafels, who presented this point of view, opined that the Sages would eventually have to delegate much of their power to the elected leader of the island (presumably Tegularius, but whomever that might be). Acceding to their current demands would not only make that elected leader impotent, but the pretense of elections would precipitate an even greater bloodbath when the people realized that they had been duped and were still living under the Sages' malevolent control. The meeting dispersed in a calm, workmanlike atmosphere, and the four deaf secretaries were sent back to the eastern side with a note composed of a single word: "NO."

Tuesday, April 18, 1978
Copy of RADIOGRAMME sent to Marius Villenouve

Cher monsieur,

Thank you for your keen interest in my work. Currently I teach piano to nineteen students, ages six to eighteen. For the past seven years (since 1971), at least five or six students have finished a nine-year-long course of piano studies. For their final examinations, they usually play four or five pieces that include a Beethoven piano sonata in its entirety and two technically demanding studies—one by Moscheles and the other by Chopin. Additionally, they play some contemporary music, specifically pieces from Bartok's *Microcosmos.* The most frequently performed composition is *Six Dances in a Bulgarian Rhythm.*

With regard to a piano competition for the best performance of a prelude and fugue from Bach's *Well-Tempered Clavier,* I assure you that I will definitely arrange for such a competition as soon as my students have prepared six preludes and fugues from the *Well-Tempered Clavier.* I would also love to receive copies of the scores of the compositions by the late Jeanne Demessieux, whom you mentioned in your last communiqué. I knew her personally and greatly admire her talent and her brilliant organ works. It is so sad that Jeanne has left us so early. If you could mail me this sheet music at your earliest convenience, I would greatly appreciate it.

Sincèrement,

Adélaïde Fourangier
Asie du Sud-Est

Tuesday, May 2, 1978
RADIOGRAMME from Marius Villeneuve
À Madame Adélaïde Fourangier, Asie du Sud-Est

Please inform us what the repertoire of your sixth and ninth graders is.

Also please name the pieces that are obligatory and those that are elective. Please inform us what musical styles and epochs are represented in your school year repertoire.

May 2, 1978
Diary entry by Adélaïde Fourangier

This situation is absurd—pupils rarely appear for more than a few weeks of consecutive study. My first piano is all but dead. It has no strings, pedals, or keys—I have used them as spare parts for the second piano. And besides, Costas took some of the strings so he could mend two of his generators. This damned island…. If I could vomit, I would.

A week ago I thought another war was about to start—they say there was an island-wide attack by the easterners, but it failed because they could not break through our lines. Having said "our" lines, I must acknowledge how emotionally corrupt I have already become. Costas and Illirio took Jean-Luc's boat and sailed to the Philippines. But instead of bringing me a new piano, they intend to bring back machine guns, hawsers, medicine, and more electrical equipment. Who knows what else will they bring? How can that small Pettersson carry so much cargo? Poor idealists, they think they will win this war.

Jean-Luc, our poor, dear papa, is dying. With Goncalvo and Zeferino tending to him night and day, he lies in bed, essentially a lonely Don Quixote—the only one on this island who knew the difference between Hummel and Moscheles and could appreciate them both "in spite of Beethoven," as he used to say. And he was so good to Costas—Costas only became a great man thanks to Papa's solicitations. I think of him now as my parent too—from him I learned what it means to be a beloved daughter. And from him I started to be able to love and give of myself selflessly, as he always did. As a pianist, how I loved to observe his hand movements—unhurried, always precise, even up to recently when his hands started to tremble. Papa, god's gift to me and all Pinto Island.

He almost never opens his eyes now. What will become of us??

May 8, 1978
Diary entry by Adélaïde Fourangier

Costas returned alone—leaving Illirio in the Philippians to make more purchases. I cannot understand how Illirio intends to come back. By some other boat or will someone from the Philippines bring him? Costas did not say. The great secret-keeper, you know. But he did come in bragging how he managed to bring four cows and much seed for our agriculture—"Children will at last have some milk! And, ah, we even brought back toothpaste!"—as well as powerful artillery and two motorbikes. He was angry that I did not answer Marius Villeneuve's radiogramme concerning the program of studies at the music school. He said my silence would cause them to cut me out of their system. So to please him I went to Goncalvo and improvised a "professional" answer that had no connection whatsoever to reality. As I am completely unaware of the new pedagogy being promoted over there in Paris with so much enthusiasm, how could I write any report that would seem adequate? This is what I sent:

Sixth grade:

MASSENET—*Melodie* Op. 10, No. 5
CHOPIN—*Mazurka in G Minor*, Op. 67, No. 2
IBERT—*A Giddy Girl*
LINN—"Les ombres de lune sur la montagne" from *Les Petites Impressions*
Obligatory: MOZART—the allegro from Sonatina 6 in C from the *Six Viennese Sonatinas*
Obligatory: BACH, J.S.—*Prelude in D minor*, BWV 935
scales in four octaves played in regular as well as in contrary motion, with one hand playing up the scale while the other hand plays downward

Ninth grade:

BACH, J.S.—*Italian Concerto*, first or third movement (Urtext)
SHOSTAKOVICH—*Prelude and Fugue in C*, Op. 87, No. 1
BARTOK—first movement from *Suite*, Op. 14 (Universal Edition)

BEETHOVEN—first movement from *Sonata in F minor*, Op. 2, No. 1 (Urtext)

HAYDN—first movement from *Sonata in B-flat major*, Hob. XVI/41 (Peters Vol. 3)

MOZART—first movement from *Sonata in C*, K309 (Urtext)

MOZART—first movement from *Sonata in B-flat*

POULENC—Novelette No. 3 in E minor from *Three Novelettes*

DE SEVERAC—Peppermint Gel from *French Romantic Repertoire Book #2*

Obligatory: HANDEL—*Air con Variazioni (Air and five variations)* from Suite No. 5 in E (Peters)

Obligatory: BEETHOVEN—first movement from *Sonata in E*, Op. 14, No. 1 (Urtext)

While there, I went to Jean-Luc's room to sit with him a bit. Taking my hand in his, he remained calm, voiceless. Then he spoke:

"When I die, please cremate my body and preserve my ashes so that when you return to France, you can give the urn to the people of the village on the coast of northern France where I was born, Bénouville Seine-Maritime. I would like my ashes to be interred there.

"You know, I haven't been to France since 1929, the year I was sent to Saigon and later to this island to build the meteorological station. When I first came here I thought that in a few of years I would surely return to my native village on the shores of La Manche...but life turned out otherwise.

"I still remember the last battles of the Great War (the one that is now called the First World War). I participated in the Battle of Soissons and from then on in continuous skirmishes until the final day of the war. I still remember at the time of the truce, the eleventh hour of November 11, 1918, that I felt like I had gulped the full dose of glory designated for my life, and from then on I had to devote myself to something tender and full of love. I liked technology so I remained in the military to study engineering at Saint-Cyr, the military academy; later on I studied meteorology there. As one of the first military meteorologists in France, I was sent to Saigon. M. Pierre Pasquier, our *gouverneur-général de l'Indochine française*, sent me to this island to scan not only the weather, but also the movements of various unfriendly countries' military vessels.

"I met Costas on the very first day I stepped onto the soil of this island. An unusually curly, sandy-haired boy, he was standing alone on the shoreline, holding out his hand and giving me a disarmingly trusting glance. I approached and lifted him up. He smiled. He must have been no more than seven years old, I think. I never had a child, you know. I left my parents' house at the age of seventeen, and only saw them twice after that, the last time a day before I left France. I always missed the warmth of home and longed for a simple girl's love so that I could establish such a home myself; a warm nest, you know. But I never met the right girl. Instead I found only neurotic prostitutes. Somewhere along the way, I lost hope. And then here was this boy...they called him Costas. I did not speak any Portuguese; however, one of our Frenchman did and he communicated with the locals for us. All of them behaved so strangely and were covered with flies and were very malodorous. Very soon I saw how many natives died due to lack of basic hygiene. Later I discovered that this filth was imposed on them by their religious ideology. I decided to save Costas and took him to our compound. We discovered a fresh water source near the western promontory and built our installations around it in order to protect it from the locals who threw feces into their own water wells.

"Costas became my son, Koty. All of us taught him French, mathematics, a bit of English, and world history. In 1937 I brought him to Saigon to study at Lycée Chasseloup-Laubat, an excellent French high school there. Costas also studied electrical engineering at a local plant there. He was highly adept at mending the cars owned by French administrators. The people there all loved him so much and urged him to enlist in the French army so that he could automatically become a French citizen. But Costas dreamed of saving this island from its plague of early death, filth, miserable narrow-mindedness, and helplessness. When he returned from that foolish journey to Hainan when he was only sixteen, he confided to me with all possible passion: "Papa, our people live in darkness! Their souls are blinded! They are slaves to colossal folly! I must free them!" Can you imagine such depth of spirit coming from such a young man?

"I convinced him to study medicine so he could pursue his dream of saving lives. So Costas returned to Saigon for more study. M. Pignon (our *gouverneur-général* at that time) noticed how gifted he was and advised that he pursue further study in Paris. By that time we had sent already at least four hundred islanders to study in Saigon, but nobody excelled like Costas.

"How I missed him when he was in Saigon and later in Paris! I consoled myself by sailing on my new boat, the Pettersson. I bought it off an old Swede who came here to buy pearls to satisfy his old wife and his three daughters. Well, he got his pearls all right, and I got mine. It was right after your last concert in Saigon. The boat, though in good shape, was not suitable for long voyages on the open sea. I had to strengthen it with iron crossbeams. I also installed an especially huge gas tank and added several cylinders to the engine. You know, it became a powerful ship....

"I was so happy to hear Koty's impressions of your concerts in Saigon, Adèle. You know, three of us—there were four meteorologists on the island—listened to your last concert in Saigon in 1949. It was such a bright, refreshing interlude for us; what brilliant, churning music. I'm so glad the two of you got together.

"Indeed Costas has changed the quality of life on Pinto Island. Fewer people die from filth and epidemics. I am sorry that his work is not finished yet. Bad forces on the other side of the island work to undermine him and they receive much assistance from members of their tribe in America, causing great pain to my dear Costas. My hope is that the wonderful Illirio will help him. Are you and Koty Illirio's true parents, Adèle? Do not answer, if you do not wish to. It is such a tragedy that in addition to his arm, Illirio has lost both his beloved Nissa and Alfi. The unbearable pain in my soul that I feel for him causes me to want to die sooner.

"Now I am tired. My strength leaves me. Adèle, please help Costas as much as you can. I still remember his palm on my cheek when I lifted him up on the beach that first time. An angel's touch…. Please bring my ashes back to my village….

May 16, 1978
Diary entry by Adélaïde Fourangier

Jean-Luc is dead.

May 22, 1978
RADIOGRAMME from Marius Villeneuve
À Madame Adélaïde Fourangier, Asie du Sud-Est

The council of senior music professors has approved your repertoire of selections for the sixth- and the ninth grades with one further suggestion: you are recommended to teach the sixth grade any three pieces from *Les Pieces de Clavecin* (Livre Premier, 1670) by Jacques Champion de Chambonnière. Next year you will receive a similar questionnaire from us. If the council obtains a positive impression of your instructional capabilities, we shall start the process of inviting you back to Paris to give open master classes.

PART FOUR: THE WARS

Thursday, August 3, 1978
Cassettes recorded by Goncalvo

In late May our people on the western side, especially those living near the border created by the guano fence, heard strange noises coming from underground that lasted for three days and nights. The alarm in our camp caused Tegularius to convene an emergency meeting of his advisors. He feared that the Sages were preparing some sort of onslaught of the western side of the island. The technically brilliant Mariafels suspected that the Sages had acquired drilling equipment that could bore diagonally underneath our soil to collect sand for the Hill while at the same time inflicting enormous damage on western territory. The council did not know what to do, especially since no one had firsthand information about what was actually going on.

Four days later, a large area of western land collapsed into a huge pit. Hundreds of people were buried alive. Access to the forest and the southeast shore where most of the pearls are collected was obstructed and required massive restoration work. But first every effort had to be made to save the lives of those buried beneath the sand. For three frantic days people dug into the rubble with whatever tools they had at their disposal in the attempt to rescue friends and loved ones. Fortunately, the lives of twenty-nine men, forty-eight women, and fifty children were saved. Still, the number of deaths approached five hundred. Tegularius convened the council again to devise an appropriate response to the Sages' murderous acts. Two plans of action were discussed:

1) An all-out attack on the Sages' compound to kill them and their fighters

2) An occupation of all eastern territory and the capture of all military hardware stored outside the Sages' compound

Tegularius rejected the first idea, claiming that killing the Sages would vilify the western camp in the eyes of all those who still revered those four madmen as sacred embodiments of the meaning of life. Hence the council decided to implement the second plan. Tegularius ordered the attack five days later. Three-quarters of all adults on the western side participated in it.

There were two main lines of attack—a frontal one along the width of the guano separation line between east and west, an offensive that was met with severe counter fire. Many of our people died on the first day. But the attack—bloody as it was— allowed our youth to carry long ropes through wide sections of the front, thus preventing any serious counterattack. On the same day toward evening, another force infiltrated the eastern part of the island through the defensive ditch that had been dug on the western side of the guano fence. On the eastern side, the entrance to the ditch was covered with huge piles of earth deposited there by the Sages' excavators. None of the eastern strategists imagined that our people would bother to clean up their debris and enter eastern territory through that opening. Consequently, that area was not defended. Our invading forces easily penetrated it and then divided into two: one group rushed the living easterners' quarters while the other, larger force attacked the eastern line of defense along the guano fence from behind.

Heavy fighting continued for two more days with sporadic skirmishes occurring over the next two weeks. Our forces succeeded in liberating the entire eastern part of the island— except for the Sages' compound! In the operation, 2,500 youths and parents on our side were killed. The easterners suffered even greater losses totaling at least five thousand. Our forces captured all the weapons and ammunition on the defeated side. Most of the eastern part of the island was destroyed.

The day before yesterday the gates of the Sages' compound opened and four secretaries dressed in gray appeared. They were clearly deaf, as they did not react to the double-voiced singing of the teenagers we sent out to meet them; we also noticed that there were no Iowa cotton ear plugs in their ears. They held up a huge white placard that read "TEGULARIUS, THE SAGES ARE WAITING FOR YOU." Yesterday Tegularius entered the compound accompanied by Eulalio, Leocadia, and Valeriano. Tegularius left Mariafels in charge in the west.

Wednesday, August 9, 1978
Diary entry by Adélaïde Fourangier

I have never seen Costas so emaciated, so tired, so sad. Although they have just celebrated an enormous victory, he's almost on the brink of despair. He along with Illirio, Eulalio, Leocadia, and Valeriano met in Jean-Luc's old house for a private council. He asked me to join them.

"The Sages once again suggest holding elections and if I get enough support they are ready to allow me to run the island with almost full power in my hands," Costas reported. "So let us analyze their position: they want their compound to be out of our control and they insist on arranging two annual festivals of Hill building and two annual festivals of 'unification of body and soul' that entail putting feces in the drinking water. They have agreed to turn voyages to Hainan into a triannual event. They demand the authority to approve all school textbooks on national identity. Everything else is in our hands."

Eulalio's immediate response was, "We need to kill those Sages before they kill us."

Leocadia said, "We do not know what forces they keep in their compound. The fact that they had highly mechanized bulldozers that could dig under our territory and bring death to so many indicates they have a strong supply source, probably those mad Pintoists in Des Moines."

Valeriano said, "We need to capture their supply sources, otherwise we are doomed."

Costas agreed, with Illirio seconding him. "We cannot keep on fighting indefinitely. Our losses are huge and our dream of liberating our people turns into a pyrrhic triumph of freedom through death."

Leocadia asked a practical question: "Do we have any estimates of how many armed people are hiding in the Sages' compound and how long they can survive there?"

Costas: "According to stories told by captured secretaries, there are more than a thousand well-armed men with heavy weaponry. They have a continuous supply of fresh food from the Philippines and an adequate reservoir of drinking water stored in containers. The live like vacationing lords in Switzerland." He asked Illirio, who then held the position of chief of staff, "How many men do we need to take the compound?"

"No less than 2,500, if your estimate is right," Illirio surmised.

Costas: "Do we have enough ammunition and food?"

Illirio: "We have enough for another two weeks of fighting and that's it."

Valeriano added, "How is it that we are so victorious in battle and yet so pessimistic in our prognosis for the future?"

Leocadia: "Because in reality we are not victorious. The true outcome of the fight between us and the Sages is a standoff. We cannot eliminate them and they cannot eliminate us. Currently we are at the outer guano fence surrounding their compound, but after some rest and refreshment, they will certainly be able to mount a counterattack and possibly succeed in overpowering us."

Valeriano: "Then why allow them to rest and refresh themselves?"

Illirio: "If we attack the compound, we will suffer huge losses. We would be called forces of evil by Sage supporters in both the east and west and they would undoubtedly resort to guerrilla warfare, killing many innocent women and children."

Eulalio: "So you ask us to sit on our hands and wait while they prepare for another attack?"

Valeriano: "Once again, our aim should be to disrupt their resupply from Des Moines."

Leocadia: "How?"

Illirio: "We could send armed fishermen to block their port."

Costas: "That sounds good. But such an operation would only have a temporary effect as our brethren in Des Moines will surely send bigger, heavily armed boats."

Eulalio: "We have no choice. We have to kill the Sages, otherwise they will annihilate us."

Leocadia: "We still have a little time to explore a less brutal course."

Costas: "If we get our hands on the next supply from Des Moines, it may give us the leverage needed to reach an agreement about sharing power with the Sages. If we accept the idea of elections with their support, we could get international recognition for Pinto Island. That would allow us to establish our own independent supply sources. With international recognition, we could also travel to Des Moines and work to change the Pintoist attitude toward our movement. I am sure that ultimately they will support our endeavor. After all, we are fighting for a lifestyle that is just like theirs and they always claim that they are devoted to our betterment."

Leocadia: "We have more armed fishermen than the Sages do, so if they send men to protect their supply lines we could overpower them."

Illirio: "How many supply convoys from Des Moines are expected in the next two months?"

Valeriano: "Usually two Arun-class boats come every three weeks. They stay for a day and then sail back. One boat, a powerful Nordhavn that apparently brings fuel, stays here longer. I think the next Arun-class boats will arrive in two weeks."

Illirio: "Then I propose that we prepare a special operation to divert the Sages' supply boats to our harbor. We could send a few fishermen to intercept the arriving vessels. Our youth could hook the bottoms of their ships with ropes and then we could tow them here."

Costas: "Let's not forget that your crazy ideas about restraining boats with ropes almost got you killed once."

Illirio, insulted by the reminder: "So what do *you* propose? Sending 240 armed fishermen to combat the much faster Arun-class boats that may have armed guards aboard? We stand to lose most of our good men and may still not bring the boats to our harbor."

Costas: "OK, prepare the operation, and let's get ready for more fighting. I hope the Sages will be more pliant once we disrupt their life support. And if our brethren in Iowa arrange for armed convoys, that will already be another chapter in our history. It seems best to negotiate with the Sages while their supplies are in our hands."

Eulalio: "I like this idea."

I returned to my abode in a state of bewilderment; these people are so determined! Having just lost hundreds, no, thousands of dear friends and relatives, they still go forth with hope in their hearts. How I wish I could share their optimism. Still, I cannot brush them off entirely either.

Wednesday, August 30, 1978
Cassettes recorded by Goncalvo

Amazing! Ten days ago our decoy, a lonely fisherman out at sea, sent a short, sun-refracted beam to our people, informing them of the approach of the incoming Arun-class boats. Immediately three boats from the southeastern promontory of the island rushed out to meet them, pulling along with them submerged ropes drawn from the west. Only later did we figure out that Illirio had built concrete columns under the surface of the water with huge reels thirty meters from shore across from the harbor next to Grandpa Jean-Luc's runway. It appears that he had constructed this apparatus over the course of the past few months, even before the plan of towing the Des Moines supply boats came up. Mariafels says that he used all the reserves of concrete that our departed Jean-Luc had amassed on the island. The underwater reels enabled concealment of the ropes when our people started pulling the captured boats to our shores, thus preventing the sailors from realizing in the decisive moments of the operation exactly how they had been trapped.

Our people swam to the boats with the heavy ropes tied to their waists. At a distance of three hundred meters from the approaching boats, they dove underwater and surreptitiously fastened the ropes to the rudders of each of the Arun-class boats and then quickly swam out into the open sea. In a moment two groups of twenty strong men standing on the shore near Grandpa Jean-Luc's runway started pulling the ropes with all their might. The sailors on both boats started shooting in all directions, but to no avail; they were dragged to our harbor. Luckily they did not see any connection between what was happening to them and the lonely fisherman in his small boat.

Mariafels sent two hundred armed fishermen into the water to overpower the crews of the boats. In half an hour our people had disarmed the seventeen-man crews on each boat and towed their vessels ashore. Taking command of the loudspeakers on the bridges of the beached boats, our men announced, "You are here with the Free Islanders." The appearance of the Des Moines sailors on our shore made a phenomenally uplifting impression on all of us; all of them had diamond-shaped eyes just like ours. They were our true brethren. We did not feel any animosity toward them. They were dressed in gray sweat suits printed with images of flies clinging to a naked human body on the front. They spoke Portuguese with an American accent. They often fumbled in finding the necessary words with which to express themselves because among themselves they spoke only English. Our people embraced them and immediately brought our children to sing our lovely two-voiced chants for them. What a stunning impression it produced! All of the Des Moines sailors wept, and kept trying to kiss the hands of our people. Some of them asked to remain on the island; the others excitedly admitted that it was the most glorious moment of their lives.

Our people examined the Arun-class boats' cargo. They found some artillery and two disassembled military helicopters complete with bombs. They also found a lot of dazzlingly white linen, three washing machines, boxes of disinfectant detergent, and plenty of canned beef and vegetables. There were many containers of bottled drinking water, and also forty-four crates of French wine.

Tegularius asked the Des Moines sailors whether they would like to remain with us on the island. With deep emotional gratitude they all agreed. Tegularius, Eulalio, Mariafels, Leocadia, and Valeriano had a long meeting with our guests and asked that only eight of them remain with us so that the rest could travel back to Des Moines to inform our brethren there about our true aims. We asked them to convey our urgent request that the Des Moines community send us their support as well, joking with the departing crew that they could skip the French wine. Our guests informed us that there were thirty-four people from Des Moines stationed in the Sages' compound around the clock. They usually stayed for an eight-week shift and then were relieved by another similar group. They also informed us that the Sages already had five battle-ready military bomber helicopters; each thirty-four-person shift included five pilots ready to execute military orders given by Sage no. 1, with sincere bows of agreement on the part of the other three.

In order not to provoke any conflict with our brethren in Des Moines, we sent both Arun-class boats back to their station on the Philippines; eight members of the crew remained with us. Two of them were helicopter pilots. Tegularius asked the rest of the Pintoists to show us how to milk our new dairy cows. All of the men asked to listen to our two-voiced chant every morning. We happily complied.

Saturday, July 29, 1978
Editorial from *OUR BELOVED ISLAND POST OF PINTOVILLE*

In recent years our brethren on our beloved Pinto Island have been severely challenged by a series of moral disruptions emanating from nearby communists in China and Vietnam. These enemies send predators to our motherland to poison the hearts of our beloved brethren. Our noble Sages valiantly struggle to protect the purity our nation from external contamination. Since the communists are infernally resourceful, they pose a mortal threat to our Sages and our nation. We, the proud Pintoville diaspora, are called upon to redouble our efforts to help our beloved peace-minded Sages to ward off this external threat. Military ordnance, especially tanks and helicopter bombers and long-term food supplies, must be provided. Our noble-hearted representatives in the Philippines act day and night to deliver these vital supplies. Our national Pinto bank account is open for your generous contributions. Those who refrain from making such contributions will no longer be held in high esteem by our community.

Saturday, August 12, 1978
Editorial from *OUR BELOVED ISLAND POST OF PINTOVILLE*

We publish the following excerpt from an article by Prof. Ilvars Siliš of the Institute of Advanced Policy Research at the Department of Political Science and Government, Ashford University, Iowa, originally published in *Far East Policy Review* (Vol. 76, No. 3, Summer 1978):

> Information on the politically interesting Pinto Island is very scarce and comes primarily from one source—the spiritual leaders of the Pinto nation, the so-called Sages. From an academic point of view, it is difficult to ascertain whether this information is accurate enough to obtain a clear picture of the situation there. It is difficult to fathom how the Chinese and the Vietnamese communists act jointly to subvert the rule of Pinto Island if they continually fight each other in all other locales in Southeast Asia. Such unique collaboration between them regarding Pinto Island should indicate a common inspirational source, and this source must clearly be centered

on the island itself or in close vicinity to it. Nevertheless, questions with regard to what happens on this island are more numerous than answers. It should be very interesting to follow developments there with utmost attention.

Editorial response to Prof. Ilvars Siliš's:

> We are sure that the information we possess on events occurring on Pinto Island is accurate even to the smallest detail. We have no doubt that our Sages keep us fully informed. Prof. Silinš's article only shows how difficult it is to maintain a clear-sighted vision of the truth when the air is poisoned by dissenting views. We therefore encourage all members of our community to redouble their effort to help our brethren on Pinto Island.

Friday, September 8, 1978
Diary entry by Adélaïde Fourangier

Complete calm has settled over the island; music classes have resumed. The eight new guests have asked me to perform Beethoven for them. I will gladly do so after I have practiced the pieces that they want to hear. These strange people have told me all that has happened in the world since I left France— like the fact that American astronauts walked on the moon nine years ago. I feel that I am slowly waking from a long coma—it's a strange feeling of resurrection. What will be the fate of this filthy island? I am afraid to allow myself to imagine. Costas went to meet the Sages. His position is stronger now, but how long will this remain the case?

Wednesday, October 4, 1978
Western Island Bulletin

We are pleased to resume publication of our newsletter. Last week our representatives Costas Tegularius, Leocadia, Valeriano, Eulalio, and Illirio Mariafels reached an agreement with the Sages to turn our glorious unified island into a political republic. The Sages offered to hold elections for the office of chief executive for which Tegularius will run unopposed. A simple majority of affirmative votes will suffice to confirm him to the post. If he does not get a majority, absolute power will remain in the hands of the Sages. The chief executive will have authority in the following spheres:

1) economy, introduction of a currency and banking system
2) food production, construction, infrastructure, sewage, energy
3) international relations, transportation
4) sanitation, with the exception of two annual five-day feces rites that will be performed by secretaries in the Sages' compound
5) educational curriculum with the exception of sacred chanting and discussion of the Sages' teachings

In addition:

1) People will be free to study abroad and learn foreign languages.
2) Free communication technology will be made available to all.
3) The administration of the chief executive is required to maintain the welfare of the Sages' compound in accordance with contracted agreements between said chief executive and the Sages in annual personal communications between them.
4) One supply boat from the Des Moines colony via the Philippines will be sent to the administration of the chief executive fortnightly.

The following was promised to the Sages:

1) the inviolability of the territory of their compound
2) the untouchability of one fortnightly cargo sent to the Sages with the right of inspection (not rejection or confiscation) of its contents by the chief executive's staff
3) the chief executive's public endorsement of the elevation of the Hill in return for cessation of the ritual journeys to Hainan
4) provision of homes for at least 1,450 secretaries in the free zone (outside the compound) who are free to procreate and bequeath their positions to their offspring; the Chief Executive's administration is required to feed these secretaries and their offspring and to provide necessary education for their future public roles
5) free circulation of the Sages' bulletins and dissemination of the Sages' teachings throughout the island

In addition:

1) Two-voiced chanting will be restricted to the area surrounding Senhora Fourangier's (Senhora Boulger's) residence, without specifically delineating the limits of the area.
2) The ritual necessity of low-ranking secretaries patrolling the island naked and covered with feces (with the exception of the abovementioned two annual five-day festivities) will be suspended.

This arrangement was accepted after receiving 60% of the votes of Costas Tegularius's council. Costas Tegularius emphasized that it was in the interest of all freedom-loving inhabitants of the island to support it, however imperfect, as it provided an opportunity to fundamentally improve everyone's lives within a short period of time. Eulalio and Leocadia nevertheless voted against it.

Monday, October 9, 1978
Diary entry by Adélaïde Fourangier

I have never seen such a thing in all my life: At midnight
Illirio gathered all the children and young adults whom he
had instructed in his art of two-part singing and they sang
his wonderful chants. It seemed to me that the sky itself—
and perhaps even the entire galaxy beyond—embraced and
welcomed this joyous sound! By torchlight I noticed how deeply
moved our new citizens from Des Moines were. I have to admit
that I was excited too.

Friday, November 30, 1978
Cassettes recorded by Goncalvo

We are living our happiest hours. Long live Costas! The elections
were held ten days ago—all islanders (with the exception of the
dwellers of the Sages' compound) cast their paper ballots into
clay urns. Valeriano, Leocadia, and two secretaries dressed in
gray supervised the ballot counting.

Costas won with 67.8% of votes! A nice majority.

Several days before the elections, our people established direct
radio contact with our brethren in Des Moines and after several
awkward initial conversations a wonderful dialogue ensued. The
Pintoist community just announced Costas's electoral victory
and we overheard the joyous applause from the other side of the
globe. It seems that all planet Earth is waiting for us to present
ourselves!

Friday, January 19, 1979
Western Island Bulletin

Our Chief Executive Costas Tegularius calls for the creation of a
legislative assembly composed of forty-one representatives to be

elected by the people for a four-year term. These representatives will discuss executive projects and formulate laws for our Free Island. Tegularius's advisory council (Eulalio, Leocadia, Valeriano, and Illirio Mariafels) have set the date of the election for March 12. Anyone wishing to run as a candidate must register with Leocadia by February 19.

Tuesday, March 6, 1979
Cassettes recorded by Goncalvo

What a mess with the elections! Fifty-five people received the same number of votes—161 each. Severe rioting began and we did not have any means to stop the brawling. Two days later Tegularius ordered the creation of a police force composed of 380 tall men and thirty-six strong women, all equipped with Tasers. Our new citizens from Des Moines sent a radio message home asking for nine hundred Tasers and nine hundred plain red sweat suits (without any pictures on the front) to serve as police uniforms. The folks in Des Moines promised that the equipment would arrive within four weeks. Meanwhile our strong men and women walk around the island shouting, "I am the police!"

Five days ago another round of elections was held—this time without any exasperating incidences. Our assembly now consists of four factions:

Eulalio's faction (strong anti-Sage orientation)—six representatives

Leocadia and Valeriano's faction (direct support for Costas)—nineteen representatives

Caring Heart faction (supporters of the late Leonor)—seven representatives

True Fidelity faction (supporters of the secretaries)—nine representatives

So Tegularius has the support of twenty-six representatives— Eulalio's faction, Leocadia and Valeriano's faction, and one member from the Caring Heart faction. To the surprise of many he invited four representatives from the Caring Heart faction and two representatives from the True Fidelity faction to join his executive committee. Only Eulalio alone from among his six-person faction was asked to be on this governing body. As explained by Tegularius, since the direction of the government was preservation of the island's unity in the interests of all, Eulalio's strident opposition to the Sages constituted an obstacle. Eulalio, furious at the outcome, nevertheless privately agreed to assist Tegularius for a while. Mariafels was entrusted with the task of coordinating development projects on the island. He is called now Illirio the Harmonizer or just the Harmonizer.

Monday, March 26, 1979
Bulletin: THE SAGES' WARNING

The elevated Sages sternly reprimand all those who participate in the idolatrous singing brought to our pure island by Illirio Mariafels, whose soul is poisoned by Satan. His life now depends only on the good will of our noble and most glorious Sage no. 1. Every islander who participates in this obscene chanting should fear immediate death, or death with prolonged pain.

Moreover, the elevated Sages now clearly inform all the islanders that the so-called assembly has no place and no moral power in our homeland. This assembly constitutes a severe breach of the agreement between the elevated Sages and Constantius Tegularius that led to his election to the position of chief executive in the first place. People who accept Tegularius's teaching are apostates who will pay a terrible price for their infidelity.

Tuesday, April 3, 1979
RADIOGRAMME from Marius Villeneuve
À Madame Adélaïde Fourangier, Asie du Sud-Est

Please supply us with your program for the fourth and the seventh grades.

Monday, April 30, 1979
Western Island Bulletin

The day before yesterday our Chief Executive Costas Tegularius visited the USAT *President Harding* and was received by her captain, Commander Edward Hayes. Our leader was accompanied by Leocadia Moniz, our minister of foreign relations, Illirio Mariafels, the chief coordinator of the executive committee, and Estácio Beltrão, minister of food production and a representative of the Caring Heart faction. Commander Hayes informed our representatives of the favorable impression our island's liberalization process had created—and not only in President Jimmy Carter's administration, but also in the heart of the president who is himself an ardent supporter of human rights. Unfortunately due to the ongoing conflict between the People's Republic of China, Vietnam, and the Philippines over sovereignty over the Paracel Islands, the United Stated was unable to extend official recognition; however, all possible humanitarian and financial aid will be provided through facilities to be created in the near future.

Our representatives expressed gratitude for the cooperation of the USAT *President Harding* with our pearl catchers over the decades, and expressed their wish for expansion of this excellent cooperation in the future. Commander Hayes expressed his personal admiration for Constantius Tegularius's long-term efforts to maintain cooperation between Pinto Islanders and the officers of the USAT *President Harding.*

Saturday, May 5, 1979
Diary entry by Adélaïde Fourangier

They are ridiculous with their tiresome questionnaires. They are sure that I have free access not only to the international press but also the music publication trade, and that I can keep up to date whenever I wish. This is so stupid; they do not invest a scintilla of effort in learning where I live or the circumstances under which I work—or do not work—as is the case in times of bloodshed and epidemics. They surely relay on the dated reports of that idiot Döpps. Oh, those formalists. And with this idiotic shallowness they shape children's musical education. Well, I answered them as best I could (straining my memory to the utmost):

Fourth grade:

HANDEL—*Allemande in A minor* (I can no longer remember the index number)
KUHLAU—*Allegretto from the Sonatina in G major,* Op. 55 (luckily I managed to remember the index number for this one)
HELLER—one of the early études from his collection of twenty-five studies (here again I fail to remember the index number)
MOZART—*Solfeggio in F,* K 393
BACH, J.S.—both bourrées from the *Second English Suite* (I do not remember the index numbers)
BACH, J.S.—both minuets from the *Fourth English Suite*

BENDA, Jiri Antonin—Sonatinas in F major and A minor
CHOPIN, F.—Waltz, No. 17 in A minor
GRIEG, Edward—*Grandmother's Minuet* from Op. 68 (oh, I see I still have some memory left!)
TCHAIKOVSKY, Peter—The Toy Soldier's March from Children's Album, Opus 39

Seventh grade:

BACH, J.S.—"Prelude and Fugue in C minor" or "Prelude and Fugue in B-flat major" from the *Well-Tempered Clavier*, Bk 1
CHOPIN—Nocturne, Op. 15, No. 3, and the second waltz from Op. 34
DEBUSSY—"Golliwog's Cake-Walk" from the *Children's Corner Suite* (how could one possibly overlook this popular piece!)
DEBUSSY—"La Fille aux Cheveux de Lin" from the *Preludes*
FAURÉ—Improvisation from the Op. 84 collection
HAYDN—the First movement of the *Piano Sonata in C-sharp minor* (I do not remember the index number)
HELLER—Study in G minor from collection of Op. 45 (thank god I remember the index number)
MENDELSSOHN—"A staccato Song Without Words" from Op. 102
MOZART—*Gigue* (K 574)
MOZART—the first movement from the *G major Sonata*, K 283.
SCHUBERT—the first and third moments *musicaux*, from Op. 94
TCHAIKOVSKY—*Tender Reproaches*, Op. 72, No. 3

Saturday, June 30, 1979
Diary entry by Adélaïde Fourangier

We just had an outstanding children's concert; my students feel so much better now that peace has taken root here. They have started smiling again. Two pilots from the Des Moines boat crew also started to study piano with me, but I suspect their goal is to study Illirio's two-voiced chanting. He will have to decide how, when, and what to teach them.

Leocadia attended the concert with smiles; she is now called Executive Leocadia. She loved the Fauré. This year one pupil performed his famous *Sicilienne* and two others performed two duets from the *Dolly Suite* that were arranged by my revered maître, Alfred Cortot. I was so moved at seeing how much Leocadia enjoyed these pieces. If only Jean-Luc could have been here.

Wednesday, July 4, 1979
RADIOGRAMME from Marius Villeneuve

Your answers are satisfactory, though they contain significant omissions from contemporary repertory, especially the French. In spite of these failings, our collegial council has agreed to start the process of summoning you back to Paris, a process that will take several years. As part of this process you will be invited to give open piano classes in the presence of our collegial committee. This will occur in the spring of 1983. You will receive further instructions in January to February 1980.

Friday, September 21, 1979
Cassettes recorded by Goncalvo

We are living in stressful times. The first feces rites have just been held according to the new arrangements. On August 28, two bulldozers from the Sages' compound proceeded along the northern coast to the area of the former youth marina. For two days the bulldozers excavated an enormous pit and secretaries dressed in gray carried thousands of buckets of sand to the summit of the Hill. The rain turned the sand into mud that immediately flowed into the sea on the northwestern corner of the island. Less than a week later, seawater flooded a mile-long stretch of the northern coastline, bringing the shore four hundred meters closer to the residential area.

The feces festivities were held between August 31 and September 2. Fifty secretaries dressed in gray with buckets full of feces arrived at both public drinking wells in two large, old trucks that our people had never seen before. Forty-five secretaries emptied their buckets into the drinking water, immediately after which five of them proudly drank from the wells. Five other secretaries approached a part of the recently constructed water system. Drilling a hole into one of the pipes, they emptied five buckets of feces into it. Under the strict orders of our chief executive, all islanders who came to watch the rites stood by observing the proceedings without making a move. Two of the secretaries who drank the water from the public drinking wells died even before reaching the Sages' compound. The feces must have been previously contaminated by fly poison since there were no flies buzzing around the wells now.

An emergency cleaning operation took place between September 3 and September 11. Luckily our people stopped the flow of water the moment information was received that the wells had been polluted. Special alternative water pipes were installed for temporary use. Nobody in the free territory died. On September 10, there was a meeting of the executive council to discuss the situation, but no announcement of the proceedings was published. Zeferino informs me that the executive council secretly ordered the installation of special devices capable of separating the contaminated water in the wells from the fresh water coming from underground. It is vital not to disseminate this information.

Monday, September 24, 1979
Bulletin: THE SAGES' WARNING

The Sages express wrathful condemnation of all those in charge of the affairs of our blessed island who do not allow our people to participate in the sublime ritual of drinking from water sources hallowed by the inner richness of our noble people. The Sages perceive such disregard for the teachings of our Founding Fathers as a punishable offense.

Saturday, September 29, 1979
Diary entry by Adélaïde Fourangier

Illirio has been staying at my house for the past three days. He was here to supervise the overhaul of Jean-Luc's runway as well as to instruct Goncalvo and Zeferino in more advanced use of Jean-Luc's radio equipment. Yesterday I had three whole hours together with him at my vegetable table. Since Jean-Luc's death, I am the one who maintains his vegetable garden and it surprises me how much I enjoy it. We also had my own delicious homemade yellow pitaya juice.

Illirio's mood was dark and anxious. He maintains that we do not have the necessary support from the outside world to help us create a modern society. The Americans send encouraging messages in elevated English and sell us some antibiotics, but more substantial aid never follows. In addition, Illirio relayed that the Des Moines supply to *our* part of the island—now only one boat a month with only three more boatloads promised—

was meager, just rolls of toilet paper, countless cans of pickles, used clothing (unwashed), old shoes, some yellowed school notebooks, old pencils (with thirty-four pencil-sharpeners!), many useless copies of their newspaper (all from the same day), and bottles of ketchup. They also sent us forty-two cheap women's necklaces (we need them as much as we do yesterday's sunrise). The crew with their latest boat is made up entirely of Filipinos who depart the same day they arrive. Thank god they speak Spanish and somehow we manage to understand them. Our new citizens from Des Moines also help us communicate with the Filipino crews in English. These American Pintoists work night and day to teach our people English.

Illirio sighed sadly. "We do not know what is going on in the Sages' compound, but we are afraid they are amassing weapons with the intent to bring us to our knees and annul all our achievements. Eulalio makes exasperating protestations over our reluctance to attack them, while on the other hand the camp of the late Leonor—that awful woman—morally blackmails Costas into passivity. Above all we still have no sustainable industry besides our pearls and we only have Grandpa's old Pettersson for trade. We must acquire more boats, but they are terribly expensive."

I did my best to cheer him up by telling him that he could have a bright future if he could only bring his children's chorus to Europe. But our goodbye kiss was rather mournful. At least he got his full dose of vitamins, my boy....

Wednesday, October 3, 1979
Editorial from *OUR BELOVED ISLAND POST OF PINTOVILLE*

In accordance with information that reached us from our support station in the Philippines, eight of our men were kidnapped by Chinese or Vietnamese communists who are hiding on our beloved island. The Sages ordered our fellow islanders to make every effort to free them. We wholeheartedly support the resolve of our glorious Sages.

October 16, 1979
Cassettes recorded by Goncalvo

Two of our new citizens just left the island. I think they may have been sent on a secret mission, the purpose of which even Zeferino with his uncanny ability to get access to secret information does not know; he only knows that Tegularius and Mariafels sent them to perform some special tasks a few weeks ago. Zeferino suspects they will not travel together, but will split into different directions. Personally I think that the time has come to infiltrate the Sages' compound and to ruin them from within. However, I cannot imagine how two men can perform such a task, and surely do not know how one man can do it. But if such a man were indeed to go to the compound on a secret mission on our behalf, I believe he would be on a suicide mission. I am already sad for him—a heroic volunteer. I do not even know his name, though I am sure that Tegularius— our leader—knows him personally quite well. Such a mission would require almost fatherly support from the commander. As to the other one—I cannot imagine where he might go. To the Philippines? To France? Or maybe back to Des Moines? How happy I would be if he exposed the villainous hypocrisy of his entire community with their shameless support of mass slaughter in their historic homeland.

Those two men cried before leaving and kissed our children.

Sunday, February 3, 1980
Diary entry by Adélaïde Fourangier

Illirio came by again and quickly fell asleep in a chair. He told me he sleeps just four hours once every two days. My boy is only twenty-five and already a widower and a bereaved father. How he has aged! He looks fifty-five. Horrible. He woke up after only twenty minutes of awkward rest. Today he was taciturn— just eating my vegetables while deep in thought. Later on he dropped a quizzical bombshell: "Perhaps we will find some method of outsmarting those Sages...." He then returned to a business-like tone: "We still have no idea how to develop our economy." This seems to cause him terrible grief. I massaged his knotted shoulders. He kissed me and left.

Wednesday, March 26, 1980
Cassettes recorded by Goncalvo

Interesting development: the spring feces festivities ended with the Sages' being embarrassed. Bulldozers left the gates of the compound and proceeded westward as usual, and just as they started digging, both their caterpillar treads and their blades fell apart. Five secretaries dressed in gray hurriedly filled their personal buckets with sand and ran toward the Hill. Two days later the old trucks carrying fifty secretaries and their cargo of feces did not even succeed in crossing the gate of the compound before they too broke down. This time no feces was dumped into the wells. An amazing atmosphere of optimism (silent in nature) reigns in many areas of the island, especially in the west. I think I was right with regard to the volunteers and their secret missions. But who knows?

Monday, March 31, 1980
Bulletin: THE SAGES' WARNING

In recent days heinous crimes have been perpetrated against the will of our glorious Sages, and our pure and elevated nation. The sacred tools for maintaining our Founding Fathers' spiritual rites have been destroyed by evil spirits. Not only will those directly responsible for these crimes suffer eternal punishment, but also those who inspire them will die awful deaths as well— now or later, in accordance with the will of our great Sages.

Friday, April 11, 1980
Diary entry by Adélaïde Fourangier

Costas came by yesterday and remained until morning. Although less worried than before, he is still very tired and overworked. I nagged him that he should concern himself more with Illirio because he has aged so under the burden of all his responsibilities. He looks like he could be the same age as Costas. Costas looked at me with consternation and articulated with great solemnity, "Illirio and I work for our people."

I said to him calmly, "Do not forget your heart. Illirio is a bereaved father and you are not."

"Bereaved or not, I am the father of so many dead people," he retorted.

"Drop your empty arrogance," I rebuked him. "Illirio's life is incomparably sadder than yours. You may be a father, but he is a bereaved father."

"A father? To whom?" he asked quizzically.

"To Illirio," I said calmly, then added, "you have a paternal obligation not to let him die before you."

Costas looked at me in complete silence for five long minutes without making a move. His eyes widened and he gazed at me with almost unbearable intensity.

"When did you manage to...when did you become pregnant with him?" he said in a hesitant voice.

"When you were working on your PhD in Paris," I said.

"Why didn't you tell me?"

"Because you left so abruptly to attend to your dear people on this island, I didn't get the chance," I said angrily.

"You—you are an impossible woman, Adèle," he said. He was angry too.

"You are wrong!" I almost shouted.

"What's wrong?" he asked.

"You are an impossible woman, *my love*," I shouted out in correction.

"Yes, my love," he whispered, smiling tenderly. He stood up and kissed me as though I were an eighteen-year-old girl. I responded by slamming my fist into his shoulder (right in the scar that united us years ago). He kissed me again.

"I should have figured out that Likki is our son all by myself. I am such a fool. Can you explain to me why?" he asked helplessly.

"You are wrong again," I said sternly.

"Can you explain me why I am such a fool, my love?" he asked.

"Because you are the father of your nation, that's why," I said, shaking my head in despair.

Then he said, "I promise you that Likki will not die, not here, and not before us."

After a long silence he asked, "Why didn't you tell him that I am his father?"

"I did not want him to experience the loss of a father, should something ever happen to you," I said.

"Wrong, I think," he mumbled.

"You forgot again," I said acidly.

"Wrong again, my love," he corrected himself.

"What is wrong?" I asked.

"You were afraid that I would manipulate Likki against you, my love."

I suddenly burst into tears. That is in fact what did happen, although by that time, I had also joined his side. He kissed me again, on my lips, the old rascal. I fed him some freshly picked vegetables from my garden and the fish that Zeferino had prepared.

Costas told me that developing the island's local agriculture on a commercial scale was now a possibility. After tense, week-long negotiations with the Sages, he finally succeeded in obtaining their consent for one more shipment for the free state from Des Moines. This shipment brought many varieties of grain and fertilizer. He also told me that two dentists from Des Moines had come to stay with us. Actually, they came in secret—Costas relayed this because in Des Moines only the Sages' side was seen as legitimate. They brought with them fifteen cases of toothpaste and toothbrushes and a complete dental office setup. It took them three days to assemble their equipment and now they work nine hours a day treating our children and adults. Immediately upon their arrival, they asked to listen to the children's two-voiced chanting. They wept with joy. Costas added, "They also want to listen to you play, especially Schubert's *Six Moments Musicaux,* so they say. Do you play them?"

"It's been years; I will look for the scores and relearn them."

"What happened with the Sages' annual craze this year?" I asked. "I heard that there was an amusing embarrassment at the compound gates."

Costas laughed lightly. "I think someone damaged their machines—an inside job. At the moment the Sages are fuming; they accuse me of treachery and threaten me in their printed bulletins. In reality it gives us some room to breathe before they can exercise military power against us again—those damned heavy armaments are constantly shipped to them from Des Moines.

We went to sleep.

Tuesday, April 29, 1980
RADIOGRAMME from Marius Villeneuve

The professional council of the IHEMdP has discussed your work and invites you to come to Paris no later than June 1983. During your visit you will be asked to give master classes for both adults and teenagers (age fourteen and above). Your future as a member of our teaching staff will be discussed with the possibility of eventually offering you a permanent position. The details and the timing of your visit will be forwarded to you later. Please confirm receipt of this message.

Wednesday, April 30, 1980
Diary entry by Adélaïde Fourangier

Looking at this radiogramme, I did not feel a thing. I asked myself if I was ever homesick for Paris. Hardly. Not even a regret about Fleurette (she must be a married woman by now, perhaps even a mother). Is Jules alive? Is that detail of any importance to me? I can hardly remember what he looked like. Did I live in Paris at all? What did I live for then? To play recitals at Salle Gaveau? What feelings did I have? The first truly positive emotions that I still vividly remember appeared only as I approached this island on Jean-Luc's boat.

And do I now feel connected to this island of crazy people? Here and there I meet some wonderful souls, but this should be the case everywhere, shouldn't it? I think I am just Costas's "half-married, half-separated" woman, nothing more than that. And somehow I have developed into the mother of Illirio, at least in my heart. Maybe this happened because of the local children, and foremost because of Nissa, that beautiful girl. She is the one who taught me to love. How I miss you, dear Nissa…. Here is what I feel: I feel pain, intense pain for Nissa's horrible, early death, and for the death of our beautiful Alfi. This crazy island killed them. And I am worried for Illirio and cannot even trust Costas to keep him alive. Now I live here on Pinto, and not in Paris, and my pain—this overriding pain—is all I have. I know Paris is beautiful. Now it must be even more beautiful than ever. But this *pain* is mine. Tomorrow I will confirm their message.

Saturday, June 28, 19
Cassettes recorded by Goncalvo

Amazing scenes. Much of the nonresidential areas of the island have been converted into agricultural fields. I have never seen such hard work—small tractors rumble across the wild grassland, plowing the soil and creating beautiful, orderly beds. The traditional smell of turtles roasting has receded into the far corners of the eastern part of the island. Soon we will have bread, potatoes, tomatoes. How exotic! Who knows, maybe we will even sell some to Hainan!

Sunday, July 20, 1980
Diary entry by Adélaïde Fourangier

Costas and Illirio came to visit me, though they were not the slight bit interested in my company. They just needed a secluded place to discuss an important matter. Still, they did ask me to join them and requested some of my pitaya juice.

Costas asked Illirio, "Should I visit Des Moines?"

"I think not, Uncle Costas," answered Illirio. "At least not now."

Costas smiled at him and then briefly glanced at me. "Why not, my son?" he asked.

"Look, we do not have any truly close friends in their upper circles so you would be stepping into a hostile environment."

"But at least they are nominally our brethren, and look, they send shipments and support us."

"Who is the *us* of whom you speak?" asked Illirio. "I know you agree with me, Uncle Costas. You just want me to play devil's advocate."

"As you like. Go ahead, my son," smiled Costas.

"Look, we do not have a clear understanding of what is going on there. All we know is that there are some seventy thousand people of our origin, divided into an orthodox camp and a more enlightened camp. We know there are about forty thousand people in the enlightened camp and these people support the orthodox community materially in exchange for their preservation of the nation's historic identity."

I interrupted Illirio's exposition, asking him to elaborate further so that I could understand his line of argument too.

"You see, Mother, the enlightened Pintoists send their children to regular American schools. They have no special aptitudes that allow them to achieve high economic status in America. Inevitably their lives would devolve into the miserably banal existence shared by the rest of assimilated Americans. Their only way of presenting themselves as worthy of respect is to cling to their orthodox relatives, displaying an aura of especially precious humanity. Our culture's fantastic spirituality and the assimilated Pintoists' intriguing devotion to it, their clannishness, and their self-obligation to support their nonworking brethren set them apart. Not to mention that their uncanny success in business makes them attractive partners for Americans eager to invest in joint enterprises with them. These traits have enabled the Pintoist community to achieve astonishing social advancement from the early twentieth century onward."

When Illirio finished speaking, Costas smiled. "Your words only prove that I *have* to go and meet them. After all, it is in their power to help us, especially since we too are willing to work hard."

"Dear Uncle Costas, it's just the opposite." He took a deep breath and then explained. "To the enlightened camp, you and your position represent the worst possible scenario, one actually close to treason. Their success in America depends on their adherence to an utterly outlandish ethnic group that purportedly carries some arcane, mystical knowledge, but one that is incapable of surviving on its own. The enlightened Des Moines Pintoists are not themselves a self-sustaining cultural entity—rather they are an appendage of the orthodox camp that is intransigently faithful to our Sages, four maniacs sitting on the other side of the globe from them. This faithfulness, by the way, is part of the same dynamic as the dependency of the enlightened Pintoville majority on the orthodox minority. When the enlightened camp learned of our revolution, it threatened their entire life view—we are their greatest enemy, dear Uncle Costas. This is why they support the Sages with such zeal, sending them lethal armaments and luxury goods beyond any reasonable limit. Why do you think they have stopped sending us any support? According to our source there, the last three shipments packed with toilet paper, outdated notebooks, and thirty-four pencil sharpeners were intended as an insult!"

"I am not sure about all that," said Costas, still hopeful. "Yet if you are right, there is no possibility of my opening a meaningful dialogue with them." Sighing again, he continued, "Unfortunately their support of the Sages is so massive that it doesn't allow us to neutralize them, in spite of our miraculous successes in battle." After a while, he asked Illirio, "What do you propose, my son?"

For once Illirio had no answer.

I ventured, "I think we may have an opportunity to visit France in the near future."

"How so?" Costas asked in surprise.

I showed them the latest radiogramme from Marius Villeneuve. Costas sank into deep thought. "We need to prepare for this trip carefully. It could really save us. But whom should I apply to?"

"What about Léon Pignon, your former patron?" suggested Illirio.

"He's been dead for four years now, son."

"Who told you?"

"Jean-Luc. He was always scanning the radio universe."

"Then we are cut off from the entire world," said Illirio glumly.

Costas was completely silent. He sat with his head in his palms. I wondered how I could help. My own contacts in Paris were nonexistent. Well...maybe Jules could help, if he was still around, but that would depend on my success at IHEMdP. Another well-laid trap, so I did not say anything to them about him. The year of my journey to France—1983—was still too far away. We still had a long time ahead and this island could produce a new craze at any moment.

Thursday, October 2, 1980
Bulletin from the Sages: A SPECIAL NOTICE

Our great Sage no. 1, the wisdom of the planet and the heart of the universe, is suffering excruciating pain. In his endless love for the sacred people of Pinto Island, he only asks that they free themselves of all sins that adhere to them since they abandoned our sacred customs. He asks that every adult pray for him at the entrance gates of the Sages' compound starting at sunset on this blessed day.

Sunday, October 5, 1980
Cassettes recorded by Goncalvo

Goncalvo's voice: Here is Zeferino's testimony of the last two days.

Zeferino's voice: A crowd of at least five thousand supporters of the Sages from the eastern part of the island gathered at the gate of the Sages' compound, ardently chanting ventriloquist hymns extolling Sage no. 1. At midnight they switched to hymns of repentance and this continued for three more hours. Their voices shook the whole island. During part of that time, it rained heavily and the huge crowd was thoroughly drenched. Nobody thought to bring an umbrella. People actually wanted to get soaked. At 4 a.m. Tegularius joined the crowd. He came by himself without his associates from the executive committee (they had arrived earlier and were in lines closer to the gates). Tegularius remained in the back as was his custom, embracing the shoulders of the other bystanders. After half an hour he left with his associates.

I came to Jean-Luc's station for rest and a day's sleep and returned once again to the compound gates the following day at midnight. This time not only was yesterday's large crowd there, but children from the secretaries' orphanages and from families associated with Senhora Leonor's Caring Heart faction were there as well. Four nine-year-old children from this camp had been studying at Senhora Fourangier's school. At 2 a.m. they started singing Illirio's two-voiced chants in their sterling sopranos. Their voices produced a phenomenally calming effect on the emotionally charged crowd. With this dispersing tranquilly, only a few hundred people remained near the fence, standing there in motionless silence. Today at 5 p.m. a bulletin from the Sages appeared with the following message:

> Last night an abominable crime was committed. Public prayers for the health of our great Sage no. 1 were desecrated by squalid howls of foreign idolatry whose vile intent was to bring early death to Sage no. 1. The evil spirit that took root in these children's hapless souls now permeates the hearts of all islanders. It must be expunged at any cost. If anything happens to our great Sage no. 1, it will be the result of the enemy spirit that infests our island. There can be no forgiveness for those who have allowed this evil spirit to take possession of our noble island.

I went to the gate of the compound and was informed that the parents of those children who had chanted so lovingly in two voices last night had been killed on their way home by the naked secretaries. The bodies of these parents were covered in feces and brought to the gates of the Sages' compound as a sacrifice. Secretaries dressed in gray pushed the stinking corpses back toward our side of the guano fence that divides east and west where they were lowered into an open pit and left to attract poisonous flies. At midnight Costas Tegularius and Illirio Mariafels arrived and they and some of their associates covered the mass grave with sand and sealed it with cement. Although at this stage there were at least seven hundred people at the site praying for Sage no. 1, nobody tried to prevent the sealing of parents' grave. I left the scene at 2 a.m. when there were still at least six hundred people praying for Sage no. 1's life.

Tuesday, October 7, 1980
Diary entry by Adélaïde Fourangier

Olivia, Manuelita, Alexio, and Renaldo—these are the names of the children whose parents were murdered because of their chanting. Last year Illirio taught them double-voiced chanting when the mother of one of the children especially asked him to do so. She thought that the chanting would be a good weapon against sudden killings. Poor woman.

Now with these innocent parents dead, I can only imagine the fate of my Illirio. Can I even hope that Costas can protect him? Those poor parents, victims of their nation's madness. How can I commemorate them? Should I even try? And why do I speak about adults, when so many children here die at any given moment, if not from epidemics then from negligence or crazy violence. Dozens of my former pupils have not reached the age of fifteen. Fifteen! I should be in perpetual mourning. Maybe I am.

Wednesday, January 30, 1981
Bulletin from the Sages: SPECIAL SHATTERINGLY TRAGIC NOTICE

Two days ago our incomparable father, the wise Sage no. 1, died in his sleep surrounded by great Sages no. 2, no. 3, and no. 4. His body lays in state in the courtyard of his mansion with his eyes open to the sky. The noble northern flies came to part from him and flew back to Hainan, our ancient homeland. We hope they will return soon. The great father, the wise Sage no. 1 asked us not to mourn him with ritual obeisance at the gates of the Sages' compound, but rather to carve his teachings into our hearts, to remember our Founding Fathers' greatness, to be faithful to their ways, to build our magnificent Hill, to keep our hearts and bodies pure and united, and to free Hainan, our motherland. His written testament will be opened and read to the public the day after tomorrow at midnight.

Monday, February 1, 1981
Cassettes recorded by Goncalvo

Sage no. 1 is finally dead. I am sending Zeferino to the gates of the compound to listen to the late Sage's testament.

Tuesday, February 2, 1981
Cassettes recorded by Goncalvo

Zeferino's voice: I went to the gate of the compound around 11:30 p.m. At least thirty thousand adults were already there— almost all our adult population (which has been significantly reduced due to the recent wars and epidemics). I sighed with relief when I verified that there were no children present. Midnight passed and nothing happened. Nobody came to read Sage no. 1's testament. The crowd stood motionless in anticipation.

Suddenly at 1:30 a.m. a huge fireball ascended to the sky. The sky blazed with blinding light for three or four moments and then darkness descended as though nothing at all had occurred. The crowd was transfixed in awe and remained motionless for another full hour. It seemed as though we might stay there indefinitely or until death overtook us. But around 2:45 a.m. the gates of the compound opened and a secretary dressed in gray said in a muffled voice, "Go home, all of you. The testament will be announced at a later time. Go."

Wednesday, February 18, 1981
Bulletin from the Sages: A SPECIAL NOTICE

We can announce now in noble ecstasy that our dear Sage no. 1 was resurrected and taken in flames to god eternal and will become his second son, residing to the left of his heavenly majesty's throne. The wisdom dispensed by our heavenly Sage will now become godly truth. It will empower our people to carry his message and redeem themselves. With our heads bowed low in deep reverence, we open the sacred last testament of our beloved Sage no. 1.

Here are the last wishes of our great and glorious Sage no. 1:

First, Sage no. 3 must become Sage no. 1.

Second, Sage no. 2 must remain Sage no. 2 and Sage no. 4 will be promoted to the position of Sage no. 3.

Third, one secretary from among those with the longest moustaches will be promoted to the position of Sage no. 4. The three current Sages and the four secretaries with the longest moustaches will elect Sage no. 4.

Fourth, there must be a purification festival held at the wells a month after the elevation of the Sage no. 4. It should include more than half of the adult population.

Fifth, there can be no forgiveness for those who deviate from our faithful ways; infidels should be killed by filling their mouths with our sacred sand.

Sixth, if not this year or the next, then during the third year our people will surely rid themselves of the evil filth that clings to their minds and hearts. They must purify themselves by resuming our sacred rites, building our Hill, and sending our valiant youth to our Founding Fathers' land. All islanders take heed: our Hill has not been built in earnest for the last three years, therefore when the work resumes, it must be undertaken with triple resolve.

The seventh and eighth points are secret directives addressed only to our elevated Sages and the most distinguished mustachioed secretaries.

Thursday, April 30, 1981
Cassettes recorded by Goncalvo

Thank god (I mean the one with only one son) we passed the "purification festival" without excessive trouble. This time it was even funny. Fifty secretaries dressed in gray marched in complete serenity and with high purpose through the gates of the Sages' compound toward the two public wells, each carrying a large, open bucket of feces. About four hundred meters before reaching the wells, their buckets fell apart and the feces spilled onto the ground. Our police force quickly buried the feces in sand.

Another group of fifteen secretaries dressed in gray marched to the aboveground connections of the water pipes, ceremoniously raising their mechanical drills high in the air. Yet the very moment that they switched them on, the drills disintegrated in their hands, wounding two secretaries. Those carrying the buckets of feces that were to be emptied into the water pipes hurriedly ran away, stumbling and falling. Their buckets broke as they approached the gates of the compound. Only three secretaries succeeded in filling their silver buckets with sand and traveling all the way west to the Hill. Unfortunately for them, high winds immediately dispersed the dry sand that they had deposited on the summit. I think—it is my own guess, of course—we should be grateful to our heroic people who succeeded once again in their courageous sabotage mission.

Sunday, May 17, 1981
Diary entry by Adélaïde Fourangier

Costas and Illirio visited me yesterday. I am so angry at Costas that after Illirio left I drove him out of the house and said I never wanted to see him again. This island is too much for me! The evening began as usual—the two of them came together after my classes were over and I fed them vegetables and my pitaya juice. I now have some local bread too, as the first grain crops have been harvested and the newly constructed bakeries have started baking. Costas reported gleefully on expectations for a bountiful harvest, though he worried that there would be no possibility of exporting our crop.

I asked about Jean-Luc's old Pettersson. Costas nodded. "Yes, you are right, my love. But it is too small and too old to carry heavy cargo for hundreds of nautical miles. Under the present circumstances, we can deliver our goods only to the Philippines or possibly to Taiwan or Bangkok. The other Paracel Islands are either uninhabited or patrolled by the communist Chinese. Mainland China and now Vietnam both have regimes without free trade, so we have a huge problem—all our development routes are effectively blocked."

"Our main task must be to acquire larger and stronger boats so that we can ship our agricultural produce abroad," said Illirio.

"Do you have any idea how we should go about it, my son?" asked Costas.

"In the usual way, by trading pearls for the merchandise we desire from the Philippines. I think Grandpa's boat can make just one more trip there."

"I am afraid it's not as easy as that, my son. The Sages—as we can see from their bulletins—are so full of rage toward us that they would readily intercept that old wooden Pettersson with the swifter Arun-class boats supplied by the Des Moines Pintoists. We will somehow have to elude them."

"Well, then the only thing I can suggest is that I swim undetected to the USAT *President Harding*, meet with Commander Edward Hayes, and ask him to transfer me to the Philippines by some passing American ship. I can swim the twenty-five kilometers to the American ship without any problem."

"Even if you reach the Philippines that way, how will you bring the boats here?"

"I will visit the Filipino base camp of the Des Moines Pintoists and sing them our two-voiced chants. If I succeed in recruiting some of them, as I hope I will, they will bring their boats to us and maybe even agree to help us. It is not as crazy as it sounds...."

Costas lowered his head. He clearly wanted to conceal his smile; our son's idea was so funny that he had difficulty remaining serious.

"What makes you think that the *President Harding* will be in the same spot where you found her last time?" I interjected. "You *are* crazy! How do you expect to find the ship when you're in the middle of the ocean?"

"We have radio communication with them from here, Mother. I will find them, don't worry. I always do."

"Are these waters free of sharks?" I screamed at him.

"No," my son answered matter of factly. "There are always sharks around."

"Then you will remain at home," I ordered.

"I can't. Mother, we are working for the freedom of our people—I must go."

I was speechless at his inner resolve. Risking his life once again? After we kissed and he left, I ranted at Costas for breaking his promise. Costas became deathly pale. "I will keep my promise," he whispered.

But I could no longer trust him. I screamed hysterically, "Get out of here and do not return until I see Illirio back alive!" I pushed him out the door with a vigor I did not know I had.

Sunday, June 21, 1981
Diary entry by Adélaïde Fourangier

A whole month has passed and still no word from Illirio. No one tells me anything. Madmen on a crazy island. All of them. And I fear I am becoming one of them.

Tuesday, June 23, 1981
RADIOGRAMME from Marius Villeneuve

You are expected to give open classes at IHEMdP on May 10–15, 1983. Your presentation will follow open classes by three other teachers who are returning from Punta Arenas in Terra del Fuego, Argentina, from the Kerguelen Islands off the coast of Antarctica, and from Wallis and Futuna in the South Pacific in the vicinity of Samoa. You will be provided with roundtrip airfare from Bangkok to Charles de Gaulle Airport in Paris plus accommodation at the Alexandra Hotel for May 5–19, 1983. Please arrange your work around this schedule.

Wednesday, June 24, 1981
Diary entry by Adélaïde Fourangier

Crazy people live in Paris too. They plan meetings two years in advance. Maybe I will be dead by then, who knows? Or a communist takeover in France may occur?? From Bangkok to Paris…but how do I get to Bangkok? And where is Illirio? Still no word from him.

July 9, 1981
Diary entry by Adélaïde Fourangier

Illirio is back. On a large cargo ship! With some guests. It appears my son promised all our future agricultural produce to the company that leased him this ship. This man is a true gambler. My hands are shaking involuntarily. I am afraid my head is starting to shake too. Horrible.

Saturday, October 31, 1981
Cassettes recorded by Goncalvo

It seems we are getting better now—our stalled economy has started growing. The first large-scale harvest has been gathered. People now eat bread, rice, potatoes, green vegetables, and strawberries. We definitely have more produce than we need for ourselves. People are extremely pleased. Tegularius says we have to organize agricultural exports to the Philippines and to Thailand. He says we have to expand our small fleet. Mariafels now insists that we have to acquire cargo planes too.

Tegularius says we have to develop a free society with personal accountability. He wants to introduce a banking system that allows people to have private accounts for their disposable income. He also wants to expand the educational curriculum. At this point we have excellent, newly recruited teachers from Des Moines who are trained in a wide variety of disciplines. Six more schools are being constructed. They are being built with imported concrete, and they have electricity and sewage! There are many adult education groups meeting in the schools in the evenings.

We have just completed the second annual feces/Hill festivities cycle. This time the fifty secretaries dressed in gray from the Sages' compound brought their buckets of feces to the wells and politely withdrew. There was no attempt to break into our water supply. Three secretaries with buckets full of sand went to the western end of the island to empty their buckets at the bottom of the Hill. The Leocadia and Valeriano factions (the nonaggressive activists) bubble over with enthusiasm; they feel vindicated, because at long last the Sages understand the spirit of the times and aren't obstructing the wheels of progress! People joyfully congratulate one another, but both Tegularius and Mariafels seem worried. The aged, always angry Eulalio is worried too. It seems that our long struggle has done irreparable damage to their spirits—they are no longer capable of joy.

Sunday, April 4, 1982
Diary entry by Adélaïde Fourangier

Costas and Illirio resumed their evening visits to my home yesterday. Of course I forgave Costas the day Illirio returned. I think I know what goes on in Costas's heart—he does not take me too seriously. Maybe he is right. After all, I am not some serene Hildegard from Bingen. Throughout the rainy winter, people toiled in the mud to expand and fortify Jean-Luc's runway. It is now wider, longer, and reasonably smooth. They paved it with concrete. Yesterday our American-born citizens landed a new light cargo plane on it—a relatively new Spanish Indonesian Aviocar. They proudly call it "our C–212."

"We will send you to Bangkok on this plane," laughed Costas, heartily praising our son's ingenuity and foresight. But the dark mood never leaves them. Neither believes that the Sages have rescinded their vow to undo the progress made by the Free Islanders.

Besides, Costas has a new, strange idea: he wants new elections in November 1982, exactly four years after receiving the people's mandate to govern. Illirio is opposed. He says Costas first has to go to France to secure international support for the Free Island and only then can he organize elections. But the earliest date for this visit to France is "after Mother's visit there," which makes it during the second half of 1983. Without "Mother's success" there can be no fruitful visit to France, you see—because only in the event that IHEMdP is pleased with my pedagogy "can she reactivate her relations with her first husband, Jules de Vermandois" who has access to the French government. If Jules is still alive, that is.

Afterward their conversation became even bleaker. It turns out that during the last feces festival the secretaries mixed feces with human bones; human bones were also found in the sand delivered to the Hill. Costas assumes that it is a message to us. The Sages must have discovered the Free Island's undercover agent planted among them and murdered him. That means no more broken drilling machines and bulldozers.

My hands shake incessantly now, though it is hardly noticeable. I have more and more difficulty holding this pen. What is it, early onset Parkinson's or a million years of repressed anxiety?

Tuesday, April 13, 1982
Bulletin from the Sages: AN ANNOUNCEMENT

The august and pure Sages follow with righteous indignation the events at our sacred wells. The chief executive willfully obstructs our rites of consolidation of body and spirit, thereby declaring himself an enemy of our sacredness. All those who adhere to his rule bear the responsibility for their treason.

Thursday, April 15 1982
Cassettes recorded by Goncalvo

There were no feces festivities this spring. However, four days ago a huge crowd of people from the secretaries' faction together with a majority from the Caring Heart faction came to the wells with placards accusing Tegularius of betraying of our Founding Fathers' spirit. For hours they chanted ventriloquist hymns. Then their 650 men protectively surrounded both wells thereby allowing another forty men in the group to quickly lower their trousers and defecate into the wells. All the others signified their approval with a chant glorifying the Sages and their eternal teachings. With ceremonious solemnity, hundreds of people bent over the wells and started gulping the water.

When Tegularius learned about what had happened, he ordered technicians to activate the recently installed aluminum diaphragms that hermetically seal the upper water level in the wells, thereby saving the drinking water reservoirs from further contamination. The fate of those ecstatic secretaries who drank the feces-contaminated water was already sealed, as was the fate of those who would now be infected by contact with the secretaries and attracting poisonous flies. Minutes after the craze began, seventy-six of our police officers rushed to the wells and started to drag away those who were still trying to get a chance to gulp the water. A huge riot ensued, and our police had to shock the rioters with Tasers. Then the assembled masses turned on the police. Fourteen policemen and 179 rioters died. Poisonous flies appeared just at sunset and started dispensing their venom. Two hundred people died over the next few days. Two days ago, in a Sages' bulletin Tegularius and his executive council were once again excoriated for angering the Founding Fathers' spirit, while the death of so many resulting from the fanatics' actions was not even mentioned.

Monday, May 3, 1982
Cassettes recorded by Goncalvo

Two-thirds of the island has been placed under protective quarantine. Huge doses of antibiotics are being administered to infected people, most of who are in the camps of eastern secretaries and the Caring Heart. Eulalio fumes that they should be allowed to die, but Tegularius, ever faithful to his Hippocratic oath, treats all patients regardless of creed, rebuffing Eulalio as usual, saying, "we work for the benefit of all islanders."

Sunday, July 4, 1982
Cassettes recorded by Goncalvo

Tegularius announced that he will run in a new round of elections to be held on November 20, 1982. Two months after that elections for the legislative assembly will be held. Leocadia announced that the deadline for candidate registration is August 20, 1982.

Thursday, August 5, 1982
Diary entry by Adélaïde Fourangier

Yesterday evening Costas and Illirio came for one of their visits. I now have a large Taiwanese refrigerator, so I can keep vegetables fresh for a longer time. I now also dress my salads with gorgeous soy sauce. We still drink my yellow pitaya juice. Although my hands tremble, I can still manage a kitchen knife. By the way, I have no problem when playing the piano—the moment my fingers touch the keys, they are as precise as ever. I hope and pray that it will remain so.

During the usual evening conversation between the two men, Illirio asserted that Costas was playing a dangerous game—he could easily lose the next election. Costas said that he is prepared to lose, as his goal is to generate a sound political process on the island. Illirio said that mental dependence on the Sages' utterances was a fact of life on the island; it would not diminish in spite of the dreadful toll such dependence takes.

"Could you explain this, son?" asked Costas.

"Uncle Costas, as you well know, because of our people's highly ingrained sense of helplessness, everyone feels that their own judgment is faulty. Afflicted by desperation, they turn to a larger, more omniscient entity that purports to address all their concerns."

"Why this sense of helplessness, son?" queried Costas. "Isn't it our job to convince people that their own abilities are sufficient?"

"You are dead wrong, Uncle Costas," asserted Illirio emphatically. Costas lifted his eyebrows in surprise at his categorical statement. I think I did too.

Illirio continued, "Most people are correct in not believing in their own capacities. Their inability to make sound judgments stems from insufficient attention to the minute details of their lives and what the true sources of their misery might be."

"So is this inability inborn?" I interrupted.

"No, Mother, I don't think so. This inattentiveness is a result of constant stress, misery, and fear."

"So?" Costas raised his eyebrows once again.

"Those who are capable of stopping their mental flight for a few moments and can reflect on their lives are the ones who take the first step into the realm of spiritual sovereignty. In our society, very few people are at this level; this is true even of our Des Moines brethren. Unbearable anxiety induces people to choose the panacea of a stronger force that embraces them from outside, the god with two sons. To see just how indoctrinated our people are, death from fly-borne poison after drinking water polluted by feces is viewed as an uplifting event, not as a curse."

"Even those with views like Leocadia's and Valeriano's?" asked Costas.

"Uncle Costas," said Illirio, "the large majority of people in these camps trust you. They are no different from the others; they have merely transferred their allegiance from the Sages to you. They feel that you are the true Sage no. 1, the true follower of our Founding Fathers."

"What would they do if I disappeared?" asked Costas.

"They would return to their former despair and start worshipping the Sages again in deep contrition."

"In spite of their Saigon education and their new studies, my son?"

"In spite of all this, Uncle Costas."

"And what about Eulalio's people?"

"These people are bursting with anger, Uncle Costas. True, they think the island belongs to them and not to the Sages, but they do not have any well thought out ideology. What motivates them is rage. All they want to do is kill the Sages and the mustachioed secretaries whom they view as satanic monsters along with all their advocates."

"So we live on a crazy island, son?" asked Costas with his sad smile.

I interjected, "So this is news, dear?"

"Anyhow, we will have elections at the end of November. If I lose, I will remain active as the hospital director and as the chief executive of public health, positions that I got after returning from Paris many years ago."

Now it was Illirio's turn to protest. "But we're far beyond that. What will happen to all our development plans if you lose? Everything that we have been striving for will be lost. How can you even think of risking it?"

"First the elections," said Costas with unconquerable serenity. "This is the only nonviolent way to bypass the defamation campaign that the Sages conduct against all my efforts."

One last thought: I think it is convenient for Costas that Likki is not aware that he is his true father. That way there can be true equality between them, and our son can contribute all his intellectual power to Costas's struggle. Oh, those lousy men.

I can't write anymore, writing has cramped my hand into a spasm.

Monday, August 16, 1982
Bulletin from the Sages: AN ANNOUNCEMENT

Almost four years ago, in October 1978, we called upon Costas Tegularius to assist us in the running of the affairs of our sacred island. We believed that his long years of foreign study had equipped him to administer public life while keeping true to the spirit of our Founding Fathers. Putting our faith in him, we gave him our written consent to function as the island's chief executive with the support of our people, whom we advised to vote for him.

Unfortunately Costas Tegularius ran the island without devotion to the spirit of our Founding Fathers. He created the "legislative assembly" composed of profane people who were never ordained to true legislative activity. Costas Tegularius made a circus of our Founding Fathers' spirit. He sanctioned the public mockery of our holy rites.

This man should have perished years ago; however, he is not the only sinner walking sacred Pinto soil. Those who follow his words bear no less responsibility for the sins committed against our Founding Fathers. Therefore the august Sages do not call for the immediate death of Costas Tegularius; on the contrary, they want to preserve his life so that everyone will realize that he, elected or not, is a source of evil.

Saturday, August 21, 1982
THE VOICE OF THE FREE ISLAND (formerly *Western Island Bulletin*)

To our dear sisters and brothers, deeply respected fellow islanders: In order to preserve the successful improvement we now experience in our lives and for the sake of our children and their children, we have to free ourselves from blind subordination to unelected religious authorities. We have to practice accountability not only to one another, but across society, so that our lives become fairer and less brutish. We have to learn to be both free and mutually supportive. This is our only guarantee of survival and personal fulfilment. In order to move in this direction, we have to elect our leadership every four years. We have to vote in new elections in order to keep on living in dignity and fairness. The date of the new election will be announced in the coming days.

On behalf of Pinto Island's executive council,

Costas Tegularius
Chief Executive

Friday, December 3, 1982
Cassettes recorded by Goncalvo

The elections are behind us. Costas Tegularius, running unopposed, received only 48.3% of the vote. Without the Sages' backing he failed to gain a majority. Visibly embittered, our leader immediately resigned from his position as chief executive and returned to his house near the hospital. Illirio Mariafels resigned from his position as chief coordinator of the executive committee. The legislative assembly disbanded.

Saturday, January 22, 1983
Cassettes recorded by Goncalvo

Agricultural work has largely stopped; the secretaries residing in the eastern part of the island have once again shed their clothes, dancing around the wells smeared in their own feces, happily humming the ventriloquist chants as though nothing had changed. Some men from the western part came over to sing two-voiced chants to them, but the naked secretaries were completely deaf. Their eardrums had been mercilessly pierced by their bosses.

Sunday, February 27, 1983
Cassettes recorded by Goncalvo

The offensive smell of grilled turtle has returned to the island. Education in the eastern part of the island has been totally disrupted. All notebooks of pupils engaged in advanced study have been burned. Two American brethren siding with the Free Island have been beaten and were driven out of eastern territory. Our red-clothed police force has been attacked by seven hundred naked secretaries with heavy bludgeons. Over one hundred of them have been stripped of their uniforms and beaten; the perpetrators even succeeded in taking some of their Tasers.

Wednesday, March 30, 1983
Cassettes recorded by Goncalvo

Rumors fly that people on the eastern side are dying of hunger. People on the eastern side have completely stopped working in their fields and gardens. No wonder they starve, getting only little portions of grilled turtle meat, prepared for them once again by the turtle-grilling women. Feces are everywhere again. Naked secretaries deliberately pour water on the excrement, bending over in order to lick this water wherever they are capable of performing this ritual. Consequently, hundreds die from poisonous flies. There are also reports that a high guano fence is being erected beyond the already existing wall separating the Sages' compound from the rest of the island. They say it has a high wire mesh netting to protect the compound from flies.

Monday, April 4, 1983
Diary entry by Adélaïde Fourangier

Costas came by yesterday and much to my surprise ordered me to leave the island tomorrow (and not next month as I had planned). They need my urgent assistance in Thailand, to get help for our severely ill children and to start an unofficial bureau that will liaise with the free Pinto movement and the Thai government. Costas wants me to use my French credentials for that purpose. So instead of preparing myself for master classes in Paris, I will run around the streets of Bangkok trying to meet with Thai officials in my capacity as a "French humanitarian on an international mission," he says. The Aviocar C-212, the plane loved by all here on the western side of the island, will fly me to Bangkok along with the two beaten American volunteers and twenty sick and wounded children. After that I leave for Paris while the American volunteers will remain in Bangkok to develop the Free Island embassy there. In spite of the fact that I should be back within two months, Costas asked me to take all my diaries, the newspaper clippings he had brought to show me, and the cassettes made by Jean-Luc and Goncalvo. He said that these are precious materials that should be preserved for future generations. He says that our struggle for freedom should be known throughout the world. He wants these materials stored in a safe place. I nodded silently, though in my view Paris was not as safe as Costas thought. Remembering the years between 1940 and 1945, I could tell him that Paris is not all that safe. But as Costas pressed me to take these materials to France, I acquiesced.

He also brought me Jean-Luc's urn, upon which he carefully wrote Jean-Luc's name, together with the name of his native village, Bénouville. He said that with Goncalvo's help he would communicate with me via radiogramme. I asked him to notify my pupils of my sudden departure and to wish them well. He said, "Of course, you will see your pupils again." Then he added reassuringly, "You will see our son too."

He embraced me tightly in his arms. I let my head rest on his shoulder—after all, he is my man, my wretched, old *prince charmant.*

No more for now—I have to prepare myself for the trip.

INTERMEZZO

Friday, August 26, 1983
Diary entry by Adélaïde Fourangier
Hôtel de Varenne
44 Rue de Bourgogne
Paris

I rested for two months at the Château de Sissi in Petites-Dalles on France's northern coast. Having received treatment for my tremors prior to this rest, my hands and head no longer shake as they once did. I can now hold a pen and write freely. Only now am I starting to regain my inner balance. It took almost three weeks to fully overcome the jet lag caused by traveling from the Far East to France; I taught my open classes under conditions of severe drowsiness in spite of consuming many cups of strong black coffee. Later, I clearly went through culture shock. I had to learn how to be French again. The steel and glass France of today is not the France of 1960 that I remember from when I left, and in my mind France is still that bleak, occupied country of 1942....

My first shock occurred when boarding the Air France plane full of French speakers who conversed so matter of factly in my own native tongue. For the last twenty-three years I spoke in French only with Costas, Jean-Luc, and Illirio, and since Jean-Luc's death I never heard French outside the confines of my own house (or should I say "cabin"?). On the plane I dined on French cuisine and listened to many new French songs on the audio system. I could hardly avoid crying when hearing the magnificent Edith Piaff. Later on, to my surprise the stewardess informed me that this was not the voice of Piaff but rather that of a young woman called Mireille Mathieu. I'm told that Mlle Mathieu with her stunning vocal range and delivery has replaced Piaff in French hearts. This stewardess also told me that Mlle Mathieu is incomparably more beautiful than Piaff and behaves with much more self-restraint—both on stage and in her private life. *Voilà!*

At the Paris airport (who would ever think it would bear the name of that tall poseur de Gaulle?) I was met by an IHEMdP representative, an elegant young lady with a strangely sad gaze. She took me to the Alexandra Hotel, deposited me there, and left. The next day she came back and took me to IHEMdP where a secretary—without any hint of a smile—handed me the scores of the music my prospective students were to play. I had to choose six compositions from a list of twelve pieces from the piano repertoire. I had to make the decision on the spot, and I did.

I chose the *Italian Concerto* by Johann Sebastian Bach, Beethoven's *Piano Sonata in E minor*, Op. 90, Fauré's *Third Impromptu in A-flat major*, Op. 34, Ravel's *Miroirs*, Hummel's *Piano Sonata in F-sharp minor*, Op. 81, and Henri Dutilleux's *Piano Sonata*. All these compositions have expansive melodic developments and deeply expressive accompaniments that I love, and my long acquaintance with these pieces made me feel that I might truly contribute to their inspired performance.

Having just two days to immerse myself in these works, I worried about the problems I might encounter during the open classes, especially since my hands and head shook incessantly (I had not yet received any medical treatment and my drug therapy began only ten days later). I was required to put on a pedagogic show for judges whose careers centered around the glittering capital of France, while I had spent most of my life on a remote, half-savage island. For two years I had hardly ever practiced, instead attending to Jean-Luc's vegetable garden. Even though—and in spite of—my shaking, I can still control my fingers on the keyboard, I am frequently too tired to sit for long hours at the piano. Self-critically, I have to admit that as a solo pianist I am out of shape, and so could not give the students examples of my own playing to illustrate my points. But all my musical knowledge remains with me, and I still do not wish to give up professionally at this stage of my life. Feeling quite sure of myself, I set out to show my metropolitan colleagues what I had learned and discovered during my long years of professional solitude.

The only thing that bothered me was my dated and inevitably unrefined French.

I took to the streets of Paris. My hotel on rue du Faubourg-Montmartre allowed me to stroll through the most beautiful parts of the city. I even took a taxi to my former house in Neuilly-sur-Seine. But somehow it did not interest me, as I could no longer enjoy the views of this beautiful city. Walking around Paris made me feel like an alien from another planet who had fallen into a world of faux images. The street noise paralyzed me, while reflections off the glitzy show windows blinded my vision. In short, I could hardly move.

Buying several newspapers and journals, I sat down at a nearby outdoor café. I started reading *Le Monde* from May 8, 1983. I was startled to learn that once he became president of France that handsome catholic Vichy minister François Mitterrand had gone almost completely bald and now he was a leading socialist with the reputation of being a former Resistance fighter! Well, he never interested me that much anyway. All the other names mentioned in the paper were totally unfamiliar. Page after page of news on things unknown to me, including photos of massive new buildings created by famous architects! And for some reason I found this all terribly boring. I could only sigh and direct my attention back to the piano compositions that I had to study.

Two days later at half past nine in the morning, the sad, elegant lady came to take me to IHEMdP. She was extremely helpful, leading me to the waiting room adjacent to the open class hall. Strangely, at the last moment she smiled and kissed me; then she entered the hall alone, saying someone else would escort me inside. I waited for five minutes, then an affable young man with long hair and a Chekhovian-style beard (perhaps the latest star in western concert circuits) came to bring me into the hall. It was lit with the natural light of a joyous Parisian spring. Along the outer wall sat the five jurors, four men and one woman, all with sharpened pencils in hand. One of the men, awkwardly holding his pencil in his left hand, slightly reminded me of my historic "colleague," Lothair Döpps, but at first I dismissed this as just a generic resemblance. A short distance away from them sat my new friend, the young, elegant lady with the sad gaze. Evidently she performs secretarial functions in these procedures.

Greeted by all of the jurors, I was asked to take a seat at the second piano. Immediately a young, nimble, long-haired lad of Asian origin approached, bowing toward me with a complicitous smile. He sat at the concert piano and started playing Ravel's *Noctuelles* (*Night Moths,* from the *Miroirs* suite).

The moment the lad set his hands in motion I was divided in two—one part followed the familiar text, now played with joyous, self-assured virtuosity (especially the right hand, whose sound radiated energy and precision), and the other part dwelled on a faraway island where people die in droves from infectious, poisonous flies. For me, flying insects would always represent mortal danger, killers of my only grandchild and his mother, whereas for this confident lad there could be no limit to the fireflies' glow.

Looking at the score, I focused on the gentle pianissimo at the beginning. I also checked the metronome indication—it showed 128 beats per minute—and this man with his great enthusiasm raced through the piece at an even quicker tempo. When he finished, I suggested that we discuss the nature of night moths as Ravel had conceived them—for example, were they poisonous or harmless? The student answered that the moths could not possibly be poisonous, because in that case the music would be alarming, suggesting anxiety and pain. I remarked that his performance—with all its technical brilliance—was in fact alarmingly anxious in its pursuit of bravura. I asked him what he thought Ravel's purpose was in composing a piece about insects. "Isn't it true that humans do not usually like insects?" I queried. The student sat like a stone, not uttering a word.

"Please concentrate on direct teaching," the juror who resembled Lothair Döpps sharply intoned. "Give the student exact and concrete instructions." The moment I heard his voice I realized that this *was* Döpps. I also realized that I had failed my open class examination. Frankly, I did not feel much distress. What saddened me was the sight of my new young lady friend who lowered her head in obvious pain.

I nevertheless persisted. "Composers usually use the dramatic or lyric character of the piano's sound to augment their musical ideas. In other words, there is a direct link between the quality of the sound and the concept of the piece. Therefore, in order to decide what kind of sound we should aim for, we need to discuss the ideas behind the composition. Why would Ravel *wish* to depict moths?" The student looked straight ahead in dead silence.

I relieved his discomfort a little by adding, "I think for Ravel night moths were symbols of innocence—dimly glowing creatures barely visible in the dark night. Their glow should by no means dazzle, but rather emphasize the night's embracing darkness." I suggested a slower tempo (I gently clapped my hands at 124 beats per minute) and I suggested a rebalancing of the left hand. In that way the triplets that represented the air around the moths could be tender but no less prominent than the semiquaver flow of the melody in the right hand.

The student rushed to play. I raised my hands in order to emphasize the unhurried pace: Ravel purposely wrote très léger as the character of the piece, deliberately refraining from using traditional tempo prescriptions like allegro or presto. The student, as indicated by the ironic expression on his face, started playing as though waiving personal responsibility for the outcome. Then all of a sudden, he smiled and started producing wonderful music—a heartrending night scene with little innocent fairies—a sheer delight to the ears. (This we accomplished by freeing the finger muscles from their habitual tension.) The female juror and two of the men could not hide their smiles. The young secretary smiled in huge relief. Döpps and the other man still looked on with stern faces. Döpps, in fact, energetically tapped his pencil on the table just as he had done during my students' examinations fifteen years ago. He urged his colleagues to maintain an "objective" relationship to the process they were assessing.

That day I also worked on the Hummel sonata; the next day on Bach's *Italian Concerto* and Deutilleux's post-war sonata; the last day I listened to and taught Beethoven and Fauré. I was glad I could finish my presentations with Fauré because from my own lifelong engagement with the composer, I felt I could contribute to a masterful performance by the young, talented Canadian woman who was nearly ready for public concertizing.

The following two days I rested in my room, even taking my meals there, as my hands and head shook quite heavily. This surely was not a condition that I wanted to display on the streets of Paris. Then Jules called and said he was sending a chauffeur to take me to Saulchery; he suggested that I take all my baggage and leave the hotel altogether. I welcomed the idea. I did not know his chauffeur, although on the other hand I no longer know anyone in Paris now. We drove to Saulchery through the beautiful late spring countryside of northeastern France, tender paysages full of sweet green deciduous forests with little villages scattered in between. The chauffeur informed me that Jules was now a bit frail, but generally well; he said that his life partner (to whom he was not married) was a former attorney for a bank once directed by M. Georges Pompidou (who I'm told later became another president of France). I kept silent, not only because my attention was more focused on the passing landscape, but also because here again I was unfamiliar with the name. We arrived at five o'clock in the afternoon. I immediately saw my former husband, tall, perfectly dressed in a three-piece suit, with a pince-nez and gray bow tie, watching the approach of our sleek, black vehicle. His right hand rested on the arm of a young, elegant woman. Getting closer, I recognized her as my benevolent assistant from IHEMdP. She looked at me with a tense, sad smile.

"Come here, Adèle," said Jules in his aging, wheezy voice. "This is our daughter, Fleurette." We embraced. I had difficulty concealing my tears. Fleurette tenderly helped me into the house. In the course of the evening I asked Fleurette about her life. She said only a few words, but she did mention her last two years in the public relations department at IHEMdP.

"An unknown life cannot be revealed in conversation," said Jules with his characteristically subtle condemnation of me and then asked his servant to invite the other lady of the house into the room to meet me. Though in her early sixties, she was still elegant. Her hair was brown and her eyes piercing, even slightly suspicious. While her attitude toward Fleurette was cool and businesslike, her emotional ties to Jules were obvious.

"So how is your life on the island?" she asked me casually.

Now it was my turn. "An unknown life cannot be revealed in conversation," I said, glancing innocently at Jules, who lowered his eyes and seemed to play with his fingers.

We—the four of us, that is—spent a tranquil evening together, and Jules suggested that he and I have a private conversation the next morning. I agreed. I had a comfortable night's sleep in the spacious, clean bedchamber that they provided for me. The next day, after breakfast (which all of us had together), Jules led me to his private office and asked me about my immediate plans. I said I wanted to rest for a while in some tranquil place and then visit a village on the northern coast, Bénouville, so I could present the remains of M. Jean-Luc Lefevbre, my longtime friend on Pinto Island and the only other European there besides me, to the people of his native village to be interred next to his parents, as was his dying wish. Then I intended to return home.

"Home?" asked Jules. "You mean you wish to return to Pinto?"

"Yes," I replied in the affirmative. "At the moment there is no other place that I could call 'home,' though I wish it were otherwise."

Jules looked at me thoughtfully and said, "Let's first visit some doctors and provide you with medical attention for your...."

"Shaking," I offered in to ameliorate his embarrassment.

"Yes," he conceded. Gratified by his concern, I asked Fleurette if she wouldn't mind helping me find suitable treatment. So during the next six days, she and I visited three clinics in Picardy. We also stopped at the Interior Registration Office at Aisne so I could obtain new personal documents. A few days later Fleurette took me to Paris and helped me settle my financial affairs. I am a rich woman now, thanks to the untouched earnings from IHEMdP that have been accruing compound interest over the years.

"How is your life, Fleurette?" I asked on the way back to Saulchery. "Are you married, do you have children?"

"I am divorced, Mama, after two years of an unhappy marriage to a gifted engineer who was successfully employed at Aérospatiale. I now rent a small apartment in one of the new buildings of Romainville, just east of central Paris." I did not know what more to ask.

"Some of the judges had very positive opinion of your work," offered Fleurette in an effort to break the uneasy silence between us.

"How many are 'some'?" I asked.

"Two, Mama. They felt that you are a great *artiste*."

"And what about the others?" I asked.

Fleurette sighed. "One was furious that you used nontechnical explanations in teaching piano, a *faute* trespassing on the most elementary principles of professionalism, or so he said."

"And the other two?" I asked.

"I think they liked you very much but were afraid to say so."

"Why?"

"I believe they were intimidated by the one who hated you," responded Fleurette.

"Well," I said, "then my fate is clear."

Fleurette looked at me with unbearably sad eyes. We sat in silence for the rest of the journey. Three days later I left Saulchery for Bénouville, having arranged a summer-long stay at the Château de Sissi nearby. Before I left I had another tête-à-tête with Jules. I asked him to help set up a meeting between Costas and some influential people in the French government. Jules asked me to tell him more about Costas, and I told him that he was a liberal revolutionary fighting ultra-religious Sages on the island whose perverse and heartless teachings caused mass death among the population. I told Jules that the Sages occasionally used Costas for their own aims and then attacked him for altering the island's theocratic culture.

"I am glad that you care for somebody at last," said Jules, lowering his head.

"I did not come here to discuss my ethical qualities, Jules," I replied acerbically. "This man needs help with international political and financial support. Otherwise his island is doomed."

"Doomed? To what?" asked Jules, with just a hint of a sardonic smile curling around his lips.

"To extinction," I said, and tapped my fingers on the table.

"Oh, that serious," said Jules. "Well, I'll call Pierre."

"Who is Pierre?" I asked.

"Do not worry, my dear," said Jules, "Pierre is in a position to help."

He promised to call me at the Château de Sissi and inform me about the possibility of a meeting between Costas and that Pierre-whoever-he-is.

The next day I left Saulchery. When parting, Jules told me that if I wanted to come back to Paris, he would help me return to my previous residence on Rue de Longchamp in Neuilly-sur-Seine. I thanked him very sincerely.

After getting settled at the château I traveled to the village of Bénouville and passed Jean-Luc's ashes to the head of the local community. I was invited to the burial ceremony that took place two days later and was asked to give the eulogy because the head of the community could not find any of Jean-Luc's living relatives or friends. Several local functionaries stood around in silence. I said that I knew Jean-Luc very well. I related to total strangers what a devoted friend he was and what a noble, courageous heart he had! I told how he saved many children from death and taught them modern science, which was an unknown field of knowledge on that remote island. I also related that Jean- Luc raised Costas, my life partner, as his own son. It was Jean- Luc who taught Costas to love people, as well as to love freedom, decency, and music, attitudes that Jean-Luc so perfectly embodied. After witnessing the urn interred in the concrete wall where the cremated remains of Bénouville residents were kept, I promptly left.

Two days later I had an unexpected guest—M. Caetano Thibault, a solfège teacher from Cambrai. He was one of the two island youngsters Lothair Döpps had brought to France thirteen years ago. Thibault was the surname given him by his foster parents in Cambrai who had also financed his education. Caetano told me about his work with the children at the local music school and about his joy in coming to class every day and singing with them. He asked me about Illirio. He said the memory of Illirio was most precious to him (he mentioned my lessons too). He said he had completely forgotten how to sing in two voices but would dearly love to relearn the skill. He said that meeting Illirio again would be for him the greatest of life's gifts. I said that I too would be happy if they could meet again.

Four days later Jules called to tell me that Pierre would be waiting for Costas, and that a meeting could be arranged for mid-August at Pierre's office in the Hôtel Matignon. Jules asked me to inform him whether Costas could come.

I immediately phoned the office of Aigle Azur and asked them to send a radiogramme to the Jean-Luc meteorological station containing these words: "Come, Costas, for an important meeting!"

The next day I received an answer:

> Do not see any justification for coming, since I do
> not hold any public office now.

I asked to send another radiogramme: "Come, for god's sake!"

Costas confirmed his arrival in late July.

I booked a room for us at the Hôtel de Varenne, which was near the Hôtel Matignon; I had already figured out that Jules had arranged for Costas to meet the French prime minister. As my hands no longer shake thanks to the treatment I received, I went out and bought a pair of good glasses. Now I can see perfectly well.

Wednesday, August 24, 1983

A separate page written in Tegularius's hand and kept between the August 1983 pages of Adélaïde Fourangier's diary

Yesterday I had the honor of a private meeting with the prime minister of the French Republic. I am submitting this summary of our conversation for his approval as per his instructions.

Currently I do not serve in any public position on Pinto Island. I came to France not as a representative of the people of Pinto Island but rather as a private individual wishing to establish personal ties with the public servants of the French people in the hope of inaugurating a collaboration between our two countries.

Our meeting lasted twenty-five minutes. For the first fifteen minutes I answered the prime minister's questions regarding my views on the current situation on Pinto Island and my projections of possible developments there. I told the PM that in the recent past I had served my compatriots for four years as chief executive. I informed my host about the spiritual and military power concentrated in the hands of four Sages, the upper echelon of the national religious institution of our little country. I explained to my host that my election to the post of chief executive had been endorsed by the Sages and without their approbation there was no way I could command the people's trust. I also told him that in spite of their calling themselves Christian, our Sages actually adhere to tribal rites that cause recurrent mass death among our people. I informed my host that during the last two decades following the departure of the French meteorological delegation that was once stationed on the island, the indigenous population has been reduced from eighty thousand (registered in the only population census ever undertaken there) to an estimated fifty thousand due to recurring fly-borne epidemics. I told the prime minister about the way of life on our island and about the progress made in modernizing our healthcare, sanitation, and education systems in spite of the Sages' negative influence. I told him about the many people in our country who succeeded in obtaining a good secondary and professional education in French Saigon and later in South Vietnam until it was overrun by the northern communists. I also told the prime minister about the conflict between the majority of the islanders and the Sages' armed forces, notwithstanding the considerable affection and respect that islanders still maintain for the Sages.

The prime minister asked me whether our Sages were aware of the tragic consequences engendered by the practice of their religion. I answered that I had no idea about our Sages' thoughts. I informed him that the Sages live in a secluded part of the island and are protected by an unknown number of well-armed troops. The prime minister then asked me about the source of their large supply of weapons. I informed him of the fortnightly shipments sent by the Pintoist diaspora residing in Des Moines, Iowa. I also informed him that our liberalization campaign was known among our faraway brethren in Iowa, but was summarily discounted. The prime minister then asked what assistance the French government might provide to Pinto Island in the event that I acquired official public status there once again. I told him that we had to introduce a money-based economy to replace our barter economy. Once this was in place, we could accept French investment, both public and private. We could develop Pinto Island as a venue for European tourism, especially for those interested in discovering exotic locales, and during the first phase of our economic development we could trade our "cash crops"—pearls and agricultural produce—for sound western currency. The prime minister expressed favorable understanding of the program I outlined.

He also expressed concern about interfering in the internal affairs of the island against the wishes of all the inhabitants. He stated quite unequivocally that the French government could not support any faction due to the international dispute concerning ownership of the island, as the continental Chinese, the communist Vietnamese, and even the Philippines claimed the entire archipelago—or parts of it—as part of their nations. However, the prime minister could envisage some form of humanitarian assistance under the right circumstances. The prime minister informed me of possible large oil deposits around our island that had been detected by French satellites. The prime minister observed that if test drilling proved these deposits to be significant, there might be much help our islanders could offer to its developers, especially if the development rights would be given to French companies.

I expressed my sincere readiness to explore most favorably all possibilities stemming from the prime minister's remarks. I expressed my gratitude to the prime minister for our meeting. The prime minister in turn expressed his own satisfaction with the meeting and wished me every success in helping my compatriots improve their lives. He extended an invitation to be his honored guest on any occasion during future visits to Paris.

Friday, August 26, 1983

A separate page written in Tegularius's hand and kept between the August 1983 pages of Adélaïde Fourangier's diary

Confirmation received from the prime minister's office for the minutes of our meeting.

Signed:

Saturday, August 27, 1983
Diary entry by Adélaïde Fourangier

We are going back to Pinto Island now. I am going to leave all my archival material, including this diary, with Fleurette. Costas is shipping a large box of piano accessories—strings, screws, nuts, plastic covers for the keys, and glue—and a lot of music scores for children and young people back to the island. He also included school textbooks on mathematics, physics, and French literature for children of different ages in addition to surgical instruments, tools for dental surgery, and a large stock of antibiotics and painkillers. At his suggestion I included some books for myself, notably works by Michel Foucault, Roland Barthes, and Jacques Lacan. I am also taking *Le Solitaire* by Eugène Ionesco, *L'Œuvre au noir* by Marguerite Yourcenar, and *Exercices de style* by Raymond Queneau.

Goodbye, Paris; goodbye, France.

Saturday, August 27, 1983
Cassettes recorded by Goncalvo

It seems that many of our islanders have become completely deranged. There is no ruling hand on the island and madness hovers over our soil. Ever since Tegularius stopped acting as chief executive things on the island have turned sour—less and less agricultural work is being done, more and more turtles are being cooked, and feces has reappeared on the paths between our clay houses, causing more and more deaths from fly poison. But things deteriorated into complete madness the moment Tegularius left the island—some five weeks ago.

The secretaries in compete self-abandon now urinate on one another and on any woman in their path; the women laugh wildly and dance ecstatically around the secretaries, some loudly begging for "golden shower." Two weeks ago twelve of them choked to death in puddles of urine. Secretaries copulate with women in the open on excrement-covered ground. Many copulating pairs die soon after reaching orgasm from the bites of the uncrushed poisonous flies beneath their bodies. Nobody works. As people dance and defecate all around, secretaries beat everyone they see with their deadly clubs, laughing all the time at people's injuries.

Zeferino has told me of the rumors about someone bringing American corn mash whiskey to our island and distributing it to the secretaries and the women who work in the kitchens at the entrance to the Sages' compound. I sent Zeferino to the Sages' gates to learn who, but he discovered nothing; the gate was locked and no one was around. I think it must be some morbid joke played by one of the American Pintoists, either from the Sages' side or from our side. We may never know.

Last month, with so much death in our country, the surviving secretaries are motivated to urinate more and more. The Sages instituted a two-week body and soul purification rite that failed to calm things down and only created more mayhem and death. Mariafels organized protective measures for the westerners, but in Tegularius's absence he refrains from ordering an attack on the Sages' compound. It seems we will all soon die unless Tegularius comes back to save us.

PART FIVE: BACK ON THE ISLAND

Monday, August 29, 1983
Bulletin from the Sages: THE SAGES' WRATH

Life on our sacred island is undergoing a sudden and severe lack of harmoniousness. Our inviolable sacred rites are being mixed with hysterical nonsense that incapacitates our people and exposes them to disorientation, abomination, and death for the wrong reasons. Abandonment of the only true and holy rite of unification of body and soul is an act of heresy that will be severely punished.

Our turtle catchers have stopped catching turtles, our women have stopped grilling them, and nobody brings wood from our forests to the grilling stoves. Our secretaries, left without their sacred turtle meat, consume poisonous vegetables instead, and this necessitates that they be drowned in our holy wells and that their bodies be covered with our soul-saving body substance by our senior servants in gray. Many of those whose deaths could be sanctified will now die without such sanctification due to the disruption of our beatific island life.

Moreover, at this troubled time Costas Tegularius allows himself to leave our island in order to spend time with alien people overseas. His behavior is inexcusable. The moment the abovementioned Tegularius returns to our island, he will be brought before us in order to receive orders on how to harmonize life of the island anew and free it from this current turmoil.

Monday, September 5, 1983
Diary entry by Adélaïde Fourangier

Immediately upon landing on Jean-Luc's runway, I was shocked by the sickening mixture of odors—dead human bodies and protective concentrates of chlorine and sodium hypochlorite, the smell of which I had learned to discern many years ago. Illirio entered the plane's fuselage and put a protective medical mask over my face so quickly that I could not even say good bye to Costas. Illirio then led me to my house, which he had covered with two layers of metal gauze. He ordered me to remain inside for a whole week, filling my refrigerator with fresh vegetables and promising to visit. Walking around the house, I was surprised to discover that air filters had been installed in the windows, and water filters placed in my kitchen sink and toilet. This is the fifth day now that I have been encapsulated in my residence, cut off even from this small crazy island.

Tuesday, September 6, 1983
Cassettes recorded by Goncalvo

Zeferino's voice: The very moment our Aviocar touched down on Jean-Luc's runway, two motorcyclists approached. Several secretaries dressed in gray jumped onto the plane and hauled our former leader Costas Tegularius from it, strapping him to a stretcher. Humiliatingly they attached this stretcher between their two motorcycles in the shape of the letter "H." Curiously, Tegularius did not even resist. The convoy drove straight to the Sages' compound, with some of our astounded western parents and even some of our youngsters running alongside, trying as best they could to keep up. I followed after them. When I got to the gate, a small crowd of people had already gathered. In the midst of the crowd stood Tegularius, shouting that he would not enter the Sages' compound without Eulalio, Leocadia, and Valeriano. Secretaries dressed in gray tried to drag him inside, but our people prevented it.

At sunset Eulalio, Leocadia, and Valeriano arrived. Eulalio in his fiery rhetorical style shouted that there could be no negotiation with murderers of the people. Costas put a finger over Eulalio's mouth to calm him. All four entered the compound around seven o'clock in the evening. All of us who were gathered outside waited anxiously for their return. We all wore protective masks so as not to be overwhelmed by the terrible smell. The territory extending far beyond our two public wells to the area of the turtle-grilling kitchens, including the area of the Caring Heart supporters in the central part of the island, was littered with unburied corpses of people felled during the last month of public anarchy. Swarms of poisonous flies circled the dead bodies and buzzed in a manner reminiscent of our ventriloquist chants. We all protected ourselves with antidote-impregnated gauze that Mariafels, as chief coordinator of salvage operations, had distributed during the month of mayhem. Now dozens of our westerners were collecting the corpses for burial near the guano fence surrounding the Sages' compound. Our leaders came out at around 3 a.m.; Tegularius had lost his voice, apparently from incessant shouting.

Leocadia said, "Now we will keep a tight rein on them."

Valeriano added, "They will publish their announcement of a complete transfer of power to us by midday. Let's all get some sleep."

Wednesday, September 7, 1983
Bulletin from the Sages: THE SAGES' ANNOUNCEMENT

We have given Costas Tegularius full authority to restore orderly life on our sacred island. We shall not insist on the performance of our rites for a period of twenty months. The arriving supply shipments from the Des Moines Pintoists will be redirected to the runway harbor, except for one monthly shipment that will bring us fresh food and clothing. We forbid the alien two-voiced chanting throughout the island with the exception of the vicinity of the alien music teacher's house.

Friday, September 30, 1983
RADIOGRAMME from Marius Villeneuve

After prolonged debate, the collegial council of the IHEMdP has awarded you the opportunity to work in our institute as a professor of piano accompaniment starting September 1985. Moreover, as the council was highly impressed by your ability to inspire young pianists, it has decided to direct the weakest students majoring in piano to your expert tutelage. IHEMdP will stop paying your international grant at the end of August 1985. Kindly respond.

Friday, September 30, 1983
Cassettes recorded by Goncalvo

Fourangier's voice: What do you think of their proposal?

Tegularius's voice: I think you should accept it.

Fourangier's voice: Don't you see how humiliating it is? After touring Europe as a soloist to be made a professor of piano accompaniment. And on top of that to be given the students nobody else wants.

Tegularius's voice: Yes I see that.

Fourangier's voice: So?

Tegularius's voice: You should accept anyway."

Fourangier's voice: What? Don't you even see what's going on there?

Tegularius's voice: I do see, my love.

Fourangier's voice: And you don't care? You just push me out after all the years that I have spent inhaling this shitty air and teaching these kids to be a little bit more civilized? You have no—

Tegularius's voice: You are right, my love. I have no heart. I have become a mass killer. Each time I see you and take you in my arms, I feel that I desecrate you; I trespass my own love for you and become a beast, just hungry to possess you.

Fourangier's voice: You are crazy. Why, we were just together in Paris, attending concerts and the theater. You enjoyed Westphal's play "*Outrage au Bonnes Moeurs*" so much...you even caressed my hand in the darkness with the endearment of a fairytale prince touching the fair damsel he just rescued from the dragon's lair….

Tegularius's voice: Yes….

Fourangier's voice: Oh my god! You mean to tell me that you deliberately chose that dark comedy for some ulterior motive? To hint that you yourself have changed exactly as the heroine of that play changed from a saint working at a clinic for the poor to a driven gambler thieving and vamping in casinos?

Tegularius's voice: Brutally changed, yes…

Fourangier's voice: You are unbearable. Put me on you damned plane, I am leaving you now.

Tegularius's voice: Adèle—

Fourangier's voice: What Adèle, why Adèle? You and I are finished. I have nothing more to say to you.

Tegularius's voice: Tell them that you will accept the position.

Fourangier's voice: Yes, I will. Their humiliation is much less evil than yours.

Tegularius's voice: Good. Write the proper phrasing for the radiogramme so Zeferino can send it right now. I will come to you this evening.

Fourangier's voice: What for? To desecrate me?

Tegularius's voice: Just to see you, my love. I must, I have to inhale your image for years to come, to keep the remaining crumbs of my soul alive.

Fourangier's voice: Your words are so meaningless.

Tegularius's voice: I love you, Adèle.

Fourangier's voice: You mean the crumbs love me.

Tegularius's voice: The crumbs love you, yes.

Friday, September 30, 1983
Copy of **RADIOGRAMME** sent to Marius Villeneuve

I agree to start teaching piano accompaniment classes at IHEMdP from September 1985. I also accept the position of teaching weak students majoring in piano.

Adélaïde Fourangier

Tuesday, October 11, 1983
Diary entry by Adélaïde Fourangier

It seems that I cannot overcome my penchant for melodramatic domestic quarreling—a throwback, no doubt, to my own deranged childhood. There was really no reason for me to shout at Costas ten days ago; he graciously presented himself as a harsh-hearted man, when in fact all he wanted to do was protect me and send me away to a safer place. After all, since my arrival on this island I knew perfectly well that one day I would return home; in fact, both of us knew it. Also it was clear to us that my stay here depended on the monthly salary from IHEMdP. Who knew then that my stay here would become my life's work? But that should not change the logic of my life; I have to return to Paris and end my career there. I must vindicate myself in the very *lieu* that exiled me years ago.

Costas? Illirio? My young pupils here? I do hope to see them all frequently. But even if I visit Pinto Island only once in a while, Costas and Illirio could certainly come to Paris to spend time with me there.

I refuse to attach much importance to Costas's moaning about his becoming a mass killer; what nonsense, though even he has a taste for melodrama! We both know that he dedicates his life to saving his people, not killing them. Anyway, I couldn't touch a mass killer. I know he is not one. He loves me, the old dreamer, and his love is pure. I owe him much in this life. Let him come and kiss me, if he wishes, or make love to me, or just sit and eat my cucumbers.

January 6, 1984
Cassettes recorded by Goncalvo

Significantly fewer people than before the last epidemic now live on our island. The eastern part, where most of the devoted secretaries and members of the Caring Heart faction live, has been decimated. When walking along the paths on the eastern side of the island, instead of the constant human presence of the recent past, you can go for minutes without encountering a single man, woman, or child (a living one, that is). Although people are now purposefully engaged in restoring the island, they are depressed despite the orderliness and the obvious improvement in the quality of life. Their mood stems from awareness that the moment Tegularius leaves the island, they collectively degenerate into a horde of beasts on the one hand and a crowd of hapless losers on the other. When they feel Tegularius's presence they remember how to act in harmony. He inspires them by his wonderful behavior; he walks around the island embracing people's shoulders and asking about their lives with genuine concern. Then he tells them how he envisions the next stage of our cultural advancement and inspires people to do their part in this collective endeavor. People begin to feel their own self-worth and gladly organize themselves to do what they do best. Amazing. Nobody but Tegularius can do this.

Well, at last all the public wells have been cleaned and are now protected by our police force, which is armed with guns and plastic bullets. We are no longer going hungry—only six months after the catastrophe—as many people have resumed farming and now raise sufficient quantities of vegetables, fruit, and grain. There are now practically no turtle-grilling kitchens on the island. Children have returned to school; our teachers lovingly teach them for long hours, trying to bring them back from their mental abyss.

We now receive regular cargo shipments of aid from Des Moines that come straight to the harbor next to Jean-Luc's runway. We have learned not to become angry when the shipments consist only of dirty, ragged clothing, worn shoes, crumbling blankets, torn notebooks, and broken pencils. We have assigned forty-five secretaries to mend whatever is salvageable and throw the rest into our compost bins behind the forest. The crews manning the cargo ships are now routinely invited to our music teacher's house where they listen to our children's two-voice chanting. How quickly they are imbued with sympathy for us and for our aspirations. The only problem is that the more sympathy they feel for us, the more the Des Moines Pintoists send deaf seamen to the Philippine entrepôt.

According to my calculations, thirty-nine brethren from Des Moines trained in agriculture, construction, pedagogy, and medicine have recently joined us. The person debriefing them is Valeriano, and he reports directly to Mariafels and to Tegularius. I hope our future will be brighter than our past.

Monday, March 5, 1984
Diary entry by Adélaïde Fourangier

In recent months life here has stabilized. I am free to walk two miles to the west and even to promenade in the forest. Nobody bothers me. Everything is very quiet. People here work hard to create a reasonable life for themselves. What I call the "craze" has receded into the invisible past. Even the air feels friendlier. I can breathe better now. To my surprise I recently overheard some birds chirping. It was so unexpected that I froze for a good quarter of an hour just to listen. While I was in Paris, fourteen students from my last year's class died in the epidemic. I have somehow learned to turn my attention to my current pupils and not succumb to heartbreaking emotion. But my hand tremors have gradually returned. I have run out of medicine.

Illirio visited me yesterday evening. He told me that Costas wants to hold elections at the end of 1984 without the sanction of the Sages. He said that Costas is fed up with their merciless idiocy, and no matter who wins, he will not collaborate with them after the elections. Illirio also told me that from the interviews Valeriano conducted with the new volunteers from Des Moines, he learned that the liberal-minded community there—in spite of its being completely secular—still reveres the Sages, overlooking the salient fact that the practices endorsed by the Sages are unacceptable to them. Like their orthodox brothers they believe that their task is to support the Sages and their supremacy on the island.

"That is classic hypocrisy," I said after he had finished.

"Maybe so, Mother," answered Illirio, "but *they* do not feel that way. They sincerely believe that the Sages are solid conservatives who preserve the best traditions of our nation's past for the benefit not only of Pinto Islanders but for humanity as a whole. The Sages' doctrines represent unique attributes of world culture that the progressives in Des Moines feel morally obliged to disseminate throughout the word."

"So the progressives intend to sell the world a message that they themselves do not adhere to?" I asked, reveling in the sarcasm.

"Yes, Mother, so it would appear."

"So they exalt their public image with a teaching that they are not ready to impose on themselves…very nice. Do you have any proof?" I hounded him for more details.

"Yes, Mother. After learning that the Sages are no longer the sole representatives of our people, and that the progressive movement led by Uncle Costas and made up of the majority of islanders is much closer to their own personal preferences, they still choose not to establish any contact with us, and even when requested by the Sages to send fortnightly supplies to our end of the island, they send us their old rags. When our new volunteers return to Des Moines and they ask the authorities there why they send us these rags, we're told that they receive the same circuitous answer: 'In a land without a Harvard, a Yale, a Stanford, or a Princeton, without even the West Point Military Academy or the Kennedy Space Center, one should not expect to be treated as if these institutions do exist there.'"

"So am I to presume this island will never grow and flourish?" I asked.

"Not with the help of our American brethren," said Illirio dejectedly.

Before leaving Illirio told me that after hearing the enthusiastic impressions of the returning Des Moines seamen to the miraculous two-voiced chanting of our children, and after a radio consultation with the Sages, the authorities in Des Moines forbade such singing in their own territory.

Monday, October 15, 1984
Cassettes recorded by Goncalvo

On September 30 we had new elections. This time Tegularius did not run unopposed; Eulalio put his name on the ballot against him. The election results were: Tegularius, 38.9%; Eulalio, 12.9%. Almost half of eligible voters did not even cast a ballot. While the people could not openly express their antagonism toward the Sages, they also could not bring themselves to vote against Tegularius, whom they regard as their savior. So they solved their dilemma by remaining at home. Fortunately, a majority—51.8%—did come to the polls. This is a clear indication that the Sages do not represent the will of the majority now. Tegularius noticed that too, but he warned his supporters not to celebrate, especially since this victory came at the price of so many deaths.

Yesterday Eulalio announced his support for Tegularius. Today they jointly announced the formation of an independent judiciary on the island. Elections to the assembly will be held at the end of November.

Tuesday, December 4, 1984
Bulletin: *Our Free Island News*

In accordance with the final vote count supervised by Senhora Leocadia, the four factions in our Assembly received the following mandates:

Strong Will faction (lead by Eulalio)—8 representatives;

Supporters of Costas Tegularius—18 representatives;

Caring Heart faction (founded by the late Leonor)—5 representatives;

True Fidelity faction of secretaries—10 representatives

The total number of people who voted in the elections for the Assembly was 74% of all eligible citizens. Naturally, Constantius Tegularius was proclaimed Prime Minister of the Pinto Island Republic and will remain in office until December 4, 1988, unless asked to resign in a no-confidence vote of the Assembly.

Monday, December 17, 1984
Bulletin from the Sages: WRATHFUL WARNING OF THE SAGES

Chief Executive Tegularius has committed a grave sin, trespassing upon the orders given him by the Sages on September 7, 1983. No less sinful are the people who take part in activities unfaithful to the spirit of our Founding Fathers. The mandate given to Chief Executive Tegularius by the Sages expires on May 4, 1985. Should he want to continue he must publicly annul all authority invested in him from the recently conducted "public games" and announce his faith in our Founding Fathers' spirit, as expressed by the will of the Sages.

It should be clear: those desecrating the spirit of our Founding Fathers do not deserve to live, since a life devoid of Their spirit negates its own reason for being. The inhabitants of our sacred Island live only to project this holy spirit onto the entire world, to endow it with the wisdom springing from the Founding Fathers elevated souls. Cutting off this spring of wisdom and purity is worse than murder—it is deicide. Therefore no mercy can be shown to these hideous spirit-killers.

Nevertheless, not all of those who took part in the heinous act of elections must die. Those who voted for our Founding Fathers' spirit bearers must not die. The "voters" who gave their support to our followers should be nevertheless proclaimed captured souls, innocents led astray by the manipulations of Diabolus. Our noble gray servants will sooner or later cleanse the Island of this abomination and will save all those whose souls can be saved.

January 19, 1985
Bulletin: *Our Free Island News*

Our prime minister Costas Tegularius visited the United States Transport Ship *President Harding* and met its captain, Commander Edward Hayes. Costas Tegularius informed his American host about the liberalization process that is taking place on our island. Commander Hayes promised to dispatch two representatives to our island to get firsthand impressions of our transformation and growth. The representatives will arrive no later than April 29, 1985. They will be housed in a well-equipped modern residence in our hospital area. Commander Hayes enthusiastically agrees to inform his superiors about the new situation on the island and as a sign of his friendly disposition decided to reconfigure his ship's patrols to make their outer perimeter only eight kilometers from our eastern coast instead of the former twenty-five kilometers. In this way his ship will frequently be visible from our easternmost shore.

Thursday, February 14, 1985
Diary entry by Adélaïde Fourangier

It seems that Costas has started enjoying flying to Paris. Yesterday he told me that he requested another meeting with the French prime minister and secured an invitation for a meeting in just two weeks' time. I will not accompany him now, as I am due to return to Paris at the beginning of the summer. I have never seen Costas radiating such a businesslike attitude—and yet he never smiles. Illirio looks worried too (I fed them both some homegrown vegetables yesterday evening as if that could do anything). Costas says he will take a large box of pearls with him to Paris and deposit them there in exchange for French currency that he intends to use to reorganize our economy.

Thursday, April 11, 1985
Diary entry by Adélaïde Fourangier

A sad mood prevails among my pupils who know that I am leaving soon even though I repeatedly assure them that I will visit the island every two months and see them often. Meanwhile, I am grooming several outstanding former pupils to expand the activity of our school, including leading children's choruses and establishing music theory, singing, and acting departments. People from the western part are constructing two additional buildings for our school. Illirio and two of my former students repaired my old piano and now it is a joy to play. Ah, those Pleyels, what unique sonority!

Costas came back from France yesterday. He looks pleased, though the tension does not leave him. I told him to relax, otherwise his hands will start to shake like mine, and I no longer have any medicine to alleviate my own malady, not to mention his. Costas laughed at me ironically and placed a fresh supply of drugs on my desk.

April 17, 1985
Cassettes recorded by Goncalvo

We have money now! After long preparation and much discussion, we have introduced the long-awaited currency system to replace our customary method of financial exchange that relied on buckets of holy sand.

For the sake of our grandchildren who may one day hear this cassette, I will now briefly describe how our now defunct economic system worked.

A bucket of holy sand served as a symbol of the Sage's benevolence to its possessor. Its worth was equivalent to a four-month supply of turtle meat and fish and one set of clothing; each adult islander was entitled to three buckets of holy sand a year, which were handed to them by secretaries dressed in gray either as actual sand-filled buckets or in corresponding quantities of goods that were recorded in the secretaries' books. It also included one hand-bound book of the Sages' teachings. Four buckets of sand were equal to the value of one clay cabin.

Problems arose with the inability to discern holy sand from regular sand, since both types of sand appeared to have the same nature; however, only sand from the Sages' compound was considered "holy." Building up the Hill used any sand from the island, and, of course, regular sand from Hainan (which the youth always passed to the Sages upon their return) that became "holy." So there could be no clear differentiation between ordinary sand and treasured sand, and as a result people rarely used these buckets for transactions; instead they would come to the Sage's gates and beg for food, and secretaries dressed in gray who were on duty would either hand some out, or not, depending on their mood.

According to our leader Costas Tegularius, the new system of currency will work as follows: the monthly haul of pearls will be valued according to its worth in the Paris market; all other goods and services will be valued according to their worth in our own market. Every family will now receive its share of the monthly haul of pearls, distributed according to the number of working family members, and will be able to exchange pearls for money using our newly established banking system. All exports to and imports from Bangkok and the Philippines will be conducted by private citizens or foreigners, *not* by our leaders, *not* in their name, and *not* on their behalf.

Both agriculture and construction will be in private hands. Only the safe maintenance of our drinking water, sanitation, education, and public defense will be governmental functions. These activities will be supported by a flat tax: young families and those without children will be taxed at 10% of their annual income, while bigger families will be taxed at 15% of their annual income.

Costas hopes to finalize these reforms in July. He has ordered the first banking arrangements to be instituted in two weeks. He claims this will allow islanders to start working for their own benefit as soon as possible.

Wednesday, May 1, 1985
Cassettes recorded by Goncalvo

Yesterday two representatives from the USAT *President Harding* arrived. They brought much film equipment with them and many bottles of their native Diamond Knot beer. This morning I already spotted them filming Jean-Luc's meteorological station. I posed for them too.

Thursday, May 2, 1985
Diary entry by Adélaïde Fourangier

My mood is already becoming nostalgic. I am starting to worry about Illirio's fate. My impression is that he has lost all interest in marrying again. He gives himself over entirely to managing the affairs of the island. He is Costas's right-hand man. Both of them visited me yesterday evening. Both were very tense. I asked them why they felt such tension when things were going so well.

"Mother, we do not know what the Sages will do," explained Illirio. "In two days the mandate they gave Uncle Costas is due to expire and they can do many awful things."

"But are you sure that is their intention?" I asked.

"Yes. You see, we held elections and organized our life in a liberal way in opposition to their wishes, and the flourishing life that you see on the island could not have been achieved without the complete cancellation of their dreadful rites," he added.

"But look, they annulled the purification rites themselves," I said.

"Yes, but according to their proclamations, this was just a temporary measure and what hasn't been done during the last twenty months will have to be compensated for in the future, as always," said Illirio.

"So what do you intend to do?" I asked.

"We will fight them," asserted Illirio.

"Do you have the means?" I questioned.

"We have the two helicopters that we assembled," interjected Costas, the former hater of war, with a bitter smile. "We will also resort to shooting all those who dare attack our people."

"Maybe they will not do anything dreadful," I said hopefully. "Maybe the Sages themselves have been impressed by the wonderful changes that you have created on the island and would not wish to disrupt them."

The two men smiled only to humor me.

"Nevertheless, please arrange a farewell party for me, both of you!" I said, making a supreme effort to sound festive. I may have succeeded; both of them embraced me. Wishing me goodnight, they left.

However, their gloom only exacerbated my disgruntled spirit. For many years during the hardships and the disgusting onslaughts of the naked secretaries, I used to be able to sleep perfectly well. Now, though, I wake up with a splitting headache just two hours after falling asleep. I feel a dull humming in my brain. I cannot determine whether the humming actually exists or is just some psychosomatic quirk. When I walk around the house I never hear the humming. After pacing for a while and feeling drowsy again, I fall sleep. But in an hour's time I'm awake again, and this time I become angry with myself, because all I hear is distant birdsong, which does indeed fill me with joy. This morning I did not return to bed.

Saturday, May 4, 1985
Cassettes recorded by Goncalvo

This evening I am going to the celebration for our departing music teacher—after many years of service she will leave for her own homeland. Prime Minister Costas Tegularius asked me to gather all my cassettes, also those made by Zeferino and our dear friend Jean-Luc, and hand them over to her. Our governmental coordinator Illirio Mariafels has fashioned a box from local wood to preserve the historical memories of our island for posterity. I think it is glorious to make the story of our island known around the world. We will at last become prominent! Mariafels informs me that he will also bring various clippings from our printed leaflets (at one point these were called newsletters).

Now, as our island looks toward the future after its healthy transformation, these materials will remain as a record of our dismal past, to look upon, smile at, and pass on to our grandchildren. I am leaving now for our music teacher's house. Zeferino will remain on duty here.

Sunday, May 5, 1985
Diary entry by Adélaïde Fourangier

What a nice evening! We have been making music for two hours, some with wet eyes (not me), and singing local chants and French ballads. Some children played the piano, and two of my former students, themselves now very able pianists, played works by Chopin and Beethoven. Their program choice was evident: Chopin's *Waltz*, Op. 70 in F minor, his *Polonaise-Fantaisie*, Op. 61, and the famous *Étude*, Op. 10 in E major, and finally Beethoven's *Piano Sonata*, Op. 81a, "Les Adieux"—all pieces with a distinct air of farewell.

Illirio gave me the wooden box containing historical memorabilia from the island, saying, "Mother, this box encapsulates our hearts. Keep it until someone with a friendly eye is ready to open it." Then all of them left, and I remained alone with Costas. It was after midnight, and we stepped outside for a stroll, walking hand in hand like old lovers through familiar places that now are lit by orange-colored electric light. The passageways between peoples' houses remind me more and more of streets. Here and there artificial ponds have been constructed and with the grassy public lawn space that has been created, the atmosphere here resembles that of a fashionable resort. As we strolled along we saw many people on the "streets" and I was surprised to see even several café bars, gloriously alight and with the wonderful aroma of our local fruitcakes pouring out of their windows.

I looked at Costas and caressing his hand said, "It's your achievement, *mon prince*."

"It's what people wish," he demurred, "and what they have achieved by themselves. Besides," his mood turned dark, "it is still too early to rejoice. When do you want to leave?"

"In two weeks."

He nodded. "Let's return to your house."

"I would still like to walk around a bit more. Something strange has been interfering with my sleep recently."

"What?" asked Costas.

"When I put my head down on the pillow, I hear dull noises that do not stop as long as I lie in bed," I said.

"You don't hear this noise when you walk around?" asked Costas.

"No, it is all in my head, I am afraid," I said self-accusingly.

"Well, let's return to your house. I want to lie down in your bed," he said.

"As you wish," I answered coyly, looking for a hint of a seductive smile on his lips. There was none.

When we returned home, Costas did not undress. He lay down on my bed and pressed his ear against the pillow. After a moment he jumped back as if stung and then lay down on the floor, pressing his ear to the floor. He asked me to do the same. Obediently, I pressed my ear to the floorboard and noticed that the sound did indeed get stronger.

"What's happening, my dear?" I asked.

"Make your preparations to leave the island as quickly as you can," he ordered. "Take just Illirio's box, your medicine, clothing for the journey, and nothing more." Then he added, "Preserve your magnificent composure no matter what happens." He almost shouted as he ran outside.

"Costas!" I shouted into the night. "You'll keep your promise to me!"

"Yes!" he shouted from a distance.

Tuesday, May 7, 1985
Diary entry by Adélaïde Fourangier

Here I sit at dawn in my camouflage gray sweat suit with high boots on, ready to run. My wheeled wooden case is ready too. I am sitting at the table with my diary open, either to register any new development or to quickly stash it in my purse and run.

Yesterday at 9 a.m. the dull noise emanating from my under bed became very loud and it was obvious that its source was underground. At 11 a.m. a cavernous hole on the lower slope of the Hill appeared and several huge bulldozers roared out of it.

They were followed by three or four hundred naked secretaries smeared with excrement who rushed to the top of the Hill with buckets full of sand, spreading both sand and feces.

Police in red sweat suits immediately appeared and started to hose down the secretaries with chlorinated water. At that moment additional secretaries numbering in the hundreds— this time in gray sweat suits—sprang out of the crater and started shooting at the police. Nearly all those in front were killed. An additional group of police started shooting at the secretaries, and the whole crater and the eastern slope of the Hill became littered with the bodies of the dead and injured, all covered with feces. The infernal stench began to spread. In a couple of minutes the crater disgorged two large tanks that started shelling the western territory's residential areas, causing huge fires and killing hundreds. Another group of secretaries dressed in gray jumped out of the crater and started directing flamethrowers at the westerners' homes. Everything transpired at lightning speed. In a moment a helicopter appeared low above the Hill and started shooting at the secretaries. Another helicopter took off from Jean-Luc's runway and soared away in the direction of the Sages' compound. Both helicopters were shot down by enemy missiles. Around half past noon a sudden, terrible silence overtook the island. Horrible flames burned in silence, accompanied by horrible smells.

I now sit at my table ready to die. It's three o'clock in the afternoon. Illirio ran in with a helmet and a radio microphone fastened to his amputated arm.

He shouted into the microphone, "When will the Aviocar land?" Then he said, "Got it, in twenty minutes," and pushed the wooden box that he had lovingly crafted in front of him. I hurriedly crammed my diary into my purse.

17:05

The plane just took off with twenty-five children, two other adults, and myself. The island is quiet now. Looking out the window, I can clearly see a small red-and-white striped craft carrying the two Americans envoys leaving the island. Oh my god, the whole northwestern coast just imploded…seawater is covering half of the western territory. God, please save them!!

Wednesday, July 15, 1992
Letter addressed to Fourangier from Fleurette

My dear mother, the remote queen, of whom I have always dreamed:

Seven years ago when encountering you again in my adulthood, you asked me about my life. I could not answer you then because I was so blinded by your presence; it was as though an impossible dream had suddenly become reality.

Today, in deep sorrow, with beloved Papa's body resting in well-deserved peace at my right hand, I feel I can write you not as an enchanted daughter, but as a mourning adult. Papa raised me with love and tenderness; I knew only kindness from him. At early dawn he used to come into my room, throw open the windows, and ask me to listen to the morning song of the birds in the forest surrounding our home. He used to say, "Your mama loved the birds' chirping so very much." At night he would give me two soft goodnight kisses—one in his name and the other in the name of "loving mama who was far away."

He told me that he caused you to leave us, because he did not love you strongly enough, but he did love me enough to fill my girl's heart with the love of both her parents. He taught me to fly his little old plane, and even ignited in me the passion to fly solo—I got a pilot's license at age twenty! Papa used to say that one day I would fly to the Far East and meet my mama, the glorious queen who played Beethoven piano sonatas! While I dreamed about flying to the Far East Papa changed his mind and started talking about your possible return to France. He was sure I would be enchanted by you—and he was right!

Papa was a wonderful man—besides working hard in our fields, he helped the locals here immeasurably. Many times he brought women about to give birth to the hospital in his own vintage car, driving many lonely kilometers in the middle of the night. Whenever this occurred, he would leave a light on in his study, so that if I woke up I would know that he would return after his night missions. He did not like to call his night rides "night missions"—this was the term employed by my old nurse in memory of Papa's heroic night flights over La Manche during the *Deuxième Guerre mondiale*.

Mother, I know you could not have been as glamorous as Papa succeeded in presenting you to my child's imagination. I figured this out only at the end of high school. Having received a diploma with highest honors, I asked Papa whether you would be proud of me. He looked at me through his pince-nez and after a moment's delay said, "Yes, of course," and then after an additional short delay smiled slightly. These two delays told me the real story—I felt that you probably would not have been greatly interested in my achievements; you probably would have been preoccupied with your own concerns. Later I asked Papa about your mother, and his story only confirmed my own feeling—that you, like me, had been deprived of a mother's love. Then I understood that you left us for your own reasons. You simply did not need us.

This awareness caused me great pain; a pain so acute that I lost my *joie de vivre*. Later, after studying art and public administration at the Institut d'Administration des Entreprises de Paris, I married a modest engineer who was successfully employed at Aérospatiale and was in addition an outstanding amateur pilot. Papa liked him too. But Maurice—that was his name—liked to run my life by maintaining private contacts with my superiors behind my back, and I could not abide this. Maurice was sure that he was only acting out of love, and that my temper tantrums were nothing less than incorrigible defamations of him. After I left him, Papa was very sad. I felt that I had betrayed Papa as well because he so very much wanted grandchildren.

Two years ago he told me that the Vermandois dynasty would cease to exist, thus paying for its historic prominence and riches. He asked me to try to love someone anew, but his glance—he lowered his dear eyes, as if not believing in the worth of his own offspring. When I was a little girl, I remember that once after kissing me, he said, "Oh, little flower! When will you blossom?" and then he left and stood at the door of the room for a moment, as if pondering my chances. I was overwhelmed by sadness then, and this feeling has never left me. I am reminded of that bittersweet Moustaki song, "*Avec ma solitude je m'en suis fait presqu'une amie.*" But I do try to help people, Mother. I would like to be like Papa. He was a wonderful man.

And now we must remain without him, my beloved mother. For you it might not be a tragedy, but yesterday with Papa's death— on a glorious Bastille Day, no less—half of my heart sank and I now feel so old and withered. But no need to worry, Mother; I will pull myself together, and I will be with you.

You know that well, Mama—after all, wasn't it me who sat at your bedside three years ago when you were ill? In near delirium, you shouted, "Don't let him die, Costas! Remember Illirio is our only son! Keep your promise to me!" This is how I learned that you have a son—a real son, your beloved Illirio. Is he a good man, Mama? Would he open his soul to a sad creature like me? Please do not worry, Mama. I now drive Papa's Hispano-Suiza and I will take you wherever you need to go.

Fleurette

May 23, 1994
Diary entry by Adélaïde Fourangier

I am dying now. This shaking ailment overpowers me. Fleurette— what a dutiful daughter she is!—has been assisting me for the past few months. We are with each other almost constantly, and it's as though I have come to know her for the first time. How regrettable that so much of our lives had to be spent apart. I do not know anything about the fate of my Illirio, my son. I only hope he is alive. I ho————————

[a long winding line to the end of the page—S.J.]

FINALE

Between July 2004 and October 2007 I visited Fleurette four times, each time for a period of no less than three weeks in order to sort out the contents of Mme Fourangier's trunk and to listen to the audio cassettes it contained. As most of the cassette recordings were in Portuguese and most of the written material was in French—two languages that I do not know—I had to get professional assistance with translation. Professor Narutowicz introduced me to his dear disciple Isidor Levada, a native Parisian and a connoisseur of the Portuguese language with whom I could communicate in English. After several months of hard work, Isidor and I sorted the material in the trunk into two groups—one that had purely anthropological value (for example, details explaining the barter system used on Pinto Island in the early years of Mme Fourangier's time there, the ventriloquial melodies, and even more information regarding the theocratic education that children received from both the naked and clothed secretaries) and the other that could be turned into a narrative. Finally, I arranged all the material to be translated into English and took it back with me to Israel.

I worked on the artifacts in two directions simultaneously. In the evenings, after returning home from lecturing or giving piano lessons, I slowly wrote a historio-anthropologic case study of the customs and rites of the indigenous people of Pinto Island. During the day, whether commuting to work or standing in line at the supermarket or the bank, I thought of how I could find Illirio Mariafels, that amazing man. And could I ever find Mr. Tegularius? I was sure from Nelly's account that they did not go to Des Moines. I was also convinced that Illirio had left Israel for good and would hardly have chosen another conflict zone in which to put down permanent roots. I wracked my brain; who might know him now?

My thoughts first turned to Commander Edward Hayes. But could he be still alive after all these decades? Even if he were, he might be so old that his memory would no longer be intact. In any case, finding him would be enormously difficult and judging by the contents of the Fourangier trunk, his connection to Costas Tegularius and Illirio was purely an official one. Most likely he would not have made any effort to remain in touch after he left military service. From Nelly Zhdanovich's narration I deduced that Illirio had a predilection to live on islands, even though he no longer had a need to do so. I could make travel around inspecting all the islands on the globe...but this of course would take two or more lifetimes....

* * *

Thinking over my promise to Nelly to find Illirio, I remembered that during her visit to France in 1983 Adélaïde Fourangier had met a young man, Caetano Thibault, the solfège teacher from Cambrai whom Lothair Döpps had brought to France. Thibault had confided to Fourangier how much he longed to meet

Illirio again and to relearn his two-voiced chanting technique. I somehow sensed that the motivation of this man might make him an ally in my quest. I decided to fly to France once again in order to find him.

A week before leaving for France I called Professor Narutowicz and discussed meeting up in Paris. Knowing that he was already familiar with my preoccupation with Adélaïde Fourangier, I told him about Lothair Döpps, who had tormented Mme Fourangier on Pinto Island and asked about the subsequent direction of his career. Professor Narutowicz clearly did not wish to get into a discussion about Döpps. He answered me brusquely, "He is both a senior functionary in the French Ministry of Culture and chair of the department of piano pedagogy and methodology at our institute."

Narutowicz's revelation made me realize for the first time that after her return to Paris, Adélaïde Fourangier had worked under the aegis of her erstwhile tormentor. Perhaps this was the reason she never wrote another word in her diary after returning to Paris, until the last moments of her life.

"If you wish, I could call him and set up a meeting for you," offered Professor Narutowicz dryly and without much enthusiasm.

"Yes, please do it, my friend," I implored. We agreed to meet after my talk with Döpps.

I arrived in Paris in mid-October 2007, meeting Döpps at his residence, which happened to be located in Neuilly-sur-Seine, the same neighborhood Fourangier lived in during her early years in Paris. I knew I could not mention Adélaïde Fourangier in my conversation lest it generate unnecessary hostility, especially since I needed his assistance in locating Caetano Thibault. So I had to invent some roundabout approach.

When I entered Döpps' residence, the professor was in the reception hall. The house very evidently was in the process of renovation. Many workmen wielding heavy construction tools moved about, repeatedly asking the master of the house for instructions. Professor Döpps stood in the center all of this hubbub, his left arm bent at the elbow with his fist tightly clenched; his right hand nervously gripped the left elbow. His posture was one of incredible tension. Using his clenched fist, he directed the workmen in their various tasks.

"Dr. Jekavpils, I presume," said Professor Döpps by way of greeting and immediately interrupted himself by giving orders to his workmen. "What can I do for you?"

"I am interested in your pedagogical treatises...."

"Then go read them," he interrupted me.

"Yes, definitely, I have already started," I said in as placating a tone as I could muster.

"They are in French. Do you know French? Judging from your accent, you most probably do not know much French. Then how can you read my books?" he asked curtly.

"I have a good assistant who helps me read," I blurted out defensively. "I would like to ask you—"

"Everything is in my books," resumed Döpps. "The books were expressly written to supply all relevant knowledge without the necessity of resorting to private questions." And with that Professor Döpps immediately gave another set of instructions to his workmen.

"What was the background of your approach?" I managed to squeeze in.

Döpps froze. "This is not a professional question. Musical pedagogy has enough inner knowledge to allow it to function without reference to personal aspects."

"Thank you, Professor Döpps. You have answered my basic question. I am so grateful to you."

"What? Did I say anything that could help you?"

"Yes, definitely, you explained that musical pedagogy is a coherent system that functions without personal idiosyncrasies," I replied with assurance.

"You are so right, Dr. Jekavpils, I could not have said it any better. Rarely do I meet people with as high an ability to refine thought as yours. One young man whom I mentored in the past—a refugee from a distant island—who succeeded in making music his profession and establishing a career here in France did so precisely because of his ability to perceive musical discipline in defined codes."

"I would very much like to meet this man; with your permission, of course," I said demurely. "Where does he work?"

"In Cambrai," answered Professor Döpps. "I was able to secure a job for him at a music school there. He teaches solfège. Although two years ago his supervisor wrote me that he started to develop some strange ways of singing that do not fit our professional criteria. When I heard this, I thought he should be forced to resign, but the people in Cambrai explained that due to their trade union agreements he could not be fired, at least not for now. Maybe he will come to his senses in the meantime. They say he met someone who taught him some awful chanting and he completely lost his head. Do you still wish to meet him?" asked Professor Döpps.

"Oh, very much. I would like to ask about his musical progress under your tutelage," I answered. "What is his name?"

Caetano Thibault was the answer.

"Thank you, Professor Döpps. Please forgive me for taking up so much of your time. I will always remember this meeting."

"I hope you will use what you have now learned and what you will further learn from reading my books to improve your professional abilities," smiled Professor Döpps obligingly and then returned to directing his workmen.

I called Professor Narutowicz and told him about my meeting with Döpps. Both of us decided that this trivial encounter did not merit prolonged personal discussion; I thanked Narutowitz for facilitating my meeting with Döpps, and he felt relieved that I did not ask his opinion with regard to his eminent colleague. Two days later I arrived in Cambrai, a town in northern France close to the Belgian border famous for its medieval music. I discovered that the local music school occupied an old, attractive four-story building constructed in the Flemish style.

Locating the solfège room, I found Caetano Thibault, who had just completed his afternoon lessons. He was a tall, slim man in his early fifties with diamond-shaped eyes and a tense smile. As he stood up to greet me, I immediately realized that he had been informed by Döpps of my interest and was expecting me. He immediately told me how indebted he was to Lothair Döpps for his successful acculturation in France and for his career in music education. I asked him about Döpps's main artistic principles and Caetano Thibault readily elucidated them for me:

1) determine the salient feature of the discussed phenomenon
2) determine the criteria by which these features could be measured
3) determine the hierarchy of the main and subsidiary features

He said that he sincerely implemented these principles during his career in Cambrai and they allowed for excellent professionalism as a music teacher.

We went downstairs into the reception hall, got some coffee from the machine, and stepped out into the street. Thibault asked me how I came to know Professor Döpps and his pedagogic methodology. I told him about my friendship with Döpps's colleague Professor Narutowicz and about our wide-ranging talks on the nature of music and the art of performance. I told him that Professor Döpps's name occasionally came up during these discussions.

"But you know, lately I have come to the conclusion that I have to supplement my professionalism with some additional insight," added Thibault hesitantly. "You see, I was born on a faraway island east of Vietnam. Have you heard of the Paracel Islands?"

"Yes, definitely," I said.

"Those of us who live on one of the islands there have there a distinct culture that allows us to express ourselves in song in a highly natural way. From my early years I was instructed in the art of ventriloquial singing, and later on someone taught me the unique art of doubling the ventriloquial voice with a chant produced in the larynx. Singing of this kind causes a person to transcend into an enlightened spiritual state; it is a divine gift."

"Are you still able to sing in this way?" I asked.

"No, unfortunately I lost this skill through lack of use, although lately I have been trying to learn it anew. I discovered that the man who first taught it to me now lives in Europe, and after our initial meeting he agreed to teach it to me again."

"Is his name Illirio Mariafels?" I asked.

Thibault froze in shock.

"Do you know him?" he ventured after a while.

"I do not know him," I answered, "but meeting him has become the overriding passion of my life." Thibault looked at me with growing surprise.

"It is a long and involved story," I said. "I came to know some details of your native island while examining the archives of the late Professor Adélaïde Fourangier."

"Then you are a friend...." whispered Thibault in amazement. "I would love to accompany you to Illirio's place, but at the moment I am caught up in my work here."

"Could you give me his address?" I asked politely.

"Illirio avoids publicity. You must promise not to share his address with anybody."

"I cannot make such a promise," I said, "because one lady—who is, in fact, in love with him and who gave up a stellar career in musicology to return to him—asked me to find him...."

"In that case, please, Dr. Jekavpils, give me your telephone number and e-mail address and wait to hear from me. I will ask Illirio for his permission to give you his address." I fully understood Thibault's discretion.

"How did *you* find him?" I asked Thibault.

"Oh, it must have been divine intervention. I was on a train to Brussels to participate in a conference for solfège teachers. In my train car I suddenly overheard two boys joyfully parodying the two-voiced chanting that I knew from home. They happened to be traveling to the Netherlands with their parents. I presented myself to the parents and asked the boys where they had learned to produce such sound. They mentioned a place off the coast not far from where they had spent a month at summer camp. After the conference I traveled there and met my dear Illirio. This meeting became a turning point in my life in spite of the fact that I also learned the dreadful fate of our island."

"What *was* the fate of your island?" I queried with evident interest.

"Everyone perished...." he said, trying to sound normal. "Excuse me, I must return for my evening classes," he announced suddenly, as if to forestall any further questioning on this sensitive topic. We shook hands and he promised to call me as soon as possible.

I returned to Israel eagerly awaiting his phone call. About a month later Thibault called and told me where I could find Illirio.

* * *

2008

Immediately after conducting my last exams in mid-January, I flew to Europe and in two days' time stood in front of the elusive Illirio. He was at a winter camp in a secluded place where he was the educational counselor. It was a windy, snow-covered island; somber pines covered the coastal cliffs and dark seawater churned mysteriously far below. The temperature was way below freezing. Heavy vapor escaped the mouths of teenagers whom Illirio was escorting from an indoor gymnasium to the dorms. Some of the youth tried to sing in spite of the temperature, but Illirio stopped them with just a gentle motion of his hand. He led the children into the building and then invited me to join him in the foyer. He was very tall, much taller than Thibault even—certainly over two meters in height. He looked to be about my age, somewhere in his early fifties; unlike Thibault, he was powerfully built and emanated a noble self-esteem.

He sat down in an armchair in a posture that reminded me of Nelly Zhdanovich when she had bewitched me with her transfigurations (clearly Nelly was on my mind, although I did not exactly know how to introduce her into the conversation). Illirio radiated calm and friendly attentiveness.

"What brings you here, Dr. Jekavpils?" he asked.

I told him about my meetings with Nelly Zhdanovich in 2003 and about our lifelong acquaintance. I told him that Nelly had quit her academic career after realizing how wrongly she had treated him. I also told him that she realized that her love for him had led her to an entirely different world outlook—one of love, devotion, friendliness, and care, especially for children and youth. I told him how ardently she wanted to return to him. I added that it was a redeemed Nelly who had inspired the five-year undertaking that had finally brought me to him.

Illirio looked at me in prolonged meditation. Feeling how rudely I had trespassed upon his privacy, I muttered in a state of total confusion, "Please forgive me." He kept sitting there in silence, his eyes looking at me but clearly not focused on me anymore.

"You are a musician, aren't you?" he asked.

"Yes," I said.

"Could you play for me?"

I nodded affirmatively, looking around for a piano.

"The nearest piano is located on the continent," Illirio said. "We need to take my boat and row there."

"Oh my god," I murmured, wondering what else was in store for me.

We took our coats and went down the cliff to where Illirio's little boat was anchored. We stepped aboard and Illirio started rowing powerfully, manipulating the edges of both oars with only his right arm. It was an amazing scene. The seawater seemed to calm itself under his will. In two hours' time we arrived at the coast of the mainland, fastened the boat to the pier, and went up to the nearby music school; it had a kitchen and Illirio prepared a hot meal of potatoes smothered in some delicious dressing. He gave me some water, and we "dined." He said that his mother had taught him to always get a bite to eat before any strenuous undertaking.

"I know," I said. He smiled slightly.

Then he led me into a small room with a midsize Hamburg Steinway grand and seated himself on a couch nearby. Adjusting the revolving piano stool to my height, I sat down and tested the piano's sound. My hands were already warmed up from the hot potatoes. Looking into Illirio's eyes, I forgot the potatoes, seeing only cosmic vastness in his pupils. I played my beloved Schubert *Impromptu in G-flat major*. Illirio's glance accompanied me through every melodic turn, filling the spaces between the melody, the murmuring accompaniment, and the sorrowful though occasionally soothing bass. I finished the piece with a flourish, glad that the piano had responded to my wishes with good sound.

"I hear in your playing that you feel the sadness of life," said Illirio. "Have you lost someone you loved with all your heart, friend?"

"I...I have never loved someone with all my heart," I stammered and used all my mental power to prevent myself from adding "sir." "And to tell the truth, I was never loved in this way."

"But surely you know what love is, friend," Illirio said insistently.

"Maybe, I'm not sure. Schubert lived a loveless life, but clearly he felt how it would be to inhale luminous love." Then I added, and I don't know from where, "Schubert felt the presence of another world."

Illirio nodded. "Most people live within their own life experiences, closed off to messages from other souls and not wishing to see anything in life from a different perspective."

"And what about your double-voiced singing technique?" I proffered, trying to get to the heart of my meeting with him. "I heard it has great mystical properties."

"Oh, it is indeed a great gift, though hardly achieved. It has inspired many to experience different perspectives all at once. It seems it splits the identity and there are many people who cannot accept this. Could you play me another impromptu, friend?" he asked.

I nodded and started playing the *A-flat major impromptu* from Op. 90 with its falling arpeggios. At first not all the right-hand arpeggios sounded good. Illirio stood up and started reproducing the sound of sea wind, although his voice had a clear, melodic shape. His melodic line covered the peaks of my right-hand arpeggios and induced me to feel a state of greater relaxation. I found I was playing with a lighter, more assured touch. Although Illirio did not offer any additional support, he stood beside me at the piano just as Fischer-Dieskau did at Alfred Brendel's piano.

A few bars before the closing chords, Illirio received a call on his cell phone.

"I must go now," he said. "A teenager sprained his ankle and they asked me to give him a massage before the doctor arrives tomorrow. Please take the boat tomorrow morning and come meet me again, friend." He changed into a wetsuit, inserted his clothes into the waist pouch, and swam away. I slept in the back room of the school and in the morning with great trepidation jumped onto Illirio's boat. I felt that this escapade might very well be my last, but at that moment I did not seem to care. I started rowing, opening my face to the northern wind. In two hours I touched shore, although in the wrong place. I was off course by six kilometers and in order to reach Illirio's camp had to row along the coast for an additional hour and a half. I was exhausted when I got there. Illirio was glad to see me again.

"You are tired; have some water, and while you rest I will sing for you," said Illirio. He sang me two wonderful two-voiced hymns. I felt my strength quickly returning and that elated me.

"Where do you find this divine inspiration?" I asked him.

"I cling to the walls of other people's friendship," he answered.

"Walls?" I queried.

"The soundboards of friendship," he corrected himself.

"So are you saying that friendships have sounds?"

"Yes, friend," said Illirio. "Perhaps Schubert helped us to become friends."

I looked directly at him although my heart wrenched with pain. Illirio's face was motionless, but still friendly.

"I'll do whatever I can to help you to love again, friend," I whispered to myself. Although I did very much want to find out what had transpired on Pinto Island since Adèle Fourangier's narrow escape, I realized I could not at this point ask any more questions. I knew I had to go.

"Tell her to come," he said pensively.

"I will gladly do so," I said, not hiding my joy.

We shook hands and I left.

I called Nelly as soon as I reached Amsterdam. Then I returned to Paris to for my return flight to Tel Aviv. Before leaving I visited Fleurette once again. I told her that I had found her stepbrother and recounted how greatly I admired him. I told her how deeply sad he was, living such a lonely life. I said I hoped his former girlfriend would join him soon and wished that they would become a couple again.

"What girlfriend?" asked Fleurette. "From this world or from that world?"

"From this world," I answered, and I told her about Nelly, the one who had in fact sparked my interest in her mother. Fleurette smiled wanly. Then her sad face suddenly acquired a shining quality.

"It would be wonderful if my brother could find love again," she said. "You know...." she continued and abruptly fell silent, turning her face to the window.

"Yes?"

"You know, Illirio visited Paris."

"Oh...why didn't you tell me this beforehand? When? Did he see your mother alive?"

"Oh yes, he was here in 1992. Mother had just resigned from IHEMdP, suffering simultaneously from high blood pressure and severe depression. She was being treated with such strong medicine that they made her drowsy. She did not show much surprise or even affection when she saw Illirio. She just embraced him, kissed his forehead, and fell back to sleep. Illirio stayed at my house for a week, and then flew back to his island. He told me to tell Mother that he would survive, and that she should not worry. By the way, since her return to Paris and to the end of her days she received a radiogramme every two weeks from Pinto Island with the exact same message: 'We are alive—I. & C.'"

"What caused your mother to suffer at the end of her life? After all, she was only seventy years old when she died," I asked.

"This is what Illirio asked when he saw her," Fleurette replied. "I think Professor Döpps slowly finished her off."

"How?" I asked.

"This is what Illirio told me. He had found one of Mother's former students, who, officially classified as a weak performer, was given the job of assistant secretary in the maintenance department at IHEMdP. Presenting himself as her son and feeling the devotion of that man to his former teacher, Illirio asked him to steal into the personnel office and get mother's dossier. He did so, and Illirio discovered it contained several handwritten documents from Professor Döpps claiming that Mother was a poisonous force at IHEMdP because she succeeded in advancing weak students and making them relatively successful."

"What's wrong with that?" I asked.

"According to M. Döpps, it was an unpardonable breach of educational ethics. Only advanced students should enjoy priority treatment and qualitative teaching. His premise was that helping the weak distorted the very nature of virtuosic performance and rarely produced outstanding results worth the effort. She and everyone who shared her school of thought should be mercilessly drummed out of the institution for the sake of the school's good name. He claimed that even the relative success of weaker students was not only a public abomination, but a moral sin on the part of the supporting teacher; a sin that needed to be publicly purged in the best interests of society."

"But what about the human factor? What about the joy weak students experience in overcoming their deficiencies? What about the later lives of weaker students whose souls eventually become enriched and enable them to turn out to be knowledgeable musicians?" I asked in rising indignation.

"Please do not shout at me," said Fleurette. I apologized profusely.

"So why did they allow your mother to stay on at IHEMdP?" I asked.

"Perhaps out of respect for my father, the late Count de Vermandois who was a generous contributor to the school's endowment fund," she said, looking at me rather sheepishly.

I kept silent for a while.

"And then Illirio came and told me that our fathers—both of them—manipulated our mother into a slow death. He then kissed Mother, who had fallen asleep once again. In her sleep she raised her hand; Illirio caught it and kissed it in both love and tribute, and then he left with just a perfunctory goodbye to me."

"Why were you so reluctant to disclose your true relationship with Illirio? When we met first you gave me the distinct impression that you had never even seen him and, moreover, you even doubted his existence," I asked. She lowered her head.

"For me Illirio was someone who had robbed me of my mother, and when he visited Paris he did not do much to alter that impression. He hardly acknowledged me, although my assistance to Mother during her illness could hardly be ignored."

"Maybe he was preoccupied with the problems of Pinto Island," I suggested.

"Maybe, I have to admit that I was not all that interested in his problems." After this acknowledgment, Fleurette mused, "Both of us must be egoists."

"I do not think either of you are," I assured her. "You should read the contents of your mother's trunk of documents," I added.

"I can't," she said, with a quivering upper lip.

I gently caressed her forearm.

"I hope to prepare a readable text about your mother soon, and you will then see what an exceptional woman she was," I said softly.

"I already know she was exceptional. At least seventy of her former students attended her funeral—many of them bankers, doctors, teachers of literature and other academic subjects, not to mention the many teachers of music theory and the successful singers. All of them spoke glowingly of Mother, revering her as their spiritual guide. I heard over and over again how deeply indebted they were to her, how she saved their souls from neurosis and depression, how she opened them up to a deeper understanding not only of music but of the human soul. There were even three internationally acclaimed pianists who had studied with her; they did not say anything, they only wept in silence. And senior officials at IHEMP who knew Mother as more than a name on the payroll laid nice wreaths at her grave," she added.

"You see...."

"Yes, I can only bemoan the fact that I, her daughter, got nothing from her rich personality," she sighed.

"I am sure you will get your mother's blessing posthumously," I said.

She smiled. "How?"

I fidgeted awkwardly and then exclaimed, "Through her life story. I will try my best to do a good job."

She looked at me with tenderness.

"Illirio is not far from you now. Maybe you two might become a loving family at last," I proffered sympathetically. We embraced each other, and then we were interrupted by the ringing of Fleurette's telephone.

She answered the call as I made my way to the door. I waited there until she hung up. I overheard her say, "Yes, I understand. When will the burial service be? Yes, I will come, of course". Then she looked at me with a prolonged glance.

"What happened?" I asked.

"Monsieur Döpps died yesterday," she said with her usual lack of emotion.

"Let's wish him good luck," I said. As I closed the door I noticed that she was blushing.

In two weeks' time Nelly called me at home in Israel to say that she had arrived at Illirio's camp. She called me again half a year later, in June, and invited me to visit them at the end of July. I was delighted. Those two looked wonderful together: a very tall, strong, tender man, and an elegant, upright, radiant woman. The way they were always touching reminded me of newlyweds. Nelly and Illirio treated me to an amazingly juicy salad ("my mother's recipe," said Illirio). I remained in their open summer kitchen for the entire evening, listening to Illirio's story.

"After Mother left, most of the western part of the island imploded and was flooded by seawater. Only the Hill stuck out of the sea, and it was connected to what remained of the island only by a narrow strip of land that included Grandpa Jean-Luc's runway and the meteorological station from which Goncalvo and Zeferino operated our external radio communications. Most of the homes of our people on the western side were demolished either by direct shelling or by fire, and our people—those who survived, that is—fled to the eastern side, begging the secretaries who resided there to take them in. They were refused, so the refugees settled down on any open ground that they could find. The secretaries began to beat them and dump excrement on them. All this transpired under a heavy rainfall that lasted for weeks. This downpour, onerous as it was, was actually a blessing in disguise because it prevented the poisonous flies from coming. My father—at that point I still did not know that he was my real father—Costas Tegularius worked night and day relocating the hospital to the eastern side of the island while at the same time treating our wounded. Our war effort was actually directed from Father's room near the operating theater. The war took the form of sporadic mutual attacks, sometimes with shelling and sometimes with collective throwing of excrement on our people.

"Although we had managed to destroy the Sages' bulldozers and tanks, we knew that they would soon acquire more. We sent our two boats and our Aviocar with all our assets to Bangkok to exchange them for arms and for means of survival. Militarily we could not attack the compound because our numbers were too few. (Later on we discovered that there were seven thousand well-fed and well-maintained men under arms in the Sages' compound thanks to the reinvigorated supply line from Des Moines, via the Filipino entrepôt). We *had* to acquire more powerful weapons.

"By that time my father clearly understood that if we allowed the Sages to remain safe and free to act there would be no future for us on the island. So at long last he ordered his advisors to prepare a plan for attacking the Sages' compound. We estimated that preparations for such an attack would take at least two years—we had to decide what military equipment we needed and to train our "soldiers" in using it effectively. Meanwhile we had to survive. Our agriculture was in ruins and it took two years to create a very poor semblance of the fields we had cultivated in the early eighties. So our youth dove for pearls day and night, completely exhausting themselves.

"We survived those two years under constant threat of physical assault from the secretaries who stole our vegetables, bread, and fruit, and of course did not participate in any of the restoration work. We were compelled to cancel our greatest achievement— our money-based economy. Barter returned, creating riots and fist fights. In 1988 a new underground strike occurred, again without our prior knowledge. This time two new bulldozers created a tunnel along the northern coastline of the eastern side of the island (apparently the idea was to excavate ground to obtain additional sand for elevating the Hill). The result was an additional implosion of ground and additional flooding. The whole area where turtles were grilled disappeared underwater. The land on which we grew our crops was disappearing. In order to save the remaining territory, we had to attack the Sages' compound as soon as possible, even if we had insufficient forces.

"We attacked from three sides—from the nearly submerged northeast, the forest-covered southeast, and the west. We mobilized two thousand troops for the assault and our two specially trained commando squads succeeded in infiltrating the compound. Our attack ended three days later with half of our combatants dead, although not before they had killed a similar number of enemy combatants in the compound. Before our attack, we constructed sixty crossbows out of our broken refrigerators, cutting slices of metal with a heavy reciprocating saw. We had three such saws. I gave the two others to my assistants and we did the job in just fourteen days. The other parts of the refrigerators were honed into arrows and iron bowstrings. We gave these crossbows to our commandos and they shot their arrows into the face of the enemy. This was the reason for our ghastly success. Our commandos inside the compound ripped the bulletproof vests off the bodies of the guards we had shot. However, they could not locate the Sages, and returned empty-handed but elated. But our larger force did not succeed in destroying the bulldozers, and we did not learn what additional military resources the Sages had. Although each of our attacks caused heavy losses for our opponents, they still had a distinct advantage over us in matters of military hardware.

"During that time Zeferino, our radio operator, came to me to say that he had succeeded in intercepting the local radio broadcasts from our brethren in Des Moines—apparently he had managed to tune into some satellite service. He said that the Des Moines Pintoists presented the events of the island as the courageous struggle of the Sages against a small group of apostates. They said that there need be no worry as to the outcome of this struggle, since the Sages commanded the absolute faith of the majority of islanders and the apostates were inept and poorly armed. One commentator added that the Sages wisely undertook the reshaping of the northern coastline to improve the islanders' fishing abilities.

"At the beginning of 1990 we organized another attack on the compound, and this time our commandos succeeded in capturing one Sage and bringing him to our side alive. This was Sage no. 3, who was almost blind, as allegedly all of them were. We treated him with the utmost care. He did not talk much. He only said that he would be replaced by Sage no. 4, and that the newly vacant position would be immediately filled by one of the mustachioed secretaries dressed in gray. We paid dearly for our victory.

"Two thousand secretaries dressed in gray from eastern part of the island attacked the small force that guarded the captured Sage. My father gave orders to abandon the Sage and allow our adversaries to recapture him. But one group of enemy attackers killed the Sage under a decree that Sagedom itself would be purified by the killing a Sage in captivity, and other enemy fighters, unaware of this decree, attacked the assassins. After a while our forces disobeyed my father's orders and returned to the battle scene. In the fog of war, no one survived.

"The Sages further succeeded in ruining our island—their bulldozers created a new tunnel even closer to the forest. Strangely enough, my father did not instruct us to attack the secretaries running, buckets in hand, along the narrow strip of land to the Hill, so these people—extravagant in their ecstasy—continued running through the tunnel undisturbed until the end of 1990. In early 1991 the place above the new tunnel imploded and the tunnel was immediately flooded with seawater. We invented a new plan—neutralize their stock of antimissile rockets and then send our new helicopter to bomb the compound. We sent several metallic devices that resembled helicopters into air and they were immediately shot down. This enabled us to detect the sites of their missile launch pads. We then sent our commandos in to blow up these launch pads and the nearby stocks of rockets. Although this mission was successful and our skies were clear for a while, most of our commandos died in the operation.

"My father ordered the evacuation of our children to Bangkok, where we had previously established a sanctuary. Later on they would be adopted by loving people all over the world. While our Aviocar was engaged in its nonstop shuttle to that faraway city, the helicopter we had acquired began to bomb the compound. The bombing continued day and night for four days, but it appeared that all the military equipment inside the compound was lodged securely underground. We used the bombing campaign to keep the Sages' soldiers underground while our forces surreptitiously entered the compound. Our men burst into all the buildings and engaged in fierce hand-to-hand combat with the enemy in the corridors leading to an underground area. This was our last battle, as all our forces died there, together with all the forces of the opposition. Afterward, my father led a group of forty men into the seemingly empty compound to inspect the contents of the enclave. The golden faucets in the bathrooms of the destroyed Sages' palaces shone uncannily in the ruins. There were shelves loaded with canned food, mineral water, clean clothing, laundry detergent, and medicine, all products that we did not have. Empty shelves gave a clear indication that weapons had been stored there as well. The glass in all the windows was broken and the remaining walls were riddled with bullet holes. Huge numbers of dead bodies lay all around. Several dozen women slowly dragged the corpses to a mass grave.

"There were no signs of life in the compound; no radio equipment was found either. No trace of the Sages or their inner circle. No sign of a Nordhavn at the compound harbor. My father gave orders to distribute food to the islanders and began to organize restoration efforts. Sleeping in the room next to his in the half-destroyed hospital, I heard him sob in a subdued voice throughout the night. Once night I overheard him call out in his sleep: 'Adèle!'

"Slowly, very slowly, we carried out the wearying work of restoration. My father had lost all his energy and whispered orders with ever-weakening resolve. But this was enough for the remnants of our people—noncombatant women, the children who had not yet been evacuated, and several support units including people like me. The island population had been reduced to some four hundred emaciated men (half of them naked secretaries), five thousand traumatized women, and perhaps a thousand children, many of them sick or lame.

"All together our side hardly had any weapons—thirty-six pistols and half a dozen rifles, and those were mainly without bullets. Then the naked secretaries—all of them deaf—raised a cry that did not stop for the remainder of the time that we lived on the island. My father secluded them in the area of the former compound, allocated food for them, and left them alone to yell day and night. We got used to this yelling and became half-deaf because of it. And this would eventually bring about our downfall. But meanwhile our sad life stabilized. Once again we started cultivating vegetables. Two of our cows survived and we had several lambs too. Our people repaired Jean-Luc's runway and the Aviocar once again occasionally took off from there, as we had once again begun exporting our cucumber crop to Bangkok.

"At that time—at the end of 1992—my father sent me to visit Mother. I flew to Bangkok and then caught a long nonstop flight to Paris, using papers issued at our liaison office in the Thai capital. I experienced a shock: I felt free. I engaged the other passengers on the plane, mostly French students returning from vacation, in conversation about their lives, their worldviews, anything. But then my sadness returned—even before landing in Paris.

"I found Mother's address with the help of IHEMdP. When I visited her, I saw how she had aged and how unwell she had become, sleeping most of the time and hardly moving. Her eyes were dim and dry, almost lifeless. Her other child Fleurette tended to her. Both of us were too sad to become friends. I only wished to know how Mother—my strong mother—had deteriorated into such a condition. My stepsister suggested that she had been emotionally abused by her superiors. I made my own inquiries and received a similar impression. All at once the festive glitter of Paris, the luminous center of civilization, lost its appeal for me. Paris was as stinking as my own native island. I lost any desire for globetrotting and desperately wanted to return to that sad, minuscule piece of Pinto Island to help my father save the remnants of our people there.

"So I returned and toiled at his side at our hospital, in our fields, and in the rebuilding of our ruined radio and meteorological station. All this we did amid the constant drone of the naked secretaries, who did nothing but lie on ground and yell day and night. We even became happy again—like the blinded Faust who, overhearing the sounds of construction, assumes that it is the exalted public works he designed rather than his own grave being prepared. The end finally came in 1995.

"We heard a rumbling noise underground. For years we had not heard this sound, as the secretaries' yelling had droned it out. But now it was growing stronger by the minute. We all knew what that sound meant. Bulldozers sprang out of four huge holes on the remaining territory. They were manned by secretaries dressed in gray who shot in every direction, and they were followed by naked secretaries who defecated in wild abandon. Breaking off the branches of the trees in the forest, these naked secretaries started beating the wounded and the helpless whom all of our able-bodied men rushed to protect. As we crawled through the forest dragging the wounded and the remaining women and children to safety, my father turned to me and said, 'My son, leave. Swim to the American ship—you can do it.'

"'I won't leave you behind, Uncle Costas,' I asserted.

"'You must. This is the only way to save your life,' he said earnestly.

"'I do not wish to save my life,' I said with equal earnestness.

"'But I do,' he said. 'I promised this much to your mother.'

"'Why?' I asked.

"'Because I am your father,' he said.

"'All the more reason for me not to let you die here,' I asserted, and pulled him on my back to carry him to the shore. To my surprise he did not resist.

"At that moment one of the Sages' snipers spotted us and shot two rounds in our direction. I felt a strong tremor in my father's body, and then total stillness. I dragged him to the waterline, and then I myself crawled into the sea, and there I parted with the man whom I had loved all my life.

"I had been swimming for only five minutes when I heard the explosion. Turning my head back, I no longer saw the island, not even the faraway Hill appeared above water. I swam directly to the northeast, keeping my eye on the USAT *President Harding*. After two hours I heard the sound of a ship's engine. Diving deep underwater and then resurfacing for a gulp of air, I saw a large Nordhavn yacht cruising alongside me. Underneath the glass-covered upper deck sat four motionless old men in dazzling white robes. They were facing southeast. I did not wish to guess where they were aiming at. Nobody noticed me, so I was able to reach the American ship without danger. I was taken aboard and given medical attention. Commander Hayes issued me a laissez-passer and I was then transferred to a passing

French cargo ship. I reached Europe in 1996 only to learn of the death of my mother.

"Only then did I realize that I was a walking dead man—no relatives, no friends, no motherland, and without a place to lay my head. Not that I could sleep. The trauma of what I had experienced filled my dreams and haunted my waking hours as well. I started to travel, looking for my place among the living. The rest you know from Nelly, my friend," he said.

Nelly went to the kitchen to bring me another cup of tea.

"The note that you recovered from Nissa's body—what did it say?" I discretely asked while she was gone.

"'Leave the island, my love,'" he said, looking aside.

The time came to depart. I went back to the living room where I had left my raincoat. On the table I noticed several scores written specifically for two-voiced chanting. One score was signed by Caetano Thibault. The title of the composition was "CHANT OF HOPE."

www.ingramcontent.com/pod-product-compliance
Lightning Source LLC
Chambersburg PA
CBHW071638260626
47170CB00001B/150

* 9 7 8 1 8 8 8 8 2 0 9 1 1 *